## ALSO BY BETHANY WIGGINS

*The Dragon's Price*

# the DRAGON'S CURSE

## A TRANSFERENCE NOVEL

### BOOK 2

## BETHANY WIGGINS

CROWN
New York

Text copyright © 2018 by Bethany Wiggins
Jacket art copyright © 2018 by Sammy Yuen

All rights reserved. Published in the United States by
Crown Books for Young Readers, an imprint of Random House Children's Books,
a division of Penguin Random House LLC, New York.

Crown and the colophon are registered trademarks of
Penguin Random House LLC.

Visit us on the Web! GetUnderlined.com

Educators and librarians, for a variety of teaching tools,
visit us at RHTeachersLibrarians.com

Library of Congress Cataloging-in-Publication Data is available upon request.
ISBN 978-0-399-55101-7 (trade) — ISBN 978-0-399-55103-1 (ebook)

Printed in the United States of America
10 9 8 7 6 5 4 3 2 1
First Edition

Random House Children's Books supports the First Amendment
and celebrates the right to read.

This story is dedicated to my daughter,
GTW,
for the water and lightning.

# Chapter 1

It is always her voice, begging me to answer, that starts the dream. *"Sorrowlynn!"* But when I open my eyes, I see two scale-covered feet with blood-tipped claws digging into black pebbles. A wave crashes over those claws, swirling the blood into the ocean and turning the water pink. I know not to look up. Looking up is what has made it impossible for me to sleep past sunrise for the past five and a half months, because if I stay asleep, I always look up at the beast and the two dragon heads attached to its one body—and every time two sets of eyes glare into mine, both heads lunge, and the only thing I can do to protect myself is throw my arms up to shield my face. The last time I did that, my arm got eaten.

Even though this is a dream, I know exactly how it feels to have my arm bitten off by a dragon—I remember the sensation of Zhun's teeth sliding through my flesh and snapping my bones before he swallowed my arm whole. I try to open my eyes, but my body, lying in a small, hard bed in an Antharian stronghold, refuses to stir. *Please wake up*, I think. *Wake up!* But my body, weary from months of hard physical training, refuses. So I do the inevitable, the same thing I do every time

I have this dream of black beaches and a woman's desperate calling. I grit my teeth and let my gaze travel up the length of the dragon's body until I am looking into two sets of blinking eyes.

A wave collides with the beast's legs and fills the air with salt water, and I taste it. I shouldn't taste salt in a dream, and yet there it is on my tongue. And now the two heads pull back and then lunge forward. Without a thought, I lift my arm to shield my head, and just as warm breath slaps against my face and sharp teeth snap down on my arm, grinding against bone, I see the woman standing far behind the beast, hands cupped around her mouth, yelling. But I do not hear what she says because pain has a sound all its own—a roaring, shrieking wail.

It is my hoarse scream that wakes me to my dim chamber, and the first thing I notice is the complete lack of pain in my arm. I whimper and hug my right arm to my chest, and burrow deeper beneath the blankets. With my mind, I probe the nearly dead coals in the hearth and pull out a spark of fire. It floats across the room and settles on the black wick of a candlestick. Next I tell the smoldering ashes in the hearth to burn. Flames jump to life, feasting as if on fresh logs, and not just their ashy remains. When autumn turned to bitter winter and no maid was sent to light a fire in the morning, I taught myself how to heat my chamber without getting out of bed. "Thank you, Zhun," I whisper, for along with his treasure of knowledge, I inherited his fire magic. I quickly get out of bed and undress, trading my nightgown for a thick woolen shirt, woolen leggings and socks, and leather breeches that are worn over the leggings. My training begins promptly at sunrise every day, and based on the amount of light in the sky, the sun is just about to rise. As I run out the door, I buckle a sword belt and sword over my hips.

No one is asleep at sunrise in the western citadel. It is where the Antharian horse lords send their youth to be turned into the world's fiercest warriors. The citadel, a massive gray fortress built into the side of a mountain, is surrounded on three sides by a stone wall at least four stories high and as thick as a house. The fourth side, the side built into the mountain, needs no wall to protect it. It is the only Antharian stronghold built to withstand dragon attacks, and that is the main reason I was sent here. Six dragons are still alive, and they are going to find me and kill me because I killed the fire dragon and learned their secrets—they have magic in their blood, and their treasures are passed on to whoever kills them.

A great, wide training field is located inside the wall, and as I cross it, the clash of sword on sword fills the dawn air. Enzio is leaning with one shoulder against the wall and talking with three young Antharian women. He pulls a black stone blade from beneath his sleeve and tosses it straight up into the air before catching it behind his back. The women gasp. "We Satari are as well known for our knife skills as your people are for the sword," he says. "If any of you would like help honing your throwing skills, I will happily oblige." His amused blue eyes meet mine and he winks. "Have I told you ladies the story of how I pledged to protect Sorrowlynn of Faodara when she saved my mother's life?" The girls, all fierce fighters, sigh and start talking.

"Flirt," I call as I approach.

Enzio pushes his dark curls aside and nods in agreement. "When the ladies are so lovely, any man would be a fool not to flirt." The women laugh, and Enzio dips them a deep bow.

"You best get to your practicing, ladies." The women nod and leave, and Enzio's gaze follows them.

"They like your pretty blue eyes, Enzio," someone calls, and I turn and face Golmarr's older brother, Yerengul, wrapped in a thick green cloak. "But just to warn you, Antharian women always initiate the first kiss, so don't try anything unless you want to taste steel." A wave of melancholy hits me at the sight of Yerengul. He is only two years older than Golmarr, and the way he moves, the angle of his jaw, and his dark furrowed brow remind me of Golmarr and how terribly I miss him. I never knew missing a person could be a constant physical ache.

"And why don't you ever flirt with the ladies, Yerengul?" I ask. "You're as handsome as Enzio."

He steps in front of me and lifts my left arm, gently pressing a scar on my shoulder, hidden beneath my tunic. "I used to flirt, but none of the women sparked that fire of love in my heart. I'm still searching for a woman who can do that. How is this feeling today?" He moves my arm above my head and backward to rotate my shoulder. Yerengul has been trained as one of the horse clan's medics. When they go out to battle and someone gets wounded, Yerengul is the man who sews him up.

"It feels fine," I say, wincing as he pushes against the muscles around the scar.

His black eyebrows draw together. "Still sore?"

"Yes, but only when you bend it backward and *push* on it."

Yerengul frowns, and a familiar gleam enters his eyes. "If your wound has healed enough that you're sarcastic when I touch it, it is certainly doing better. I want you to only use your left arm today." He walks to an old, wooden wine barrel, which has several rust-speckled sword hilts sticking out of it. The term *waster sword* materializes in my mind. Though I have never laid my hands on a waster, I know exactly what they are for—cheap, sturdy, dull swords made exclusively for practicing. Yerengul lifts a sword and smiles a sly, slightly malicious grin.

"You're scaring me, Yerengul," I say. He laughs and slaps the sword hilt into my left hand.

"No need to be scared. I figure you can work out a little of your sarcasm this morning."

I lift the sword, testing the weight of it. "This weapon is not balanced. It is heavier than I remember waster swords being."

"So you *have* trained with a waster before?" Yerengul asks, though his dark eyes are skeptical.

The truth is, the memories I have of practicing with a waster sword are not my own. In fact, I don't know whose they are. There is so much information crammed into my head, transferred there from when I killed Zhun, the fire dragon, and inherited his treasured knowledge, that sometimes I get lost in other people's lives and forget what I have learned myself versus what other men and women learned and passed on to me. I grip the practice weapon tighter and force my left arm to lift it. "I have never touched a waster, but I know what one is. This is heavier. A *lot* heavier," I add, frowning as I try to swing the weapon.

"That is a *weighted* waster sword, Sorrowlynn. An Antharian rarity, and the reason we horse lords are reputedly the strongest swordsmen in the world," Yerengul says, his voice filled with amusement. "It weighs more than twice what a normal sword weighs. It is meant to build up your strength and endurance. This"—he rests his hand on a wooden post as tall as his shoulder—"is a pell. Did you ever practice with a pell in Faodara?"

I shake my head. Never, not even once, did I practice the sword in my homeland. My time was spent in my bedroom or being tutored, with occasional dancing and riding lessons. Images of swords sinking into wood flash in my mind. "It is used for building strength and precision in sword-fighting . . . right?" I look at Yerengul, with his arm wrapped around the pell like a woman's waist.

"Yes. This pell is for you to practice against. Pretend it is your enemy. Focus your strength on every strike like you mean to kill." He steps away and loosely folds his arms. "Let's see how much wood you can hack away with your left arm before it gives out."

I nod and adjust my left hand on the hilt. I know exactly how wide to space my feet to counter the unbalanced sword, how to hold the weapon when gripping the hilt with my weaker hand, and the precise angle to strike to cause the most damage. Practicing with a pell is an exercise of focus and force. This I know, just as surely as I know how to read, though I have never held a weighted waster sword in my hands before, and I have never struck a pell.

I squeeze my left hand on the sword hilt and clench my teeth. With every muscle in my body tightened to lend power to my swing, I strike with all the strength I possess. The blade hits the wood and sinks in. I tear it back out and swing again, and one tiny chip of wood falls to the ground. "I am still so weak," I say, looking at my left arm.

Yerengul walks to the pell and puts his arm around it again, running his thumb over the shallow gouge. "I disagree," he says.

"You do?" My voice is skeptical.

He nods. "Nearly six months of intense training with me has made you incredibly strong. A few more weeks of practicing with a weighted waster and your left arm will be as strong as your right, and then you'll be ready to leave. You can go search for my little brother without being turned into prey."

Those are the words I have been waiting to hear all these months. *You can go search for my little brother.* Hope seems to render me weightless, and the thought of seeing Golmarr again makes it hard to keep myself from throwing my arms around his brother in gratitude. I recall the words of Golmarr's parting letter, for I have read it so many times it is memorized: *There are myths about an Infinite Vessel that holds all the history of the dragons. As surely as you are reading these words, know that I am, at this very moment, on a quest to discover the Infinite Vessel.*

"Do you know where he is yet?"

Yerengul shakes his head. "I have received no word from him or of him, but as soon as I do, I will—" A horn blares, ringing above the sound of Yerengul's voice. He snaps his mouth shut and looks toward the wall's tunnel at the exact moment I hear the pounding of hooves. He draws his sword and takes a tiny step so he is between me and whoever is about to come through the tunnel. I know that Yerengul has been given the job of protecting me with his life. He has taken that charge very seriously, never letting me out of his sight unless I am in my chamber, and always standing between me and any possible danger. He is doing it for Golmarr.

King Marrkul and his oldest son, Ingvar, ride into the yard

with a small mounted party on their heels. Marrkul halts and instructs the other riders to continue on to the stable. Still mounted, his eyes sweep the yard, quickly scanning the trainees, who are now standing still as stone and watching him. When his eyes find me, he turns his horse and rides to my side.

"Father, what brings you out of the city of Kreeose?" Yerengul asks.

"My son's betrothed," he says, nodding at me—the woman his son followed into a dragon's lair in the hopes of keeping her alive. King Marrkul reaches down and clasps my hand in his, giving it a gentle squeeze. "Good morning, Princess. It is always a pleasure to see you." He lets me go and takes Enzio's hand. "And how are you faring in my fortress, Enzio? Are you learning a lot about sword-fighting?"

"Yes, sir, and growing stronger every day," Enzio says. He pushes the sleeve of his tunic up and flexes, showing off his toned biceps. King Marrkul throws his head back and laughs.

Yerengul offers his father a hand down. King Marrkul stiffly dismounts and presses on his lower back. "My bones are getting old, son."

"You must have traveled through the night to get here. Is all well?" Yerengul asks, his voice quiet with concern.

King Marrkul nods, but his black brows pull tight together as he runs a scarred hand over his long, bushy beard. "I have brought Nayadi. She keeps having visions, but refuses to speak of them without Sorrowlynn present. She insisted I bring her here *today*, before the midday meal. Hence, the night of riding and the early arrival."

My empty stomach drops. Nayadi is the Antharian's ancient witch. Six months ago, she accused me of bringing darkness to the grasslands. The next day was the worst day I have ever experienced. An ice-wielding dragon attacked the kingdom of Anthar. When Golmarr killed the beast, he inherited its treasure, which was hatred for Zhun, the fire dragon, and since I had killed Zhun and inherited his treasured knowledge, that hatred was transferred to me. Golmarr tried to kill me before riding away. I can practically feel the icy ground under my back and see Golmarr's furious eyes as he stabs his sword into my left shoulder. A warm hand squeezes my arm, and I find Enzio at my side. "I won't let the witch touch you," he whispers fiercely.

"Nayadi might look terrifying," Yerengul says, "but I assure you, she's harmless. She's never hurt anyone, or anything."

I nod to let Yerengul know I've heard him, but that does not mean I believe him.

# Chapter 2

My hands feel covered in frost as I step into the dark, quiet citadel. I rub them together and realize how insecure this makes me look, so I force my arms to be still at my sides and follow Ingvar to the great hall. The wooden tables are empty. No one is in the hall except the old, half-crippled warrior who cooks for the citadel's trainees. When he sees his king, he touches his forehead and then crosses his arms at the wrists—a warrior's salute of honor.

"We are looking for Nayadi," King Marrkul says.

The old warrior points up at the ceiling. "She said she'd meet you in the princess's chamber." His voice is as hard and rough as his scarred face.

I fight a shudder of repulsion. "She is in *my* chamber?"

The warrior shrugs. "You're the only princess here."

I look askance at King Marrkul. "Why is she in my chamber?"

"I may be king, but I have never claimed to know the reasons behind Nayadi's actions," he says, and waves his arm for me to lead the way to my chamber. I hurry upstairs to the second floor.

At my door, King Marrkul presses his finger to his lips—a reminder that Nayadi demands utter silence when she is having a vision unless she asks a question or speaks directly to someone. The door swings open on silent hinges, and Marrkul steps aside, letting me enter first.

Nayadi is sitting on my small bed with her knees drawn up against her chest, wearing my dark gray blanket over her head like the hood of a cloak. Her face is in shadow, making her pale, blank eyes look like black hollows above her protruding cheekbones. Beside her sits an old, white-haired man I have never seen before. He has broad shoulders and sits with his spine as straight as a sword. Beside the bed stands Ingvar, heir to the Antharian throne. His black hair, which is turning silver at his temples, is tightly braided. "Good morning, Princess Sorrowlynn," he says.

"Good morning, Prince Ingvar." As I walk across the room, I feel the old man scrutinizing my every move.

I stop in front of Nayadi and stare down at her. Enzio steps up beside me, his black knife already in his hand. Yerengul takes his place on my other side. Nayadi's lips are moving, but no sound comes from her mouth. When she doesn't so much as acknowledge me, I crouch on my haunches in front of her and peer beneath the blanket. She stares at the wall behind me, and a small smile makes deep creases form in her cheeks.

"Two bound as one. The blood of three kingdoms will be on your head," she whispers. "Two bound as one. The blood of three kingdoms will be on your head." She says it again and again: *Two bound as one. The blood of three kingdoms will be on your head.* And each time she says it, her smile grows broader.

I look to Ingvar for an explanation, but he shakes his head

and frowns, so I look at the ancient man sitting on my bed, but his attention is focused on Nayadi.

Nayadi inhales a breath that rattles in her chest, and I can't help but jump. Her blind eyes lock onto mine, and when she speaks her voice is no longer hushed. "From a grave of ice they will rise and color the sky like a glorious sunset blackened by smoke."

*Grave of ice?* Unbidden, an image opens inside my mind.

⁘ ⊠⬥⊠ ⁘

*The ice moans and creaks overhead and I shiver, pulling the ermine-lined cloak tighter around my shoulders and then patting my numb, beard-covered cheeks. "Where are you hiding?" I ask, my voice that of a man's. I stop before a wall of sleek ice and stare at my blurred reflection: shoulder-length brown hair, fur-lined boots that go half-way up my legs, square shoulders beneath a calf-length cloak. Something in my reflection moves, though I have not so much as blinked my eyes. A darkness rises up, overpowering my reflection. When I step aside, my reflection moves, but the dark mass does not move with me. "There you are," I whisper, but it is not my voice I hear. It is the deep, patient voice of Melchior the wizard—the man who predicted that I would die by my own hand. Even though it is Melchior's voice, and Melchior's memory, it feels just like my own.*

⁘ ⊠⬥⊠ ⁘

"From a grave of ice they will rise and color the sky like a glorious sunset blackened by smoke," Nayadi wails, drawing my attention back to the present. Warm air stings my frigid cheeks, and the biting smell of snow is replaced with the smell of warmth and food. "That is all." She yawns and pulls the blanket tighter under her chin, and then lies down with her greasy head on my pillow. "Now I need to sleep. I rode all night to get here, you know, and my bones are old and brittle."

"That is all? The vision has ended?" King Marrkul asks.

Nayadi wiggles deeper into my goose-down mattress. "Yes."

"But what did you see?" he asks. "You always tell us of precise events about to occur."

Nayadi closes her eyes and yawns. "It was different this time."

"I don't believe you," I say. Still crouching in front of her, I lean closer to the tiny woman. "What does 'two bound as one' mean?" Nayadi sucks her bottom lip into her mouth and starts breathing deeply, as if she's already asleep. "*What* is rising from a grave of ice?" I ask loudly. "Is it a dragon? Is it going to destroy three separate kingdoms in its search for me?"

One of her eyes pops open. "No, it is not *a* dragon. I have no more to say about what I have seen." She turns her face into my pillow.

I clench my teeth and stand, yanking my blanket off Nayadi. The old stranger sitting beside her startles and stands, looking at me as if I am an ill-behaved child. "What does your vision mean? You have got to tell me so I know what to do to make things right," I say, my voice so loud I might be yelling.

Nayadi wails and covers her head with her arms. She pulls her knees to her chest and whimpers.

Ingvar steps forward and places his broad hand on Nayadi's shoulder. "Let me help you to your room. I will bring you breakfast." She jerks her shoulder away.

Taking a calming breath, I look at Ingvar. "You're not going to make her tell us what her vision means?"

Ingvar spreads his hands. "I cannot make her do anything. I am sorry, Princess."

I look at King Marrkul, but he shakes his head. "I am king, yes, but Nayadi is not one of my subjects. She has never followed anyone's desires or rules but her own. It is by her own choosing that she aids my family."

"But—"

A warm hand closes around my arm. "Come. The breakfast bell rang. Let us go and break our fast," Yerengul says. "We can discuss her vision while we eat."

Something tugs on the blanket still clasped in my hands. Nayadi is pulling on it, draping it on her bare feet. The fabric slides from my fingers, and the woman covers herself, tucking the wool beneath her chin and closing her eyes.

"She's going to take a *nap* in my bed now?" I ask, wondering if I will ever be able to sleep in that bed again. I put my hands on my hips. "Nayadi, get out of my bed."

Without opening her eyes, Nayadi shakes her head. "I like it here," she says. "I feel him."

"Him?" King Marrkul asks. "Who is 'him'?"

"The bed is mine—it has been mine for almost six months, and no man has slept in it—no *him*," I say.

Nayadi's glossy eyes slowly open and travel up the length of me. "I feel Zhun," she says.

I take a small step back and shudder. "The fire dragon is dead."

Nayadi shakes her head. "Not all of him. He is right . . ." She lifts her scrawny hand from my blanket and points at my forehead. "There, waiting to take over your mind."

Something ancient and dark, and slick like moss touches my thoughts. I try to lift my arm to shove Nayadi's hand away, but am unable to move. I open my mouth to speak, to cry out for help, but no sound leaves my parted lips. Without a thought, I use the only weapon I possess that does not require physical movement, and swing a blade of *something* through the air between us: magic. Her touch is removed, and though I see nothing, I feel the sharpness of what I have wielded and it scares me.

Nayadi shrieks and pulls the blanket around her head, and I stagger backward as my ability to move returns. With a flick of my wrist, I pull the black stone blade from my sleeve and point it at the witch. Enzio's knife is still in his right hand, and has been joined by a short sword in his left.

"Sorrowlynn?" Enzio asks, quivering with energy. "Give the word and I will kill her right now."

King Marrkul steps in front of Enzio and me, shielding Nayadi. In a booming voice he says, "There is no need for weapons! She is a harmless old woman!"

Yerengul gently moves his father aside and glares. "Will you two please put your knives away?" he says through gritted teeth. "I already told you Nayadi is harmless."

I shudder. "Harmless? She touched my mind with magic, Yerengul."

Nayadi throws the blanket off herself and sits up. Two trails of blood have trickled out of her nostrils and frame her lips. "It was a tiny touch! You don't have to be so rough. You need to learn how to control Zhun's magic."

My entire body begins to tremble, and I blink back tears of frustration. "I am doing my best." Sheathing my knife, I turn and stride out of the room.

"Wait!" Nayadi wails, and then she laughs. Her peal of laughter stops me dead in my tracks as a tremor of ice creeps up my spine. I peer through the doorway, waiting. Nayadi tilts her head to the side, as if listening to something, and swipes her hand across the blood dripping from her nose, smearing a streak of red across one cheek and into her hair. "Your . . . *husband* . . . is on his way here, Sorrowlynn. He will arrive before sunset. That is why I insisted we travel through the night."

"My *what*?" I ask.

Nayadi giggles and claps her hands. "He brings two armies on his heels. The blood of three kingdoms will be on your head if you do not play this right." She falls back into my bed.

My boots pound the floor as I hurry from the chamber, and her laughter follows me all the way down the stairs. "I am leaving to find Golmarr in the morning. If you would like to come with me, we need to make preparations for a journey," I announce to whomever has followed. "But first, breakfast."

# Chapter 3

The smell of roasted meat and fresh bread permeates the citadel, and though I have no appetite, I know I must eat. When we reach the great hall where the food is being served, an unfamiliar voice says, "You walk like a sword fighter." I drag my attention from thoughts of Nayadi's vison and turn around. Enzio and Yerengul stop, too. A wizened old man with broad shoulders and a straight spine is walking toward me—the man who was sitting on the bed beside Nayadi. Yerengul gasps and starts whispering furiously in my ear, but the old man speaks.

"Sorrowlynn of Faodara," he says, his voice steady despite his aged appearance. "I have heard much about you." He dips a deep, respectful bow. "I am Leogard, the oldest living sword master in the world. Before I retired, I trained your betrothed, Golmarr, and his father, and his father's father. Though I arrived this morning with Nayadi, I came for a different reason."

When he does not continue, I ask, "Why have you come?"

"To see if your reputation with the sword is deserved or exaggerated. Yerengul speaks very highly of you." He eyes the sword at my hip and quirks an eyebrow. "Would you be opposed to stepping outside and letting me watch you practice for a few minutes?"

I look between Leogard and the food being set out on tables, and Yerengul jabs me in the ribs with his elbow. "That is Leogard! You can't say no to him!" he whispers.

I want to tell Yerengul I can say no to whomever I want, but instead choose to be respectful. "I am not opposed at all, sir," I say, forcing a polite smile to my mouth.

Leogard holds his arm out and I rest my hand on it, letting him escort me past the great hall and breakfast, and outside to the deserted courtyard, with Yerengul and Enzio trailing behind us. When we have reached the very spot where I was practicing earlier, Leogard stops. "To arms," he says, his eyes scrutinizing.

My hand is on my sword hilt, sliding the weapon free before I even have time to think.

"Thrust," Leogard orders. I position my feet and thrust. The deep creases around Leogard's brown eyes deepen. "Your form is good for a Faodarian princess. Thrust and parry."

Again, I do as he asks, letting the memories I was given from the dragon—from the hundreds of warriors that he killed—take control of my mind and body as he calls out a dozen commands.

Leogard's white eyebrows crawl up his forehead and he rubs his chin. "*Surprisingly* good for a Faodarian. Will you humor an old sword master and let me study your form a little longer?"

A smile lights my face. I nod, and Leogard starts calling out commands. Every time he does, my body knows exactly how to respond without thinking. Fighting for me has become as natural as walking and breathing.

The commands keep coming, faster and faster, and I keep swinging, jumping, lunging, retreating until my body is damp with sweat and my muscles are heavy from executing the exercises.

"One more," Leogard says. "But without the sword."

"As you wish." I hand my weapon to Enzio.

Leogard's dark eyes meet mine. *"Vinctar,"* he says.

The single word connects with my body and I swing my sword arm through the air in a wide arc at the same time as I jump in a fast spin. Landing on one knee, I thrust my arms toward the ground, giving a death blow to the imaginary opponent whose legs I just cut out from under him. Letting my arms drop to my sides, I look at my companions. All three are staring at me with wide, surprised eyes.

"Have you taught her the Vinti commands, Yerengul?" Leogard asks.

"No, sir," Yerengul says.

"Who taught you to speak Vinti, Sorrowlynn of Faodara?" Leogard asks.

I frown at the aged man and wipe away the sweat that has dripped into my eyes. *"Vinti?"*

"Vinti is the ancient language of warriors and scholars, spoken long before my great-grandfather's time. It is the language my family has passed down from generation to generation to train warriors. I did not know any other sword master still used that ancient language. *Ind vi fante Vinti?"* Leogard asks and holds out his hand. I clasp it and wobble up to my feet.

I know that what he just asked me, *Ind vi fante Vinti?*, was in a different language, but his words are as familiar to my brain as sword-fighting is to my body. He asked: *Do you speak*

*Vinti fluently?* At least one of the dead warriors whose knowledge I have absorbed spoke Vinti. "I don't know if I am fluent, but I understood what you asked."

"The last ten commands I spoke were in Vinti. And you executed them . . . perfectly, though with an antiquity I have not seen since I was a boy." His awe-filled eyes scrutinize me. *"Anta vi vesco atala en gredi?"* he asks quietly, almost reverently, and again I understand him. *Who has taught you the sword?* "Who has your queen mother hired to turn her people into warriors? More important, *why* is she turning your people into warriors? Why is she turning her *daughters* into warriors?"

"I did not learn to fight in Faodara," I admit, taking my sword from Enzio and sheathing it. "My mother abhors fighting and weapons. I learned . . ." Uncertain what to say, I uncurl my left hand and study the calluses on it.

"Did I hear you correctly?" Yerengul asks, studying me with a frown on his face. "You didn't learn to fight in Faodara?"

I clear my throat, but don't look away from my palm. "That is correct."

"If you didn't learn to fight in Faodara, then where did you learn to move like that?" Yerengul asks. "You fight as well as Golmarr, who has been trained from the moment he was strong enough to hold a sword. I was under the impression that you grew up in your mother's castle, learning to fight."

I swallow and look up.

Leogard is studying my body, Yerengul is frowning, and Enzio is staring at me with curious, expectant eyes.

Do I dare tell them that everything I know about fighting was learned in less than a heartbeat? Learned in the moment the fire dragon died and forced his thousand years' worth of treasure—men's and women's memories—into my brain?

An arrow zips through the air, piercing the ground five paces from Yerengul's feet. He jumps back and shades his eyes, peering up at the top of the wall. Sentries are up there, communicating with the Antharians' hand signals. *Strangers approaching, two men, mounted, armed,* their hands say, their movements sharp and frantic. Yerengul sprints to the entrance of the tunnel that leads under the wall and pulls a metal lever. Chains clang and groan as a giant portcullis is dropped in front of the tunnel, making the ground shudder beneath my feet. A moment later, the sound of galloping horses reaches us, and then the hooves are clopping and echoing through the tunnel beneath the wall.

Yerengul positions himself in front of the lowered portcullis, his mouth set in a thin, grim line. "Who are you, and what business do you have in my kingdom that has brought you to our threshold armed and frantic?" he demands.

"I have come to warn you that an army approaches. They will arrive within a day," a familiar voice states.

My heart lurches to a painful stop and then starts pounding against my ribs. I stride forward until I see the riders on the other side of the portcullis. There are two of them, but my eyes settle on the closer man. Even hidden beneath the shadow of the stone tunnel, and with my view limited by the metal bars of the portcullis, I recognize him. The man's gaze flickers to me and holds. Though I can't tell from here, I know his eyes are green.

"What army?" Yerengul asks.

"The Faodarian army. They are being led by Lord Damar and are coming to collect their princess."

My stomach seems to double in weight and drop. Lord Damar is my mother's husband, and since my mother is the queen, Lord Damar holds nearly as much power as if he were the king. He is the man I called my father until I learned my father was actually a palace guard named Ornald. Lord Damar is the man who whipped my legs when I displeased him and insisted I spend my days secluded in my bedchamber. Yerengul looks at me, his dark brows drawn together. When he turns back to the newcomers, he asks, "Who are you?"

"I am Ornald, a former Faodarian palace guard. I am—"

"He is my father," I blurt, walking to the portcullis and wrapping my fingers around the cold metal separating us. Ornald dismounts and smiles, and for the first time in my life I look into his eyes to see if they are the same color as mine.

"Ingvar! Your presence is needed at the tunnel! Bring reinforcements," Yerengul yells toward the citadel.

# Chapter 4

Within minutes, the courtyard is filled with somber, silent warriors, with Ingvar at their front and King Marrkul watching from the citadel. At a hand signal from Ingvar, the portcullis is raised just high enough for Ornald and his companion to dismount and enter, and a young man carrying a message to exit.

My father steps beneath the gate and stops before me. I look up at him, searching for my likeness in his square chin, his arched eyebrows, and the slant of his tired green eyes—which *are* nearly the same color as mine. Hands grab my arms from behind, and I am yanked off balance as three swords are thrust between me and my father, mere inches from his chest.

I fight against the hands holding me. "Let me go!" I demand.

"Sorrowlynn, stop it," Yerengul growls in my ear, his hands tightening on my biceps. "I am only trying to keep you safe."

"Don't hurt him!" I command and stop struggling.

Ornald raises his hands. "They're not going to hurt me. They are simply protecting you." A small smile touches his mouth despite the fact that he is being stripped of the belt and short sword hanging at his waist.

My father's companion, at sword point also, slowly releases his horse's reins and puts his hands up in the air while he is disarmed. I gasp when his eyes meet mine. "Hello, Princess Sorrowlynn," he says. His attention moves beyond me to Enzio. "Hello, son."

"I am Ingvar of Anthar, heir to the Antharian throne. Who are you?" Ingvar asks, taking the man's measure.

I know exactly who he is. I sat at this man's table eating porridge with Golmarr half a year ago. It was in this man's wagon camp in the Glass Forest that Golmarr first gave me the Antharian hand signal for "I love you." I can still see Golmarr, the dappled sunlight glinting off his black hair, his pale eyes solemn as he put a fist to his chest and then crossed his index fingers. *I love you.* The memory brings with it two emotions: a flicker of joy followed by deep sorrow.

"I am Edemond, patriarch of the Black Blades of the Glass Forest," the other man says, drawing me out of my memory. "My people were formerly known as the people of Satar, who were driven from their stone home one hundred years ago by a dragon. I am Enzio's father." I'd never imagined I would lay eyes on the leader of the Black Blades again. He winks and adds, "Sorrowlynn is my niece."

The word he called me, *niece*, rattles around in my brain for a moment as I try to figure out where it belongs in the relationship I have with the patriarch of the Black Blades. Confused, I peer into Edemond's eyes, and my heart speeds up. His eyes are the exact shade of green as my father's. Edemond grins and chuckles. "Who knew, when I married you to the young horse lord Golmarr, I was officiating over the wedding of my own niece! How unfortunate that it was a pretend wedding."

My attention moves from Edemond to Ornald, and I wonder how I didn't notice the resemblance the first time I met Edemond: the curly dark hair, green eyes, expressive eyebrows. They are brothers. Turning, I study Enzio, my closest friend and guardian these last months, and my eyes grow as wide as his. If Edemond is my father's brother, Enzio is my cousin. A wide grin splits his face, and he steps up beside me and bumps my hip with his. "No wonder we get along so well. We share the same blood," he says. I laugh and throw my arm around his shoulders.

"Come inside and refresh yourselves," Ingvar says. He raises his left hand and flicks his littlest finger, and the men holding my father and Edemond at sword point back away. "As we eat, you must tell me about the approaching army." Turning, Ingvar holds his arm out. "Princess?" he says.

Squaring my shoulders, I lift my chin and place my hand below Ingvar's elbow, allowing him to escort me inside the fortress. Ornald and Edemond follow, along with the armed guard.

We walk through a dark foyer decorated with antique armor and weapons, and enter the great hall. The rows of wooden tables are still occupied by the youngest warriors-in-training, as they finish the last of their breakfast. When we enter, an immediate hush falls over the hall. As if on cue, every person in the hall quickly stands, picks up his or her plate and cup, and leaves the room.

Ingvar pulls out a chair. "Princess Sorrowlynn? Will this suit you?"

Startled at his formality, I nod. "Yes, thank you." Reaching to lift my skirt so that I don't trip on it when I sit, my fingers close on stiff leather pants. I ball my hands into fists and sit, startled at how easily I slip back into the role I used to play.

Ingvar sits on my left, Yerengul on my right. An older woman carrying a pitcher and a tray weaves her way around the tables and stops at ours. She places a basket of bread and cheese on the table, and then sets a tankard in front of each of us. Instead of filling the tankards, she leaves the pitcher and Ingvar fills everyone's cups.

When the cups have all been filled, Ingvar sits and crosses his arms on the table, staring directly at my father. With his thick shoulders and long braided hair, his scarred knuckles and the worry lending a pensive gleam to his eyes, he fits the part of future warrior king. "How long do we have before the army arrives, and how large is it?"

My father takes a sip from his cup and sets it on the table. "We rode out from Faodara four days ago. For one man, riding hard, it takes three days to get here. I left the Faodarian army on the morning of the second day, as soon as I had the cover of the Glass Forest to hide my retreat, but I did not travel as swiftly as I would have liked." He carefully stands and lifts his shirt, showing a pale, broad chest covered with dark brown hair, and just below his ribs, on the side of his stomach, is a bloodstained bandage. He gingerly lifts the bandage, exposing a swollen, oozing hole in his flesh—an arrow wound on the brink of festering. "Lord Damar had his archers shoot at me when I fled. One hit his mark." He grits his teeth and cringes, as if experiencing being shot again. "I do not know how far behind me the army is, but no more than one day—if that."

"And what is their destination?"

"Kreeose, the capital city of Anthar. Rumors say that is where Princess Sorrowlynn is staying." He cautiously touches his stomach and grimaces. "It is only because of the wound in my side that we stopped here in hopes that you could dispatch a faster warning. We did not know my daughter was here."

*My daughter.* His words send a flurry of emotions through me.

Yerengul leans forward, elbows on the table, and looks past me to Ingvar. His eyes hold none of their normal lightness. "They left four days ago. They will reach the city tomorrow, and pass by here either at last light, or dawn."

"How many men?" Ingvar growls.

Ornald's face hardens. "Three hundred, but Lord Damar has been housing a foreigner at the palace since shortly after the winter solstice, and I believe this foreigner might be aiding him somehow."

Yerengul slaps the table and barks a laugh. "Three hundred soldiers and a foreigner? So few? They hope to defeat us with a mere three hundred?"

My father's green eyes meet mine a moment before they shift to Yerengul. "They have no wish to fight you. They are coming to retrieve what they see as rightfully theirs." He nods his head at me, and for an instant I feel like I am falling, but don't know from how high.

"Regardless of whether or not they have the aid of a foreigner, they have only sent three hundred," Ingvar says, voice disbelieving. "They have come to retrieve their *princess* with a mere *three hundred*? I do not understand."

*I* understand and close my eyes against a sudden wave of shame.

"Do they think we will simply give her to them if they ask nicely?" Ingvar's voice has grown in volume, and if I hadn't learned not to fear him during the past months, I would cower under the sheer power of it.

"No," Ornald says. Surprised, I open my eyes and look at him. "Lord Damar doesn't think you will hand her over to him if he asks you." He clears his throat. "We all heard the rumors that Sorrowlynn's betrothed tried to kill her before fleeing and never returning. It has been almost six months and still Prince Golmarr has not come for her." My father pauses and looks at me, and there is compassion in his expression. "It is obvious that her betrothed does not want her," he continues quietly, "so Lord Damar assumes you will be glad to be rid of her."

Yerengul barks a disbelieving laugh. Ingvar lifts his massive fists and pounds them on the wooden table so hard that the tankards bounce. "Insufferable, heartless miscreant!" He looks at me, and his dark eyes are so full of fury, they would be his deadliest weapon if they could draw blood. His gaze shifts above my head, to Yerengul. "Ride out to Golmarr. Tell him what is happening."

I whip around and grip Yerengul's arm. "You know where Golmarr is? You said this morning that you had not heard from him!"

Yerengul presses a hand to his heart and glares. "You wound me. Are you implying that I lied to you?"

"I hope you have not."

"I have not heard from Golmarr, Sorrowlynn. That is the truth. Golmarr has sent one letter to Kreeose—to Ingvar and my father. Seeing how I have been here with you, and have not visited the city of Kreeose for months, I was not informed of the letter until they brought it with them this morning."

Again, I think of Golmarr's parting letter: *Every time I touched you, I savored it like it might be the last. Every word you spoke, I memorized for when we would be apart.*

I turn to Ingvar. "Where is he? Did he ask about me?"

Ingvar puts a hand on my shoulder. "The first thing he wrote was to ask about you, Sorrowlynn."

"Does he still . . ." *Does he still hate me? Does he still love me?* That is what I want to know, but I cannot ask it.

Ingvar nods. "He does."

"Which one? Love or hate?" I whisper.

A gentle smile softens Ingvar's concerned face. "Knowing Golmarr, both probably. Be patient. Be strong." He squeezes my shoulder and then looks at Yerengul. "He is at the Royal Library of Trevon. Make haste. Tell him he is needed."

Yerengul stands and gives his brother a formal bow, then strides away from the table, but stops before he has crossed half of the great hall. A boy in his early teens has entered the hall. He sees us and sprints across the room and slides to a stop beside me, gripping the table's edge to keep from crashing into it. Sweat plasters his black hair to his head, and the dust of hard travel covers his golden skin. His dark eyes are alive with excitement as he looks to Ingvar. I know this boy. He is thirteen years old and the eldest son of Ingvar. His skill with a sword is good, but his aim with a bow is as perfect as anyone's I have ever seen.

"Father," he gasps, and wavers from side to side.

Ingvar stands and strides to the boy, gripping his shoulders to keep him from toppling to the ground. "What is it, son? Speak."

The boy swallows and pulls air in and out of his lungs so fast, he cannot speak. Yerengul takes his tankard from the table and presses it into the boy's hands. The boy takes a single sip before he gasps for more air. After a moment, his breathing has slowed enough for him to say, "An army approaches."

Ingvar nods. "We know, Gilliam. Three hundred strong."

Gilliam's black brows jerk together. "No. Not three hundred strong. Uncle Olenn says they are closer to one thousand."

Ingvar's face flushes with anger and he turns his smoldering gaze to Ornald and Edemond. "You said the Faodarian army is only three hundred strong."

All the color drains from my father's face as he slowly stands. "The Faodarian army *is* only three hundred strong." He turns his guarded gaze to Gilliam. "From which watchtower do you come?"

"The south tower," Ingvar states before his son can respond. "He is stationed there with my brother Olenn."

Gilliam nods. "Yes, sir. From the south. The Trevonan army approaches, not the Faodarian." Gilliam sinks into Yerengul's empty chair and leans back. "They will reach the border of Anthar by sundown."

Unbidden, Nayadi's words from earlier echo in my mind. *The blood of three kingdoms will be on your head.* Three kingdoms—Anthar, Faodara, and Trevon—are ready to start a war.

There is a long moment of uncomfortable silence. Finally, Ingvar says, "Yerengul, instead of riding to find Golmarr, send riders to the other two towers. Tell them what danger approaches, and then tend to Ornald's wound. I will dispatch another messenger to Golmarr. You . . ." He turns his steely gaze on me. "You need to prepare to meet Lord Damar." He looks at my sweaty, dusty clothing. "Do you have a dress?"

"Yes."

"Do you think you will be better received by your Faodarian people if you wear it?"

A deep sigh escapes me. "Yes." The Faodarians do not *feel*

like my people. They would be horrified to see me dressed in pants and wielding weapons.

"Then prepare yourself to meet Lord Damar. I will send riders out to intercept him and have him direct his army here. When he arrives, we will request an audience." He looks at his son. "Gilliam?"

"Yes, Father?"

"Go to the stables. Tell them to prepare twenty horses. We will ride out and intercept the Faodarian army."

"Yes, sir."

"Enzio?" Ingvar says. "I need to speak to you alone."

# Chapter 5

After I have forced myself to eat a very late breakfast, Enzio returns from his meeting with Ingvar and accompanies me to my quarters. I am grateful for his friendship. At my door, he unsheathes his sword before stepping in and surveying the room. "I am making sure the witch is gone," he announces, poking my covers with his blade even though it is obvious Nayadi is not beneath the flat blanket. Falling to his knees, Enzio peers under the bed. "Definitely gone," he says, yet he glares at the table and washbasin in the corner as if she might be hiding there. Convinced we are safe, he puts his sword away. "We need to talk," Enzio says, closing the door and leaning against it.

"Yes, we do. How are we going to leave tomorrow if two armies are approaching?"

Enzio pulls the black knife from his sleeve. He puts the tip on his outstretched middle finger and balances the blade upright. He only fiddles with his knife when he is either trying to impress pretty girls, or he is worried. Now I know he has bad news. "Leaving tomorrow is not our biggest concern, cousin. Nayadi has seen a dragon approaching," he says without taking his focus from the blade.

My insides turn to jelly and I sit down hard on the side of the bed. "What? When did she see that?"

He tosses the knife up and catches it by the hilt. His eyes meet mine. "Ingvar had her removed from your bed after we left, and she threw a fit. She screamed something about hoping the dragon eats you before you can kill it."

I remember the feel of dragon teeth on my flesh, and then I see walls made of ice, and something moving behind. "So that *is* what she saw in her vision . . . what she didn't want to tell me." I frown. "Why did Ingvar not tell me himself?"

"He thought if you knew you would be too upset to eat breakfast, and a warrior's body is her most important weapon. We were going to inform you after you'd had a chance to eat, but he needed to ride out with his men to see how far away Lord Damar is." Enzio scowls and starts pacing my tiny room. "I do not know if we should trust Nayadi. There is a certain . . . hungry attention about her when you are around. I don't like it."

"I don't like it, either," I admit, glancing at my disheveled bed and wondering who to ask to get the bedding changed out.

Enzio grunts. "I have met some incredibly unsavory people in the glass forest, but none have repulsed me quite like Nayadi. I wish you had asked me to kill her this morning." He stops pacing. "Do you need anything?"

"I need nothing."

He puts his hand on my arm. "Tomorrow, we will leave

and find Golmarr. All will be well. Do not worry . . . cousin."
He smiles. "I like the sound of that."

Despite everything, I smile, too. "So do I, Enzio." Without another word, he lets himself out of the room, quietly shutting the door.

Kneeling at the foot of my bed, I open the small trunk that holds my meager belongings and take out a wide-hemmed light blue skirt, black tunic, and pair of embossed gray boots—the clothing Golmarr gave me to wear on the first day I spent in Anthar. I remember the way he'd studied me and said: *"Tell me this is real . . . You. Here. Betrothed to me. Wearing the clothing of my people and looking at me in a way that makes my heart start pounding like I've just fought a battle."* My eyes slip shut as the memory makes my chest feel hollowed out. I do not know how to fill it. Next, my clean but dingy lace bloomers join the pile of clothing. They were to be my wedding bloomers, in case King Marrkul claimed me as a bride for one of his sons. They have survived a dragon attack. I hope they survive many other things.

I undress quickly. With hardly a second thought, I pull the lace bloomers on and wish I had a camisole to wear beneath the black tunic; its sleeves are short, made for summer and warm weather, not the final weeks of winter and biting cold. I slip the shirt on, and as my arms come out of the sleeves, I notice the lean muscles beneath my skin. I pull the skirt on and lace it up the back, then thrust my feet into the gray boots.

My gaze wanders to my soiled tunic and the discarded leather pants and weapon belt, and I can't help but wonder if I *should* wear the pants instead of the skirt to meet Lord Damar. I will freeze in the clothes I am wearing. But to arrive in pants—*leather* pants—will give him such a shock, he will probably try to throw me across his knee and spank the living daylights out of me.

"That will not happen," I whisper to myself. I am betrothed to a horse lord, which makes me part of their clan. I no longer need to follow Faodarian rules. The man I grew up thinking of as my father, Lord Damar, has no power over me anymore. Even so, I do not put the leather pants back on.

My attention lingers on my belt, which holds my sword and hunting knife. My waist feels too light without it, too exposed. I reach for the belt but ball my hand into a fist. To arrive armed when noblewomen of my kingdom loathe even the sight of weapons would be too much. Crouching down, I strap my black stone knife to my calf, right above my boot. When I drop the wide hem of my skirt, it is impossible to tell I am wearing a weapon.

I wash my face in the basin of water on the table, and then unbraid my hair. It is still damp from sweat. As I run my fingers through the light brown length of it, I expect to feel the kinky, frizzy curls I was born with, but since the fire dragon's death, when the great beast's blood circulated through my body and I was engulfed in its death fire, my hair has changed. It is smooth and sleek in my fingers, hardly ever tangled, with loose waves running through it. My skin also changed. Every scar that marked my flesh has been erased.

With nimble fingers, I twist two-thirds of my waist-length hair into a bun at the crown of my head. The other third I braid and twist around the bun to hold it in place. It is sloppily done, but I have never before had to do my own hair for a formal occasion. And this is most definitely a formal occasion— one that could result in war if it is not handled properly.

Squaring my shoulders, I look into the small mirror above the basin and force my face into indifference, though my stomach is roiling at the thought of facing Lord Damar and the Faodarian army (even if they are only three hundred strong). Satisfied with what I see, I sit on the edge of my bed and wait.

It is long after the midday meal, when the aroma of supper makes its way to my chamber, that there is a quiet knock at the door. I open it and find Enzio dressed in full armor.

"Ingvar has asked us to join him in the foyer," he says. "And bring a cloak."

I retrieve a finely woven red wool cloak from the chest at the foot of my bed and swing it over my shoulders. "Are we meeting with Lord Damar?"

"I believe so."

My gray boots are almost silent on the stone floor of the fortress, unlike my noisy heart against my ribs. As I descend the stairs, the air gets cooler and cooler, until I step from the stairwell to the foyer. Frigid air swirls beneath the hem of my skirt, and the evening sun is shining in through the open front door.

"Princess Sorrowlynn." Ingvar, sweaty and windblown, wearing full chain mail, is striding toward me. His father is at his side, also dressed in armor. King Marrkul looks older at this moment than ever before, like a horse whose back is swayed from years of being burdened. His shoulders sag beneath an invisible weight.

"Have you intercepted the Faodarian army?" I ask.

Ingvar nods, face grim. "Your father asks that we meet him a half mile from the fortress, unarmed. Enzio has agreed to accompany us."

"Lord Damar is not my father," I remind him, my body stiffening with tension.

"I apologize. Your *mother's husband* has asked us to meet him. He would like to talk. I believe he will ask you to return to Faodara."

"Ask? He never *asks* for anything. He demands and takes and punishes when he does not receive."

King Marrkul clears his throat and puts his hand on my elbow. Concern darkens his eyes. "I need to speak frankly. Considering everything that has happened with Golmarr . . ." He pulls his lips tight against his teeth and scowls. *Since my son tried to kill you and has been gone nearly half a year without sending you so much as a letter,* is what he means. "After everything that has happened with my son, do you wish to return to Faodara and your family? Do you want me to release you from your betrothal to Golmarr? As king of Anthar, it is in my power to do so."

"No!" I shake my head vigorously. "I do not want that. I still have hope—" My voice catches in my throat. Swallowing, I continue, "I have hope that one day we will be married. I do not want the betrothal broken."

King Marrkul smiles a smile that deepens the crow's-feet around his eyes. He wraps me in his arms, hugging me against his cold, solid chain mail so tightly it imprints against my skin through my clothes. "That is what I hoped you would say," he says. "Sometimes our hearts do not choose wisely, but I sincerely believe my son's heart chose well when it attached itself to you. He was sensible to follow it, even if it did lead him into a dragon's cave." He pushes me to arm's distance. "Dewdrop has been saddled for you."

Ingvar rests his hand on his hip, and I realize there is something wrong. He is unarmed. A horse lord without weapons is like a porcupine without quills. I look at Enzio and realize he, too, has no weapons. Unease snakes through the pit of my stomach. Stored away in my head are the memories of dead men having meetings just like this. They almost never ended well. "Must we go unarmed?" I ask.

Ingvar nods. "It has already been agreed upon."

"I do not trust Lord Damar." I flex my calf, feeling the press of knife against skin. I never agreed to Lord Damar's terms; therefore, I will not go unarmed. I simply will not tell anyone I am carrying a blade.

"I do not trust him, either, and that is why I am going and not my father," Ingvar growls, pressing his hand to the spot on his hip where his sword should be hanging. "But we will grant him this audience and find out what he wants. And then, if we have to, we will fight. Even bare hands can be a formidable weapon when used properly."

The unease snaking through my belly turns to cold, nauseating dread. "I don't want to be the cause of a war."

Ingvar puts his hands on my shoulders. "Why do you think Lord Damar wants you to return to Faodara so much that he has sent an army?"

"I assume he wants me for my ability to wield magic. If Lord Damar owns a wizard, Faodara will be the most powerful kingdom in the world. Lord Damar wants me because I will make him incredibly powerful."

"That is the same thing I was thinking. Because you are

magic, does that take away your freedom to choose where to live, whom to marry, and what to do with your life? Does that make it all right for Lord Damar to turn you into a slave?"

His words kindle anger. "No."

"Then we go hear him out. If we have to fight for you, we fight. If it turns to war, so be it. Antharians do not fear dying for a worthy cause, Princess."

A mounted army of one hundred fully armed men and women wait in the outer bailey. Most of them are the oldest trainees from the fortress, the rest are the trainers. Even Leogard is present, his ancient sword hanging at his hip. I mount Dewdrop and guide her beneath the raised portcullis. The small army follows me out but stops, spreading out in the shadow of the fortress wall, where they will wait for our safe return or heed the call to arms.

"The sun is going to set shortly," I say. "Shouldn't we wait until morning to meet?"

Ingvar quirks one eyebrow. "Antharians train to fight at night. This is our land, and we know it well. Do not fear, Sorrowlynn. Night gives us the advantage, not the Faodarian army." He waves his hand at the mounted army. "If anything goes wrong, all I have to do is whistle and they will rush to our aid."

"Whistle?" I ask, skeptical.

Ingvar nods, and I can tell he is trying not to smile. "My whistle carries. They will hear it, even from half a mile away. Have faith. Be brave."

I sit taller, more confident, as we leave the small Antharian army behind, and proceed to our meeting. The horses gallop through grass painted with the orange glow of evening. Half a mile ahead, a small blue tent has been erected. Half a mile beyond, a line of black and shimmering silver divides the grass from the sky. It is the Faodarian army, the sun gleaming off their armor. I turn my attention from them to the blue tent. A red flag hangs limp above it. Were the wind to blow, the flag would spread open to show a rearing griffin with its wings unfurled, as I recall from my life before the dragon transformed it.

As we cover the last stretch of ground, a tall man with pale hair that gleams in the sunset exits the tent. Though he is unarmed (as far as I can tell), the way his body moves and flows makes me think one word: *lethal.* He is nearly as wide from front to back as he is from side to side, and his arms are so thick they don't hang straight down against his ribs, but bow out slightly. Despite his bulk, he doesn't merely walk toward us; he swaggers with the grace of a man half his size.

Ingvar dismounts beside me. "Who is that man? He looks familiar," he says, voice hushed.

I shake my head and dismount without taking my eyes from the stranger. "I have never seen him before, but I lived most of my life confined to my chambers. I don't think I would forget him if I ever saw him." Enzio takes Dewdrop's reins from me, and Ingvar's reins from him.

"You wait here," Ingvar instructs Enzio, and then he positions himself between me and the stranger and slowly takes the man's measure, his eyes probing for weapons hidden in his finely made clothing as thoroughly as his hands would.

The man stops beside Ingvar and glares back at us. This stranger is as tall as an Antharian horse lord. He points at Enzio. "Lord Damar asks that your man stand twenty paces from the tent." My eyes narrow. His accent is not Faodarian.

Enzio's eyes take on a slightly panicked look. "Why?"

"He would like to discuss things with Princess Sorrowlynn in privacy," the foreigner says.

Ingvar and Enzio look at each other, and then Ingvar gives a reluctant nod. "Twenty paces, but not a step more," Ingvar instructs. Enzio mutters something under his breath, but walks the horses twenty paces away.

The stranger flexes and closes his fingers before asking Ingvar, "Are you unarmed, as per Lord Damar's agreement?"

"Of course I am unarmed! I am Ingvar, son of King Marrkul. I am a man of *honor*," he growls. "Not a slippery Trevonan. Are *you* unarmed? And why are you at this meeting? I did not know the Faodarian queen was on speaking terms with royal Trevonan swine."

*Trevonan swine?* This man is from the kingdom of Trevon, yet he is with Lord Damar? My mouth goes dry. This cannot be good.

The stranger's face hardens. "I am Prince Treyose, *heir* of Trevon."

I gasp and take a small step back. Prince Treyose is the only living heir of the ruthless King Vaunn, ruler of Trevon. When I was a child, my history teachers taught me of King Vaunn's merciless rampages and victories against the kingdoms that bordered his. Under his grandfather's instruction, Treyose led the army that conquered the small kingdom of Belldarr and forced its people to pledge fealty to Trevon and King Vaunn. Treyose was fifteen when he conquered Belldarr a decade ago. It is *his* army of one thousand approaching from the west. I try to swallow the lump of fear forming in my throat.

Without thinking about it, I center my weight over my feet as the knowledge of how to engage in combat with someone of Prince Treyose's stature bursts into my conscious mind.

Were I to engage him, my best chance at winning would be to throw my knife directly at his heart. If I have to engage him in hand-to-hand combat, the only way I could win would be to take him by surprise, outsmart him, or kill him before he has a chance to retaliate. Never could I match his brute strength, no matter how skilled a fighter I became.

I step around Ingvar and crane my neck to look the Trevonan man in the face. "What are you doing here, Treyose, with Lord Damar and the Faodarian army? And why is *your* army approaching from the west?"

His dark blond eyebrows slowly crawl up his forehead as he lets his gaze peruse my figure. "You must be Princess Sorrowlynn. I have come to escort you to Trevon."

"I will not go anywhere with you. I am betrothed to Prince Golmarr of Anthar, and I will go where I please."

He shakes his head and grins, showing big, straight teeth. "Betrothed but *not* married. That won't keep us apart, Princess Sorrowlynn."

I put my hands on my hips and tilt my head to the side. "You are mistaken. I am bound by an oath that cannot be broken."

He takes a tiny step closer to me, and his breath moves against my face when he says, "You cannot be betrothed to another man if you are already my wife."

# Chapter 6

My hands grow damp and frigid all at once, so I curl my fingers into my palms. Beside me, Ingvar shifts uneasily. Letting my eyes lazily travel down and then up the length of Treyose, I say, "No. You are mistaken. *Sorely* mistaken, Prince Treyose. I have never seen you before. I wouldn't forget a face as cruel as yours. *Especially* if I spoke wedding vows to it!"

He grins and reaches a hand toward my face. I slap it away, hard and fast, before he can touch me. Prince Treyose's eyes widen. "Your father warned me you don't act like a Faodarian lady, but I didn't believe him. He says you are a pigheaded rule-breaker, and you do not know when to hold your tongue."

"I will speak when I want to speak," I snap. "And I will only follow the rules I want to keep."

He shrugs. "Then let us talk with your father, shall we?" In two long strides he is at the blue tent, lifting the flap aside.

Chin held high, I walk past Treyose and glance at his hand holding the tent flap open. It is covered with scars, and the littlest finger is missing just above the first knuckle.

The last rays of sun shining against the blue fabric of the tent have turned the air a dismal gray. A small table has been erected, with a lit oil lamp on it and two wooden chairs facing each other on either side. Lord Damar sits in the chair facing the tent door. "Sorrow," he says without standing. He speaks my name like an insult, and for the first time in months, I feel the weight of it and the suicide prophecy that shadowed my youth. Lord Damar motions to the chair across from him. I peer over my shoulder, meeting Treyose's gaze, and then turn back to Lord Damar. When I don't move toward the chair, he sighs and says, "You may bring one escort inside with you."

Ingvar enters the tent, scanning the flattened grass floor, the fabric walls, the table, and Lord Damar. Satisfied with what he sees, he nods for me to proceed and stands to my right. Treyose moves to the left side of the tent and glowers at Ingvar. The tension brewing between the two practically makes the air crackle.

I unclasp my cloak and toss it to the side. The air is uncomfortably cold, but if I need to fight, I do not want to be burdened by the cloak's bulk. Crossing the uneven ground, I sit in the chair across from the man I used to think was my father. He is short in stature and narrowly built, with soft hands and slender wrists. Were I to face him in hand-to-hand combat, I would overpower him easily. He stares at me, his jaw muscles pulsing as if he's gnashing his teeth.

"A Faodarian princess should not be wearing Antharian peasant clothing. Those sleeves are too revealing. You look like a *barbarian*," he says.

"Your rules no longer apply to me," I answer, slowly folding my bare arms atop the table so he gets a thorough view of them.

"You never did follow my rules."

I clench my teeth and shake my head in disgust. "Of course I didn't follow your rules! You told me I wasn't allowed to *hug* my own mother, and when I did—when I broke that rule—you whipped my legs. I was only five years old! How could you do that to me?" I lean closer to him and lower my voice. "You whipped me because Melchior the wizard left, as if I was the one who made his choices for him. You sawed *grooves* into the willow branch so it would tear my skin!" I do not mean to yell, but waves of long-repressed anger are coursing through me, and my mouth is the only release I have. "You are a vile man!" The sun chooses that moment to set, bleeding darkness into the tent as if my memories have blackened the air.

Lord Damar clears his throat. "Are you finished having your tantrum?" He reaches for the ornate copper-and-glass lamp with trembling hands and turns the flame higher, chasing out the worst of the shadows. "I have made an alliance with the kingdom of Trevon," he says, and snaps his mouth shut. I stare at him, waiting for him to proceed. After a drawn-out moment, he continues, "We heard you survived the fire dragon, and Prince Golmarr killed it. We also received reports that Prince Golmarr tried to kill you, and when he did not succeed, he fled." A mocking smile stretches across Lord Damar's face, and my cheeks start to burn. "Several months after the embarrassing news reached us, Prince Treyose came to me. He asked for my permission to take you to his kingdom since your betrothed obviously wants nothing to do with you."

I shake my head. "I am not your property to give anymore."

Lord Damar smirks and his eyes bore into mine. "You are my daughter and your mother's daughter. You are a subject of your mother the queen. You are mine to do with as I please."

Placing my hands flat on the table, I lean forward, until the heat from the lamp warms my face. "I am *not* your daughter. My father is Ornald, the Satari guard. I never have *been* your daughter, and I never will be. I am betrothed to Golmarr, son of King Marrkul of Anthar, and you cannot change that no matter what rumors you have heard. *I* will choose where I go and with whom." To my left, Prince Treyose shifts.

A slow leer twists Lord Damar's face. "Because I am wed to the queen of Faodara, you are my subject and I have the authority to break every promise you made to the Antharian prince no matter whose daughter you are. Do you not realize that? You have no authority. You spoke simple words of love to a boy, and then he tried to kill you. When he fled, you remained *unmarried*, leaving you a pawn in my hands, Sorrowlynn. You may have been betrothed to the horse lord once, but now you are wed to Prince Treyose of Trevon. Now *he* holds your fate."

I frown in confusion and look at Prince Treyose. His eyes meet mine, his face impassive. "I have never seen this man before in my life! And I most certainly never spoke vows with him. I would *remember* being wed to an oversized, overbearing Trevonan prince," I say.

"Despite your less-than-stellar reputation, Prince Treyose asked for the right to take you to his castle in exchange for"—he glances at Ingvar and his eyes narrow—"peace between our two kingdoms, not to mention he paid highly for you. Faodara's coffers are well padded, thanks to the kingdom of Trevon. I agreed to his proposition, but I wasn't willing to send you off with a man again unless you were wed." He sighs and shakes his head. "The rumors of you and the barbarian prince are already bad enough. I couldn't have more rumors of you and Prince Treyose sullying Faodarian royalty, could I? So I insisted Treyose wed you first. We held the ceremony four days ago, the morning we set out to find you."

Incredulous, I try to find my voice. "No, *we* didn't. I was in Anthar four days ago."

Lord Damar laughs. "It was a proxy marriage, Sorrowlynn. Diamanta stood in for you and spoke your vows."

"No! Why? The Trevonans are known for their mistreatment of women. Why would you ever agree to give me to a man like . . ." At a loss for words, I swing my hand toward Treyose. The very air around him seems to radiate violence. He shifts beneath my scrutiny. "Why would a man like you want to wed *me*?" I ask Treyose, my voice too loud. "You don't even know me."

Treyose clears his throat. "You will be a strength to my kingdom, my lady." His guarded eyes gleam in the light of the lamp, the golden reflection of fire shining against them, and a wave of understanding settles over me. It is not *me* he wants. He knows about my magic. *That* is what he wants.

Lord Damar thinks by marrying me to Treyose, he is hurting me. Causing me pain and sorrow are his motivation. I was wrong about him wanting me for my magic—in fact, I do not believe he knows I possess the ability to wield it. "You don't know, do you?" I ask Lord Damar, shaking my head in disgust.

"Know what?" he asks, his words heavy with derision.

"You are too stupid to even wonder why the heir of Trevon wants to marry me—the youngest Faodarian princess who has a 'sullied reputation.' You have no clue."

Lord Damar leans close and lowers his voice to a whisper. "He wants you so we can make an alliance and together conquer Anthar, absorbing half their land into Faodara, and half into Trevon."

Ingvar growls and steps forward, and Lord Damar quickly leans away. I hold out my hand and Ingvar stops. "Lord Damar, that might be what Prince Treyose told you, and he probably *is* planning on attacking Anthar once he has me." I glare at Treyose. "*If* you ever have me." I swallow the bitter fear of being wed to him and look back at Lord Damar. "You are a fool to think he is your ally. An alliance is not why he wants me."

"Well, he certainly doesn't want you for your disrespectful tongue and belligerent disposition." His eyes narrow. "And you're not even *half* as beautiful as your sisters. What other reason could there be for him to marry you?"

A flood of anger sets my blood boiling. "I am strong, and brave, and smart, and kind," I say, letting the anger fill my words with power. I focus my energy on the flame in the lamp and hold my unsteady hands out, palms up. "But despite those qualities, this is why Treyose wants me." I call to the flame with my mind. Half of the fire lifts off the oily wick and splits in two, landing in a walnut-sized ball on each of my upturned palms.

Lord Damar stands so abruptly, his chair overturns and clatters to the ground. "You *are* a witch!" He looks from me to Treyose. "Did you know she could do this?"

Treyose hesitates a moment, and then gives a firm nod.

"You *lied* about why you wanted her," Lord Damar growls through gritted teeth, and fury darkens his pale eyes.

"No, I did not," Treyose says. "You are the one who assumed I wanted her to create an alliance between our kingdoms. The only thing I misled you about was joining our armies and conquering Anthar. I do not want the grasslands, so I used your greed for them to get what I needed, which is your daughter."

Lord Damar's face flares crimson. "I am returning to Faodara and taking Sorrowlynn with me. When I get there, the marriage will be annulled by the queen."

"I refuse to go with you." My voice is barely louder than a whisper, but it catches Lord Damar's attention as surely as if I'd slapped him across the face.

He points at me and shouts, "Acting in the name of Queen Felicitia of Faodara, and with the rights and power granted to me as her husband and your father, I hereby command you to submit to my will and return home with me. If you refuse, or use any type of magic against me, it will be considered an act of high treason, and thereby punishable by death. And so help me, if you so much as lift a finger against me, I will knock you unconscious and carry you back to your mother in a box!"

My fingers close around the flames burning on my palms, and the fire winks out, plunging us into shadow barely brightened by the tiny flame left spluttering in the lamp. "I will go nowhere with you."

Lord Damar reaches across the table and grabs the bun at the crown of my head, yanking me to my feet and pulling me around to his side of the table. Treyose takes a step forward, but Ingvar stands still and watches; he knows I can beat Lord Damar in a fight. I bend my right arm, prepared to ram my elbow into Lord Damar's ribs, but freeze. Something cold and sharp is pressing against my temple. Treyose halts in midstride, and Ingvar reaches for his missing sword. From the corner of my eye I see a long, silver needle, much like a knitting needle, clutched in Lord Damar's soft hand, its tip held firmly to the skin beside my eye. A bitter scent wafts from the needle, and I recognize the odor of poison even though I have never smelled it with my own nose.

"It is poisoned," I breathe out, my voice calm. As I stand there, every possible scenario to get away from Lord Damar flashes through my head in the blink of an eye. And every one of them includes the likelihood of my being poisoned. Depending on the type of poison in the needle, even a single drop on my skin could be deadly.

"She is leaving with me, or she dies here," Lord Damar warns, winding his hand so tightly in my hair my eyelids stretch toward my hairline and my scalp feels like it is on fire.

"I do not like either of those options," Treyose says, and pulls a metal throwing star from his sleeve. With a flick of his wrist, he throws it. The small weapon passes so close to my ear it brushes it. Lord Damar jolts and the poisoned needle catches on my skin. I slam my elbow into his ribs in the same moment Ingvar reaches for me. Ingvar shoves me to the side a breath before Lord Damar thrusts the needle forward. The sharp tip barely misses my back and instead slides between the chain links of Ingvar's armor and plunges into his stomach.

"Bloody Faodarian pig!" Ingvar yells. He reaches for his attacker but misses as Lord Damar stumbles backward clutching his throat, the silver throwing star visible between his fingers. Ingvar falls to his knees beside me and pulls the needle from his stomach. He looks at it for a moment, where the blood has turned the silver crimson, and then sways sideways.

"No!" I cry, lunging for him. Before I can grab him, hands close around my arms, and I am pulled away. Ingvar falls to the ground, his face pressing against the sharp blades of broken grass. His skin is ashen and covered with sweat, and his mouth is open. "Ingvar? Can you hear me?" I ask. The silver needle slips out of his fingers and falls silently to the trampled grass. "No! Ingvar!" I fight against Treyose's hold on me, trying to wrench my arms from his grasp. "I can help him!" I cry. When Golmarr was on the brink of death, I healed him. I might be able to heal Ingvar.

The tent flap is thrown aside. Enzio takes a step in and freezes, his eyes sweeping the chaos. "Help Ingvar," I plead. Enzio hesitates, studying Treyose's hold on me, and then falls to his knees beside Ingvar. He presses two fingers to his neck, and then looks like he is on the verge of being sick. "He is dead." My stomach roils, and I wonder if *I* am going to be sick.

Treyose cinches one arm around my neck, the other around my waist, pinning my arms at my sides. "If you make a single move against me, the princess dies," he warns Enzio. "Why did you have to do that?" he asks me and curses under his breath.

"Do what?" I growl, struggling against his hold.

"Why couldn't you have simply agreed to come with me like a meek Faodarian bride?" I pull one arm free and ram my elbow into his ribs, making him grunt. His hold only tightens.

"Why did you have to put up a fight?" I ram my elbow into his ribs a second time and wish I could get my knife out from under my skirt. Enzio is patiently watching us, waiting for the perfect moment to come to my aid.

"Why?" I ask and stomp on his foot. "Because I will choose my own destiny!" I reach my free hand toward the tiny flame still flickering in the lamp, prepared to use it to burn him to a crisp.

"Won't work," Treyose says, tightening his hold on my neck until I can barely breathe. "I am wearing an amulet that protects me from magic—fire, to be more specific. I came prepared for you, Princess Sorrowlynn."

I clamp my teeth down on the side of Treyose's hand. He yelps but still does not release me.

Enzio uses the distraction to step toward me, but Treyose has already dropped his arm from my waist and is holding another silver throwing star. As he lets it fly at Enzio, I shove his arm upward and ram my elbow into his ribs as hard as I can. The star sinks into Enzio's arm instead of his chest.

Treyose tightens his hold on my neck, completely cutting off my air. Focusing my strength into my arm, I ram my elbow into his ribs three times in a row, as hard and fast as I can. His hold on my neck loosens enough for me to slide out from under his arm. I grab the lamp from the table, and with the copper handle clutched in both my hands like a sword hilt, I swing with every ounce of strength I possess.

He throws his arm up to block, and the lamp collides with the side of Treyose's head and arm. Glass shatters. Oil splatters Treyose and fire flares on his face. He screams and tears off his tunic, extinguishing the fire and plunging the tent into stifling blackness. I kick the blackness in front of me, feeling the satisfying impact of my foot against Treyose's stomach. There is a grunt and a thud as he lands on the ground. My hands wave through the dark until they contact the solid warmth of Enzio. Gripping his hand in mine, I pull him out of the tent and we sprint to the horses.

"How much are you bleeding?" I ask. My words sound wrong—thick and slow, as if my tongue is too big.

It takes him a moment to answer. "Not enough to kill me."

I run my hands along his arm and find the star still embedded in his biceps. His clothes around the weapon are barely damp with blood. "Don't pull this out until you are back at the fortress and have someone to sew it up," I instruct. "Did you read the letter from Golmarr?" I am talking too fast now, and my skin feels like it is on fire.

"Yes. He's in Arkhavan. At the Royal Library of Trevon, looking for something called the Infinite Vessel," Enzio says.

Something black buzzes by my face, and I swat my hand at it. "Did you see that?"

Enzio leans closer. "See what? You don't look well. Are you all right?"

I nod, but my blood feels like it has turned to liquid fire beneath my skin, bursting with so much energy and so many emotions, my flesh can barely contain it. My head is throbbing, too. The ground tilts, and I grip Enzio's tunic to keep from stumbling. I take a deep breath, trying to gather my wits about me and say, "Treyose killed Lord Damar, and Lord Damar killed Ingvar. You need to tell the horse clan. *Damar* killed . . ." My voice cracks with emotion and I cannot speak.

Enzio sniffles and wraps his arms around me. "I am so sorry. I will tell them." My body, suddenly freezing, shudders against his, and I grip him more tightly to keep from falling.

Enzio helps me regain my balance and studies me. "Are you injured?" he asks. I shake my head, so he presses his hand to my forehead. "Are you sick? You feel too warm." I push his hand away and stumble toward Dewdrop.

"I need to go."

"Come back to the fortress. Let the horse clan protect you."

"No! I will not have the Faodarian and Trevonan armies wage war on Anthar just to get me." Even in the dark, my foot slips effortlessly into the stirrup, and I swing my leg over Dewdrop's back.

"Then I will come with you."

"Please get your arm tended to first. I would never forgive myself if anything happened to you, Enzio. And someone needs to tell the Antharians that Ingvar is dead." I do not wait for his reply. As I ride alone into the night, icy wind rushes against my face.

# Chapter 7

The grassland blurs as tears fill my eyes, and I bury my face in the warmth of Dewdrop's mane. Using the darkness to hide my retreat, I head south at a slow, quiet canter, between the two lines of opposing armies camouflaged by the night—the Antharians on my right, the Faodarians on my left. Before long, the night is filled with the clamor and wailing of the Antharian army. They have learned Ingvar, their future king, has been murdered.

"I'm sorry, Ingvar. I'm sorry, Golmarr. I'm sorry, King Marrkul," I whisper, and shudder at the thought of Golmarr learning that it is my fault his brother was killed. He already hates me because he inherited the glass dragon's hatred. Now he will have a reason of his own. Taking a deep, steadying breath, I sit back up. The world is a wavering blur of silver moonlight against the deeply shadowed grass, and I feel as if I am riding through rising and falling water. I blink hard, and tears stream down my cheeks, but the land doesn't stop moving. Giving my head a firm shake, I lean forward and signal Dewdrop to a gallop.

When I have ridden several miles south, I slow to a trot

and turn west toward Trevon and Treyose's approaching army of one thousand, toward the city of Arkhavan and the Royal Library of Trevon: the biggest and oldest library in the world. Before I reach the army, I will veer north again and cross into Trevon that way.

Dewdrop continues cantering across grassland swelling and dipping like ocean waves. "I never knew the grasslands had hills," I whisper. No maps of Anthar show hills, and none of my inherited grassland memories ever have hills. We crest a swell as tall as a mountain, and as we start down the other side, the ground grows steeper and steeper, until I have to cling to the pommel of the saddle to keep from falling out of it. And then, though there is not a single visible cloud blocking the starry sky, the night darkens.

I signal Dewdrop to stop and look up. Darkness drops from above, and a moment later I am surrounded by a black cloud of bugs. Their noisy drone scatters my thoughts. I swat at the bugs, but it does nothing to stop the buzzing. Dewdrop flicks an ear and peers at me, and I wonder why she isn't swishing her tail and shaking her mane to scatter the swarming insects. The air grows darker as the bugs become so numerous they completely hide the moon. Their buzzing grows deeper and unbearably loud, rattling my teeth and vibrating my very bones. As if oblivious, Dewdrop lowers her head and starts grazing.

I press my hands to my ears and insects land on my bare arms. Their tiny feet are covered with spines that stick into my flesh as they walk. I try to brush them off, but they cling to me. They crawl up my neck and into my ears and nostrils, and climb on the slick, wet skin of my eyeballs. My eyelids slam shut, trapping bugs beneath them. I scratch at my ears, my nose, start clawing at my flesh, digging at the bugs burrowing into it. The insects pour down my shirt and find my delicate skin, and I open my mouth to scream, but they fill it with blackness that wedges into my throat so firmly, I cannot draw breath, and Dewdrop keeps calmly eating grass.

Above the vibration of bugs, the rhythmic pounding of galloping reaches me. With my eyes still closed tight, I topple from Dewdrop and land hard on the side of the hill. I cram my fingers into my throat, trying to claw out the bugs so I can breathe. So I can scream to the rider for help.

The ground shudders as a horse trots to my side and stops. I open my eyes to see who has come, but the bugs have crawled inside of my eyeballs and are swimming through my vision: little black dots whirling slowly in front of the moon.

A dark figure crouches beside me. I open my mouth to beg for help, but still can't breathe, so I cram my fingers down my throat again, trying to clear it, trying to make myself vomit. Rock hard hands clamp my wrists and pin them to the ground beside my head.

"I can't breathe," I whimper. "There are bugs in my throat."

"If you can talk, you can breathe," a deep voice says.

I thrash against the man, trying to break his grasp so I can remove the bugs. "Get them off me!" I wail, shocked I can speak around the insects crawling in my mouth.

"What? Get what off you?" he asks, holding my wrists more securely.

"The bugs! They are everywhere! In my eyes, in my ears." I open my mouth, suck in a breath of air that draws hundreds of tiny bodies into my lungs, and scream. A warm, solid hand slaps my face and my head jerks to the side.

"Princess Sorrowlynn, you need to get up." He tightens his hold on my wrists and pulls me to my feet. The ground tilts so steeply, I tip into the man's arms before I can gain my balance.

"We're going to fall off!" I throw my arms around his neck.

Warm fingers probe my neck, my ear, and slowly make their way to my temple. When they press against my hairline, the world snaps, flattening out beneath my feet like a sheet whipped straight atop a mattress. I am standing upright, and the ground is flat as far as the eye can see; the starry sky once again is overhead. In a unison burst, the bugs fly away, but I hear them close by, waiting.

"Your father's needle nicked you. You should be dead," the deep voice says. Fingers wipe something sticky from my temple, and I smell blood. "I think you are hallucinating from the poison."

"No, I'm not hallucinating. The bugs." I lean closer to him and pull his head down so my lips are by his ear. "Can't you hear them?" I whisper.

Gently, he pushes me away. "I hear nothing, Sorrowlynn."

The man's voice is not familiar. I try to make out his face, illuminated by the moon and stars, but black spots are still swimming against my sight. I press the balls of my hands against my eyes. When I remove them, the man in front of me becomes clear as the sun rises in the north and shines on his face. He studies me with familiar hazel eyes framed by black lashes, and a bright smile pulls his lips away from white teeth. It is the smile I have been longing to see. At the sight of it, the sorrow that has been my constant companion these last months is replaced with joy. I hear Golmarr's voice in my head, from a long-ago day in the Glass Forest, as he placed my hand on his chest, directly above his heart. I could feel his heart beating, slow and steady. When I asked him what he was doing, he replied, "I want you to feel what you do to my heart when I kiss you, Sorrowlynn."

"Golmarr!" I laugh and throw my arms around his neck, savoring the feel of him. "Where have you been? I have missed you so much." Leaning back, I place my hands on his warm cheeks and sigh with contentment.

Golmarr furrows his brow. "What?" His voice is wrong, but everything else about him is perfect. My attention moves from his eyes to his mouth, and my heart starts to pound. I stand on my toes and kiss him. His lips are cool beneath mine, and completely unresponsive. Hands wrap around my wrists and he takes a step away. My joy is once again replaced with emptiness.

"Do you hate me? Is that why you don't want me to touch you?" I ask, and that is the moment the swarming bugs come in for a second attack. As they fill my eyes and pour into my nostrils and down my throat, I scream. Layer after layer, they cover my body until I cannot move. My arms and legs are pressed beneath such a massive weight, I cannot lift them. Even my ribs barely expand as I try to force air into them. Only my eyes work, darting from side to side, filled with so much black I barely see a thing.

Something cracks against my jaw, and as my head is wrenched to the side, straining so hard against my neck it feels like it is going to snap off, the bugs devour me into a silent, cold blackness.

# Chapter 8

The ocean is rising and falling, back and forth, up and down, and a woman keeps calling my name, her voice begging me to answer. Shores of shimmering black and dragon claws flit through my mind until I realize the front of my body is like ice, my dangling legs are stiff and numb, but my back is toasty warm. *Time to roll over so the other side of me is facing the hearth*, I think, but cannot move. My lips part and I taste blood on my tongue. A long, hoarse groan scratches out of my throat.

"Drink this," someone says, and I open my eyes. The world is tilting back and forth, and I am sitting astride a horse. A leather water skin is being held in front of me by a hand missing half of its pinkie finger. The sight of that disfigured finger sends a wave of concern through me, but I take the water skin and drink.

My throat burns when I swallow. It is swollen and thick, covered with raw patches. When I bring the water skin down from my mouth, I see blood dried on my fingers and caked beneath my nails. The water sloshes in my stomach, and my body rejects it and tightens. I scramble in the saddle, yank an arm from around my waist, and fall from the horse, thudding onto my side on brittle, dry grass. My stomach clenches again. Oily slime and black pebbles the shape and size of my thumbnail shoot from my mouth and stain the ground. They look exactly like the rocks from the beach in my dream. Pushing onto my hands and knees, I vomit again; more slime filled with black pebbles. No, not pebbles. Bugs. They are still squirming, trying to crawl out of the vomit and toward me.

I squeeze my eyes shut against the sight and moan. Bugs are wriggling in my belly and throat. I vomit a third time, a fourth, a fifth, until my stomach clenches but nothing comes out. When I open my eyes, I expect to see a mountain of bugs writhing on the ground, but the vomit has changed. Instead of slime filled with bugs, a puddle of yellow bile is seeping into the dirt. There is nothing black in it or around it.

"What happened to the bugs?" I ask.

Heavy leather boots thud down beside me. I wipe my mouth on my bare arm and squint up.

"What bugs?" the owner of the boots asks. "It is the end of winter. All the bugs are dead." He has short, pale hair, and his chest is as wide as a barrel of ale. *Prince Treyose*, I think. *My so-called husband.* He hands me an embroidered handkerchief, and I wipe my mouth with it, leaving traces of vomit on the expensive silk. The water skin plunks to the ground beside my vomit and I lift it to my mouth with trembling hands, swishing the water around and spitting it back out.

I look at the vomit again—plain, frothy bile and not bugs— and a word whispers into my mind. *Strickbane.* Dragon poison. Strickbane is lethal to humans if it is so much as absorbed through the skin. Only a dragon can be dosed with Strickbane and survive. In tiny doses, it causes hallucinations before killing its victim. Anything more and it kills almost instantly. I press on my hairline and feel the scabbed spot where the poison was introduced into my blood. "How did Lord Damar get his hands on Strickbane poison, and how am I still alive?" I whisper, and totter back on my heels.

"Better?" Treyose asks.

"Not really. How did you find me?"

"I knew you headed south, so I followed. When I couldn't find you, your screams of terror led me right to your side."

"I wasn't screaming," I say. "I couldn't even talk."

"You were screaming so loudly, I thought someone was murdering you." As he talks, I glance at him from the corner of my eye and quickly lift my skirt, exposing my leg to my knee. An empty knife belt is strapped to my calf. "Are you looking for this?" he asks, holding my black stone knife in his hand, testing its balance. He thrusts it into the back of his waistband and then wraps his hands around my arms and lifts me to my feet like I weigh nothing. My entire body begins quivering, and I hug my arms around myself.

"Cold," I say through chattering teeth, and my breath comes out as white mist. My mouth tastes terrible.

"I have no cloak or I would let you wear it." He smirks. "And I have no tunic, because you set fire to it." I look at his shirt—a plain, thin long-sleeve undershirt made to wear beneath a heavier garment. "When we reach my army we will get provisions."

My back goes rigid and some of the trembling leaves my body. "No," I say, my voice weak. "I am not going with you. Where is my horse?"

His lips press into a hard line, and his hand darts out, cinching around my wrist. Without a word, he drags me to his horse and mounts. "Do you want to climb up, or do you want me to drag you into the saddle?" he asks, eyes cold as stone.

Twisting my wrist toward his thumb, I break the hold. Before I have moved out of reach, his other hand tangles in my hair, dragging me so my chest is pressed against his leg. Once again my scalp burns from the strain put on it, and I silently swear I am going to cut my hair as short as a Trevonan man's the first chance I get.

Treyose digs his fingers into my armpits and hauls me onto the horse so I am lying across the animal. My poison-ravished body is too weak to fight him, so I lie there trying to catch my breath.

"I heard you were a tenacious woman, but I never would have believed it of a Faodarian-raised princess, had I not seen it with my own eyes," he growls. He hauls on my shoulders and together the two of us work to get me astride the animal. As soon as I am sitting, Treyose's arm cinches around my waist and pulls me tight against his chest. "As your husband, I command you to stay on this horse." I grunt in response, and swallow against the lump forming in my throat. He puts his mouth against my ear. "If you try to jump off, I will tie you to me with a rope."

Despite the tears trying to fill my eyes, I muster up every ounce of dignity I still possess and I lift my chin. They fall anyway—the tears—trickling down my cheeks and raining from my chin, splattering Treyose's hand. Leaning to the side, he studies my profile. With a groan of frustration, he digs his boot heels into the horse's flanks, and we start forward at a fast trot.

As the sun rises at our backs and the Trevonan army comes

into view, I lift my skirt and use it to dry my cheeks. Instead of riding to the army, Treyose pulls the horse to a stop and waits as five riders approach.

To our left and ahead a little way is a small hollow in the grass, and I know immediately an archer is stationed there, probably lying on his belly, arrow nocked and pointed at us. "Would your own archer truly shoot you?" My voice is sour with derision.

"The sun is in his eyes. I would rather not find out if he can tell it is me," Treyose says, looking toward the concealed man. "And it is you his arrow would hit."

As the five riders near, Treyose raises his hand and signals them to come close. They slow their horses and stop in front of us. All five men have the close-cropped hair worn by Trevonan nobility, and all carry well-made swords, not the mass-produced, standard army issue. These men are noblemen, probably Treyose's top ranked. They study me, eyes curious, but not one of them asks who I am. *It must not be unusual for Trevonan men to bring unwilling women home*, I think. *Even an unwilling bride.*

"Rally the army. There will be no fighting with Faodara or Anthar today," Treyose says.

"Then why are we here? Why have you been in Faodara these past weeks?" one man asks. He is middle-aged and lean—the kind of lean that begets speed and strength in a fight.

"I had business with Faodara, and it is now concluded. I asked you to meet me on our border as a simple precaution to make sure I made it back without an army on my heels. I was not sure how things would turn out with Lord Damar,"

Treyose answers. Though his men's eyes shine with curiosity, none of them question Treyose further. "Anslow."

A young man with pale red hair rides forward. "Yes, my lord?"

Treyose holds a creased and rather worn-looking sealed letter out to him. "Send a man out with this. I was supposed to give it to the King of Anthar before leaving his kingdom, but I was forced to flee before I had the chance." He looks accusingly at me. "It needs to be delivered to King Marrkul of Anthar, right into his hand. He is at their mountain fortress."

"Yes, sir. I will get provisions and then leave immediately." Anslow bows and turns his horse, trotting into the ranks of the army.

"And what is our destination, Prince Treyose?" the middle-aged man asks.

"We ride for home, Reyler." Treyose guides his horse closer to his men and adds, "Warn everyone if they linger here, they risk being killed by the Antharian army and the Faodarian army. I need a fresh horse. You are dismissed." The men nod and turn to leave, but Treyose calls, "Wait!" The four riders turn to him. "My companion needs food. Reyler, stay." The men's eyes flicker to me with renewed interest, and then all but one man ride away.

The lean man's eyes linger on my long, loose hair for a moment, and I wonder what I must look like. He quickly takes in my rumpled clothing and Treyose's arm cinched around my waist. "She is wearing Antharian clothing, but she does not have their black hair and darker skin. Who is she?"

"She is . . ." He studies the side of my face. "A Satari woman from the Glass Forest."

Reyler looks at me again. "You've taken a Satari woman hostage?" he asks, and his eyes move to my bloodstained hands.

Treyose nods. "Yes, Reyler, I have taken a Satari woman hostage," he says so loudly my ears ring. Every man within hearing distance stops what he is doing to study me. "I like the look of her," he adds. I open my mouth to protest, but he claps his hand over it. Leaning close to Reyler, he quietly says, "In truth, this is Princess Sorrowlynn of Faodara, and she is my wife. But that information is not to go beyond you. Do you understand?"

Reyler's gray eyes light up and he grins. "Of course, my lord. It is about time you were wed." The grin falters. "She does not look happy."

"No, *happy* is definitely not a word I would use to describe our union. Be sure to give her the utmost respect, and protection if she ever needs it." There is a hard edge to Treyose's voice.

Reyler, his eyes still taking in every detail about me, whispers, "Is she why you have been in Faodara these past weeks? You have fallen in love with her, and married her against her will?"

"I have been in Faodara for many reasons, but my grandfather is not to know I brought a woman home with me. I do not want him to find out," Treyose explains. Reyler's eyes grow dark, and he nods. "I will explain more later, when we have privacy. Come with me." He kicks his mount and we ride forward, though the horse's hooves stumble with exhaustion.

"Where, exactly, are you taking me?" I ask.

"Prince Treyose," he says, his voice cold.

"You *are* Prince Treyose, so you cannot be taking me to him."

With his mouth against my ear he quietly says, "When you speak to me, you address me with respect. You can either call me 'my lord' or 'Prince Treyose.'"

My lips pucker. "Then I will not speak to you."

He shrugs, and I feel it against my back, so I lean as far from him as I can. "I *prefer* silence from most women," he says.

Every muscle in my body grows taut as a bowstring. I grit my teeth and ram my elbow into Treyose's ribs as hard as I can, and then brace for the recoil of his anger. He laughs under his breath, and then chuckles out loud. "I don't know why any man would want to be wed to you," he says. I ram my elbow back a second time, but he catches it before it hits his ribs.

"Then have it annulled," I say. He doesn't respond.

At a simple, linen tent, he dismounts. "Reyler," he says, not taking his eyes from mine. "I would like you to nock an arrow and keep it trained on this Satari woman's thigh. If she dismounts, wait until she is far enough from my steed so you can shoot her in the leg without hitting the animal. But shoot first, and ask questions later." Eyes still boring into mine, he adds, "And I can guarantee you she will run."

I glare at Reyler. "Not when I see with a glance your man knows how to use his weapon."

Reyler grins, and Treyose laughs as he enters the tent. A moment later he exits and tosses a fur-lined Trevonan-purple cloak to me. Desperate for its warmth, I swing it around my shoulders and hook the golden clasp at my throat—a quill crossed with a sword, the royal seal of Trevon.

After a few minutes of metal clanking and ringing from inside the tent, Treyose steps out, armed with a sword at his hip and a bow slung over his back. He's wearing sleek Trevonan armor that makes his barrel of a chest look even bigger than before. Instead of chain mail and leather, his armor is made up of small metal scales that overlap each other. He looks like a dragon. I eye his sword and wonder how to get it away from him.

"I do not like how you are studying my weapon," he says. He runs his fingers down the front of his armor. "Now your elbows will do no damage." He turns and bellows, "Where is my fresh horse? We need to ride."

As if on cue, a young man guides a well-groomed, saddled bay mare to us. He hands the reins to Treyose and bows. Squinting against the sun, Treyose looks up. "Are you going to trade horses like a good girl, or am I going to have to drag you into the saddle again?"

I clench my jaw and stick my nose in the air.

"My men would love to see me force you into the saddle," he says quietly. Stepping close, he rests his hand on my knee and adds, "I would prefer not to."

Feeling like I am giving up my freedom, I slide from the saddle of the weary horse and gracefully swing up onto the bay.

Treyose nods his satisfaction. "At least you can see sense."

# Chapter 9

The army is like a slow-moving beast, skulking across the land and flattening everything in its way. Every few minutes, I peer back around Treyose's broad, armored shoulder, expecting to see another army darkening the horizon we have recently trodden. The horizon never changes. When the sun has crawled halfway across the sky, and I peer to the east yet again, Treyose grunts and says, "No one is coming for you, so you might as well stop looking."

His words muddy the hope I have been clinging to—the hope I have used to anchor my emotions since the day Golmarr tried to kill me. Hope. It is getting harder and harder to hold on to it. "I am betrothed to Prince Golmarr, son of King Marrkul. That makes me Antharian," I say through a tight jaw. "They will come for me."

He pulls me tight against his chest and puts his mouth beside my ear. "My arrangement to wed you was agreed upon by your mother and father, and was put into motion by one of the Antharian princes. King Marrkul was informed of it this morning—that is what was written in the letter I gave to Anslow. King Marrkul will not send an army for you because the letter was from his own son. This arrangement is part of a bigger plan."

My stomach clenches and then sours. "One of the Antharian princes agreed to this? As in one of Golmarr's brothers?"

"Yes, one of King Marrkul's sons agreed to this, but I am not at liberty to say who it was."

I think of Golmarr's eight brothers and wonder who betrayed me. "I do not believe you," I say after a long silence. "Golmarr's brothers pledged to protect me."

He laughs under his breath. "The horse lords are fighters and warriors. They will pledge to protect you one minute, and then change their minds when they find a worthier cause to fight for. Unfortunately for you, one of them has found a worthier cause."

"What cause?" My voice is barely louder than a whisper.

"Something they have sought for hundreds of years: peace with Trevon."

I shake my head as a swell of dizziness hits me and tilts me sideways. "No!" The word comes out as a breath. "They wouldn't trade me for peace." *Would they?*

"You have to understand how they think," he says, firming his arm around me and pulling me back upright. "Your life is but *one* life. Giving you to me in exchange for peace will spare thousands upon thousands of lives, Princess Sorrowlynn. It will be the key to preserving fathers and mothers, the means to having children grow up in whole families, not as orphans who are instantly recruited to one of the Antharian's citadels to train to be a warrior in place of being a son or daughter. It will change the way they live for the better, and all because of you."

What he says makes sense. My hope takes wings and

flutters just out of reach. I swallow past a growing lump in my throat and ask, "Am I truly wed to you?"

"Truly, legally, and inescapably."

"But I did not give my consent. I did not say 'I do.' I did not plight thee my troth, and I never shall!" My voice trembles with emotions I cannot name. I have never experienced these feelings before today. They take my hope and shatter it.

"But Queen Felicitia did. She holds double stewardship over you, as your mother *and* your queen. It is a written law in your land that the queen can marry any of her subjects by proxy marriage, with or without the person's consent, to further the good of the kingdom," he says.

A sheen of sweat coats my palms and my breathing accelerates. I was taught Faodara's laws at an early age, and I remember this particular law well because of its unfairness. I cover my face with my icy hands and fight the sting of tears. "I do not want this," I whisper.

Treyose exhales. "I have been commander of my grandfather's army since I was fifteen years old. Not *once* have I wanted to lead this army and watch hundreds upon hundreds of people lose their lives. But we are tools, you and I. We are used to do others' bidding, to fulfill their desires and schemes. You, at least, are being used to spare lives. I have *always* been used to take them." Were his voice that of a dragon, I would be killed by its venom.

I lower my hands from my face and hang my head. "What of my betrothed?"

"If you are wed to me, you are no longer betrothed to another." His voice has lost its edge.

A disturbance shudders through the army, like a stone has been thrown into a pond, making ring after ring of soldiers ripple out from its center. When the ripple reaches us, we stop riding and look toward the commotion. Two unknown riders have come upon the rear of the Trevonan soldiers. They are encircled by Trevonan archers, their bows drawn.

Treyose turns his horse toward the new riders and we gallop forward. Instantly, I recognize them. It is Yerengul and Enzio. With their appearance, a tiny, fragile piece of hope returns to me.

Treyose rides forward and stops in front of Yerengul and Enzio. "Stand down," he orders his men, and the bows are lowered, but not put away. He turns to Yerengul and Enzio. "For the sake of this woman, I request you hold your tongues until we have privacy." Yerengul looks at me, and then nods. "Follow me. Reyler, accompany us," Treyose calls. We ride the horse to the head of the army, and then a little way beyond, before Treyose asks, "What business do you have with me?"

"We have come for Sorrowlynn," Yerengul says, his glare so sharp I can practically feel it slicing my skin. Reyler guides his horse closer to Treyose's and places his hand on his sword hilt.

"You and what army?" Treyose asks, voice quiet.

"She is sworn into the horse clan, and I have pledged to protect her until she is united with my brother Golmarr," Yerengul says. "Our army will come for her, and so will the Faodarian army, once Lord Damar's wound has been treated."

Treyose's arm tightens around me. "Damar lives?"

Yerengul nods.

"Damar's army might come, but the Antharian army will not. Have you spoken to your king? I dispatched a letter to him this morning."

"When I left my father in the middle of the night, the only thing we had received from you was my eldest brother's body. The Antharian army is making preparations to follow me."

Treyose lifts his left hand—the one that has been holding the reins—and flicks it in a series of Antharian hand signals so fast I barely see them. Though I have been taught the Antharian hand speak, I do not recognize what Treyose said. Yerengul's fierce glare falters, turns to confusion, and then shock as he studies Treyose. "Now you understand I am working with your brother. I swear on my life that I will not harm Princess Sorrowlynn," he adds. "I am not your enemy. So, unless you want to risk the wrath of your own brother, I suggest you take your leave. If you do not, I cannot protect you against my army."

Yerengul looks from me to Enzio and shakes his head. "I cannot stay," he says.

Enzio's nostrils flare with anger. "Why not?"

"Prince Treyose is working with one of my brothers. To fight him will be to go against my own flesh and blood." He grips Enzio's arm. "Stay with her," he pleads, and then he looks at me one last time before turning his horse east.

"Wait," Treyose calls.

Yerengul glares at him. "I do not take orders from Trevonan princes."

"Make sure your people know I am not working against Anthar in this," Treyose says. "And I did not kill Prince Ingvar. Lord Damar did."

Yerengul clenches his teeth, holding in the fury burning behind his eyes. He leans over his horse's neck and gallops away, and I am left staring at the trail of dust left in his wake.

"What did you tell him with your hand?" I ask. *What gesture does this Trevonan prince know that will convince the horse clan to abandon me?* I wonder.

"You claim to be part of the horse clan, but you do not know the Antharians' hand talk?" Treyose asks.

"I have been taught all their battle signals, but I have never been taught what you just did."

"Then you are not supposed to know what it means."

"And how do you know it?" I ask.

"The prince I am working with taught it to me. It was his secret hand signal I gave Yerengul."

Golmarr has eight brothers. I try to think why one of them would work with Treyose and have me wed to him, when they knew I was planning on marrying Golmarr.

Treyose points at Enzio. "By the look of you, you are a Satari forest dweller. Why would Yerengul of Anthar ask you to stay with Sorrowlynn? I know you are not her sweetheart because she has told me *so many times* she is betrothed to Golmarr of Anthar. So what allegiance do you owe her?"

Enzio dismounts and kneels beside Treyose's horse. "You are correct that I am a humble Satari forest dweller, from the band called the Black Blades. I beg of you, let me stay with Sorrowlynn. She is my cousin, and I owe her my mother's life. I have vowed to protect her until the debt is repaid."

"I am not a prince who makes people grovel at his feet," Treyose snaps. "Stand, man. If you wish it, you can come with us. But know this. I was sincere when I said I mean Sorrowlynn no harm. You must give me your solemn vow you will do as you are told while in my company. If you do not, you will forfeit your life."

Enzio climbs to his feet and a calculating gleam flashes in his blue eyes. "So long as you do not harm Sorrowlynn, or command me to do anything to put her at risk, I will do what you ask for now."

"Then mount up. We are still half a day's hard ride from Arkhavan." Treyose shifts behind me and then something comes over my head and settles around my ribs. Rope. I gasp and try to pull it off, but he yanks it tight around my waist and then cinches it into a knot. I am bound to him, and my hope of escape is destroyed.

⊷ ⊰✦⊱ ⊶

We travel until the sun sets, its last orange rays lighting up a horizon of houses built so closely together, they look like a single structure divided only by the narrow roads that snake between them. A black stone wall as tall as a house surrounds the city. *Arkhavan*, the memories encased in my conscience whisper. Arkhavan is the city where Golmarr is rumored to be. It is the seat of the Royal Library of Trevon. If I escape Treyose, maybe I can find Golmarr . . . and tell him what? I have been wed to another, his brother died trying to protect me, and at least one dragon is coming for me? He will hate me more than ever.

We ride a short distance from the army, and Treyose reigns in the horse. "Reyler," he calls. The slender nobleman rides to us, and Treyose leans in close to him. "I need you to wait until morning to bring the troops inside the wall. Set up camp here," he whispers. He pulls up the hood of his cloak, which I am still wearing, so my face is hidden deep in shadow. "I will enter the city tonight with Princess Sorrowlynn. Before sunrise, I will return and we will come inside together. I do not want my grandfather to know I have returned until tomorrow."

Reyler studies my face, hidden beneath the cloak, before nodding. "Yes, my lord. I will see to it." He unfastens his dark gray cloak and hands it to Treyose. "Although there is no point trying to sneak her in if everyone sees you."

"Thank you." With the hand missing half a finger, Treyose takes the cloak. He puts it on and fastens it, pulling the hood so it hides his face.

Something is very wrong. "Why are you sneaking me into your city, especially if I am your new bride?"

Treyose's body grows so taut behind mine, it feels as if I am leaning against stone. "My grandfather, King Vaunn, is not kind to women. I would protect you from him. Enzio, I assume you will insist on coming with us?"

Enzio nods, and his worried eyes meet mine.

"Then I need your weapons," Treyose says.

Enzio laughs and shakes his head. "I think not, sir. A Satari man without his blade is like a sky without stars—unnatural and undesirable."

Treyose gestures at his army of one thousand. "Do you truly think you have a choice in the matter? Hand over your weapons and come with me, or I will have my one thousand men watch you for the night. The choice is yours."

Enzio's face grows stony, but he unhooks his belt and removes his short sword and scabbard and hands them to Treyose.

"The knife in your sleeve, too," Treyose says.

"What knife?"

Treyose laughs. "I have been commander of the Trevonan army for ten years. You cannot pull the wool over my eyes so easily." He holds his hand out. "Give me the knife now, or stay with my army tonight."

Enzio growls and slides the knife from his sleeve. He tosses it in the air and catches it by the blade, and then hands it pommel-first to Treyose.

Treyose looks at the black stone blade and frowns. "This is the twin blade to the one I took from Sorrowlynn."

Enzio nods. "Those blades were wielded by my ancestors before they were forced to flee the kingdom of Satar more than a century ago."

Treyose studies the blade more closely. "This is one of the fabled Black Blades that cannot be broken?"

"It is, and I would like your oath that you will return both of them to Sorrowlynn and me."

"I swear to return your blades," Treyose says, sliding it into his belt. "Follow me. We only have a few minutes before the city gate is shut for the night."

We pass through a wide opening in the wall and into the city while I'm still tied to Treyose. He chooses dark, deserted streets for us to follow, and when anyone looks our way, he hangs his head so the cloak shadows his face. I should be dwelling on escape plans, but all I can worry about is how I am going to avoid our wedding night. Even with his armor pressed tight between us, shielding my body from his, I am repulsed by his closeness.

Soon, the castle, located in the heart of the city, comes into view. It is made of slick black granite that reflects the light off the torches lit in the inner bailey. Silhouetted against the starry sky is a tower so tall I have to crane my neck all the way back to see the top. I know there is a massive copper bell in the tower, hidden from view by the darkness. Beside the bell tower is the Royal Library. It is so close, and yet it has never been as out of reach as it is at this moment.

# Chapter 10

We are stopped by guards at the gates to the inner bailey. When Treyose lifts his hood enough for one man to see who he is, the gate is opened, and we are quietly ushered inside. No grooms or pages come to assist the prince. We are like ghosts.

Treyose cuts the rope binding me to him, but not before taking a firm grip on the back of my tunic. Enzio steps forward to help me dismount, but Treyose blocks my cousin. "I do not trust you," Treyose says. He dismounts and puts his hands on my waist and lifts me out of the saddle. Taking both my hands in one of his, he wraps the rope that bound me to him around my wrists and ties it tight enough that I cannot wiggle out of it.

"Why are you binding me?" I whisper, too scared to raise my voice.

"This wouldn't be necessary if you'd simply behave," Treyose says, glaring into my eyes. "I thought escorting a Faodarian princess to my kingdom would be one of the simpler things I have done in my life. It is not."

"But I do not wish to be escorted to your kingdom. I do not want to be your wife." My voice comes out laced with repulsion. "I do not . . . wish to share your bed."

He grunts and looks right into my eyes. "That is the most refreshing thing that has ever come out of your mouth. Most women want to be in my bed for no better reason than I am a prince. I am weary of it, Sorrowlynn. *Weary*." He ties one more knot in the rope and gives it a hard yank to make sure it holds. "To be honest, I do not want you in my bed, either, and even if I *did*, I wouldn't be fool enough to force you into it."

"Why?" I ask.

"Mostly because I will never force any woman into my bed, but also, you'd kill me in my sleep."

I stare at him, mute, for a long moment. Finally, I am able to ask, "You will *not* make me share your bed?"

He shakes his head. "I will not. But you must swear if I give you your own chamber, you will not run away this night." He takes my elbow and starts guiding me through the quiet bailey, toward the castle. Enzio falls into step behind us. "Swear it," he says.

I clench my teeth and clamp my lips over them.

His grasp on my elbow tightens. "Swear it, Sorrowlynn, or I *will* have you share a bed with me for the purpose of making sure you do not escape. And I have no qualms about tying you to me for the night."

Evidently, there *is* a way he can make me swear. "Fine." The word trembles. "I swear I will not try to escape *this* night. But I make no promises beyond that." We pass through the doors of the black castle and I remember the interior as if I have walked these very halls every day of my life. It feels like *my* castle, and I have come home after a long time away.

"You will not want to leave after tomorrow," Treyose says, his voice light, almost teasing.

"I will."

"No, you will not. This I know as surely as I know my ribs are aching, and my eyebrows are singed, and I have not slept in two days, and all because of you." He gives me a pointed, superior look, and I study his dark blond eyebrows. They *are* singed.

I fight a smirk and ask, "How is it the rest of your face is not burned?"

He reaches down the front of his shirt and pulls out a medallion, the same he showed me in Lord Damar's tent. "This was given to me by my new wizard. It shields me from fire," he says. He tucks the medallion back into his shirt. "Unfortunately, it does nothing against glass." He holds up his left arm and rolls back the sleeve. His arm is black and blue, and covered with shallow cuts, but I hardly see them as his previous statement registers.

"You have a wizard?" My mouth goes dry and I look at Enzio to make sure he is listening. His eyes meet mine, and I see the worry there.

Treyose nods. "The first wizard we have had since Melchior disappeared from this castle more than sixteen years ago."

I come to an abrupt halt and Treyose takes another step, yanking on the rope before he realizes I have stopped walking. I lurch forward and catch my balance. "Melchior was the royal wizard of Trevon?" I ask.

"When he chose to be. He was only here for a few months

of every year. He attended special occasions, like births and weddings, but no matter how my grandfather and father tried to cage him, the old wizard always disappeared."

"He was *my* family's wizard," I say, falling into step beside him again.

"Yes, I know. It was your birth that took him from us permanently."

I nearly trip. "Why do you say that?"

"Mere weeks after he disappeared, the rumor of your birth blessing traveled to us: *This baby will die by her own hand.* I was nine. My father and brothers died soon after that."

"Your father was an evil man," I say.

Treyose shrugs. "He was. The last time Melchior was at this castle, he told my father unless he stopped killing and plundering and giving women to his soldiers against their will, he and his sons would die. And then Melchior disappeared. My father was furious. He didn't want to stop killing and plundering, so he took my two older brothers and went after the wizard, determined to bring him back to the castle for good, since every war-hungry ruler needs a wizard to tell him whether he is going to win a battle. All three of them got sick and died within a day of leaving." We stop at a massive stone door carved to look like the sun is rising on it. Behind me, I hear Enzio's quiet breathing.

"Your chamber for tonight," Treyose says.

"You are making me sleep in the throne room?" I ask, before he has opened the door.

His eyes narrow. "How do you know this is the throne room?"

I startle at his words. How *do* I know it is the throne room?

I know this castle like I have lived a lifetime inside of its walls. "Am I wrong?" I ask, curious.

He shakes his head, calculating eyes taking my measure as if seeing me for the first time. "The throne room is the safest room in the castle. No one can get in, no one can get out, depending on which side of the door is locked," he explains. "I am putting you in here so I can get a decent night's sleep. Your palace in Faodara is very beautiful, but the beds are hard, and it is drafty. I have been away from my own bed for weeks." He takes one of the black stone blades from his belt. Enzio makes a muffled sound of alarm. "It is for her ropes, forest dweller," Treyose says, and starts carefully sawing at the rope binding my wrists. "You will be locked in until morning, Sorrowlynn."

"And what happens if the castle burns down while I am locked inside?" The moment the question leaves my mouth I know the answer. The throne room is constructed from marble walls so thick, not even a dragon's fire can penetrate them. This vast castle is built for more than the stark splendor it emanates. It is a safe hold, and this room, at the castle's heart, is the safest of all.

"Hopefully the castle *won't* burn down tonight," he says, his voice a cold, hard warning.

I incline my head. "I will not burn your castle down tonight." A small smile quirks my lips. I sounded just like my regal mother.

The massive stone doors swing silently open and I step inside the room. Sounds echo from the sleek walls, every fall of Treyose's and Enzio's boots amplified. At the far end of the room, centered before cream-colored velvet curtains that stretch all the way to the high ceiling, is a purple velvet throne.

Stone benches line the outer edges of the room. "There is a chamber pot behind the curtains," Treyose says.

"In the throne room?" I scoff.

"My grandfather is an old man. He needs a chamber pot close when he is in here." Treyose removes his cloak and spreads it out on a bench. "Your bed for the night. You can use the cloak you are wearing as a blanket."

I walk to the bench and press on the cloak. It offers almost no padding at all.

"No royal complaints about your sleeping arrangements?" Treyose asks.

"I will admit a pillow would have been nice, but you probably know I slept in a dragon's cave without a blanket or pillow, for days. This is better than that. And . . ." I slowly peruse Treyose's formidable body and pucker my lips in distaste. "I don't have to sleep with you. I'd pick a dragon's cave and no blankets for the rest of my life over your bed."

His face hardens. "I, also, would rather spend the night in a dragon's cave than have you in my bed." Without another word, he turns on his heel and clasps Enzio's elbow. "You can sleep on the cold stone floor outside the doors," he says, and stomps out of the room with Enzio in tow, slamming the heavy doors so hard a gust of air ripples across the room and stirs the velvet curtains. A moment later, I hear the loud grate of a metal bar being slid in place in front of the door.

When the air has settled, I pick up Treyose's discarded cloak and carry it to the purple-lined throne. The throne has been built for an old, frail man who obviously likes his chair thick with padding. It will make a much more comfortable bed than a stone bench.

I wad the cloak up for a pillow, cover my body with the

purple cloak, and curl up like a cat. The ocean and black sand beaches fill my dreams.

---

It is midday before the stone door swings open, and dreams of black sand beaches, a two-headed dragon, and a woman's voice calling above the crash of waves still fill my mind. I miss the ocean like I have lived on its shores my entire life. But I have not.

I am sitting sideways on the gaudy purple throne with my legs dangling over the armrest, my feet swinging back and forth. Treyose steps inside the room with a bundle under one arm and a washbasin balanced on his other. When he sees me, he freezes for a moment and then slams the door shut behind him, sliding a thick metal bar across it.

"Get off," he whispers, his face burning with rage.

I stop kicking my feet, stretch, and then slowly rise, smoothing the wrinkles out of my travel-stained skirt. "It was more comfortable than the bench," I say.

He sets the basin down on the bench, spilling half the water, and then stomps to me, his boots echoing through the room. Thrusting his face close to mine, he grabs my arm, and says, "Were King Vaunn to find you on his throne, he would have had you beheaded!"

He is squeezing my arm too hard, and I have to fight the instinct to slap his hand away. "My being beheaded would probably void the peace treaty you fashioned with Lord Damar!" I snap. "Oh, wait, you threw a metal star into his neck and nearly killed him. It was probably already voided. Oh, wait, you *lied* about why you married me in the first place!

I think *that* probably voided it." His grip grows tighter and I can't stop the yelp that escapes my lips.

He flinches and drastically loosens his grasp on my arm. "He was holding a poison-filled needle against your head. What was I supposed to do? Let him murder you while I stood by and did nothing?" Though his words are fueled by anger, his voice is soft. "I might be Trevonan, but I will not stand by and watch an innocent woman be murdered, especially if I am partially to blame." He uncurls his fingers from my arm and I yank it away, rubbing the ache his grip left. He holds the bundle out to me, and when I take it, he turns his back. He starts taking off his finely made tunic, and I take a giant step away.

"Please stop!" I blurt, my cheeks flaring with heat, my belly twisting with fear. "Why are you getting undressed?"

"I am not getting undressed. I am showing you something." He pulls his dark purple tunic up until it is around his shoulders, and then stops. Without thinking, I take a step closer to him, and my eyes grow wide. I recognize the thick white scars crisscrossing his broad back. "*This* was my punishment for touching my grandfather's throne. Even if the hem of my cloak so much as brushed it, he noticed, and I got whipped. Ten lashes each time, put there by my own father." He yanks his tunic down. "When I saw you on the throne, it was fear for *your* life that made me act so roughly. For that, I apologize."

I swallow and nod, thinking of the whippings Lord Damar, who I thought was my father at the time, gave me for touching my mother. "I wish you'd killed him," I whisper.

His eyebrows shoot up. "Who? My father, or my grandfather?"

"Lord Damar."

"Any man who would kill a woman because she will not obey him deserves to die. There is no honor in hurting women." He glances at my hands. "Unless she is a trained fighter. But even then, only in self-defense." He walks to the other side of the room and stares at the wall, his hands clasped behind his back. "Get dressed," he orders.

"What?" I ask.

"You're holding clean clothes. Get dressed."

I shake out the bundle and discover it is a dark green Trevonan-style dress and a pale green underdress, finely made if slightly worn. I walk around to the far side of the throne, where I am shielded from Treyose's eyes, and quickly remove my travel-stained clothing. My tunic smells faintly of vomit and strongly of sweat, and I am glad to have something clean to wear.

I pull the pale green underdress on. It is loose and baggy around my body, with a full skirt that almost covers my feet, and fitted sleeves down to my wrists. Next, I slide my head and arms into the dark dress. It smells of cedar and dust, and I wonder where Treyose got it. It is sleeveless, with stays that crisscross up both sides of my ribs and tie beneath my arm-pits. It takes me a few minutes to properly fit the dress over the underdress and tie it. When I am done, I step out from behind the throne. "Whose dress is this?"

Treyose turns. "It belonged to my first wife. She is dead." There is no emotion in his words or his face. He strides to my side. Pulling a mother-of-pearl comb from a satchel attached to his sword belt, he hands it to me, careful not to let our fingers touch. "Brush your hair and wash your face. We are visiting the Royal Library."

My heart starts to pound against my ribs. I might be able to find Golmarr, if he is in fact at the library. I start running the comb through the ends of my tangled hair and force my voice to nonchalance. "Why are we visiting the Royal Library?"

"So you no longer want to leave."

I clench my teeth. Prince Treyose obviously doesn't know me at all if he thinks thousands of books will entice me to stay with him. Nothing could tempt me to stay with the heir of Trevon. "I would like my stone knife back," I say.

He looks me over, once, twice, and then shakes his head. "Not yet."

When I am brushed and washed, he picks up his cloak from where I dropped it to the floor and holds it out to me. "You need to wear this for now, hood up," he says, and we step out into the hall.

# Chapter 11

The library is a separate building attached to the granite castle by a series of torch-lit, winding passageways. Treyose and I pass several maids and one boy with soot-blackened hands as we wander the deserted halls. When they see us coming, they all press their backs to the black stone wall and stare at the floor until we pass.

"Where are all the nobles?" I ask.

"Eating the midday meal," Treyose says, his voice hushed.

Even though I am relieved we are not joining the Trevonan nobility for the meal, I ask, "And why are you not bringing me *there*? I am your new wife, after all. And I am hungry."

Our eyes meet, but he says nothing. A moment later, he opens a pouch at his belt and removes a thick piece of jerky. He hands it to me, and I devour it.

We stop before two massive stone doors with the Trevonan quill and sword carved into them, and Treyose pulls a gold chain from beneath his tunic. On it are several keys and the amulet given to him by his new wizard. Never before have I seen an amulet that is magic, and I wonder again where he found a wizard. He selects the biggest key and leans down, inserting it into a keyhole. The lock clicks and Treyose removes the key. Before opening the doors, he glances down the passage we just came through and then pushes. One door swings open on silent hinges, and the scents of paper, wood, and dust float out.

Once inside the library, he shuts the stone door, tugs the hood of the cloak from my head, and then takes a small, unlit lamp from a hook on the wall.

"Why do we need that?" I ask. The library has narrow glass windows on its exterior walls, which provide more than enough light to see the books. I know this because I remember the glaziers working for months to build and install the windows.

"It is dark where we are going," he says. He holds the lamp out toward me. "Will you light it?"

I am so startled by his request I take a small step from him and the lamp. No one has ever asked me to use my fire magic before.

His blue eyes grow smug, and I want to slap the look off his face. "You can't even light a lamp?"

Without taking my eyes from his, I step back to the door and crack it open. His mouth grows taut, but he doesn't stop me. I hold my hand out and pull a tiny piece of fire from one of the torches. It floats down the hall and settles on the tip of my longest finger. Opening the small glass door of the lamp, I deposit the flame onto the wick. When it has caught fire, I smirk at Treyose.

His face pales. "Follow me."

The library is utterly deserted, and step by step, the deeper we walk into the quiet structure, my hope that Golmarr is here is crushed. "Why was the library locked?" I ask.

"So no one can get in," Treyose answers.

"You don't allow your people inside the library?"

He looks sideways at me. "King Vaunn does not—not without written permission. Does your mother let people in her library?"

I think back on my childhood, to the tall, stately windows that let the sun drench the library, and the velvet-lined chairs pushed up by the library's many hearths. The few times my tutors took me to the library, the chairs were always empty, the hearths always cold. "No, she does not."

He stops walking and frowns. "If you became queen, would you change that?"

"If I became queen, as in, when your grandfather dies and you are the king?"

He looks shocked by what I've said. "No, that's not what I meant. If you became the queen of *Faodara*, would you open your library to everyone?"

"I have never thought about what I would do if I were queen because I will never be queen," I say.

He turns and keeps walking past shelf after shelf of unused books, running his fingers across the leather spines. "I will change the rules when I am king of Trevon."

I follow Prince Treyose up three flights of stairs, and every time we reach another level of the library, the scent of dust and old leather grows stronger and the windows grow smaller. The fourth level of the library has no windows. The only light comes from Treyose's oil lamp. Cobwebs stream from the ceiling and brush the tops of the bookshelves as our arrival stirs the still air.

"This is where the oldest scrolls and texts are kept," he

whispers, as if afraid his voice will shatter the ancient silence permeating the fourth floor.

He keeps walking. I stand still and watch his retreating back, wondering why he has brought me up here to this silent, dark, deserted room. I swallow hard and remind myself that even though I possess no weapons, fire can be a weapon—I used it to help Golmarr defeat the glass dragon—and I know how to fight with my bare hands. Reassured, I follow.

The rows of shelves grow closer and closer together, until Treyose has to walk sideways to fit between them. Instead of books, the shelves hold either scrolls of paper rolled up into cylinders and capped on each end, or metal tablets pounded so thin they look like books made of brass and copper sheets. We pass the end of the last shelf and step into a wide black space with a lone table at the farthest end. A lamp is lit on the table, and the weak light is illuminating a man sitting in a high-backed chair.

"Golmarr," I say. My breath whispers through the air, making the cobwebs hanging from the ceiling flutter toward him. The mere sight of him makes my heart stop beating and then jump back to life again. His black hair has grown enough that it is tied in a very short tail at the nape of his neck, and his bangs fall forward, nearly hiding his eyes. He is studying a scroll and frowning. His eyes slip shut, and he tilts his head against the chair's high back. Worry lines tighten his face. When he opens his eyes, they grow round with surprise and focus on Treyose's lamp. He stands. "You're finally back?" he asks, and the familiarity of his voice tugs at my heart. Treyose nods his head in my direction and Golmarr's attention moves to me.

"Sorrowlynn." His lips form my name, and the cobwebs sway from his breath. He looks down at himself, at the cream-colored tunic laced to his throat and the brown Trevonan leggings that hug the curves of his long legs. He slides a knife from his sleeve and lays it on the table beside the scroll. Next, he slowly draws his sword. The reforged metal gleams bright in the dim lamplight. His eyes meet mine and then focus on my left shoulder. Carefully, almost reverently, he lays the sword across the parchment.

With deliberate slowness, he clasps his hands behind his back and steps out from the table. Exhaling a deep breath that sends the cobwebs into a waving frenzy, he walks toward me. Not once do his eyes leave mine, not even when he walks so close to Treyose that his sleeve brushes against the glass casing of the lamp. Every step he takes seems to wind my body tighter with swirling emotions, until I can barely force my feet to stay planted on the library floor when all they want to do is run to him.

He stops in front of me and peers down into my eyes, searching them. "Sorrowlynn," he whispers. He is beautiful, with his tired hazel eyes and hair that looks as if it has been pushed from his forehead dozens of times. When the familiar smell of him—cedar and soap and *Golmarr*—reaches my nose, my feet refuse to follow sense. They push up from the ground, flinging me through the air so my arms can wrap around Golmarr.

I bury my face against the warmth of his neck and hold on as if he is a cliff face and I am about to fall. I hold on like I am in the boughs of a tall tree and the wind is trying to throw me to the ground. His body is firm where it meets mine, his heart beating hard against my ribs. Right here, right now, this dark forgotten library feels more like home than anywhere has in my life. And yet his arms are dangling at his sides, his body held taut and still. "I know you still hate me," I whisper, and open my eyes.

Finally, he lifts his arms, and I think he is going to embrace me, but he gently pushes me away. His eyes are filled with a palpable agony that makes my pounding heart slow. My feet meet the hard, cold floor and Golmarr takes a step back. "Yes, I still hate you. If I let my guard down, or if I'm exhausted, the hatred creeps in. It hits me in spurts." He looks at his discarded weapons. "I think I hate *myself* more than anything. I am so sorry about your shoulder." He grimaces and presses on his shoulder as if he can feel the pain of the wound he gave me.

I watch his lips as he talks and remember exactly how they felt on mine, and how the simplest touch of them would make me forget the world around me. Folding my arms across my chest, I fight the longing to grab his face and kiss him until we both forget everything that happened in the past, and ask, "What are you doing here?"

"I am trying to figure out how to remove the glass dragon's treasure, because being away from you is the best revenge the dragons could have taken on me. I left my heart with you, Sorrowlynn, and I have been miserable. You consume my thoughts and fill my dreams and drive me to distraction. Even though I have inherited the glass dragon's hatred for you, I have never stopped loving you." I whimper and reach for him, but he steps away. "Please don't touch me."

With a nod, I let my hand fall to my side.

"I need to find the Infinite Vessel." He pushes the hair from his forehead and excitement fills his eyes. "Do *you* know where it is?"

I know what he is asking: *Are there any memories from other people stored in your mind that know the location of the Infinite Vessel?* I shake my head. "I know nothing of an Infinite Vessel."

The anticipation in his eyes is replaced with disappointment and a flicker of hatred. He motions to the dark room with his hand. "This is the oldest library in the world, with scrolls and tablets so ancient, no one knows how to read them anymore. I was hoping the Infinite Vessel was here, but I am losing hope." He reaches out and clasps a strand of my hair, his knuckles brushing my collarbone. That tiny touch seems to awaken my skin and make my heart pound like I have just obliterated a pell. Golmarr twines the curl twice around his index finger before letting his hand fall back to his side. "I have missed you," he says. I laugh, and a small smile lights his face. His smile feels like home. Finally, I have come to a place where I fit in and am accepted for who I am. Only the place isn't a *place*. It is a person. And he hates me.

"I've missed you, too," I say. Behind him, Treyose shifts, and all the warmth and joy at finding Golmarr are squelched. I look at my feet as a familiar hollowness consumes my chest. Seeing Golmarr again made me temporarily forget that I have been wed to another, and I do not have the heart to tell him.

Treyose clears his throat. Together Golmarr and I look at the Trevonan prince—my *husband*—and sorrow washes through me. "I brought her like you asked," Treyose says to Golmarr.

I turn on Golmarr. "You? *You* are the Antharian prince Treyose has been working with? *You* are the brother who has betrayed me?" He nods, and my throat tightens as I fight to keep my despair and fury from consuming me. "How could you?" The words barely squeak out.

Golmarr opens his mouth to answer, but Treyose cuts him off. "There is one aspect of this arrangement we didn't foresee in the beginning. There is a problem," he says.

Golmarr's eyes turn guarded. "We plotted this out for weeks before you left for Faodara. How can there have been an unforeseen *problem*?"

Treyose clears his throat again and lifts his hand to the back of his neck. "After her reputation was sullied by a certain Antharian prince, Lord Damar blatantly *refused* to put her in my care if I did not marry her first."

Golmarr jerks as if he's been slapped. "She would never agree to that," he states, but then he turns to me and asks, "You aren't wed to him, are you?"

I swallow against the lump in my throat and try to explain that it was a proxy wedding, but I cannot find my voice. It has been overridden by the desire to cry, and I know if I speak, the tears will start to flow.

"Are you Treyose's wife?" His voice is as sharp as daggers.

Still unable to find my voice, I shake my head, and then close my eyes and nod.

# Chapter 12

Golmarr presses on his chest, and his face hardens into a mask of fury. "You married him?"

"I did not marry him. It was a proxy wedding," I say.

Anger darkens his face and he reaches for his sword, but his hand comes up empty. Almost faster than I can follow, Golmarr darts behind Treyose and pulls my stone knife from the Trevonan prince's belt. I open my mouth to warn Treyose, but Golmarr leaps past the man and thrusts the blade at my throat. The sharp edge presses against my skin and I stop breathing as I stare into Golmarr's feverish eyes, eyes I hardly recognize. "You are *married* to him?" he snarls again. The same hatred from the day he tried to kill me darkens his face.

"What are you doing, man?" Treyose asks, drawing his sword. "I thought this was the woman you loved more than life itself!"

"It is!" The knife blade starts to tremble as Golmarr's entire body grows so taut it shakes with effort. Sweat breaks out on his forehead. With a great groan, he pulls the knife from my throat and flings it across the room. "I'm sorry," he whispers, and then turns his fury and hatred on Treyose.

Treyose quickly sets the lamp on the floor and places the tip of his sword at Golmarr's chest. "I do not wish to fight with you, Prince Golmarr."

"But you married her!" he growls.

"It was a proxy wedding," Treyose calmly explains, keeping his sword point on Golmarr's chest. "Princess Diamanta stood in for Sorrowlynn. Sorrowlynn was not even present for the ceremony. I—"

Golmarr slams his forearm against the blunt side of Treyose's blade, knocking it from his chest, and leaps at the Trevonan prince. They fall to the ground beside the lamp and crash into a bookshelf. Ancient dust and books rain down on them. Golmarr wraps his hands around Treyose's throat, squeezing, and shouts, "How could you do that to me?"

Treyose slams his fist into Golmarr's face, but Golmarr doesn't loosen his hold.

"Stop it!" I shout. "Golmarr, stop it!"

Treyose punches again, and Golmarr topples sideways, sprawling on the ground at my feet. There is blood on his chin. Treyose lunges for him and pins him down with a knee to his chest. Golmarr fights, thrashing and roiling beneath Treyose so ferociously the floor beneath them groans and the cobwebs on the ceiling swing. Golmarr swings his leg up and slams his foot into Treyose's head, and they roll sideways. In his struggle to wrap his hands around Treyose's throat again, Golmarr kicks the lamp. Glass shatters. Oil splatters the wooden floor, the spilled books, the nearest bookshelf, and in one audible *whoosh*, fire erupts on every drop of oil and starts consuming it. The flames rapidly grow and spread, feasting on brittle, ancient parchment and antique wood as they climb up the bookshelf.

I grab my skirt in my fists and leap away. Golmarr and Treyose jump apart from each other and start working together to stomp out the flames, but they are spreading too quickly. Thick black smoke is billowing around the flames and filling the air. Golmarr slams the sole of his boot atop the biggest flames, but instead of being extinguished, the fire jumps onto his fitted Trevonan leggings—to the spots of oil darkening the fabric. And then I see the dark splotches on his tunic. The fire curls up his legs and latches on to his tunic.

"Golmarr, your chest!" I yell. Treyose starts slapping his bare hands on the bright flames burning Golmarr's clothing.

Golmarr lets out a howl of pain, his eyes grow tight with anguish, and something happens to me. The thoughts and memories stored in my brain take control of my body and mind. I know fire. I can control it—I have done it before, though never in such high quantities. I hold my hands out, palms forward, and draw the heat and light and power of the fire to me. It is like watching water rush down a riverbed, how the fire condenses to one thick stream and flows to my hands. Every flame in the library simply lifts off whatever it is burning and joins the flow of light. All of the fire pours into my outstretched hands and shrinks until it is the size of my head.

Even though the fire has shrunken, the energy of it is massive. It fills me up and feeds me, and erases every ache in my body, every weariness left from the journey to Arkhavan, and the last lingering residue of Lord Damar's poison. It fills me *too* much. The energy is burning so intensely inside of me, I feel made of wax on the brink of melting, not flesh and bone. "I need somewhere to put it," I say. "Quickly!"

Treyose stares at me dumbfounded, but Golmarr holds out

his hand. "Take my hand. Magic can be shared from one person to another."

I study his hand but do not take it. "How do you know?" I ask, horrified that I will burn him if I touch him.

"I have read an entire library of books on magic. You have to trust me." Still I hesitate, so he grabs my hand. His skin feels like ice against mine, and some of the excess energy surging through me passes from my palm to his. He jolts as the energy enters him, and the heat flaring beneath my skin cools a bit, but not to the point of comfort. I release Golmarr's hand and take Treyose's, and this time purposely pass energy to him. His body leaches it away from mine, as if he is riddled with cold, and my skin cools. I sigh and my shoulders sag. With the release of energy, the fire has shrunken to the size of a candle flame. Not knowing what to do with it, I balance it on the tip of my middle finger.

"You just healed me," Golmarr says, his voice a deep, close rumble. He wiggles his jaw back and forth and wipes the blood from his chin. Leaning down, he examines the skin peeking through the holes that have been burned into his leggings.

"What in the world was that?" Treyose asks, pressing against his chest. "My heart feels better than it has in years." He closes his eyes and shudders.

"How did you know I could share the fire's power with you?" I ask Golmarr.

"I have read hundreds of books and scrolls about magic in the last months. I probably know more about magic than any living person, save Nayadi." He looks at my hand holding the fire. It has started shaking. "Are you all right?"

Physically, I feel *fantastic*. I feel like I have wings, and I am about to take flight. But I am trembling with the shock of what I just did and the realization I might have melted myself if I didn't have an outlet for the fire. "Yes. I am . . . fine," I say, but my voice is unsteady. Golmarr studies me, and I know he can tell I am lying. He opens his mouth to speak, but Treyose speaks first.

"Golmarr, you need to listen to me."

At the sound of Treyose's voice, Golmarr's jaw clenches. Slowly, he turns and faces the Trevonan prince. "I'm listening."

"Sorrowlynn was not present at her wedding ceremony. She didn't know she had been wed to me until her father informed her of the arrangement, four days after the ceremony took place. She had no choice in the matter."

Golmarr freezes, his only movement the rise and fall of his chest.

"I had no choice in the matter, either, if I was to fulfill my part of our bargain. I do not want to be wed to her," Treyose says. He hastily looks at me. "No offense meant, Princess."

"None taken," I assure him.

He looks at Golmarr again, his eyes guarded. His stance changes the slightest bit, and I know he is preparing for a possible attack. "I have completed my part of our bargain by bringing her here. I will annul my marriage to Sorrowlynn when you have completed *your* portion of the bargain."

*Annul.* The relief that single word brings makes my knees weak, and the flame on the tip of my finger flickers.

Golmarr clasps his hands behind his back, and I wonder if he is doing it to keep himself from punching Treyose. "Why not annul it now?" he asks, his voice hard. "I will complete my part of our bargain no matter what. You do not need to hold being wed to her over my head to get what you want."

Treyose leans closer to Golmarr and whispers, "I cannot dissolve the marriage until our arrangement is settled and I am king of Trevon. While many have the power to wed two people, none but a king of Trevon has the power to break such a union with a single word."

Golmarr curses and runs his hand through his hair. "Fine. As long as you promise not to touch her. No kissing, no consummating the marriage." Golmarr peers sideways at me. "Unless, of course, you would prefer being wed to him?"

I shudder at the thought and shake my head.

Treyose laughs. "She would attempt to kill me with her bare hands—again—if I tried to touch her. I agree, gladly, to your terms."

Golmarr raises one eyebrow. "You tried to kill him with your bare hands?"

"Not *kill* him, just knock him unconscious," I explain.

Golmarr laughs and looks past me, to the dark rows of shelves Treyose and I came through. "Is Enzio here?"

"Yes," I say.

"He needs to always be between you and me, Sorrowlynn. I do not trust myself to stand within arm's reach of you. Corritha's treasure is a cruel thing. Any negative emotion I have, whether fear, self-loathing, guilt—even anger—it is as if the hatred I inherited finds them in me and feasts on them, eventually transforming them all into hatred. It finds my weaknesses and twists them into animosity. If I feel fear, it gets twisted until I hate the thing I fear. When I experience sorrow, the hatred latches on to that emotion and I find myself hating whatever is causing me sorrow. Rationally, I can see it, but hatred is not rational." He takes a step closer to me, so he is barely an arm's reach away, and quietly says, "Sometimes I hate how much I love you almost as much as I love you. I live with this constant inner battle, and it is tearing me apart." He takes one tiny step toward me and gives my hair another gentle tug and then walks to the table and picks up his lamp. When he returns, he holds the dark lamp out and opens the glass door. "For your fire, Princess," he says, and his thoughtfulness makes me weak in the knees. I have missed everything about Golmarr so much. Reaching my finger into the lamp, I transfer the flame I've been holding onto the lamp's wick. Golmarr's eyes grow wistful. "You are amazing. We need to figure out how to break the glass dragon's curse."

"Curse?" Treyose looks from Golmarr to me, his pale eyebrows halfway up his forehead. "When we made our agreement, you said nothing about a curse."

"The curse won't affect our agreement. I will still help you overthrow—"

Treyose sucks his breath in through gritted teeth and presses a hand over Golmarr's mouth. His pale eyes dart around the silent library, prying into the darkest corners. "Beware of what you speak when there may be others who will overhear," he whispers. "The king has ears everywhere." Golmarr nods and Treyose steps away, picking up my stone blade. "If I give this back to you, do you swear not to use it against me?" he asks.

I nod and snatch the weapon from him before he can change his mind about returning it.

Golmarr eyes the knife as if it is a snake about to strike. "We need to break the curse quickly," he says. "I have been studying historical documents and texts about magic day and night. Only, the closer I get to finding anything about the dragons, the harder it becomes. It is as if whole chunks of history have been removed or destroyed, or the information is unreadable."

"Unreadable?" I ask, unable to take my eyes off Golmarr as he speaks. He looks older than he did six months ago, as if the burden of hatred has turned him from a young man into an adult; the planes and angles of his face are sharper, his shoulders appear more square, and his eyes—a swirl of green and gold and brown—are guarded. He might even be a little taller. I stare at his lips, at the way they form words as he talks, and remember them against mine. His lips are incredibly soft and supple despite all his hard angles. My heart accelerates and my cheeks grow warm at the thought.

Golmarr's mouth stops moving, and I shift my attention back to his eyes. "Sorrowlynn? Have you heard anything I've said?" he asks.

I blink and clear my throat, and search my memory for what we were talking about. "Uh, yes. You were saying the information is unreadable?"

Golmarr's eyebrows slowly rise. "And *after* I said that, I explained how the oldest scrolls are written in a different language even the Trevonan scholars have forgotten." He tilts his head to the side and his eyes narrow. "Did you hear any of that?"

I shake my head and then blurt, "I mean, yes."

Golmarr grins like a rogue. "Oh, good. For a minute I thought you might have been distracted by something." He rubs his hand across his lips.

Heat creeps up my neck and burns my cheeks. "What is the language?" I ask.

"Vinti," Treyose answers.

Golmarr nods. "I have learned some Vinti; we use it when we are trained to fight in the antediluvian, Vintian style, but most Vinti is beyond my comprehension."

"None of the scholars I sent were able to help you?" Treyose asks.

Golmarr shakes his head. "They hardly know more than I. The answers are there, I *know* it, but they are out of my reach. We need someone who can decipher Vintian."

Heart pounding, I say, "Let me see the scrolls." I take the lamp and follow two steps behind Golmarr, Treyose at my side, to the table with Golmarr's weapons and the scrolls. Golmarr stands on the opposite side of the table, arms behind his back, and watches me with so much excitement, the smoky air quivers with it.

Moving the reforged sword aside, I place my hand on the curled edge of the parchment to keep it from rolling closed. It is as thin and fragile as butterfly wings, and has turned light brown with age. I lean close to the faded writing and squint.

Never have I seen letters and figures like the ones before me, but as I stare at them, I start to remember the sound each individual letter makes, and then, sound by sound, a single word forms. I place my finger on the next word and quietly say each letter sound until the word has meaning. I do it with the next word, and then the next, and my head starts throbbing, and my eyes hurt, but I am eventually able to read an entire sentence.

When I start on the next sentence, Golmarr says, "I should have known you would be able to read this. What does it say?"

"Give me a few more minutes." I sit down in the chair and lean even closer to the parchment. The reading is painfully slow, but I eventually read half of the text. "This is an account of a war." I move my finger to the next line, then the next. "It was fought between two men: King Relkinn and Prince Zhun." I look up. "Prince *Zhun*? They must have named him after the fire dragon."

"The Great War," Golmarr muses, bringing my focus back to the parchment beneath my finger.

I continue reading and then paraphrase what I've read. "Prince Zhun beat King Relkinn, and then became the new king. When the war was over, the male population had been depleted to such an extent that most of the women had to take care of themselves. Many of the women who survived starved to death that winter because there weren't enough people to harvest the crops that endured the war, and most women didn't know how to hunt for food." A sudden, over-whelming sadness pierces my heart as the memory of this very event feels trapped within my body. "The women gave what food they had to . . ." My throat tightens, and I find it hard to continue. "They gave the food to their children. Only the children survived . . . and the two kings, with their hand-ful of men."

At the bottom of the scroll is a signature. I have seen it before, with my own eyes, and then I see the young, strong hand as it signs this very parchment. *Melchior.* A shiver runs down my spine. "Melchior the wizard wrote this." And now I know from whom I inherited the ability to speak and read Vinti.

"Melchior couldn't have written that," Treyose says. "That parchment is probably more than a thousand years old. Mel-chior didn't look over sixty years old."

"You're right. He didn't look a millennium old, but he was ancient," I say.

"And the Great War?" Treyose asks, uncertain. "I thought the Great War was a legend."

I tuck a strand of hair behind my ear and look up. "I did, too. I guess I still don't know everything."

Golmarr smiles. "No, not *everything*." He is still leaning over the parchment, and his face is mere inches from mine, his eyes sparkling. He takes in a deep, deliberate breath of air, as if he is inhaling me, and his smile trickles away. "I have missed you so very much," he whispers. With a heavy sigh, he takes a step away, and it makes my heart feel like he has stomped on it.

"How can you look at me like that when a few minutes ago you almost killed me?" I ask.

"I still love you, Sorrowlynn. Never doubt that. But the struggle of trying to cope with the hatred passed on to me by the glass dragon is exhausting. I'm so sorry I threatened you when I found out you were married to Treyose. The hurt and anger overtook my ability to stay in control, and the hatred became too strong to bear. I didn't mean to touch you with a weapon. I would rather die than hurt you." His eyes are pleading, begging me to understand. "So if we can keep a little distance between us for now, that will make it easier for me to be around you—easier to trust myself with you. My greatest fear is that I will kill you, and because of that I am too scared to touch you for now." His eyes are dark with sorrow, and I recognize the same emotion in myself.

"I will die by my own hand," I say.

"I wish I had as much faith in your birth prediction as you, but I have been trained to fight and take lives since I was eight years old." He holds his hands up and studies them. "I know what I am capable of, and it terrifies me."

An ache fills my chest, accompanied by the desire to take him into my arms and tell him everything will be all right. But I don't know if it will be all right. Maybe we are destined to lead our lives side by side but never be together.

"Does it say anything about dragons in there?" Golmarr asks.

"Aside from the prince being named after the fire dragon, no."

"Then I will get more scrolls for you, and then find Enzio." With a sad smile, he hurries off into the shadows and returns a moment later carrying several scrolls and two metal tablets. With utmost gentleness, he lays them on the table. "I should have known," he says as he takes the end caps off a scroll and starts unrolling it.

"Known what?" I ask.

"That Suicide Sorrow was the answer to this problem." He smiles, and it lights his eyes, chasing away some of the sadness. My heart starts pounding as emotions I haven't felt for months swell within it—love, desire, acceptance. Golmarr's gaze slowly moves from my eyes to my lips. Frowning, he presses against his chest, slowly moving his hand up to his shoulder, and then backs away. "Treyose, will you stay with her until I come back?"

Treyose nods. "Of course."

"I will be back with Enzio." He turns and strides into the darkness.

"Wait," I say, the single word freezing Golmarr where he stands. "I need to tell you something." My chest tightens, and I find it hard to breathe. I cannot find the words I need, for I am terrified at how Golmarr may react.

When I do not continue, he walks back to the table, staring

at me across its width. "What is it?" he whispers so gently a tear slips out of my eye. Golmarr's eyes follow the tear as it drips down my cheek and gets caught in the corner of my mouth.

I wipe the tear away. "Your brother was killed. Ingvar. My father . . . I mean Lord Damar killed him."

Golmarr groans and leans forward so he is bent at his hips, elbows resting on the table, his face buried in his hands. I stare at the top of his head, at his glossy black hair.

"How?" Golmarr asks, his words muffled.

"The way spineless Faodarian nobility always kill their enemies," Treyose says, voice filled with loathing. "With poison."

A low moan escapes Golmarr.

"I am so sorry," I whisper, wishing I could wrap my arms around him.

"He died protecting you, didn't he?" Golmarr asks.

I cannot speak, so Treyose answers. "Damar was trying to stab Sorrowlynn in the head with a poisoned needle. Your brother blocked him and was stabbed in her stead. Your brother died to save her."

Golmarr slowly stands and wipes the heels of his hands across his eyes, and I study his face for signs of rekindled hatred but see only sorrow.

"Who is the new heir to the throne?" asks Treyose quietly, respectfully. "Is it Jessen or Arendinn?"

Golmarr shakes his head. His black lashes gleam with tears. "Neither. Me. I am the new heir," Golmarr says.

"What?" Treyose asks.

"But you are the youngest!" I say.

Golmarr nods. "I am also supposed to marry a Faodarian

princess. That makes me the automatic heir to the throne of Anthar. But I declined the honor on the condition that if anything happened to Ingvar, I would rule in his stead, and Ingvar is no longer heir."

Treyose looks at Golmarr's sword lying useless on the table. "I am housing the future Antharian king in my grandfather's castle, and he is unarmed." He gestures to me. "And I am married to his true love. Yet here we all are, having a civil conversation." Treyose shakes his head and laughs under his breath.

Golmarr's eyes turn fierce. "It is a good thing you and I want the same things right now. Otherwise we might be tempted to kill each other. I will be back shortly with Enzio." Without another word, he turns and walks into the dark library.

"You don't have a lamp," I call after him.

"I don't need one." As sudden as lightning but as subtle as a breath of air, pale blue light swells in the dark space between two narrow rows of books, and for a split second I see Golmarr's silhouette before he has moved from sight, taking the light with him.

# Chapter 13

I spend the entire day in the cold library, wrapped in Treyose's purple cloak, painstakingly studying and deciphering parchments with Enzio at my side, while Golmarr practices hand-to-hand combat moves in the dark, open space in front of the table. His bare feet are silent on the dusty floor, and despite the cool air, sweat gleams on his brow and soaks the front of his tunic. Enzio is fully armed, but Golmarr remains weaponless, and I find my attention drawn to him far more than it should be. The way his body moves, with the fluid grace and strength of a warrior, is distracting to the point I almost ask him to stop moving. But I like watching him. I like it a lot.

Golmarr's eyes sweep over me every few minutes. They are hungry for the knowledge contained in the parchments and tablets strewn before me, and yet heavy with mourning.

By late afternoon, dozens of records have passed beneath my aching eyes, and not one of the ancient histories mentions dragons. All the wars, skirmishes, famines, and disasters were created by either man or natural forces, like weather or the shaking of the earth.

I finish reading a particularly difficult metal tablet, with letters and images scratched on its surface, and press on my throbbing temples. "I can read only about half of these symbols, but there is no mention of dragons. None of the histories I have read mention the beasts. It is as if they didn't exist," I snap. "I do not think your Infinite Vessel exists, either, Golmarr."

He walks to the opposite side of the table and lays his hands flat on the polished wood. The heat from his warm, sweaty body fills the small bit of air between us. "It has to exist," he says. "If it doesn't, there is no hope for us, Sorrowlynn." He raises his gaze to mine and whispers, "We need to keep looking."

I place my fingertips on the back of his hand, but Golmarr pulls away. "I will read every tablet and scroll and parchment in this library if I have to," I say. He nods and takes the histories I have read back to the shelves before bringing me more.

When the library has grown colder with the onset of night, Prince Treyose returns dressed in a deep purple velvet tunic with gold thread sewn into the cuffs, and suede boots over pristine white leggings. He has replaced his plain leather scabbard for one made with gold and jewels, and a narrow silver crown sits low on his forehead. Despite his royal finery, he is carrying a tray of food like a lowly servant. He places it on the edge of the table and the smell of fresh-baked bread and meat makes my stomach rumble.

Enzio grabs a small loaf of bread and starts eating. I lean back in my chair and frown. "You look nice, Treyose—much too nice to be bringing us food in this musty, old, frigid library," I say, my voice disapproving.

"Thank you," he says, not meeting my eyes.

I stand and put my hands on my hips. "Midwinter eve is long past, and the first day of spring is more than a week away, so what is the occasion for such finery?"

Treyose clears his throat. "My grandfather is honoring my return and my success in Faodara," he says, frowning.

My toe starts tapping the wooden floor. "Success in Faodara? Does he celebrate the peace treaty you made with Lord Damar, or our wedding? Because I was under the impression you were hiding our matrimonial state from him. And, if it is the latter, shouldn't I be present?" I look down at his purple cloak, still wrapped around my shoulders, and my borrowed green dress beneath. Though the dress is well made, it is plain and covered with dust and a few strands of cobweb, nowhere near as fine as Treyose's formal attire. Golmarr, holding a small book titled *The Power of Air*, walks over to us.

"My grandfather is celebrating neither of those things," Treyose says, clasping one hand behind his neck and studying his feet.

I look at him sidelong. "Then what is the success you are celebrating? If it is success with Faodara you celebrate, shouldn't I be in attendance?"

Treyose rolls his shoulders. "My grandfather does not know that we are wed. Word of my nearly killing Lord Damar has reached him, and that is what he is celebrating."

"What?" I step directly in front of Treyose, forcing him to look at me. His pale blue eyes meet mine. "You bring home a Faodarian princess as your bride—albeit an *unwilling* bride—and your grandfather wants to celebrate you putting a star in the neck of the man who is supposed to be your new father-in-law?" The urge to shove him is so strong, I have to ball my hands into fists and force them to remain at my sides.

"What is wrong with you Trevonans?" Strong hands clasp my shoulders, and I turn and glare at Enzio.

"Easy, Sorrowlynn," Enzio says, yet he is glowering at Treyose.

Golmarr steps between me and Treyose. "King Vaunn has no idea you're married to Sorrowlynn of Faodara, does he?" Golmarr asks. "He still believes you went to Faodara to gather information on their army and castle so you can conquer their kingdom this spring." It is not a question.

"My grandfather does *not* know I am wed to her. No one does, except my closest, most trusted confidants. It is a secret, and I would prefer to keep it that way, seeing as I will not be wed to her much longer if all goes as planned."

"What would Vaunn do to Sorrowlynn if he discovered her in his castle?" Golmarr asks.

"He would kill her," Treyose admits. "Slowly and painfully." Now I understand why Treyose insisted on sneaking me into his grandfather's castle.

Golmarr curses under his breath and glances at his discarded sword. "And you didn't think to warn me?"

"That is why I had her dress as a Trevonan noble," Treyose explains. "She looks Trevonan enough, and it is not unusual for a nobleman to bring a common woman to the castle and dress her as nobility if he fancies her. If Sorrowlynn follows Trevonan tradition, no one will know she is Faodarian. Unless she talks. Her accent is thicker than her older sisters'."

Golmarr's eyes fill with fire. "If we are risking your grandfather killing her by simply having her here, then I insist she shares a chamber with both Enzio and me."

Treyose scowls. "You are going to insist Sorrowlynn sleeps on a pallet in the library with you?"

"No," Golmarr says. "We need a room with a door that locks."

Treyose studies Golmarr. "In that case, you should probably cut your hair in the Trevonan style—short on top and even shorter on the sides. The clothes alone don't hide your heritage, and the only doors with locks are bedchambers and the throne room, which means you will be walking through the castle."

"I will not cut my hair," Golmarr snaps. "I trust you can find a bedchamber that will fit the three of us, while at the same time keeping our presence in the castle a secret. Remember the benefits you will be getting from our agreement."

"Fine. But if my giving you a bedchamber alerts the king to your presence and you end up dead, or Sorrowlynn does, you are the only one to blame." Treyose motions impatiently to the scrolls piled high on the table. "Have you found what you are looking for? I am ready for you to fulfill your part of our bargain and be gone."

Golmarr shakes his head and picks up a thin slice of meat. "I need more time." He puts the meat in his mouth and starts chewing.

Treyose nods. "I will send someone to fetch you and show you to your new chamber after the feast, but don't complain to me if you dislike the chamber." He turns on his heel and strides away.

After a long moment, Enzio asks around a mouthful of bread, "What does Treyose want from you?" I hold my breath as I wait for Golmarr to answer.

"An alliance with Anthar, and me acting as his wizard."

"He wants you to be his wizard?" I cannot hide the skepticism in my voice.

Golmarr's eyebrows rise. "You have so little faith in me, Sorrowlynn, but yes, he does."

I don't mean to laugh, yet it bubbles up out of me. "Does he know you cannot do magic?"

Golmarr shrugs. "He seems to find my abilities believable enough. Once an alliance is established, we agreed to begin open trading between our two kingdoms, and I am going to send my best farmers to Trevon to teach the Trevonans how to grow better crops and grain. Also, I will give Treyose half a dozen Antharian horses, and he will stop attacking Antharian ships that attempt to sail to Ilaad. Plus, and more important, if Treyose has the backing of the horse clan, he might have the power to overthrow his grandfather. If he has the horse clan's support *and* a wizard aiding him, he will be able to claim the throne and put an end to his grandfather's madness."

"And you trust that Treyose will not come after Anthar when he is king?" I ask.

Golmarr presses his lips together tightly and nods. "More than anything, Treyose wants peace for Trevon. He is sick of fighting. I know because he pulled out of the last battle he fought against Anthar. I could see his hate for war in his eyes when he killed my brother Jessen's wife." Golmarr's eyes darken, and he lowers his voice to a whisper. "King Vaunn is insisting Treyose lead an army against Faodara this spring. When he conquers Faodara, Vaunn wants him to combine armies and finally vanquish Anthar. Once Anthar is Vaunn's, he will use all the armies to overpower Ilaad and be the ruler of all. Treyose wants to be done with war because he knows that to defeat Anthar, he will have to kill every man, woman, and child. But his grandfather is very . . . persuasive when it comes to getting Treyose to do his bidding."

Enzio glances over his shoulder at the darkened library before furtively whispering, "Does he want you to assassinate the king?"

"No," Golmarr says. "He wants to win the support of the nobles and then lock King Vaunn away in one of the castle towers where he can finish out his life in comfortable confinement." He picks up a small loaf of bread and tears it in half, giving me the bigger piece. "Let us eat before this gets cold."

---

The food Treyose brought up has been gone for hours, and still no one has come to fetch us. I pull my borrowed purple cloak more tightly around my body. I am still sitting in the chair, my arms crossed over the table, my head resting on them. If I didn't shiver every few minutes, I would give in to the exhaustion dragging at my body and fall asleep. Golmarr, sitting on the floor beside Enzio, their backs pressed against the wall, notices every time I shiver. Enzio, on the other hand, is fast asleep with his arms and head resting on his bent knees. Every few minutes he snores and mumbles something about pretty ladies in his sleep.

I shiver again, and Golmarr jumps to his feet. "Every time you shiver, I have the urge to come over there and warm you up with my body. It is almost painful, knowing you are so cold," he whispers.

"I would like that," I say, sitting tall and imagining his warm arms wrapped around me, his breath against my neck. Just the thought warms me a bit.

"So would I," Golmarr says, but shakes his head and strides to a dark corner of the library, too far to be illuminated by the weak lamplight. He returns with a wool blanket and drapes it over my shoulders.

I stifle my disappointment and pull the blanket close. "Where did you get this?" I ask.

"From my pallet."

"You really *do* sleep up here? I thought Treyose was joking."

"I have been sleeping up here for months," he says. "It is the easiest way to avoid a chance meeting with King Vaunn."

"Look." I tap the glass lamp. The oil is gone, and only what remains saturating the wick is feeding the fire. "It is a matter of minutes before it goes out," I whisper, my jaw tight with cold.

"I'm not worried about the light," Golmarr says, studying me with tired eyes.

"Why? Have you been hiding out up here so long you can find your way around in the dark?"

Something in his face changes, a spark behind his eyes, and he smiles. I can't help the smile that jumps to my lips. "I'm not worried about the dark," he says. He lifts his right hand, palm facing up. All the cobwebs lining the ceiling whoosh toward Golmarr, as if they are being blown at him, and then a tiny ball of blue light the size of a grain of sand is hovering above his palm. It grows bigger, as big as a pebble, an acorn, a chicken egg, and then stops. The cobwebs go limp.

I blink and sit up tall. "What is that?"

Golmarr looks at the light and dances it between his fingers, spinning it around like a knife. "I told you earlier that I've read hundreds of books about magic, hoping to learn how to break the dragon's curse, but they taught me nothing like that." The blue light reflects off his eyes. "But they did teach me this. Apparently I have a talent for magic. As I studied the books, I memorized and practiced the magic, and the more I did it, the better I got—just like with sword-fighting. Now I can pull energy and moisture from the air. Not a *lot* of energy, but enough to do things like this." He throws the blue light against the ceiling and it turns into a thousand separate, tiny stars that slowly orbit around their center, Golmarr.

I reach up and touch one, but feel only cool, damp air. "Is that all you can do?"

"No, that is not all." Mischief fills his eyes. "I made Treyose a medallion. By pushing cool, damp air into the metal, it makes him immune to fire."

I gasp and smack his arm. "You are the one who gave him protection from my fire? Why?"

Golmarr grins and looks at his arm, touching the spot where I hit him. "Because I had the feeling you might try to set him on fire. I read about how to infuse metal with magic in one of the ancient scrolls. I have also learned about healing with magic and transferring fire energy from place to place, or person to person. That is why I knew how to help you when you were holding too much fire. When we are not focused on history, I will teach you what I know, if you'd like."

I tilt my head to the side and study him. "You truly are his wizard."

He shrugs, and all the little stars slowly fade to nothing, returning us to the dim light of the lamp. "You look exhausted, Sorrowlynn. Why don't we forget about Treyose's promised escort and go to your chamber? Can you find it from here?"

"I don't have a chamber. Treyose locked me in the throne room last night."

Golmarr makes a noise of disgust deep in his throat, and his eyes flash with anger.

"But," I say, and a small grin tugs at my lips, "I know this castle better than I know the castle I grew up in. I could probably find an empty chamber for us to sleep in." I stand and stretch. "And if not, I could find us a pantry or closet close to the kitchen that would most definitely be warmer than up here." I fold the blanket and hand it to Golmarr. "Enzio," I whisper, giving his shoulder a shake.

Enzio jumps to his feet and brandishes his black stone blade. When his bleary eyes focus on my face, he quickly puts the knife away and presses on his stomach. "I'm starving. Is it breakfast yet?"

"Probably," Golmarr says with a frown. His eyes meet mine. "You've been wed to an *incredibly* thoughtful man," he adds sarcastically.

"Don't remind me."

Golmarr walks to the table and places his hand on his sword hilt. His breathing quickens and he yanks his hand away like he's been burned.

"What is it?" I ask.

Golmarr presses on his eyes. "Every time I touch a weapon, all the different ways I can kill you with it assault my brain. Enzio, will you carry this down to the chamber for me?" He slowly steps away from the sword.

"It will be an honor," Enzio says, though his eyes are troubled as they move between Golmarr and me. Enzio was there the day Golmarr tried to kill me with this sword. He is the one who carried me from the battlefield and put pressure on my wound to keep me from bleeding out.

When Enzio has fastened the reforged sword to his belt beside his short sword, I pick up the lamp and we leave the quiet solitude of the library's fourth floor. As we descend the first flight of stairs, with me in the lead and Enzio keeping Golmarr from my back, Golmarr whispers, "Sorrowlynn, exactly how well do you know this castle?"

I pause and the lamp splutters, contorting our shadows against the stairwell wall. "I know it like I designed it," I whisper, pressing my hand to the sleek black wall. "I know it like I built it."

Golmarr takes a step closer, so Enzio is sandwiched between the two of us. Enzio clears his throat. "I do not do so well in tight spaces," Enzio whispers, shrugging his shoulders. "Especially with another man breathing down my neck."

Golmarr laughs under his breath, and Enzio leans as far away from him as he can. "I will move in a moment. Sorrowlynn, are there secret passages in the library?"

"Yes. The only room that does not have any is the throne room. It was built to keep dragons out." Without warning, I see scales the color of wheat and eyes like fresh-spilled blood, and a shroud of long-forgotten fear settles around me. "Not *dragons*, just one particular dragon." I shudder.

"If we need to escape for any reason, can you get us out of here without using any of the main passages?"

I frown at Golmarr. "Why? Are we going to need to escape?"

"Should I be worried?" Enzio asks, carefully maneuvering his short sword from his belt in the limited space between Golmarr and me.

Golmarr nods and claps him on the shoulder. "Always be on your guard, my friend. Be prepared for anything. Treyose,

I trust. But King Vaunn? If he discovers we are in his castle, using his library, he will try to kill us. He will set his entire army on us, if need be." Golmarr takes a step away from Enzio. "There you go, my friend. No more man breath on your neck."

Enzio rubs his neck, but he laughs.

At the bottom of the stairwell, I open the door leading to the third floor and gasp. Five armed soldiers are striding toward us. When they see us, all five of them slide their swords from their scabbards.

# Chapter 14

When staring at five armed men, one does not expect to live long. Instinctively, I reach for a sword at my waist, but my hand grasps air. Enzio leaps in front of me, his short sword ready.

"What is this?" Golmarr demands, sounding every bit like the prince he is. He strides past Enzio and me, placing his unarmed self between us and the soldiers.

"We were sent by Prince Treyose, my lord," a soldier says. Despite his bloodshot eyes and weary face, I recognize him. It is Reyler, Treyose's man who was instructed to shoot me in the thigh if I tried to run. At a signal from Reyler, the Trevonans sheathe their swords.

"Five of you?" I ask, stepping forward. Golmarr's hand clasps my shoulder, staying me.

"As he saw fit, my lady," Reyler says with a small smile. "It is not my place to question my future king. I was instructed to show you to a chamber for the night."

Golmarr's hand drops from my shoulder, and I feel its absence like I have shed my cloak in the middle of a blizzard. "Then, by all means, lead the way," Golmarr says. He presses his hand to the small of my back, giving me the slightest nudge forward.

The lower levels of the library are dark, the windows filled with the black of deep night. I follow Reyler silently, but when we reach the bottom floor, it occurs to me Treyose has not assigned five guards to protect his people from us. *We* are the ones being protected, and neither Golmarr nor I are in possession of a sword. I pretend to stumble and fall to the floor, my green skirt pooled about me. Groaning, I wrap my hands around my left ankle and rock back and forth.

Golmarr is kneeling on the floor in front of me before the armed escort has even noticed I've fallen. He unlaces my boot and carefully pulls it off, and then his long, strong fingers wrap around my left ankle, probing the soft tissue around the bone. Enzio and the five guards gather around, frowning down at us.

"Is it broken?" Reyler asks, crouching beside Golmarr.

Golmarr slowly twists my ankle from side to side. His fingers slip beneath the hem of my skirt and slowly move up the length of my calf, pressing and kneading. Despite the six men surrounding us, despite the cold stone floor beneath me, my heart jumps into my throat and my mouth goes dry. I stare at Golmarr as he slowly trails his hand back down to my ankle. One of his eyebrows slowly lifts, his face questioning. I shake my head the slightest bit and, as if he knows exactly what I am doing, he nods.

"It's not broken," Golmarr announces, slowly standing, "but she would benefit from a sturdy walking staff. One about this high"—he lifts his hand just higher than his shoulder—"and solid enough to hold most of her weight."

Reyler studies me for a moment. "A quarterstaff is about that size. They're tipped with iron, so it's not going to be lightweight, and for that I apologize."

"It sounds like the perfect thing," I say, and hobble to my feet. Without a word, Golmarr lifts me from the floor, cradling me in his arms. He looks into my eyes and I stare back, so shocked by his actions I cannot speak. I loosely wrap my arms around his neck. Even though he is wearing Trevonan clothing, he smells exactly the same as I remember, and I breathe in the soap-and-cedar scent of him. Beneath my chest his heart is beating a quick, steady rhythm, much faster than it should be, and his hands are trembling. He inhales a deep breath. On the exhale, he whispers, "I cannot do this. It is too hard for me to be this close to you," and sets me down. "Enzio, can you help her?" Golmarr growls, staring at the floor like he wants to kill it.

"Of course." Enzio steps to my side and pulls my arm over his shoulders and I start limping along. Reyler commands one of his men to fetch me a quarterstaff, and then we leave the library through a door that is also a bookshelf. We pass through a dark, dusty passage that Enzio and I can barely fit through side by side. At the end of the passage, Reyler holds a thick tapestry aside and we enter the slightly warmer castle. The halls are silent, and only our lamp lights their dark depths. Gauzy cobwebs hang from empty sconces, and the smell of mildew saturates the air.

We ascend a flight of narrow stone stairs and continue down a silent passage, past several shut doors, before Reyler stops in front of one. "Wait," he says. He draws his sword and opens the door, confirming my suspicion he was sent by Treyose to *protect* us. Reyler and two of his men sweep through the room before he gives us the signal to enter.

The room is big and drafty, with a freshly laid fire burning in the hearth. On one side of the room, two moth-eaten chairs face the fire. The other side has a big bed with bright purple linens and a rotting canopy hanging above it. Beside it are a dusty table, two water basins, and a small stack of cloths.

"My men and I put fresh linens on the bed for you," Reyler says, "since this part of the castle hasn't been used for nearly a century. The roof leaks, and until it is fixed, it is inhabitable only in dry weather." Golmarr makes an irritated noise and Reyler glares at him. "Since Treyose did not feel comfortable alerting your presence to the cleaning staff, my men and I did our best to scour and prepare this room for you. It is the safest place you can sleep."

I smile and try to look gracious. "Thank you, Reyler. It will suit us just fine."

He nods. "We will be stationed outside your door, my lady. Your men can sleep in the chairs. There are two extra blankets at the foot of the bed. If you need anything, simply call my name and I will be here." Before Reyler has passed through the door, a man enters carrying a staff. My heart soars at the sight of the weapon—tipped with iron on both ends. The guard hands it to me. The wood is smooth and worn from hours of weapons practice, and the metal makes it much heavier than a simple wooden staff. I take the staff and use it to help my limp, then nod my approval.

"This will be perfect."

When Treyose's men are gone, I center my weight on my feet and swing the staff, testing its balance. The iron tips lend a new speed to my swing—a more forceful swing—and the weapon feels good in my hands. I work through several exercises while Enzio and Golmarr stand beside the fire quietly talking. When I have worked up a sweat, I place the staff beside the bed and wash my hands and face at one of the basins.

Golmarr moves to the bed. He pulls the covers back and plumps the pillow before sitting in the chair by the fire. The small gesture warms my heart. "Thank you," I say.

"You are welcome. It is the closest thing to a good-night kiss I dare give you. Enzio, sleep with your sword out," he adds.

"I don't need the reminder. Yerengul has taught me well these past months."

"Your skill with the sword has improved immensely since I last saw you. I can tell simply by the way you draw your weapon," Golmarr says. He glances at me. "Who typically wins in sword fights—you or Sorrowlynn?"

Enzio takes a deep breath before admitting, "Sorrowlynn beats me every time we practice with swords."

Golmarr's eyes fill with approval, and I smile as I loosen the stays of my dress and climb into the bed, which smells strongly of mildew. Staring at Golmarr's dark, brooding profile, I fall asleep.

---

I thrust my hands into the ground and they come up spilling black pebbles the size and shape of my thumbnail. The ocean crashes and swells over the pebbles, wrapping around my ankles, and I know if I look up, I will see a two-headed dragon. I close my eyes and inhale the smell of brine and realize I miss this place almost as much as I miss the way Golmarr was before he killed the glass dragon.

The tide crashes to shore again, burying my feet beneath a shallow layer of black rocks when I hear someone call my name. I open my eyes, and the dragon is there waiting for me. Beside it walks a woman. Her hair is like clouds blowing around her face, her skin the deep brown of tea, and even though she is walking toward me, the distance between us never narrows. I look up at the dragon, and the woman follows my gaze. When her eyes alight on the beast, she jumps with surprise and swishes her hand at the creature as if it was a pesky fly. The two-headed dragon shivers and then slowly disappears until it is only the woman and me on the beach. She walks and walks, never getting close enough for me to see the details of her face. I try to step toward her, but the rocks on top of my feet grow heavy, rooting them in place. I grip my leg and yank, but the ground refuses to relinquish me.

The woman cups her hands around her mouth. It moves, but I hear nothing. She yells again, but only the in and out of the tide, the crashing and receding waves, fills the air.

*Sorrowlynn.* The voice does not penetrate my ears, instead forming inside my head. *Come find me. Please.*

The urge to run to the owner of the voice is so strong, I sit up in bed, throw the covers off, and leap to my feet. "I'm coming," I blurt before I remember I am in King Vaunn's castle. I need to leave the suffocating black stone walls and run to the ocean.

"What is it?" Enzio asks from the chair beside my bed, sword in hand. He blinks sleep from his blue eyes.

Golmarr stands from the chair by the hearth and strides over, his bare feet silent on the sleek stone floor. He stops three paces from me, and his tired eyes take in my rumpled dress and tangled hair. He clears his throat and looks down at his tunic, double-checking it is tied tightly beneath his chin. "You said, 'I'm coming.' What does that mean?" he asks, his voice rough with sleep.

I shake my head and rub my eyes, plopping down on the side of my bed. "I don't know. I keep dreaming of the ocean and a beach with a woman on it. She wants me to find her." Golmarr and Enzio look at each other, and Enzio shrugs.

"Who was she?" Golmarr asks.

"I don't know. I couldn't see her face." I gather my hair and start combing my fingers through the tangles. "Have either of you ever seen a beach with black pebbles instead of sand?"

Enzio's face drains of color, and Golmarr curses.

My hands freeze in my hair. "What?"

"The only place I have ever heard of with black rock beaches is Draykioch," Golmarr says.

I shiver at the mere sound of the name. "What is Draykioch?"

"The Serpent's Island," Enzio replies. "A sea creature as long as a ship and as black as night controls the sea around the island. My gran used to put me to bed with horror stories of that place—ships being sucked down whirlpools, waves as tall as a mountain. When I was fourteen, a man with hair bleached white as bone wandered into our forest. He asked if a stonemason could turn his metal flask to stone because it contained something more precious than gold. I was training to be a mason, so my father gave me the flask even though it is not possible to turn metal to stone." He rubs his thumb over his fingertips and his eyes grow unfocused.

"What was in the flask?" Golmarr asks.

Enzio blinks. "Dragon tears."

"A dragon's actual tears?" I ask.

"No. Black rocks that glow in sunlight," Enzio explains. "The stranger claimed he was a sea captain. He said he got the dragon tears from the Serpent's Island, from Draykioch, after the sea divided and marooned his ship on dry land where the water used to be. He said when he and his men got off the ship, the sea rose up and crashed atop them, and he floated on an empty keg all the way back to the Antharian shore, but not before he filled his whiskey flask with the black rocks from the sea floor."

"What happened to the man?" I ask.

"When I gave his flask back to him, in the exact state it was in when he gave it to my father, the man thought it had been turned to stone, so he paid me for my work and wandered away. He was so muddled in the head he couldn't even tell that his flask hadn't undergone any change. Fortunately, I never saw him again."

Golmarr starts pacing back and forth at the foot of my bed, right arm folded across his chest, hand above his heart. "I have lived by the sea my entire life. I have traded goods with sea captains from around the world. No one goes to Draykioch and comes back to tell the tale."

Enzio reaches under his rumpled, gray tunic and removes a small leather pouch fastened to a chain around his neck. He holds one hand out flat and cautiously dumps the contents of the pouch onto his palm. Two small black rocks the size of my thumbnail tumble out. "This is what he paid me with."

Golmarr and I peer into Enzio's hand. "How do you know they aren't simply black pearls or onyx?" Golmarr asks.

"I tried smelting it in the blacksmith's furnace. No matter how hot I got the fire, I could not melt these. When the sun shines on them, they shimmer differently from anything I have ever seen. It looks like there is a flame inside. Watch." He walks to the sunlight streaming into the room through a window and holds the stones in it. The black rocks light up as if there is a live coal inside of each. "See?" he says, and then carefully returns the stones to the leather pouch. He pulls the drawstring tight and tucks it beneath his shirt. "The man might have been crazy, but these are not ordinary rocks."

"No sea captain I ever traded with would go within fifty miles of Draykioch," Golmarr says.

Enzio stares off into space. "I have always wanted to see the fabled Serpent's Island."

⟞ ⟩⟨ ⟞

We break our fast with fruit and cheese and poached eggs given to us by Reyler, and then Golmarr, Enzio, and I are escorted to the fourth floor of the library again. I sit in the chair, with a lit lamp on the table before me, and begin the painstaking chore of deciphering scroll after scroll, parchment after parchment, looking for the word *dragon*, but nothing ever turns up. We haven't been there half the morning when I roll up the last scroll left on the table and hold it out to Golmarr. "Nothing about dragons in this one. I need more," I announce.

Instead of taking it, Golmarr growls and thrusts his hands in his hair, tightening his fingers in it. "I have had you look at every scroll that is written in Vinti," he says, eyes touched with panic. "That was the last one."

I glance at the rows and rows of shelves. "Surely we haven't checked them all." I stand and return the scroll to its proper shelf. "What about the shelves back there?" I point toward the door.

"Those shelves contain archived music, art, and other antiquities," Enzio says. He walks to a shelf and lifts a heavy necklace, holding it up for me to see. It is made from several separate plates of metal and formed to look like a gold dragon, with red rubies for eyes.

"And I read everything else over the last few months." Golmarr starts pacing back and forth, his hands still in his hair, eyes intent on the floor. "We could go to the abandoned library in the Ilaadi desert once I complete my bargain with Treyose."

"You mean the library located out in the middle of the wasteland, which was abandoned because the sandworm eats anyone who so much as sets foot on the sand?" I ask.

Golmarr stops pacing and gives me a fierce look. "Yes. That is the one to which I am referring."

I groan and stand, pressing on the small of my back. "Unless you have learned to fly, we will die if we try to get to that library."

"Then we die trying," Golmarr says, and starts pacing again.

"I don't think we should risk it." When he doesn't respond, I step into his path, forcing him to stop. Golmarr pauses, raises one eyebrow, and then steps around me. I don't think before I act, and grab his wrist, flipping him around to face me again. He looks from my hand, holding his wrist, to my eyes. I recognize the deep, dark emotion rippling over his face, and my fingers grow cold on his skin. His hatred feels like a tangible pressure, like a wall of swords has been thrust up between us. I drop his wrist.

Enzio steps to my side, black knife in hand. "Your eyes are like weapons when you look at my cousin like that," he says, voice sharp with anger. "Do I need to protect her? Because you know I will."

Golmarr pushes his hair off his forehead and glowers. "I don't think so, but please stay here just in case Sorrowlynn's stubbornness drives me to the point of madness."

I lean forward and put my hands on my hips. "*Me,* stubborn? You are the stubborn one, Golmarr, insisting we go to the Ilaadi library and risk being eaten in the process!"

"Of course I am being stubborn! If we cannot figure out how to break the curse, I will never be able to be alone with you because I am so scared of *killing* you!" He takes a step toward me and, in a quiet voice, adds, "I can hardly even touch you with people around because I am so scared of losing control, so what will happen if we are ever alone?"

I flinch. He might as well be trying to wound me with his words.

"Loving you, being this close to you . . ." He reaches out to touch me, but before his fingertips so much as brush my cheek, he lets his hand drop to his side. "It is killing me. Do you remember how hungry we were when we came out of the fire dragon's cave? When we had gone seven days with almost no food?"

I nod. Nearly every thought I had was about food. I would fantasize of the best meals I ever ate in my mother's palace.

"I hunger for you the same way I did for food. And now you are here, standing before me, looking at me in a way that makes me want to touch you, and hold you, and kiss you, and spend every night of the rest of my life in your arms. I want you, Sorrowlynn." His eyes move to my lips, and he swallows. "You are like a feast being offered to a man who is slowly starving to death, and I am too scared to eat. My willpower is waning, and every time I let my guard down and touch you, I hate myself for being so weak and putting your life at risk, because even bare hands can be used to kill." He takes a giant step away. "I am not fit to be alone with you." Clasping his hands behind his back, he glares at the floor. "And I hate *myself* more than I ever hated you because of it."

He growls, and Enzio steps between Golmarr and me. Golmarr shakes his head and strides to the table. He lifts the chair, and I worry he is going to throw it across the room or slam it against a bookshelf. Instead, he carries it to the closest shelf—the one with the oldest tablets—and sets it down. Golmarr climbs onto the chair and sweeps his hand across the top of the shelf, disturbing clouds of dust so thick they fill the air and stifle the lamp's pale glow. For his efforts, he finds a single brass tablet.

He blows the dust from it, rubs the tarnished brass with his sleeve, and then slams it down on the table. The metal clangs, echoing through the library. "Is this the fabled Infinite Vessel?" he asks me, his voice taut with unspent anger.

I carry the chair back to the table, sit down, and rub my thumb over the brass, wiping a thousand years of grime from it and exposing shallowly engraved symbols. As I slowly read, my heart starts beating faster. "Golmarr, Enzio!" The excitement in my voice has them instantly alert.

"Please say it says something useful," Golmarr whispers, placing his hands flat on the table across from me. Enzio, still gripping the stone knife, steps up beside him.

I touch the date on the top of the tablet. "This was written about thirty years after the Great War. It says, 'I and my uncle journeyed to the north to check the—*something*, I'm not sure what that word means—holding King Relkinn in his stone prison, but when we arrived, all we found was a great beast with scales the color of gold and eyes that shone like rubies. We assumed the beast had eaten the king, and were glad to finally be rid of him, but it was not so. The king was alive in the beast, as the beast had always been alive in the king. It is only a matter of time before the beast destroys the rock it is held under, and now it falls to my uncle to travel the world and gain knowledge so he might defeat King Relkinn and protect these people.'" I look up. "That is where it ends, but it is the first piece of writing that mentions dragons."

"Not the Infinite Vessel, though," Golmarr whispers. He rubs his hand on the unshaven whiskers growing on his chin. "Does it say *where* King Relkinn was imprisoned? Maybe they stored the vessel with him."

I run my finger below the symbols as I look for the answer he wants. "In the north, and in stone."

"My gran used to put me to sleep with a story about King Understone, who was sealed beneath a mountain," Enzio says.

"Your gran has a lot of scary stories," I say, and then realize his gran may also be my gran. "Is she my father's mother?"

Enzio nods. "You are feisty like her, Sorrowlynn. You are going to love her. She always said King Understone was imprisoned thousands of feet below the tallest peak in the world because no one could kill him."

The fire dragon's knowledge seems to swell in my head, and then I feel King Zhun there.

*Stacks of books and scrolls and tablets are piled on two tables: one table holds the books I have read in the past few days, the other holds the books I have yet to read. I slam the book* Spirits and the Unseen Realm: How Blood Binds Souls *closed and carefully toss it to the "already read" table. There are only a handful of books left to read. "Is this all there are?" I ask, looking up. Melchior, leaning against the wall, has his nose in a book of spells and seeing. He looks up and glances between the two tables.*

*"Yes, my king." Amusement flashes in his young eyes.*

*"What are you secretly laughing about?" I demand.*

*He closes his book with a snap, and a gust of air fans his brown hair back from his forehead. Turning in a slow circle, he looks at the rows and rows of books lining the library shelves. "Well, Uncle, it has taken you almost six years to read every book in this library, so, yes, six years' worth of reading is all this library contains."*

*"There must be information somewhere about how to kill the beast." Its blood-red eyes flash in my memory, making my blood grow cold. When I return to Arkhavan, I will devise a way to make a dragon-proof room, for every day that we do not find answers, the great beast is one day closer to destroying his stone prison. "I wonder if any of our other council of nine have found anything."*

*"Considering you have brought the smartest and strongest men and women to help in your quest, it is likely."*

*"Good. As soon as we finish with these last books, we need to gather them and see what they have found." I run my thick, callused finger over the embossed title of the book at the top of the stack,* Almanac of Desert Plants, and How to Transfer Their Energy, *and sigh. Plants are my least favorite subject to read about. "When we return to Arkhavan, I am building the biggest library in the*

*world. It will contain fifty years'—no, one hundred years' worth of reading. It will hold all the knowledge in the world, so that when someone else is desperately seeking answers, they will all be contained in the same place. And if they know the mistakes we have made, Melchior, they won't be foolish enough to repeat them." I open the book and start reading about the plants that thrive in the Ilaadi desert.*

---

"Where are you?" Something shakes me, and when I blink, I am back in King Zhun's library, which contains well over one hundred years' worth of reading. Enzio releases my shoulder, but he frowns with worry.

"The fire dragon must have killed King Zhun, because I have his memories in my head," I say, my voice light and dreamy. "Before he was eaten, King Zhun built this library to contain all the knowledge he could obtain, in the hope his people's mistakes would never be repeated. When he couldn't find the answers he sought, he must have gone to the fire dragon for help, since the fire dragon hoarded knowledge."

"What answers was he seeking?" Golmarr asks.

"He needed to know how to defeat the gold dragon locked beneath stone. He sought the brightest minds and the strongest warriors and delved into histories and magic and darkness." I search my head for more, but hit what feels like a void in my brain, where the knowledge and memories of King Zhun simply disappear. "Golmarr, are there any more tablets where you found this one?"

Golmarr shakes his head, and I peer at the tablet again, rereading it, hoping I missed something that will help me better understand what happened. There is nothing. Golmarr reaches for it, but before he even touches the tablet, he jerks his hand back as if he's been burned. He squeezes his eyes shut and presses on the bridge of his nose. Instinctively, I reach out to him, but stop myself before my skin makes contact with his. After what he said about hating himself for touching me, I dare not touch him. "Are you all right?" I ask.

Enzio gently shakes Golmarr's shoulder. "Can I help you?" he asks.

Golmarr stands tall. "A dragon is here. I can feel its hatred mingling with mine."

# Chapter 15

The sound of a clanging bell echoes through the library. Another closer bell starts ringing. I meet Golmarr's unblinking eyes. They are filled with fear. A third bell gongs, so close the ceiling cobwebs shudder from the vibrations rattling the library's very foundation, and dust floats down from the rafters. I know this bell.

"That is the dragon bell from the tower. They have finally come for me!" I stand and wrap my fingers around my staff. A moment later, the bell rings so loudly it makes the floor beneath my feet vibrate. And then it is silenced. "Something is terribly wrong."

Enzio grabs the lamp in one hand and frees Golmarr's reforged sword from his belt with the other. He holds the blade out to Golmarr, but Golmarr backs away. "I dare not," Golmarr says, his eyes haunted.

"But it is the only weapon that can kill a dragon," Enzio says. "How else are we going to beat it?"

"I do not trust myself to wield it with Sorrowlynn in the vicinity!" He wraps his arms around his chest and tucks his hands under his armpits.

Enzio's blue eyes flash with anger. "Then you will leave her to die?"

Golmarr's face darkens with loathing. "I hate myself enough already for attempting to take her life once. If I *killed* her, I would not survive it." He clenches his hands into fists and turns his spiteful gaze to me. "I am sorry!"

Without taking my eyes from Golmarr, I switch the staff to my left hand and hold out my right hand. "Give me the sword," I say.

"No!" Enzio takes a step back. "I will use the sword if Golmarr will not. You are a . . ."

My jaw tightens when he does not continue. "A . . . woman? I *am* a woman, and I am also a better swordsman than you. Give me the sword." Enzio hesitates for only a moment before he lays the hilt on my palm. My fingers wrap around it, the metal pressing against my skin. I swing it in a fast figure eight, its blue blade blurring as it slices the air. Despite the hilt being slightly too thick for my grasp, the sword feels familiar. Holding it is like waking after a long sickness to discover my body is completely healed. It feels good. "I will wield the reforged sword until Golmarr trusts himself to." Once the words leave my mouth, a shock of fear makes my knees tremble. I have just volunteered to fight the dragon.

"No! I cannot ask you to fight it!" Golmarr says.

I glare at him. "You did not ask, Golmarr. I have chosen, of my own free will, to wield the sword, and there is nothing you can do to stop me unless you dare to touch me. Because you will have to physically pry this weapon from my hands if you do not want me to fight." He opens his mouth to protest, but clutches his left shoulder and grimaces.

"What is wrong with your shoulder?" I ask. This is not the first time I have seen him grip it.

He looks down at his chest and grasps the laces of his tunic, cinching them as tight as they will go. "Nothing is wrong."

I stride to him, determined to examine his shoulder, but both of my hands are holding weapons.

"It is nothing!" He turns away. "Stop worrying about me. A dragon is here." He says it so simply, I almost laugh.

"Is *now* when you want me to find those secret passage-ways through the library? Are we leaving this castle?" I ask.

"No. If we go now, you will still be married to Treyose. And besides, I can't leave until I find the location of the Infinite Vessel. There has to be something we missed." He turns to me, his eyes pleading. "You don't understand. I *have* to figure out how to break this curse before—"

Booted feet are pounding up the stairs. Golmarr steps to my side and wraps his fingers around the quarterstaff, just above mine. "Do you know how to use a sword against a staff?" he asks.

I nod. "Thanks to Zhun's knowledge and Yerengul's training, I think I know everything about fighting."

"Good. Let me fight with the staff. If I attack you, do not hesitate to kill me." He takes the staff, and his entire body ripples and firms with the anticipation of battle. I do not tell him I don't think I could kill him, even if I am wielding a sword. Because I love him, I would not be able to take his life—even to save my own.

I know the moment the owners of the booted feet reach the top of the stairs. Light fills the far end of the library. Golmarr takes a step forward. "You two stand behind me on either side. If it comes to fighting and I cannot hold them off, move forward and take your places at my sides. If we can keep the enemy squeezed between the bookshelves, we can kill them one at a time," Golmarr instructs. I know this formation. It is an ancient technique used to fight an enemy who outnumbers you.

The lamplight moves closer, growing brighter between the narrow shelves, and then Reyler and another man are before us. "Treyose has sent me to see you safely out of the castle. A dragon is here. It is perched on the castle's bell tower, practically above our heads!" Reyler shouts. He doesn't wait to see if we follow.

As I take the first step forward, an outpouring of bravery I never knew I possessed steels my body. I straighten my spine and move forward with the confidence of a true warrior.

"Where is Treyose?" Golmarr asks.

"He is organizing the palace guards and soldiers to protect his people from the dragon," Reyler explains.

When we exit the quiet of the library, I stop walking and stare. The air is heavy with humidity and the jarring scent of sweat. Maids and manservants, their uniforms askew, are wailing and screaming, filling the halls with panic and chaos that seems to bleed into the guards trying to herd them efficiently out of the castle. Lords and ladies are mixed up in the mess, screaming insults, insisting on order, and cursing everyone around. For once, no one listens to their threats or cowers beneath their murderous glares.

Above the ruckus and pandemonium, the air shudders with a bone-deep blast that shakes the black castle. A clap of thunder follows. The panic in the passage freezes for a split second as everyone stares up, and then, with renewed horror, people start screaming and trampling each other.

Reyler is leading us in the same direction the masses are heading: out. I dig my feet against the stone floor, hold myself solid against the current of people fighting past me, and turn in the opposite direction.

"What are you doing?" Golmarr yells, his voice barely rising above the din of terror.

"I am going to the top of the bell tower!" I yell. "The dragon has come to kill me, since I have Zhun's knowledge. If I go outside with these people, the dragon is going to kill them to get to me! I'm going up there to fight it!"

Golmarr studies me for a moment and then smiles. "I'm coming with you."

"And so am I," Enzio says, though his face is pale, his mouth a hard line.

A hand grips my arm and pulls me to a stop. I meet Reyler's concerned eyes. "I have been ordered to get you out of the castle, my lady. I am to protect you with my life," he says.

"No. I am going to the bell tower." I twist my arm out of his grip.

"Then I will not be able to protect you, for I was told to bring you to Treyose and then help him lead the soldiers."

"Go, Reyler. Tell Treyose we are going to fight the dragon."

He nods and lets the pull of people sweep him away. I struggle against the crowd, forcing a narrow gap between the press of sweaty bodies, and pause at the base of a staircase so packed with people I cannot see the stone stairs beneath their feet. The castle's blueprints and secret passages instantly unravel in my head, and among them all, one clear pathway seems to light up—a narrow passage hidden behind a giant Trevonan crest, which leads to the bottom floor of the bell tower. With certainty making my steps firm, I shoulder my way through the people blocking the stairway and come out on the other side of the maelstrom of bodies.

A hand grips my elbow. "I thought we were going up," Golmarr says, mouth against my ear. Even in the midst of chaos, his mouth and breath on my skin make my heart leap.

"We are," I say. "I know a better way. Stay with me."

"I will," Golmarr says. His hand slides from my elbow, and I instantly miss his touch.

Now that we are farther from the castle's exit, the people in the passages are few and far between. We quicken our pace, pass the open door to the empty throne room, and two steps later, come to the crest on the wall. It is made of wood and has been replaced with a more modern crest than I remember. I lift the reforged sword and hack at the top of the crest. The silver blade shatters the wood, and I leap away as it clatters to the floor and splits in two. Where the crest had been is a cobweb-filled passage barely wider than the width of my shoulders.

"Make way for the king!" someone bellows. I turn away from the hidden passage and find myself staring at a wall of six steel-clad soldiers standing shoulder to shoulder. Behind them is a litter being carried by two more soldiers, with an ancient man covered in purple blankets sitting atop it.

"Make way for King Vaunn," the soldier before me commands. He looks at my sword and his eyes narrow and move to Golmarr, taking in his darker skin and long black hair. The soldier gasps and takes a step back. "Antharian brutes are infiltrating our castle!" he says. In one chilling, unison hiss, the six guards unsheathe their swords.

"Antharian brutes?" The old man on the litter leans forward, his beady eyes focusing on Golmarr. "The Antharians have woken the dragon! I should have known!" he cries, flinging aside the purple coverlet. It is then I see the jeweled gold crown sitting atop the man's brittle hair. "They are trying to take my kingdom!" King Vaunn climbs from the litter onto spindly legs, wearing nothing but a thin nightshirt hanging down to his knees. His hair is gray and stringy, his skin thin and wrinkled, but his eyes are sharp with a cruel hatred that makes me recoil.

I open my mouth to defend Golmarr, but then remember what Treyose said about me speaking. My Faodarian accent will give me away, and his grandfather will try to kill me. I close my mouth and grit my teeth.

King Vaunn grabs the sword of the man closest to him and runs forward, knocking his guards aside. For an old man, he is deceptively agile. He thrusts his weapon straight at Golmarr's heart, and the world seems to stand still. I cannot lift my sword in time to block the king. As his sword tip comes even with Golmarr's chest, metal rings on metal as the king's blade clangs against the steel tip of Golmarr's staff. Golmarr slams the king's blade aside, and the sword ricochets straight at my neck. King Vaunn turns his body with the sword's momentum, and as his eyes focus on me, he lends his strength to the blade, just as eager to take *my* life as he was to end Golmarr's.

Golmarr shouts. Enzio screams. I grunt and thrust the reforged sword between my skin and King Vaunn's weapon right before it can kill me. Our blades send a mighty crack through the air that seems to rise above every other sound. I twist my sword around his, our blades hissing as they slide against each other, and then the blade falls from his knobby hand, clanging to the floor between us. King Vaunn stumbles back a step and eyes the fallen weapon in shock.

Golmarr's booted foot covers the Trevonan blade where it lies. "If you lift your weapon against me or either of my companions, I will be forced to kill you, King Vaunn!" Golmarr bellows, holding his staff firmly between them.

The withered king opens his mouth, showing jagged yellow teeth, and screams, "Attack! Kill them!"

Even before the soldiers move to follow their king's orders, I know what to do. My sword darts low, aiming for the closest man's ankle. My blade slices through the back of his leather boot and finds its mark, severing flesh and tendon and toppling the big man. He crashes to the granite floor, metal armor clanging, creating a momentary blockade between me and the other soldiers. A heartbeat later, they are upon us, seven against three, with King Vaunn behind them screaming orders so fast they are mere gibberish.

Golmarr is a blur of motion, his long staff spinning and knocking two men unconscious before they are close enough to reach him with their swords. Enzio is like a viper, darting in and out, and attacking fast and hard with his short sword. I back away, loath to kill, horrified at the thought of having another person's memories and knowledge forced into my brain.

Though only five soldiers remain standing, Golmarr says, "Let it be known King Vaunn started this fight, and I have no intention of taking his land or his life. If he dies, it will not be an act of war by the Antharians. It will be an act of self-defense!" A soldier lunges at Golmarr.

"On your right!" I cry. Golmarr dodges the blow. "You would kill a man for proclaiming his desire not to fight with your king?" I ask, enraged.

King Vaunn's attention turns to me once again. "Though your dress is Trevonan, your accent is not," he says. He looks me up and down. "You are from Faodara! Faodara is infiltrating us with the horse clan?" His eyes grow wild. "The Faodarians have declared war on Trevon! Treyose! I need you!" King Vaunn falls to his knees and pries a sword from the hand of one of his fallen men.

Enzio pulls his sword from a soldier's thigh, and the man falls to the ground. "You stay away from her," Enzio snarls, but before he can lift his sword to stop Vaunn, another soldier engages Enzio. Golmarr swings his staff into another man's head with so much force, the man goes limp in the middle of swinging his sword and falls to the ground. "Go to the tower stairs, Sorrowlynn. We will meet you there," Golmarr says, but before I can take a step, something hits me hard in the shins, and I fall forward, landing on my stomach on something solid and uneven. It is a man. I am chest to chest with the soldier whose Achilles tendon I severed. He slams his fist into my face and then wraps his hands around my throat.

I am too close to use my sword against him, and his metal armor is a barrier against my fists, elbows, and knees. I jab my finger at his eye, but he whips his head away and I gouge his cheek instead. I look down at the soldier strangling me, and rage fills me with so much heat it seems to boil my blood. Grabbing his short hair in my hands, I lift his head and slam it hard against the granite floor. His grasp on my throat loosens, but doesn't release. I slam his head into the floor again, and the soldier goes limp, his hands falling to his sides.

In my peripheral vision I see movement, so I turn my head. Golmarr and Enzio are fighting with the last three Trevonan guards, and King Vaunn is standing over me, a sword in his wiry hands, about to run me through the back. Before I have time to react, a short sword clashes against the side of King Vaunn's head. The old man whirls around and comes face to face with Enzio. Golmarr is one step behind, his teeth bared. King Vaunn thrusts his sword at Enzio, but Enzio leaps to the side. The weapon keeps moving forward and stabs Golmarr in the chest, the tip disappearing beneath his tunic, right above his heart. King Vaunn jerks his sword back out and Golmarr stumbles backward, pressing on his chest. Everyone freezes—the guards, Enzio, King Vaunn—as Golmarr gapes at his torn tunic.

"No!" I scream. I leap to my feet and raise my sword at the same moment King Vaunn turns to me. Without meaning to, without my giving it conscious thought, the point of my sword lowers to his stomach. King Vaunn lunges forward, and his momentum carries him onto my blade, until it is buried deep in his flesh. Even when he is stabbed through, his eyes don't lose the hatred and anger burning in them. He glances down and sees my sword piercing his stomach, and the anger multiplies.

I pull my sword free and stab again, this time aiming for Vaunn's heart. In the blink of an eye, all the passion is stripped from his face. Vaunn's skin goes slack, his eyes lose focus, and he totters backward. He lands on the floor with a loud thud, and that is the moment the worst part of the fire dragon's inherited treasure takes over—the unstoppable curse of absorbing the knowledge of any living thing I kill. My conscience seems to fill with thick, rotting sludge.

"Your king is down! Do not lift your swords against us again!" Golmarr orders. I fall to my knees and press the heels of my hands against my closed eyes as images fill my brain.

I see Treyose screaming, his arm tied to a stone table as a blade slices through his littlest finger. Next, I see King Vaunn plundering city after city, killing men, raping women, forcing allegiances. As the images continue, I do not regret killing him, even if the price of his death is my head being assaulted with his filth.

I shake myself, trying to stop the onslaught of knowledge so I can rush to Golmarr's aid, but I cannot stop seeing King Vaunn's memories. Warmth clasps my wrists, pulling my hands from my eyes. When I blink them open, I still see piles of dead men and weeping women, but I also see Golmarr staring into my eyes. His tunic is torn above his heart, and the cream-colored fabric is slowly turning red as his blood soaks it. I reach for it, but Golmarr tightens his grip on my wrist.

"I am fine. You killed King Vaunn," Golmarr says, his voice soft. I spin away, fall to my knees, and vomit, trying to force the taint of King Vaunn from my body.

The castle rumbles and groans, and the distant screams of people fill the halls.

Golmarr pulls me to my feet, his eyes tight with worry as he examines my body. "Are you hurt?"

I shake my head and spit the acrid tang of bile from my mouth. Three guards are still standing, their backs against the wall and their swords on the ground, while Enzio holds his sword ready. "If any of you so much as *sniffs* wrong, you will taste Satari steel," he warns.

"Golmarr, your chest is bleeding. Are you sure you're not mortally injured?" I reach toward his bleeding wound, but he backs away.

"It is not deep, and we do not have time to spare."

I nod and take a step forward, but stop again as Treyose and Reyler stride into the passage, surveying the guards at my feet and the three standing against the wall. When Treyose sees his grandfather's motionless body, I grip my sword tighter, ready to fight the Trevonan prince once he realizes I have killed his king.

Instead, Treyose looks at Golmarr and asks, "You killed him?"

Golmarr shakes his head. "Sorrowlynn did. It was self-defense."

Treyose exhales a trembling breath and pushes on the bridge of his nose. Golmarr puts his hand on Treyose's shoulder. "Your troops are assembled and keeping your people safe?"

"The troops are assembled, but the dragon is killing my people one by one," Treyose says. "How do I defeat it?"

"Come up to the bell tower with us. The beast wants Sorrowlynn. We will draw it up there and you can help us slay it. You will not have to do anything more to get your people to follow you," Golmarr says quietly. "You will be your people's hero as well as their rightful king. They will follow you willingly."

Like a swelling wave, the muted shrieks of people outside the castle grow, reach a climax, and then fade to nothing. Thunder shatters the silence and vibrates the granite beneath my feet.

"Will you fight the dragon with us?" Golmarr asks Treyose again, his voice urgent.

"I will," Reyler says.

"I will, too, but wait." Treyose picks up his grandfather's

body and carries it through the open throne room door, laying it on the hard stone floor. He pulls a torch from a sconce in the throne room and strides out, shutting and locking the door from the outside. To the three remaining guards, he says, "Stand watch and keep his body safe. I have a dragon to battle with."

# Chapter 16

The bell tower is the tallest man-made structure in Trevon, standing ten stories high, like a black granite needle thrusting all the way to the clouds. At its highest point sits a huge bell, with four open windows exposing it to the air. There is a balcony around the bell's windows, built wide enough for a small army to stand atop and fight a dragon.

Today, we have no army, just two Trevonan soldiers, an Antharian warrior, a Satari forest dweller, and me. And even though I am the woman, *I* am the one wielding the only weapon in the world that can kill a dragon.

A spiral stone staircase with no handrail twists up the interior of the bell tower, lining the sleek black wall, all the way to the top. Up the steps we climb, circling the bell's thick rope, which dangles down the exact center of the tower. We reach the last step, and I stop at the stone door leading from the bell tower to the balcony. Placing my hand on the rusted steel bar locking it, I try to slide it away. But it doesn't budge.

Golmarr steps up beside me and lends his strength to mine, but the bar still does not move. Enzio joins us, and the metal groans with our combined effort.

"Stand aside," Treyose says. He hands me the torch and steps up to the door, placing his big hands on the bar. My focus moves from the metal to his missing finger, and again I see a flash of his arm stretched long across a stone table and tied in place as a sword swings down and severs his pinkie. And then I hear King Vaunn's voice: *That is what you get for refusing to lead my army! Your hand will be next.*

Treyose groans with effort, his biceps strain against his sleeves, and the tendons bulge in his neck. With a shriek of metal on metal, the bar slides free and clatters to the ground. It topples over the side of the stairs, and a moment later, far below, we hear a quiet clang as it collides with the ground.

Treyose shoves the door open, and a blast of cold air hits me, accompanied by a cloud of smoke. The balcony is wider than I remember, and its once-glossy granite floor is covered with centuries of dirt, dead birds, and bugs.

I squint against the weak sunlight and step out onto the balcony. The bell tower is whole and untouched. Shading my eyes, I look to the sky, but there is no dragon in the haze. I cross to the edge of the balcony, my feet crunching the littered ground, and look down.

Far below, a dragon flies and people are running from the beast while Treyose's men stand in organized columns, ready to fight the creature. The dragon dives down and the soldiers fire arrows, but the beast doesn't slow. Two voices echo in my thoughts: **Let us grab us a handsome soldier.** No! That pretty maiden there! I want to eat her. I want to ruin her milky skin! I shudder at the realization that I am hearing the dragons' conversation. I heard the fire dragon, but only when he intentionally spoke to me.

"I can hear them," Golmarr says, his eyes wide. "Look!"

Just out of the soldiers' reach, the beast touches the ground, and then whips its wings against the air as it takes flight. The way it flies is nothing like the way the fire dragon or the glass dragon soared. This creature lurches in clumsy, lopsided jolts. It turns and starts flying toward the bell tower, and I understand why it cannot fly well. One of its wings is the vibrant, shimmering hues of a sunset fading from light to dark to purple; the other wing is the dull, grayish color of putrid mud. The purple wing is wide and delicate, like a falcon's. The gray wing looks like the stubby wing of a dead and plucked chicken, with skin pulled so taut between bones that light shines through it. Above the wings, the neck divides in two, and on the end of each neck is a single dragon head.

"God save us all," Reyler mutters as he gapes at the beast.

Beside me, I hear Enzio swallow. "Are you truly going to fight that thing, cousin?" he asks.

I cannot speak around the fear clenching my throat closed, so I nod.

He swallows again, an audible gulp. "Give me the sword. I will do it," he says, holding out an unsteady hand.

My heart hurts at his offer, at the obvious motivation behind it. Enzio cares for me as deeply as I care for him, which is why I shake my head and tighten my hold on the sword. "I will not let you fight in my place, friend."

The dragon continues its struggle upward, passing the edge of the balcony and flying above us. It lurches its mass onto the very top of the bell tower, just above the four windows exposing the tarnished bell. The dragon curls its tail around the black stone so the end of it, a massive, weapon-like spike, is resting on the balcony. In its talons the creature holds a young woman with hair as pale as flax and skin like cream. The woman is arched back, her body limp, and she is wearing the uniform of a castle servant. My focus moves from the woman to the dragon, and I take a step back, pressing my body against the balcony's railing. I do not know how to fight such a massive beast.

Two sets of eyes are blinking down from two separate heads. One head is covered with gleaming purple feathers, and its eyes rival the beauty of the bluest summer sky. The other head is misshapen and covered with bulging lumps that ooze yellow liquid. Beady, sunken eyes the color of dried blood glare from that head, and long yellow fangs jut out of its lipless mouth. It is so repulsive, I can hardly stand to look at it.

The female finds me hideous! a voice shrieks in my head; it sounds like the high-pitched grate of metal scraping against metal. The ugly head looks at me and hisses with its forked tongue, then lurches forward. In horror, I watch as it opens its mouth and eats the flaxen-haired girl in one gulp.

"No!" Reyler shouts.

Treyose curses and asks, "What is that monstrosity?"

I wade through the memories in my head, and just as I start to glimpse the creature, my mind seems to hit a solid wall. "I don't know," I say.

Golmarr groans and pushes on his left shoulder—the one that is bleeding. "Those are two sisters," he says.

Of course it is the handsome one who recognizes us. Let's eat him first, says a deep, silky female voice.

*No, let us sizzle the woman! I cannot stand to see her judging me,* shrieks the other voice.

"Move!" Golmarr slams his foot into my hip, throwing me sideways. I twist in the air and land on my hands and knees just as a spear of lightning strikes the balcony where I had been standing. The floor explodes, and heat fills the air. Energy crackles against my skin, and I *know* it: it is the same source that fire comes from. Without standing, I pull the energy to me the way I pulled the fire from the library shelves, and turn it into a dancing, orange flame the size of a man. With a thrust of my arms, I throw the fire at the dragon, but the beast stretches its wings—one beautiful, one hideous—and flaps. A gust of wind scatters the fire, whipping the heat back at us. My companions scream and throw their arms over their faces.

*She can wield fire! Sister, she is the one who killed Zhun,* the silky voice says, slithering through my thoughts like oil. *She killed him and stole his treasure. She is the one we have been seeking. Kill her!*

I climb to my feet and stare up at the two-headed monster pushing its words into my conscience. "For a person to steal something, she has to want it first!" I yell. "This power, this *curse*, was forced upon me, and I want nothing to do with it."

Golmarr steps up beside me and asks, "How do we break the curse?"

For an answer, the dragon swings its tail. I jump away as the spike slams into the balcony railing, shattering stone and leaving a gaping hole.

I adjust my grip on the reforged sword, grasping the hilt in both my hands, and run the two steps to the tail. With all of my strength focused in my shoulders and torso, I slam the sword down onto the creature's tail, just above the giant spike on the very end of it. The blade carves through scales, glides through flesh, melts through bone, and comes out on the other side, ringing against the granite floor. The end of the tail rolls away from the beast and falls through the wide hole in the railing.

Treyose steps up beside me and swings his sword at the dragon's tail, where it connects to the beast's body. When his blade hits scales, it ricochets off them, and he is thrown backward by its momentum.

The beast shrieks and whips its tail away, splattering Treyose, the balcony, and me with hot crimson blood.

She can hurt us! wails the ugly dragon. Now we are even uglier than before! She made us even uglier!

You will all die for that! The beautiful dragon opens its mouth and pulls back its neck. I prepare to leap out of the way of lightning, but a jet of water sprays from the creature's mouth. The beast doesn't aim for any of us, but simply covers the ground with warm water until I am standing in a puddle tinged pink with dragon blood and seeping into the seams of my leather boots.

Yes, sister! Yes! There is nothing tastier than sizzled human for lunch! the ugly head says, its thought so loud my skull vibrates.

"No!" Golmarr shrieks, sprinting toward me. "Run! Run! Onto the railing!" He slips once in the water and then reaches my side, gripping the fabric of my dress, yanking me off my feet, and placing me so I am sitting on the railing. I start to fall backward, so I grab the edge of the stone as Golmarr jumps up onto it. He grips my shoulder to keep me upright. Across the balcony, Enzio leaps for the railing, landing on his stomach, feet flailing. Treyose climbs up beside me, balancing on the balls of his feet, and Reyler is one step behind.

I stretch my hand out to the Trevonan nobleman, and as he reaches for it, lightning forks out of the ugly head's mouth and hits the soaked balcony with a glaringly bright explosion that deafens my ears, rattles my bones, and nearly blinds me. Golmarr kicks my hand away from Reyler just as the tips of my fingers touch his. The nobleman's body turns hard and stiff, and spasms midstride. Treyose reaches out for Reyler, but Golmarr screams, "If you touch him, you will also die!"

I close my eyes against the sight of Reyler dying and feel the power of the lightning as it crackles the very air around me. I pull the energy to me again, every bit of it, until my skin feels like wax on the verge of melting, and then I focus it on the bell tower. I push the heat from me, as hard as I have ever pushed anything in my life, and white flames burst from my fingertips, slamming into stone.

The granite explodes, and chunks of it liquefy from the fire's heat. Melted rock flies through the air, and one giant piece lands on the neck of the feathered dragon, conforming around it like a black molten collar. The ugly head shrieks, the pretty head roars a deep, throaty sound, and the top of the bell tower snaps beneath the dragon's weight, collapsing onto the balcony and pinning the beast beneath it.

"Give me your sword," Treyose says, and I place the reforged sword into his hand. He jumps off the railing, but when his feet touch the balcony, it creaks and shudders. Treyose freezes and stares at the stone floor as a vein shaped like a jagged piece of lightning cracks its surface, dividing it in two.

The dragon, still pinned beneath the top of the bell tower, is writhing and struggling, thrashing its stump of a tail from side to side, flapping its mismatched wings. The balcony makes an audible crack and splits wide open, dividing the floor into two halves. The half where the dragon lies, where Enzio is still gripping the railing, starts to tip and break away. Enzio leaps and sprints up the wet, tilting floor. He jumps over the stump of the bleeding dragon tail, and then catapults his body across the crack between the balcony's two halves. His arms pinwheel through the air, and it is obvious he isn't going to make it to our side.

Golmarr jumps from the railing, takes three steps, and then slides across the granite on his knees. Just as Enzio's head disappears beneath the balcony's broken edge, Golmarr thrusts his hand down. His shoulders strain beneath his tunic, and he starts sliding forward. "Treyose!" Golmarr shrieks.

Treyose presses the hilt of the reforged sword into my hands and flings himself to his stomach beside Golmarr, reaching below the balcony. In one giant heave, they drag a pale, trembling Enzio up.

With a gust of wind, the other half of the balcony breaks completely free and drops from sight, carrying the dragon with it. The bell's thick rope speeds past us as the bell, still inside the tower, plummets with the dragon. When the whole length of rope has zipped past, a hollow gong fills the air, followed by the distant screams of the people below.

I jump from the railing and freeze, staring at my feet. The floor is crumbling.

"To the stairs!" Treyose screams. He bends and picks up Reyler's body, swinging it over his shoulder. I run to the gaping hole, where the door leading into the bell tower used to stand. Five feet below the missing doorway, the stairs start, as if the top of the bell tower took a chunk of stairs with it when it fell. I leap to the stairs and start descending, but the tower tilts, throwing me into the wall.

"Go, Sorrowlynn!" Golmarr cries. I push off the wall and run down the stairs, skipping three at a time as rubble rains onto my head. The tower tilts again, to the other side, and my feet stumble, tipping me toward a fall that would mean certain death, but just before I plummet, the tower starts swinging the other way.

"The entire tower is going to fall! Go faster or we all die!" Treyose screams.

"I am going as fast as I can!" I scream back just as loud. I am sprinting, leaping and flying downward so fast my bones shudder every time I land. When I am almost at the bottom, I forget the stairs and launch myself over the side of them, landing so hard the wind is knocked from my lungs, and my knees buckle. Treyose, Golmarr, and Enzio land around me. Someone drags me to my feet, and together we run into the castle as the bell tower moans and crashes to the ground with an explosion of wind and debris that slams against my back and throws me to the floor.

I lie there, eyes closed, body paralyzed with fear. "Suicide Sorrow," Golmarr whispers. I open my eyes and find myself face to face with him. A smile graces his beautiful, dust-covered face. "I think it is time for us to go from this castle."

"What about the dragon? The people?" I whisper, unable to find my voice.

He shakes his head. "It is going to hide away and lick its wounds before it comes for us again. And wherever you go, there the dragon will be." He sounds so certain.

I blink the dust from my eyes and look at him a little more closely. "How do you know?"

His eyes slip shut. "Just trust me for now. When we aren't lying on a hard stone floor, covered with pieces of an ancient tower, I will tell you."

I nod and simply breathe the dusty air. Even dust-filled air is a pleasure after thinking I might never draw breath again.

# Chapter 17

Inside my chamber, I brush the remnants of the bell tower from my face, my dress, my hair, even my eyebrows and eyelashes. Enzio yanks his shirt off and shakes his head from side to side, flinging rubble from his dark curls. Golmarr stands in the doorway and stares at nothing, his eyes far away. The blood on his tunic, from his sword wound, is caked with dirt. I walk to him and reach for the strings of his tunic, but he catches my fingers in his. "What are you doing?" he asks.

"Checking your wound."

"I'm fine," he says gently, giving my fingers a squeeze before letting them go.

I step in front of him, so close he can either back himself up against the shut door or physically move me to get by. He backs himself against the door and stares at me with suspicious eyes. "Golmarr, I watched King Vaunn stab you in the chest. You're bleeding. Let me at least check it."

He shakes his head and scowls. "Please do not worry about it. I have seen hundreds of injuries—enough to know mortal wounds from flesh wounds. I assure you, I have nothing more than a flesh wound." He puts his hand on my shoulder and moves me aside, then steps away.

I open my mouth to insist he let me check it, but booted feet echo in the passage. Golmarr cracks the door open and peers out, then swings it wide. Treyose enters. Every step he takes, small clouds of dust rain down around his feet. "The tower destroyed the library," he says.

"I know," Golmarr replies, dropping into the chair that has been moved beside the bed. Rubble topples from his shoulders and hair.

Treyose's filthy eyebrows rise. "You know?" he asks.

Golmarr leans forward and rests his elbows on his knees. "The tower was built beside the library. Of course the library is destroyed."

Treyose narrows his eyes and nods.

"Treyose, we need to leave tonight," Golmarr says.

Treyose nods again. "Where will you go?"

"Ilyaro."

"The capital city of Ilaad? They do not like foreigners in the desert. Not even *I* dare go there, and they are my neighbors."

Golmarr laughs. "Of course you can't go there. Your grandfather conquered a large portion of their land. *You* are their sworn enemy. *I* am an Antharian prince—they should have no quarrel with me. And I need to go to their famed desert library," Golmarr explains.

Treyose takes a step closer to Golmarr and quietly asks, "Is the Infinite Vessel worth dying to find? Because the ancient Ilaadi library is located in the middle of the desert, where the sandworm rules. It has been abandoned for two centuries. There is probably nothing left of it."

"The Infinite Vessel *is* worth dying to find," Golmarr whispers.

Treyose throws his hands up in the air. "I don't think you should go to Ilyaro. My grandfather's library . . . *my* library is the largest in the world." He scowls. "*Was.* If you didn't find what you were looking for there, I guarantee you the Ilaadi won't have it, either. In the desert, death, knives, and poison are ranked above wisdom and knowledge. I would like to invite you all to stay here as long as you like, as my honored guests."

Golmarr's eyes briefly shift to me. "I thank you for the offer," he says, "but I need to go. As far as I am concerned, our deal has been met. Your grandfather is dead, and now you are king. I am no longer bound to you."

A small, sad smile touches Treyose's mouth. "You did not meet the terms of our deal." His eyes shift to me. "But Sorrowlynn, by her actions, has made me king, and I accept that in place of our deal. And, since I am now the king, I have the authority, by Trevonan law, to break marriage vows. It is finally within my power to annul my marriage to Sorrowlynn." Treyose crosses the room and stands before me. Taking my hand in his, he says, "Sorrowlynn of Faodara, wife of Treyose, King of Trevon, with the power vested in me, I absolve our marriage wholly and completely. Any vows that were spoken to bind us—no matter where or by whom they were spoken— I break with my authority as king. From this moment forth, you are wed to no man, bound to no man, betrothed to no man. You are no longer my wife and are free to pursue whatever and whomever you choose henceforth. I hold no power or authority over you, save that of King of Trevon, and I swear I will never use that power to take away your freedom. Neither do you hold any claim or power over me. We are free to pursue separate lives."

I close my eyes and laugh. When I inhale, my body feels lighter than it has in days. "Thank you." I glance at Golmarr and feel the sting of tears even though he is unaware of my gaze. He is still leaning his elbows on his knees and staring at the floor, deep in thought. Finally, I am free to love him and act on it.

"There will be a brief ceremony declaring me king this evening, and I would be honored if you would all attend," Treyose says. "You can leave after the ceremony, if that is the course you choose."

"Though I cannot speak for my companions, I would like to attend," I say.

Enzio nods. "If you can promise me a bath and find me something presentable to wear, I also would like to attend. I shall represent the people of Satar."

Golmarr stands. "You've proven to be a good man, King Treyose. I am glad to know you. It would be an honor to attend and represent the agreed-upon peace between our kingdoms." Golmarr grins. "I can perform a few feats of magic, too, if you'd like, to prove that Trevon once again has a wizard backing it."

Treyose grins and claps Golmarr hard on the back, making a cloud of dust billow out from his clothes. "Thank you . . . friend." Treyose holds his hand out to Golmarr and they clasp wrists. "I will have travel supplies ready for you before the sun sets. And a hot bath and meal for each of you, and fresh clothes." He turns to me and holds his hand out so we can clasp wrists—a warrior's salute. I wrap my fingers around his wrist.

"You are a commendable fighter, Princess," he says.

I inhale to thank him, but my vision clouds over. I am seeing the world through the eyes of King Vaunn as my mind opens up to one of his memories.

*"Why can't you be more like your brothers?" I ask, but the words come from King Vaunn's mouth. I pace in front of a younger Prince Treyose, my hands clasped behind my back. "Your brothers always did whatever I asked of them," I snarl.*

*"I am not my brothers!" Treyose yells, and I wonder how he can have so much passion when it comes to defying me, his king and only living relative, and yet abhor war. War is what makes a boy into a man. War is what has built Trevon into the largest kingdom in the world.*

*I step up to my grandson and look at his mutilated hand, the nub of his pinkie still scabbed over. I threatened to cut off his whole hand if he did not do my bidding, and he has not. But without a hand, how will he lead my army to victory? He needs that hand to wield his weapons. "A pity. I hoped removing your finger would buy your loyalty, as nothing else seems to. Since it has not, I will be taking something else of yours." Giddy excitement tempts my mouth to smile, but I force it to remain neutral as Treyose clenches his hand into a fist.*

*"Are you truly going to take my hand?" he asks.*

*I shake my head, and he sighs with relief. "No. I have something infinitely more precious than a hand at my disposal."*

*Treyose's face pales. "What are you talking about?"*

*King Vaunn's mouth pulls up into a smile despite his best efforts to control it. "If you fail to lead my army to victory against the Antharians, your wife dies a slow and painful death."*

*"Where is she?" Treyose yells, his muscles bulging against his sleeves as he fights to control himself, fights to keep his hands from suffocating me. I take a step closer, daring him to lose control. Daring*

*him to raise a hand against me so I have the right to hang him. It takes him several long moments before he reins in his anger, and when he does, my smile slips the slightest bit. Of all my offspring, this young man, who hates war, who loves a single woman, scares me more than any of my ferocious, warmongering sons and grandsons. But they are all dead. I sigh a bored sigh. "Will you lead the army against King Marrkul, or have your wife killed before your eyes? And I promise you, it will not be a fast death."*

*"Fine," Treyose whispers, his entire body trembling. "But if you hurt her . . ."*

I stumble back a step and look at Treyose. "He killed your wife because you couldn't defeat the horse clan."

Treyose recoils and looks to Golmarr. "Does she also possess the sight?"

Golmarr studies me and shakes his head. "No. At least, not in the way you imagine."

Treyose stares at the floor. "He killed her," he confirms, his voice rough with emotion. "And from that day forward I have done everything in my power to put a stop to his madness, while at the same time doing everything he asked. And now his madness is over." He falls to his knees at my feet and takes my hand again. "Thank you, Sorrowlynn of Faodara. You have rid the world of an evil man. I swear on my life, that from this day forward, I will strive to undo all the evil he has worked."

Chills spread down my entire body as I recognize the truth and passion behind his words. This famed warrior kneeling at my feet, with his scarred body, broken heart, and missing finger, is going to make a good king.

Because of the terror and damaged wreaked by the two-headed dragon, Treyose, who is dressed in mourning black instead of Trevonan purple, keeps his kingship ceremony short and quiet. He stands on a raised dais, the setting sun shining orange against his somber clothes and gold crown, and swears before the gathered nobility and peasants to earn their trust and respect, and put an end to all war. Whether his people will support him in his quest for peace is yet to be seen, but they cheer at his declaration. Golmarr stands at his side and the two men pledge peace between their neighboring kingdoms. When they shake hands to seal their promise, Golmarr fills the air with shining blue stars. The Trevonans gasp, some weep, and as the sun dips down behind the horizon, it silhouettes something perched on the black city wall. The two-headed dragon is watching.

# Chapter 18

We ride out as the very last light of dusk frames the horizon, and right before we pass beneath the black wall of the city, I see the two-headed dragon perched on the westernmost end of the wall. I pull my hood up and peer at Golmarr. He nods. "It is watching to see if we leave. Take your hood off. Hopefully it will follow us."

I pull my hood down and study the deserted road. When I look back, the wall is empty. "I think the beast is following."

Enzio cranes his neck, searching the dark sky. "We should ride faster," he says. "I do not want to meet that creature in the dark."

All three of us coax our horses into a steady trot. The air is bitterly cold and filled with the dusty remnants of battle and destruction. I cough on the dense air and think, *I am breathing in the ancient bell tower. I am breathing history.*

Icy wind whips against my back and tugs on my clean, tightly braided hair. I am wearing men's wool leggings and a brown tunic beneath a plate armor shirt. Golmarr's reforged sword hangs from my new sword belt, and I have been given a wrist strap for my black blade. Sturdy leather boots are laced up to my knees, and in the top of one boot is a second knife—a parting gift from Treyose. Once again, I am wearing Treyose's deep purple, fur-lined cloak, the back of it draping the hind quarters of my Trevonan horse.

Golmarr rides on my right, Enzio on my left, both of them outfitted similarly to me—wearing thick, dark cloaks with the hoods pulled low around their faces. My steel-tipped staff is attached to Golmarr's saddle. Every few minutes, he reaches out and grips the wood in his hand, clenching and releasing it as he studies the black sky, looking for the dragon.

I guide my horse until I am riding right beside him, my knee bumping his. He looks from my knee to my face, and his eyes are heavy with an emotion I cannot name. Maybe sorrow, maybe suspicion, maybe fear. "How is your shoulder?" I ask, raising my voice above the howling wind. "I could use fire to heal it."

"I already told you, I barely have a scratch." He swings his left arm in a wide circle, proving there is no pain.

"How is that possible? I watched King Vaunn plunge his sword into your chest with the entire force of his body!"

He lifts one eyebrow. "There was hardly anything left of his body besides skin and bones." His gaze lowers from mine, and his hand shoots out and cinches around the staff, kneading the wood. "Sorrowlynn, I . . ."

My stomach drops into my hips at the tone of his voice. "You what?" I reach out and cover his hand with mine, stilling the constant movement on the staff.

"Lord Damar severed our betrothal. You are free of me."

His words take me so off guard, I am struck mute. *Free* of him? As if I can simply tell my heart to stop loving something? As if I can tell my mind to cancel all thoughts of him—tell my body to stop craving his touch, and my soul to stop longing for his friendship? I shake my head. "I don't wish to be free of you."

He looks at our touching hands and his face hardens. Pulling his hand away, he says, "You don't know everything about me." His words are so soft they almost get lost in the wind.

I sit taller and glare at the road, a straight line of black that slowly blends into the darker world ahead. "You are right. I do *not* know everything about you, but I know *me*, and I have the knowledge of hundreds of men and women infused in my brain—maybe even *thousands*. I know what love is. I know it hundreds of times over, from hundreds of different people, from hundreds of unique perspectives!" My heart presses against my ribs as the truth of my words hits me, and I find it hard to draw breath. "*I know what love is!*" Anger courses through me. "And no matter what you say or do, you cannot change how I feel, Golmarr. I cannot choose for you, but for me, I choose to hold on to my love for you."

His eyes slip shut and he takes a few deep breaths before he answers, "I am simply saying, if for any reason you do not want to spend your life with me, I will let you go with no questions asked. Because I love you, I will give you freedom to choose whatever path you want to take in life. I will never force you to stay with me. *That* is what love is."

"Yes, it is," I agree. "And with that freedom, I choose to love you." I ride away from him, so I am once again centered between him and Enzio, and stare straight ahead, chin thrust stubbornly forward. The miles pass in cold, miserable silence.

By the time the middle of the night has come and gone, I am sagging in the saddle, and my hands are stiff and numb from the frigid air. The plate mail seems to hold the cold, and its weight is making my head and shoulders throb. "I need to sleep," I say through chattering teeth and a stiff jaw. Without waiting to hear Golmarr's or Enzio's response, I guide my horse off the road to a small copse of trees and dismount. With unbending, numb fingers, I fiddle with the plate armor until I have it off and drop it to the ground. It lands with a noisy jangle.

"Wait here," Golmarr says to Enzio. He follows me to the copse and dismounts. Moonlight glows against the planes of his jaw, and his hood shadows his eyes. The wind whips his cloak out from his body, sending it soaring behind him like midnight wings that hide the stars. He reaches back and yanks his cloak tight around his shoulders, and the smell of him and the warmth from his body envelop me. I close my eyes and take a small step closer to him; the desire to bask in his warmth is so strong I have to dig my toes into my boots to keep myself from taking another step.

"We need a safe place to sleep since the dragon is following us. The outskirts of Harborton are about five miles farther south. That is our destination." His deep, quiet voice sends a shiver through me. He starts to fiddle with his plate armor, and by the way his fingers fumble with the metal, I know they are just as stiff and cold as mine. "We will stop at an inn there and sleep." He removes his armor, tosses it beside mine, and shrugs his shoulders. "The lack of armor will help, too." He turns to the road and calls, "Enzio, if you want to stay warmer, remove your armor."

I shiver and wrap my cloak tightly around my body. "I can't keep going, Golmarr. My hands . . . I can't even feel the horse's reins in them anymore. They're so cold, I can hardly bend my fingers." For a moment, he stares into my eyes, and then he reaches beneath my cloak and takes my hands in his, though his are no warmer. But his touch sends a rush of energy through me that makes the night seem far less cold. I miss him so much, miss this closeness. I pull my hands out of his and take a second step forward, wrapping my arms around his waist beneath his cloak and laying my head on his shoulder before he can protest.

His muscles stiffen, so I tighten my hold and close my eyes. The warmth from his body enfolds me, and I breathe it deep into my lungs, letting it fill me. A tentative weight settles against my back as he rests his hands there. "No sudden movements," he whispers. A moment later, Golmarr wraps his arms and cloak around me, holding me so tightly I cannot take a full breath. Unexpected tears fill my eyes.

*This* feels like home—out on a dark, deserted, windy roadside in the early hours before sunrise. His arms around me, and the smell of him in my nose, with his breath in my hair and his warmth against my body, is where I belong. My home is not a place. It is a person. We stand there and let the wind whip at us with its fury, let the iciness of the night try to squeeze between us, yet warmth grows everywhere our bodies touch. Minutes pass and neither of us moves or speaks.

From the roadside, I hear the polite clearing of a throat and Golmarr loosens his hold on me. "Warmer?" he asks, his voice rough.

"You held me and didn't hurt me," I say. "Please don't let me go yet."

"I held you and didn't hurt you," he repeats, voice filled with awe, and he tightens his arms around me once more. I bury my face in his chest. Beneath his thick tunic, I feel something more solid than skin and muscle and bone. I frown, pull away, and press my fingers to his chest, just below his left collarbone. The fabric of his tunic slides against a hard, smooth surface. The hair at the nape of my neck stands on end.

Golmarr growls deep in his throat and spins away, his cloak flaring around him like shadow wings once more. I stare at his dark silhouette and ask, "Are you wearing armor beneath your clothing?"

"No," he says, the word clipped.

"Are you bandaged there? From where King Vaunn stabbed you?"

"His sword barely left a scratch. Just remember what I said about not having to love me."

"What does that have to do with your shoulder?"

"We need to keep going." He bends to pick up his armor, so I put my foot on it. His eyes meet mine, and I expect to see anger or hatred in them. Instead, they are brimming with sorrow. He swallows and opens his mouth, as if to say something, then closes it. Finally, he says, "I choose not to answer that question right now. It is not the right time or place."

"When will you answer it?"

"I don't know, but definitely not when we are on the side of a cold, deserted road in the middle of the night, with a dragon chasing us." He shakes his head, picks up his armor, and then strides to his horse, swinging up into the saddle in one swift, graceful move. I pick up my armor and follow.

⊹⊱❈⊰⊹

We set a faster pace. Our horses' hooves clopping on the well-worn road and the whistling wind are the only noises. For a moment, the wind shifts, surging up from the south, and carries on it the smells of wood smoke, sewage, and beneath those, brine.

Unlike the city of Arkhavan, Harborton has no wall around it, so we enter the outer fringe of dark buildings unopposed. An eerie fog is hovering above the cobblestone street, dancing when the wind sneaks through. We pass ramshackle structures with dark windows, and even darker alleys between them, and I put my hand on my sword hilt despite the cold that has made the metal like ice.

"Are we safe here?" I whisper, wondering if it was wise to remove my armor. My words get stripped away by the wind, so I guide my horse closer to Golmarr's. He hasn't once looked at me since our encounter on the side of the road. "Are we safe here?" I ask again. "I don't like the feel of this place."

He presses a finger to his lips and pointedly looks at my sword. I nod and loosen it from the scabbard. Enzio guides his horse closer to mine, his black knife in his hand. "Don't worry, Sorrow, I will keep you safe." Without looking away, he tosses the knife into the air and then catches it by the hilt.

Despite my heavy heart, a small smile finds its way to my lips. "I am sorry for any man who dares to come between me and your black blade."

"There will be no need to be sorry for a dead man." He grins and spins the blade around his fingers before it disappears up his sleeve.

After we have passed a dozen dark buildings, I hear the low sound of music. A moment later, we stop at a two-story structure with a dim, flickering light coming from its lower windows. I am fairly certain the music is coming from within.

Above the red front door, a sign is blowing in the wind, flapping back and forth and squeaking with the movement.

FISH HEAD INN AND TAVERN is written on the sign, the words barely visible in the orange glow coming through the window. Golmarr dismounts, and Enzio follows suit.

"*This* is where we are going to stay?" I whisper, dismounting and trying to peer through the grime on the window. "I think I'd rather have frozen on the side of the road."

The sides of Golmarr's mouth twitch, as if he's fighting a smile, and he looks right into my eyes. His gaze moves from my eyes to my lips, and I feel like my heart has been caught by his and it is drawing me in. Instead of fighting it, I give in to the pull and step forward so there isn't room for the wind to move between us. I reach up to touch his face, and his eyes grow round with surprise. He stumbles away like a clumsy boy. With an audible gulp, he opens the inn's door.

The sound of music—a lonely pipe playing a sad tune— seeps out the open door as Golmarr steps inside. He pulls the door closed behind him, and a gust of cheap ale and warm air blows out and is whisked away on the wind.

The music stops dead, replaced by the deep rumble of voices followed by silence. A minute passes, then another. A noise disturbs the night, and I pull my sword free. A dark, small shadow shuffles out of the black alley beside the inn. When it steps into the light of the window, it is a young boy with mussed hair and eyes heavy with sleep. He limps up to Enzio and holds his hand out.

"I'm to stable your horses, sirs," the boy says, glancing at my weapon with mild interest. His accent is thick.

Enzio hesitates before putting his and Golmarr's reins into the boy's hand. The child holds his hand out to me, but I shake my head. "I will come with you," I say.

The boy shrugs and stifles a yawn, then turns down the

dark alley, horses in tow. I sheathe my sword and take a step to follow, but the door to the inn opens and Golmarr walks out. Without a word, he takes my reins and gives them to the boy. When I open my mouth to protest, Golmarr says, "I am paying him well to care for our horses. Let him earn his pay." He presses his hand to the small of my back and guides me into the inn with a little too much insistence.

The warm, moist air stings my frozen cheeks and nose, and seems to leach into my clothes as we enter the inn's common room. Tables are set up in it, the floor is strewn with fresh rushes, and the last dregs of a fire smolder in a hearth as tall as me. Two men sit at a table close to the hearth, sipping pints of ale. They don't even look at us as we cross the room to the stairs.

On the second floor of the inn, Golmarr guides us to the door at the end of the hall and opens it. The room is colder than the rest of the inn, but a freshly lit fire is starting to lick at the logs in the hearth. A narrow bed is in one corner, and a bleary-eyed girl is laying out a pallet on the floor beside another, right in front of the fire. She stands from the pallet and curtsies low to Golmarr, and then she rushes out of the room. With a thought, I make the fire blaze, and the room quickly grows warm.

"Sorrowlynn, you take the bed. Enzio and I will sleep on the floor," Golmarr says, his eyes holding mine, daring me to protest. I wish I was sharing the bed with him, even if it was only for the warmth and comfort his presence brings. I want his conversation, his smile, and his attention the same way I want food when I am hungry, or water when I am thirsty. I miss the way things were with Golmarr and me before he killed the glass dragon. But I nod to him, not giving voice to my thoughts, and sit on the side of the bed.

Keeping my cloak on for added warmth, I remove my boots and sword belt and then loosen the strings that have been holding my tunic tight all the way up to my throat. Enzio has shed his cloak and undone his tunic strings, too, but Golmarr has tied his even tighter, so the tan fabric is cinched up above his collarbone and digging into the skin at his throat. He presses on his left shoulder, but when he sees me watching, his hand drops and he busies himself with removing his boots. I narrow my eyes and stare at the neckline of his tunic. Before he was in Trevon, he wore shirts that plunged deep, showing his lean, tan chest. I want to know why he has stopped.

I climb into the bed, relieved the sheets are crisp and fresh. "Good night," I say, pulling the covers up to my ears.

"Good night," Enzio and Golmarr reply in unison.

I curl up on my side, watching the fire and the two men lying before it, and wait. My body is aching and exhausted from the aftermath of battle and the long ride through the cold night, but I force myself to stay awake. When two sets of deep breathing fill the room, I slowly peel my covers back and sit up. I climb from the bed and silently pad across the wood floor, and stare down at Golmarr.

# Chapter 19

Golmarr is sleeping on his back, with his right arm behind his head. The blanket covers him to the height of his armpits, and one of his stocking feet is sticking out the other end. I crouch beside his head and listen to his breathing. It is deep and even. His closed eyelids move and flutter with dreams.

I ease down onto my knees beside him and study the laces of his tunic. He has tied them in a bow beneath his chin. Carefully, I pick up the end of one string, and then the end of the other, and ever so slowly pull. The loops of the bow get smaller and smaller as I pull the ends longer and longer, until they slip completely out. Reaching beneath Golmarr's chin, I hold my breath and undo the last bit of the knot.

Next, I pinch the two divided sides of his collar, but before I have the chance to ease it open, a hand darts out and cinches my wrist, and then I am being flipped onto my back. Golmarr lands on top of me, his legs anchoring my feet to the ground, his hands pinning both my wrists above my head. His breathing is ragged, his face so close to mine our noses bump.

"Sorrowlynn?" he asks, and some of the tension leaves his body. He glances down at his loosened tunic and frowns. Anger darkens his eyes, followed by a nearly tangible wave of hatred. "Once again it seems you couldn't keep your hands off me."

Beside us, Enzio clears his throat. "Is this a time when you want me to save you, Sorrow, or go sleep in the common room? Because I can't tell if he is trying to kill you, or about to kiss you."

"Hopefully kiss me," I say.

A roguish gleam enters Golmarr's eyes, and the hatred dissipates. "I wish I trusted myself enough to tell you to go sleep somewhere else, Enzio, but I don't. Stay. Please." He rolls off me and sits cross-legged on the floor beside the pallet. Without meeting my eyes, he pulls the tunic over his head and drops it on the floor. "Is this what you wanted to see?"

I kneel in front of him, and Enzio crouches beside me.

Golmarr's torso is a deep, golden tan, and lean and muscular from years of training to be a warrior, but on the left side of his chest, right above his heart, is a patch of skin as black as coal. I lift my fingers and gently place them on the discolored skin. It is covered with perfectly symmetrical ovals. "These are . . ."

"Scales," Golmarr says when I cannot finish my thought. The scales curve up over the hollow dip of his collarbone and end. I trace my fingers over his collarbone, from the scaled side to the flesh side, and Golmarr closes his eyes. The scales are as warm and supple as his skin, yet as firm as armor. When firelight hits them, there is a deep blue glow in their depths. At the top edge of the scales, the spot where chest turns into shoulder and scales become skin, is a scabbed-over wound. I slide my fingers up to it.

"This is where King Vaunn's sword hit you?" I ask, sitting back on my heels.

Golmarr shakes his head and presses on the scales directly above his heart. "*This* is where he stabbed me. He would have killed me if I didn't have these . . . scales." The word comes out a hiss. "The tip of King Vaunn's sword stabbed right above my heart, but the scales stopped it. His sword slid up the scales and scratched me here." He touches the scab, and his face contorts with anguish. "I'm turning into a dragon," he rasps, kneading his shoulder. His eyes meet mine. "This is why I have given you the option of not pursuing a life with me, Sorrowlynn. I will not force you to stay at my side, or ask you to love me, or burden you with marriage vows. Not when I am turning into a beast."

For a brief moment, my heart falters. He is turning into a *dragon*. Before the full impact of the realization hits, Golmarr places his hand on the sleeve of my tunic. "May I look at your shoulder where I stabbed you?"

I nod. Enzio clears his throat and stands, turning his back to us.

"Enzio, take my bed and get some rest," I say. "I will sleep on your pallet."

"But what if you need me? What if Golmarr tries to kill you again?"

"I will scream if I need you, so have a knife ready. I know you can hit him from the bed." I glance at Golmarr's chest. "But don't aim for the left side of his chest." Enzio grins and walks away. The bed groans beneath his weight. With his back to us, he pulls the covers up to his shoulder.

Golmarr's eyes meet mine and he nods at my shoulder. "May I?"

"Yes."

He tugs the sleeve of my shirt and the laces at my throat

expand and loosen as the tunic's neckline is stretched down, revealing my collarbone and shoulder. He stares at my exposed skin and blinks once, twice, then swallows hard. I peer at the faint scar in the soft flesh below my collarbone, the remnant of his attack.

"The first scales I got were in the exact place your scar is," he whispers. "I am so sorry." He lifts his hand and gently traces the healed wound with his fingertips. His every exhaled breath cools my skin and makes it harder for me to inhale. "If you want nothing to do with me after that"—he nods at the scar—"and this"—he nods at his scales—"then I will help you defeat the dragons, and then leave your life and never come back. You simply have to ask, and I will do it."

For a long moment, I stare at him and try to catch my breath. And then I reach for his face with both my hands and do what I should have done the very first time I saw him in Treyose's library—press my lips to his. He stops breathing and his eyes go wide. For a long moment, he doesn't move or breathe. And then he starts trembling. His hands frame my face, the tips of his fingers in my hair, and he kisses me with the same overwhelming desire that courses through me. His breathing quickens, and his hands shake against my face. I slide my hand to the back of his head and pull his lips harder against mine.

"*Now* do you want me to go find somewhere else to sleep?" Enzio blurts. "Because I will. I absolutely will. I'd be happy to, even. I would *gladly* sleep on the rushes in the common room if you're going to keep kissing like that!"

Golmarr laughs into my mouth and pulls away. "No, Enzio. We are going to sleep now. I promise." He gives me a firm look and pulls his tunic back on. There is not even a trace of hatred in his eyes. "For the sake of Enzio, try and keep your hands off me," he whispers sternly, but a small smile lights up his face.

"You don't hate me right now. I can see the difference in your eyes," I say. "Why?"

Golmarr's brow furrows as he studies me. "I'm not entirely sure. But I think after what we've just been through, the intensity of my love for you is stronger than the hatred. They are both always there, but right now, my love for you is overpowering everything else. The hatred has no negative emotions to feed on."

I smile and scoot Enzio's—now my—pallet beside Golmarr's. Without asking, I lie down and twine my fingers through his. He freezes, but before he can pull his hand away, I say, "You have proven twice tonight that you can touch me without hurting me. I promise not to bite, I promise to keep my hands to myself, and I promise not to kiss you again tonight." One of his eyebrows slowly rises, but a moment later he closes his fingers around mine. I pull my blanket up, and, warm and content, I am asleep within moments.

◈

I see black rocks and water peeking out from the cracks between my toes. Sunshine burns warm against my back, and I close my eyes, absorbing the heat into my skin. This feels like home, this place of salty breezes and crashing waves, almost the same way Golmarr feels like home.

*Look!* someone says, the word deep inside my head. It feels wrong there, that single word, as if my mind is being probed against my will.

I take a deep breath of the balmy air and lift my gaze from my feet, expecting to see the two-headed dragon. Instead, a woman stands before me, the woman from my dream, with hair as white and soft as goose down. If I reach my arm forward, I will be touching the billowing fabric of her long-sleeve white dress. Her mouth is moving, but no sound comes from it. She is repeating the same thing over and over again, and by reading the movement of her silent lips I know what she is saying.

*Find me quickly. Find me quickly. Find me quickly! Find me quickly! Quickly! Quickly! Quickly! Quickly!*

A wave breaks close to shore and slams into the back of my legs, jolting my attention away from the woman. My cares seem to melt away as water rolls up the black beach, spreading across the pebbles. In the sunlight, they shimmer with an inner glow, as if lit from within, and for a moment I know I have seen them before. But then the sun loses some of its warmth. The pebbles return to their depthless black, and I shiver. I crouch down for a closer look at the rocks, trying to remember where I have seen them.

*Look!* the voice in my head demands, grating on my thoughts. I do not want to look when I am on the brink of remembering where I have seen the black rocks. *Sorrowlynn, look!*

I force my attention from the ground and glare at her.

The woman is rolling up her sleeve, her fingers fast and nimble. Curious, I stand. When the sleeve is up above her elbow, she holds her arm beneath my nose.

Her skin is a deep, rich brown, firm and healthy, almost like that of a child despite her white hair. Just below her elbow, something shimmers. I lean closer and see delicate pearly ovals that reflect sunlight. My heart jumps into my throat as my eyes meet hers. I know why the pebbles look so familiar—they remind me of Golmarr's scales, and the dragon tears from Enzio's purse.

"Scales?" I ask, but no sound leaves my mouth.

*Find me quickly,* she mouths, pushing her sleeve back down. And then her eyes—pale blue like the winter sky—shift a fraction, staring at something behind me. They grow round and she lunges forward. I look over my shoulder just as the woman shoves me. A man is standing on the beach, and blackness swarms around him like a living, moving cloak of bugs, and I am falling into him. I pass through the blackness and it scatters in the air. I keep falling, falling, until I am certain I have been shoved from the edge of a very high cliff and am about to hit the bottom when I collide with a body. I feel my arms slip inside of her arms, feel my legs lock into hers, feel my head absorb her brain as it is fitted to a skull it has known forever.

The smell of wood smoke and frying meat are floating on the chill air. My nose is icy cold—my fingers and toes, too. The only warm thing on me is my back, where it was warmed by the sun in my dream. I try to move, but something is wedged behind me. Turning my head, I open my bleary eyes to a barely lit chamber and Golmarr's sleeping face. The front of his body is pressed to the back of mine, his arm wrapped tightly around my waist. I lean away, but he sighs and tightens his hold, pressing his face into the warmth of my neck.

"Golmarr," I whisper.

His black lashes flutter, and his eyes open. When they focus on mine, a wide, lazy smile stretches across his face. "Good morning," he says, tucking a strand of hair behind my ear. His hand freezes and he clears his throat. Quickly, he rolls away, but I grab his shoulder and hold him still so he cannot put a single thread's width more distance between us.

"Will you stop doing that?" I whisper, glaring.

"Doing what?" he asks, studying me like I might bite him. Or kiss him again. With that thought, I look at his lips and then squeeze my eyes shut. I need to focus, and it is hard to do being this close to him.

"Stop cringing away every time I touch you! Why do you do that? Is it because you hate me so much you can't stand my touch?"

He shakes his head and grimaces. "No, that's not why I pull away. I already told you why I can't touch you."

I tighten my grip on his shoulder. "Refresh my memory," I say. It is not a request.

"I do it for three reasons. At first, when you came to Treyose's library, you were his *wife*. I am not the type of man who will ever steal another's wife. Second, I do it because I am too scared of losing control around you." Anger flares in his eyes, but he keeps his voice quiet and asks, "What if the hatred I inherited from the glass dragon overpowers me again and I try to kill you?" He stops talking, waiting for me to answer his question, but I have no answer.

I blink and shift my gaze to his throat. "What is the last reason?"

He puts his finger under my chin and tilts my head up so I am looking at him again. "How can I pursue you when I am growing scales? It is incredibly unfair for me to ask anything of you when I know one day I will be a monster. How could you love me when I am so flawed?"

Without taking my eyes from his, I slide my hand beneath the laces of his tunic and touch the scales growing on his chest. Golmarr shudders.

"Sorrowlynn," he whispers, gently pushing me away.

"What?"

"You can't . . . just . . . *touch* me like that."

"Why not?"

"Because the simplest touch of your fingers against my skin is intoxicating. I can't think clearly when you touch me like that—I can barely think at all! And then the lines between why I can never ask you to love me and how much I want to be with you start to blur and bleed into each other." He lies down and closes his eyes.

Propping my head up with my hand, I say, "Maybe the lines need to blur until they become one."

He looks at me. "You need to know something else." His face darkens. "When I killed the glass dragon, I started seeing glimpses of the future. Before I killed the beast, I thought nothing was more important than us ending up together forever. But then I saw what happens because of it."

My body freezes. "What happens if we end up together?"

"Sorrowlynn, I love you more than life itself. I would die for you more than one thousand times over, in every way imaginable. I know because I have seen it. You are *my* world, and you will be until the day I die." He sweeps the hair away from my cheek and tucks it behind my ear. "But the world is bigger than the two of us. What we have—this love—it is beautiful, and wonderful, and I cherish it above anything I have ever known, but there is so much more we have to think about."

His words send ice through me. The muscles in my

shoulders tighten, and I find it hard to breathe. "I don't understand what you are saying."

He squeezes his eyes shut and presses the heels of his hands over them. "The night before the battle with the mercenaries and the glass dragon, I gave Ingvar a letter and begged him to take care of you if anything happened to me. The next day, I had the dragon's hatred thrust on me. From that moment on, I saw glimpses of Ingvar stepping in to save your life, in more than a hundred ways, and every time he ended up dead. I tried to do things to keep you safe and remove from him the burden of protecting you so he wouldn't die." He lowers his hands. "That is why I made a bargain with Treyose to bring you to me in Trevon in exchange for me agreeing to be his wizard and backing his claim to the Trevonan throne. But it still didn't work. Ingvar died despite my best efforts to remove him from the situation."

I swallow against the lump that has formed in my throat and force myself not to blink at the water pooling in my eyes.

"Two things changed, though," Golmarr continues. "One: He lived several months longer than the first vision I saw of his death. In the very first vision, Lord Damar heard of your survival and rushed to Anthar to force you to return to Faodara. He poisoned Ingvar when he was trying to kill you. And two: I sent a letter to Ingvar telling him what I kept seeing. He was able to tell his wife and children how much he loved them before he died."

"Why not just tell him to stop protecting me?"

"He *did* stop. He sent you to the citadel and asked Yerengul and Enzio to protect you," Golmarr whispers. "But he still died."

Ingvar, unarmed and vulnerable, put himself between me and Lord Damar's poison needle. "He *knew* there was a good chance he was going to die, and yet he chose to protect me?"

"Yes."

I blink, forcing the tears from my eyes. "Why?"

"Because you are worth dying for. You are the key to everything. You have Zhun's knowledge. Together, we have the opportunity to change the world or die trying. But if we don't *try*, the dragons are going to destroy the world."

My body seems to fill with stone. "I don't want this," I whisper.

"I don't, either. I just want you, and I want to be happy. But what if that means the dragons destroy the world? Could you live with that when you have the power to stop it?"

"I don't know," I say, and the tears keep streaming down my cheeks.

"I couldn't live with that, Sorrowlynn, not when we have a chance to change everything."

"So you're saying you are giving up on us?"

He shakes his head. "I don't know."

Curling into a ball, I pull my blanket up to my chin. "We need to go to the black island."

*"What?"* he asks, rolling onto his side so he can see me better.

"We need to go there."

"No one who goes there comes back." He tentatively wipes the tears from my cheeks, but his touch makes more fall. I move his hand away and use the corner of the blanket to soak up the tears.

"We need to go. A woman with scales on her arm is waiting for us. She says we need to find her *quickly*."

"We can't go there. What if it is a trap?" he whispers, eyes pleading. "What if we are being lured there by one or more of the dragons? We will either be trapped on a boat, or stuck on an island with nowhere to go when they attack. A dragon could simply smash our boat while we sailed, or trap us on the island's shore and then eat us. I don't want to put you in that much danger."

His words make me bristle. "You go ahead and choose your fate, Golmarr, but I will choose for myself how much danger I am willing to be in." I glare at him. "I also choose to never give up on loving you and will do everything in my power to be with you for the rest of my life. Evil is coming? Fine. Let's fight it. Dragons want to destroy me? Yes. I already know. There might be a lot of things I cannot control, but I will choose whom I love!"

Despite the sorrow in his eyes, he smiles. "Calm down and put away your claws. There's no need to fight with me. I am not your enemy."

"I will choose whom I will or will not fight with, Golmarr! And I think Draykioch might hold the answers we are looking for. I am willing to take the risk of sailing there if it means helping you. Besides, you're prepared to get on a boat and sail to the desert. I don't see what the difference is."

"You don't?" he asks. I shake my head. "The difference is, when we sail to Ilaad, we stay close to shore. If a dragon smashes our boat, we can still swim to land. To sail to Draykioch, we have to cross the open sea for *five days*." He exhales so deeply his ribs visibly deflate. "Do you really think we need to go there?"

"Yes!"

"All right. I trust you to make that decision for us. Instead of taking a boat to the desert capital, we will sail to Draykioch." He throws his blanket aside. "Enzio?"

Across the room, the lump on the bed stirs. A moment later, Enzio sits up, scrubbing a hand through the unruly curls on his head. "Don't tell me it is already morning," he says, and then he sniffs. "Something smells good."

"There has been a change of plans, my friend." Golmarr puts his foot into his boot and cinches the laces tight over his Trevonan leggings. "We are going to Draykioch."

All traces of sleep scatter from Enzio's face. He grins and stands, and starts combing his hair to the side. "I will be a legend among my own people when we return."

"You know nobody returns from Draykioch, right?" Golmarr asks.

Enzio nods. "But we have Suicide Sorrow. She will die by her own hand. That means she will live to return from the Serpent's Island, and I believe that greatly increases our chances of survival."

"Let's hope," Golmarr says with a frown. I flinch at his doubt.

Enzio's nostrils flare, and he stomps across the room to Golmarr. "What is wrong with you?" he growls.

Golmarr ties the laces on his second boot and stands, glowering at Enzio. "Plenty of things are wrong with me. Would you like to point out something specific?"

Enzio glances at me and lowers his voice, but I can hear every word he says. "You are one of the few men I know who has the good fortune to fall in love with a woman as amazing as Sorrowlynn. And she has been given a fate blessing by the most powerful wizard ever known that says she will die by her own hand. Yet you choose to disregard it! You need to stop thinking that you are the best warrior in the world and could kill her on a whim, because you can't! She is Suicide Sorrow, and even though you already tried once, *you couldn't kill her*! She has worked so hard to get strong enough to find you despite having her heart utterly *broken* by you, and how do you repay her months of effort?" He puffs out his chest and takes a tiny step closer, making me wonder if this conversation is going to come to blows. "This is how you repay her effort, and sorrow, and pain, and work—by treating her like you cannot stand to be in the same room with her? Where is your faith? Your hope?"

Golmarr stares at Enzio, utterly dumbfounded. And then he steps around him and wraps me in his arms. "I am so sorry," he whispers. "So incredibly sorry." I hear Enzio cross the room, and then the door opens and closes, and I am alone with Golmarr for the first time in half a year. He leans away just enough to look into my eyes. There is no hatred there, only pain that matches my own. "I have been so scared of hurting you that I haven't been thinking clearly. I *cannot* kill you." He says it like he is trying to convince himself.

"I know. And you are alone with me, and you are touching me, but there is no hatred in your eyes."

He cups the side of my face and leans his forehead against mine. "The hatred is still there, but right now, the other emotions I am feeling are stronger. *Much* stronger. That seems to help—focusing on something stronger than the hatred." He lowers his lips to mine and leaves them there, soft and still. With both his hands he frames my face and holds on to me with such care—as if he's afraid I might break. But then he lifts his mouth from mine, and his eyes are filled with anguish.

I press my hand to his chest and ask, "What's wrong?"

"I shouldn't be kissing you like this right now. We have so many problems."

"Problems can be worked out," I say.

"Yes, but if we put our love for each other above everything else and turn our backs on the dragons, they will win."

My heart drops. "Then we will not prioritize our love over the dragons."

"There is also this." He tugs the tunic off his shoulder, showing me his black scales.

"And that is why we are searching for the Infinite Vessel."

"And if we don't—"

I press my hands to his lips to silence him, for each word he says lands on me like a weight. "One thing at a time, Golmarr."

He nods, but the sadness doesn't leave his eyes.

# Chapter 20

Today, Golmarr rides close to me, so our knees bump. Every so often, he touches the back of my hand with his cold fingers. When our eyes meet, the worry in his softens, and he smiles.

Harborton is the second-largest city in Trevon. The buildings are tall and built too close together, and on every street corner, children dressed in rags hold their hands out, hoping for a coin or a morsel of food. The icy wind presses their thin clothing tight against their bodies, showing legs barely thick enough to hold their weight, and ribs that have no fat. Before I have eaten a single piece of the breakfast we took from the inn, I give it all away. Neither Enzio nor Golmarr speaks a word in protest.

"If Trevon is such a wealthy land, why are these children not being fed?" I ask.

"Taxes are high here," Golmarr explains. "All the money goes to the capital so King Vaunn can employ the largest army in the world, while the rest of his subjects barely have enough to eat. Because of you and Treyose, things are going to change. Treyose plans on turning his soldiers into farmers, merchants, tradesmen, and teachers, and lowering taxes so they can afford to feed their families. Now how do you feel about killing King Vaunn?"

I sit a little taller and look straight forward. "I feel the same as I did before you told me."

Enzio maneuvers his mount closer to us. "And how did you feel before he told you?" he asks.

I frown and study the sleek brown fur between my horse's ears. "I feel bad for taking a life, but when I realize how many people will be affected for the better because of it, it takes the majority of the sting away. Vaunn was evil."

Enzio claps me on the shoulder. "I am glad I get to call you *cousin*."

I put my hand over his, grateful for his presence in my life.

Long before I see the ocean, the sound of gulls and the tang of brine fill the air. The sky is a dismal gray that the morning sun barely burns through, and the cracks between the road's cobbles are filled with pale sand and crushed shells that crunch beneath the horse's hooves.

The tall masts of docked ships come into view, stabbing above the cramped buildings. And then, gray and white and moving with a life of its own, the ocean appears.

Taking the lead, I guide my horse forward onto the stone wharf and survey the docked ships. Enzio stops beside me and quietly asks, "Do you really think one of these ships will willingly sail to the Serpent's Island?"

Golmarr reins in on my other side. "The one we pick won't have much choice," he says, face fierce as he studies the ships in the harbor. "We need a fast ship, but more important, a sturdy one that can withstand whirlpools and waves as tall as mountains. Sorrowlynn, what do you know about ships?"

I close my eyes, and then I am standing on a ship, my masculine hands holding on to the damp railing as I study the horizon. "I have traveled by ship before, but only as a passenger," I say, and my eyes startle open. "I mean, not me. Melchior traveled by ship." I press on my forehead and look at Golmarr. "Sometimes I feel like I'm getting lost in my own head, as if the memories that have been transferred to me are so big, and the space of my memories are so small in comparison."

Golmarr swallows so hard, his Adam's apple bobs up and down. Reaching beneath my cloak, he wraps his fingers around mine and squeezes. "We have got to find the Infinite Vessel." He dismounts and turns to Enzio. "You're Satari. Every Satari I have ever met could barter me out of my clothes in the middle of a snowstorm. How good are your bartering skills?"

Enzio grins. "Better than most, unless I am trading with a pretty woman."

"And what happens when you barter with a pretty woman?" I ask.

"I typically get swindled in exchange for a kiss," he says with a grin. His cheeks grow pink, and I laugh.

Golmarr removes his saddlebags and staff from his mount, and holds his reins out to Enzio. "I need you to go sell our horses and tack for as much gold as you can get. We might possibly get enough money to *bribe* a ship to take us where we need to go. Just find an ugly old man to barter with."

I dismount and hand Enzio my reins, and then remove my saddlebag. "Thank you. We couldn't do this without you," I say.

"My pleasure. Bartering for the Satari is like horsemanship for the Antharians. Not only are we skilled at it, we enjoy it." He adjusts his cloak, finger-combs the curls off his forehead, and rides off.

Golmarr begins studying the ships again, mouth firm, eyes narrowed. I step up so our shoulders are touching, waiting to see if he steps away. When he doesn't move, I ask, "Are we going to board a ship and tell the captain we want to sail to Draykioch?"

Not taking his eyes from the sea, Golmarr shakes his head. "I was thinking of something more along the lines of paying for passage to Ilaad, setting sail, and then pirating the ship once we have left the harbor."

I start laughing. When Golmarr remains silent, I tilt my head to the side and study him. "You're serious, aren't you?"

He grins, and a spark of excitement lights up his eyes. Speechless, I look back at the ships. Even the smaller vessels have crews of a dozen thick, brawny men. My hand moves to my sword hilt and my thumb glides back and forth over an emerald dragon eye. "Three of us against an entire crew, and you don't even have a sword, Golmarr. They'll throw us into the ocean if they don't kill us first."

"That *would* be a problem, except . . ."

I stare at him, waiting. When he doesn't continue, I ask, "Except what?"

He grips my upper arm, and his face grows serious. "You've gotten a lot stronger. I see and feel the strength in you. So I'll let you take care of the crew, Suicide Sorrow."

I smack his hand from my arm and glare. "Me? Against a dozen men?"

Golmarr starts laughing. "I sent word to Anthar, asking for four of my brothers to meet us here."

"Your brothers are coming?"

"Yes. They should be here by midday." He looks so smug; I am tempted to wipe the grin from his face. Or kiss it away, but he turns back to the docked ships. "We need to walk the wharf until we see the ship we want. That way, when my brothers arrive, we will be ready to go."

"How did you get a message to your brothers so fast? We've only known since this morning we are going to Draykioch."

A sailor walking past jerks to a halt and stares at us for a long moment before hurrying away. Golmarr presses a finger to his lips. "Not so loud, Princess. I had Treyose send the message the day before the dragon attack."

"The day *before*? The day before the attack, we were still sorting through the tablets and scrolls. We hadn't even spoken of taking a ship anywhere. . . . You saw it in a vision."

Golmarr presses against his chest, against the scales, and grimaces. For a moment his gaze flickers to mine, guarded and cautious. "Yes."

Anger fires through me. "And you waited until now to tell me?"

Mischief lights Golmarr's eyes, and the side of his mouth pulls up into a half smile. "You are absolutely breathtaking when you are angry, Sorrowlynn." He reaches a hand to my face and cups my cheek.

I smack his hand aside again and ask, "Why didn't you tell me?"

He looks away and the smile fades. "Because I knew

I would have to tell you about the possible futures I have glimpsed."

His words from this morning return to me, and I can't bear to look at him, not when my eyes have filled with tears. Behind Golmarr, I see Enzio approaching. "Enzio is back," I say, and quickly blink the tears from my eyes and force the frown from my face.

Golmarr turns. "That was fast. How did the bartering go?" he asks, his voice light.

Enzio holds up a fat purse and grins. "Better than even I would have expected. I don't think the Trevonans are used to dealing with Satari. Let's go find a ship."

Golmarr nods and puts his hand against the small of my back, gently urging me forward. We haven't taken more than a dozen steps along the pier when Golmarr stops walking and shades his eyes. Out in the bay sits a small ship with two masts. Its sails are down, its anchor dropped against the tide. Three large ships surround it, and even here on the wharf, it is obvious the bigger ships are barring the smaller ship entry. "That one there," Golmarr says, pointing to the small ship. "That's our ship."

I study the flag atop the highest mast, flapping in the frigid wind, and a shiver of anticipation prickles my skin. The flag is bright yellow with a black curling serpent on it. "That ship has the royal flag of Ilaad."

Golmarr tilts his head to the side and squints at the flag. "So it does," he says. "That was unforeseen."

Enzio frowns. "That explains why they aren't letting it dock."

"Why?" Golmarr and I ask at the same time.

"Because according to the man who bought our horses,

Princess Yassim of Ilyaro is on that ship, and she is here to declare war on Trevon."

I laugh a bitter laugh under my breath. "How do you think our newly formed truce with Treyose will hold up when we pirate his enemy's ship?"

"Probably very well." Even though I see the sorrow in his eyes, Golmarr winks. "We'll know soon enough."

We sit on the wharf, our feet dangling over the edge, my mind replaying the things Golmarr told me about our future. All I want is to live in a peaceful kingdom, where I never go hungry and never have to kill again. Instead, I feel like I have been handed a life sentence where everything I want has been torn from me and replaced with a life of fighting and struggle and pain. I feel as if I am standing on the side of a cliff, being forced to choose a destiny I do not want. Only this time, there is no dragon to give myself to. Sadness fills me, shuddering through my entire body until it feels like the very marrow of my bones is weeping.

"What do you know about how the Ilaadi fight?" Golmarr asks.

His words jerk me out of my dark thoughts, and I don't have to think about his question. I scowl and shake my head. "Too much. They take pleasure in assassinating, and like to kill with their bare hands. For them, that is the greatest measure of skill."

He nods. "I once had a hand-to-hand combat tutor who claimed he was a former Ilaadi assassin—he *did* have an Ilaadi accent, and he was the best hand-to-hand fighter I had ever seen. No one could beat him in a weaponless match. He started to teach me, but that was when I was thirteen years old. I didn't have enough time to learn much."

"What happened to him?" Enzio asks. "I thought no one was allowed to teach the Ilaadis' way of fighting."

"The poor man was assassinated before I turned fourteen. His neck was broken while he slept in the citadel's great hall with nearly one hundred others. No one saw anyone come in or go out of the hall, and the soldiers standing watch on the fortress wall didn't see anything, either."

"The best assassins in the world are trained in the Ilaad desert," Enzio says.

"True, but the best *warriors* in the world are trained in Anthar." Golmarr gives Enzio a meaningful look, and Enzio starts laughing.

We have been staring at the anchored Ilaadi ship all morning, quietly studying it and its crew. As far as we can tell, there are eight people aboard: seven men and one child. We see no princess, so assume she is either sleeping or belowdecks.

"I have met only three Ilaadi in my life," Enzio says. "They are worse than my people if you steal from them. If you rob one of the Black Blades, we get our money back by any means necessary, short of killing, and then take everything else the robber has, down to his skivvies. If you rob an Ilaadi, you will be dead before you can blink."

I nod and shudder. "They prefer to fight with their hands or small weapons, like knives and needles, because they kill cleanly and quickly, with less room for error if the assassin is well trained, less chance of being detected, and minimal blood, if executed properly." A pair of mean eyes flickers in my memory, eyes I have seen with my own—not something forced upon my mind by the dragon. "The mercenary I killed in the Black Blades camp the day after we came down Gol Mountain." I look at Golmarr. "Do you remember him?"

He nods, and hatred flashes in his eyes. "His face still haunts me. That man weighed at least twice what you weighed. I thought he was going to be the death of you."

"I killed him by cutting an artery in his gut, assassin style." My stomach turns. "I think I know every possible way to kill a person." Images of killing start flashing through my head. I squeeze my eyes shut and try to think of anything to replace them. My hands grip the damp, rough stones of the wharf and squeeze as the images flash faster behind my shut eyes. A small moan slips from my parted lips as I try desperately to grasp any thought or image that will free my mind from its layers and facets of unwanted deathly knowledge, but nothing works. Warmth encircles my face, I turn my head to the side, and something soft presses on my lips.

I open my eyes and am staring at Golmarr's close face. My hand comes up and tightens in his hair, holding his kiss to my mouth as the images assaulting my mind flitter away, replaced by the caw of gulls and slap of waves, the feel of Golmarr's breath on my face, and his soft lips against mine.

I suck a breath of cold, clammy air through my nose and relax. Golmarr opens his eyes. "Better?" he asks against my lips, gently brushing his thumb over my cheekbone.

I swallow. "Better. Thank you."

A roguish smile curls his lips. "My pleasure. What were you remembering?"

I shudder and shake my hands in the air, hard, like I am

flinging off water, when in reality I am thrusting the taint of memories from myself. "I was remembering every possible way to kill a person."

Beneath me, the wharf begins to vibrate, and then rumble. A moment later, the deep thunder of trotting horses rivals the constant rhythm of lapping water. "It sounds like my brothers have arrived," Golmarr says, standing. I hop to my feet beside him and give Enzio a hand up. Everyone bustling around the docks stops what they are doing and stares in the direction of the sound.

Four horses burst out from between two buildings and slow from a gallop to a trot. The merchants and sailors gasp and back away as the words *barbarian horse lords* are spoken from one person to another. Golmarr's brothers are here.

# Chapter 21

The people milling about on the dock move far away and stare as the riders pull their horses to a halt. Two riders have long black hair and vivid red cloaks, which do little to hide the chain mail and leather armor worn beneath. Behind Golmarr's brothers are two other riders. One is a middle-aged man with a metal breastplate beneath his deep green Faodarian cloak, and a short sword in his hand. A small smile finds its way to my face at the sight of my father, looking fierce and travel-worn and lethal despite the gray hair at his temples. His face softens when he sees me, and he sheathes his sword.

I cannot see the fourth rider because of the cloak hiding his face, but he is small and slightly hunched, though seems well at ease atop his black stallion.

"Jessen! Yerengul!" Golmarr calls, waving his arm. They ride to us and dismount.

Jessen's dark eyes narrow when he sees Golmarr. He is the second-oldest of Golmarr's brothers and rarely smiles. When I crossed into the grasslands for the first time, he threatened to kill me until he realized who I was. Jessen wraps his younger brother in a hug and quietly asks, "Where is your sword?"

Golmarr pats his brother's back hard. "It is on Sorrowlynn's sword belt. How is Father since Ingvar's death?"

Jessen frowns. "He is taking Ingvar's death hard. Father yearns for your safe return, especially since he learned you've been working with Treyose."

"As you can see, I am safe. I will come home as soon as I am able to."

Jessen steps away from Golmarr and bows to me, his attention momentarily flickering to the sword at my waist. "Princess Sorrowlynn, it is very good to see you again," he says, and a rare smile lights his eyes.

Yerengul frowns and slowly looks Golmarr up and down before wrapping him in a hug. "You've only been gone six months, and already you're cinching your shirt up to your chin and wearing Trevonan tights," he says, his voice accusing. His gaze lights on Golmarr's staff. "And carrying a staff in place of a sword? Every warrior knows a staff is a defense weapon, not a killing weapon. Did Treyose turn you into a weakling?"

"You wish," Golmarr says. "I guarantee you I can beat you at every weapon except throwing knives, but that's why we have Enzio with us."

"I still cannot get over the shock of Treyose giving me your hand signal," Yerengul says quietly. "You should have at least warned me you were working with him. I could have gotten myself killed trying to save Sorrowlynn."

"Wait . . . are you admitting it is possible for a Trevonan to beat you?" Golmarr asks. Yerengul shoves his brother away with a laugh, and then hugs me, squeezing me tight against his chain mail.

"Good to see you, Sorrow. It looks like your months of training paid off. You managed to not get killed."

"Unless you do the job right now," I gasp out. He laughs and loosens his hug.

When Yerengul steps away, my father takes his place, his brown eyebrows drawn tight as he studies me. "Hello, Sorrowlynn," he says. He bows to me, the formal greeting of a Faodarian soldier to his superior.

I press against his shoulders with both my hands. "Please don't bow," I say, and am overwhelmed with the awkwardness of standing in front of the man who is my father, but hardly knowing a thing about him.

"As you wish." He smiles. "It is good to see you again."

We stare at each other for a moment.

"He is your father," Golmarr says, gently elbowing my ribs. "Give him a hug!"

I step up to my father and quickly wrap my arms around his neck. "How is your arrow wound?" I ask.

"Getting better, thanks to Yerengul." He smells like cinnamon and pipe smoke, and has the solid feel of a soldier. "I brought you something." He rifles through a saddlebag and pulls out a small, cloth-wrapped bundle. I take it and open it. Inside are candied pecans—my favorite treat.

I smile up at him. "You remembered that I loved these."

"Of course. I remember everything about you. It is a pleasure to be here with you, daughter." He gently pats my back, and memories of this man overwhelm me. Every year on my birthday, he would give me a small packet of candied pecans and one colored ribbon for my hair, and a matching ribbon for my doll. If I ever got sick, Nona would give me a sachet of eucalyptus leaves to help with my stuffy nose—delivered to her by Ornald. He paid close enough attention to me that he knew every time I got sick. And more often than not, he was the guard who requested to stand watch outside of my bedroom door. Whenever I saw him, he would do magic tricks for me until I smiled. For the first time in my life, I realize what a father's love feels like. I've had it all along and didn't know it.

Jessen guides the last horse to us and assists the rider down. A gnarled hand comes out of the oversized brown cloak, and I take a small step back. I know who the final rider is without even seeing her face. She moves the hood of her cloak aside enough for me to meet her blind yet ever-seeing eyes. "Hello, Sorrowlynn," Nayadi croaks.

Golmarr steps between the witch and me and tugs the hood back up, hiding her face in shadow once more. He glares at Yerengul. "I asked you to bring four warriors, and instead you brought three warriors and Nayadi?"

Yerengul turns his palms up. "She insisted on coming." He leans closer to Golmarr and whispers, "She said if we didn't let her come, she would curse us with baldness and hairless chests."

"And you believed her?" Golmarr asks, his eyes flashing with anger. "She can barely heal a scratch!"

Nayadi cackles and pats Golmarr on the stomach. "Always so confident," she mumbles. "So, why are we meeting on a smelly Trevon dock, hmm?"

"We need to secure a boat as quickly as possible." Golmarr turns north and glances at the sky. "A two-headed dragon is following us."

"Two from a grave of ice," Nayadi whispers. "Then I was right. And they are only . . ." She closes her eyes and sniffs the air. "They will be here very soon."

"We need to set sail before it finds us and wreaks havoc on

this city," Golmarr says. "One swipe of its tail could topple an entire block of these dilapidated buildings."

"Have you already secured our passage?" Jessen asks.

Golmarr points at the Ilaadi ship. "We are sailing on that one, there. With the lowered turquoise sails."

Nayadi makes a small noise. "So that is how the Ilaadi figure into this," she muses. "You are going to try and win them over, then?"

"If we are lucky, yes."

"Lucky?" Jessen asks, and Golmarr flinches. "They're Ilaadi, brother. We will be *lucky* if they don't kill us before we have a chance to talk to them."

Golmarr nods. "I realize there is a strong possibility we will have to fight them for possession of their ship."

"Well, I for one would like to try my skill against an Ilaadi," Yerengul says. "What are we waiting for?"

<hr />

We pay a man double what is fair to row us out to the Ilaadi ship, and even so, the rowboat's owner—an old sailor with greasy yellow hair and massive hands—acts like every dip of the oars pains him. Before we pass between the Trevonan war ships blocking the Ilaadi vessel, one of the ships lowers a small boat and intercepts us. Five men wearing purple livery are on the boat, and the man in front is standing. His curious eyes quickly scan Golmarr, me, and then Enzio, all dressed in traditional Trevonan clothing. When his scrutiny turns to Yerengul and Jessen, the man's eyes narrow and he draws his sword.

"I am Swain, captain of the warship *Eventide*, and I

command you to halt in the name of King Vaunn and the Royal Trevonan Navy," the man with the drawn sword says, his Trevonan accent thicker than any I have heard before. "What business do Antharian barbarians have with this Ilaadi ship?"

"Row us closer," Golmarr says to the boat's owner. The man grumbles something but dips the oars into the water, easing our boat up to the side of the Trevonans'. The other four soldiers draw their swords. Golmarr reaches into his saddlebag and pulls out a gold chain. He lifts it toward the sailors, and a small gold pendant swings from side to side. Captain Swain reaches forward and Golmarr lets him finger the pendant. When he looks back to Golmarr, his eyes are blazing with curiosity.

"Why do you have Prince Treyose's royal seal?" Swain asks.

"I am on official business of your new king ... *King* Treyose," Golmarr says.

There is a collective gasp from the sailors. Captain Swain schools his face to mild concern and asks, "King Vaunn is dead?"

"He is," Golmarr confirms.

The sailors look at each other. Two of them smile.

Golmarr clears his throat. "King Treyose asked me to inform you, on his behalf, of his grandfather's death. He will send a formal announcement, but he wants you to prepare to bring all warships ashore. He says, and I quote, 'It is time for Trevonan soldiers to remember how to be fathers, brothers, and sons again. It is time for them to come home.'"

Captain Swain glances at the necklace once more, as if he

doesn't quite believe Golmarr's news, and then nods. "How did it happen? How did King Vaunn die?"

My heart starts pounding.

"He was killed by a woman who was forced to defend herself from him or die," Golmarr says, voice grim.

Captain Swain grunts and shakes his head. "Fitting, a woman taking his life after all the pain and suffering he has caused them. He deserved to die at a woman's hands. And what is your business with the Ilaadi ship?"

A slow smile forms on Golmarr's mouth, and the malice that jumps into his eyes has all five armed sailors gripping their sword hilts a little more tightly. "We have come to remove their ship from your waters."

"And how do you plan to do that? They've been here three days trying to dock, but we've refused to let them through. They are requesting safe passage to Arkhavan and will not leave until they have been granted an audience with King Vaunn . . . er, King Treyose, I suppose."

Jessen holds up three bulging purses—the money acquired from both the sale of our horses and his brothers' famed Antharian horses. "We will offer to pay them," Jessen says. "If they do not take our offer, we will fight them for control of their ship."

The naval soldiers grin at this. "Then, by all means, proceed," Captain Swain says, sheathing his sword. "Row aside, men." With a few hard pulls on the oars, we glide past the massive Trevonan warships and then slowly ease into the shadow cast by the Ilaadi ship.

Up close, the vessel is small but striking, with intricate designs carved into the dark wood railings, and turquoise sails that shine bright even in the foggy gloom of the afternoon. Two men are looking down at us, their hair and faces hidden behind thick white turbans, so only their eyes show.

"What do you want?" one of the turbaned men calls, his accent different from any I have ever heard.

Golmarr stands, and he is so steady on his feet, the boat doesn't even rock. The railing of the Ilaadi ship is even with the top of Golmarr's head. If he wanted to, he could grab the railing and pull himself aboard. "I am Golmarr, son of King Marrkul of Anthar. I request an audience with Princess Yassim."

The man who spoke nods and steps out of view. A moment later he returns with another turbaned person, whose head barely reaches the middle of his chest. The small person, the passenger we assumed was a child, loosens the bottom half of the turban, revealing the delicate face of a young woman with a smattering of freckles on her olive skin.

Her dark eyes lock on Golmarr and start examining him, pausing at his shoulders, hands, and feet, as if she is reading everything about him simply based on the way he stands. "I am Princess Yassim, of the city Ilyaro, in Ilaad. Are you here to grant me safe passage to Arkhavan and an audience with King Vaunn?" she asks, her accented voice as smooth and rich as cream.

Golmarr shakes his head. "I am not. I am here to offer you an audience with the future king of Anthar."

Princess Yassim's eyes narrow. "I am not interested in an audience with your future king, unless he wishes to join his army to mine and overthrow Trevon once and for all."

I startle at the bluntness of the desert princess's statement, but Golmarr doesn't seem the least bit surprised. In a voice calm and placating, he asks, "Why are you declaring war on Trevon, Princess Yassim?"

Her cheeks flush with anger. "King Vaunn has woken the sandworm, and it is destroying what is left of my kingdom! The worm is digging out the ground beneath Ilyaro and making the city cave in."

Golmarr turns, and his eyes meet mine. An unspoken understanding passes between us. The Ilaadi princess is declaring war on Trevon for something I inadvertently did—waking the dragon that lives in the desert. He turns back to the princess. "Why do you believe King Vaunn woke this dragon?"

She stares at him for a quiet moment before answering. "Who, besides King Vaunn, would have a reason to wake the beast and have it destroy my kingdom? For his entire reign, since long before I was born, he has been forcing the borders of his land northward into mine. No other kingdom covets our land so desperately. Already, both of my brothers have died trying to defeat the worm." She snaps her mouth shut and her entire body trembles in an effort to control her emotions. "I *demand* a meeting with King Vaunn."

"The worm will not stop destroying her kingdom until the one who woke it is dead . . . or it is killed," Nayadi says.

Yassim recoils at the sight of Nayadi. Looking back at Golmarr, she says, "I demand to speak with King Vaunn!"

Golmarr lifts his hands, palms to the sky, and asks, "What if King Vaunn is dead?"

Princess Yassim laughs, but it holds no humor. "We have been trying to assassinate him for two decades. The man is impossible to kill."

I shake my head and, without thinking, say, "Not impossible."

This makes her look at me—a dismissive yet irritated look. "You are obviously not an Antharian barbarian. Who are you?"

I slowly stand, trying to remain perfectly balanced so I do not rock the boat. It shifts beneath my feet. By her suddenly pursed lips, Yassim has noticed my imperfect balance. "I am Princess Sorrowlynn of Faodara," I say, putting on the mantle of regal importance I was made to practice as a child: shoulders squared, chin up, proud indifference burning from my eyes while on the inside, I am trembling. "I killed King Vaunn, and I am the one who woke the dragon—the sandworm."

Yassim reaches beneath her turban at the exact moment Golmarr gasps and takes a lurching step backward that sends the boat bobbing from side to side. Before I have time to throw my arms out to reclaim my balance, Golmarr turns and wraps his arm around my waist. My feet leave the ground and we are flying through the air as Yassim lifts a long, narrow cylinder to her lips. A tiny dart flies past my neck a split second before the ocean slaps against my back, molding my heavy winter clothing around my body and pouring into my open mouth.

For a moment all we do is sink, and then Golmarr gives me a firm shake. Beneath the water's murky surface our eyes meet. I hear his unspoken question: *Can you get back to the surface?* I nod. He releases me, and I fling my arms and legs out, pushing myself toward the dark oval of the rowboat's belly.

Muted by the water are the yells and screams of fighting, and just when I am about to reach the water's surface, a man draped in white clothing and a turban splashes into the ocean above me. I kick against the water to move out of his way. A halo of red spreads around him, and as he sinks past me, I see one of the horse clan's arrows protruding from his neck. And then everywhere I look, everything I see, is through a cloud of red.

With one more wrenching pull against the water, I surface and grasp the side of the rowboat with fingers made stiff by the icy water. Golmarr surfaces beside me and pulls himself into the boat. He grabs his staff and jumps onto the railing of the Ilaadi ship, swinging himself up onto the deck. Both of his brothers are already aboard, and Ornald is hefting Enzio onto the ship. I slither gracelessly into the rowboat and my eyes grow round at the sight of Nayadi holding a knife to the boat owner's throat.

"He was going to row away and leave you," she says, her scratchy voice joyful.

"Sorrowlynn!" Golmarr calls. A rope ladder is dropped down the side of the ship. I walk to the ladder, close my dripping hands on it, and climb. As I step onto the deck, I draw my sword.

My companions stand on one side of the deck, the Ilaadi on the other, and no one is moving. That is when I notice the Ilaadi princess clasped against Yerengul's chest, his knife pressed against the hollow below her ear. His lip is split, and a thin stream of blood is dripping from one nostril.

Yassim's eyes are filled with anger, her breathing is ragged. She starts to turn toward me, but Yerengul says, "One move and you die, Princess." She rams her elbow into his ribs, and his hold on her tightens. "I am an Antharian barbarian, re-member?" he growls. "Those are *your* words, my lady, not mine. Do you *doubt* I will kill you if you do not do as I say?"

The princess grits her teeth, and her body goes perfectly still. Yerengul grins, and I wonder if he is enjoying himself.

"We have no wish to kill or fight you, Princess Yassim," Golmarr says, though he never takes his eyes from the six Ilaadi sailors standing opposite us. "We need a ship and are prepared to pay for our passage."

Yassim trembles with outrage. "This is a royal ship! We are not for *hire*. Especially to a band of spineless Antharian ruffians!"

Golmarr's stance visibly stiffens. "Spineless? You call *us* spineless when you outnumber us? If we were spineless, we wouldn't have had the courage to fight your crew. The Ilaadi are reputed to be the best assassins in the world, yet it is not one of *my* men lying dead at the bottom of the sea with an arrow in his neck." He takes a deep breath and in a calmer voice says, "I ask again. We need a ship and we are prepared to pay handsomely for passage."

"Passage where?" the princess snaps. "If you want me to take you to my kingdom so I can feed the woman to the sandworm and put an end to his havoc, there is no need to *pay* me. I will do it for nothing."

Golmarr is silent for a long moment, measuring and re-measuring the princess. His hands tighten on his staff and he says, "We need passage to Draykioch."

Yassim looks askance at her crew. The shortest man shakes his head. "As I said before, this is a royal ship. We do not transport passengers," she says, glaring back at Golmarr. Her gaze moves to me. It is so cold, I am surprised it does not freeze my sodden clothes to my body. "Why do you want to go to the Serpent's Island? So this *princess* can wake another dragon, like she has woken the sandworm?"

"He is already awake and waiting for us," a grating voice calls. Every person on the ship turns toward the voice. Nayadi is tottering on the boat's railing, her bare feet curled around the wood like a bird's talons clinging to a branch. She cautiously lowers herself to the deck and points at me. "She woke *all* the dragons when she killed Zhun, the fire dragon."

I am so stunned by Nayadi's words that I stumble away from her. No one was supposed to know I, not Golmarr, killed the fire dragon. Enzio and Golmarr's brothers look at me, all three of their faces shocked. Ornald simply nods, as if he's known all along.

"What is Nayadi talking about, brother?" Yerengul asks.

"I will tell you at a more secure time."

Enzio nods, his eyes filled with pride as he studies me. "That is why you were not afraid to fight the two-headed monstrosity. You already know how to slay dragons. For some reason I am not surprised."

Nayadi lifts her hand, and everyone falls silent. "But the sandworm and the two-headed dragon are not the only ones eager for her death. There is a dragon patiently waiting for her in the mountains of Faodara, and the stone dragon of Satar is making the earth rumble again. He will bring the entire Satar mountain range down if Sorrow doesn't kill him first." She cocks her head to the side. "And the sea serpent . . . he is much closer than any of you realize. Yes. They all want to destroy the girl who killed the fire dragon, for she has his magic, and his knowledge. She is the first threat to their kind."

Yassim studies me the way she studied Golmarr the first time she saw him: like she is reading everything about me—every strength, weakness, fault, and flaw—by my posture. "You expect me to believe *this* Faodarian girl killed a *dragon*?

I live half a world away from her, and still we hear stories of how Faodarian women abhor weapons almost as much as they abhor physical intimacy. Even their men do not know how to swing a sword or throw a dagger. They do their killing with poisoned wine, like the cowards they are. So how did she kill a dragon? With her bare hands?" She laughs a cruel, mocking laugh.

I swallow the anger swelling in my throat and raise Golmarr's sword. My wet hand slips on the handle, and the weapon wavers to the side. "I killed the fire dragon with this sword," I say, and shrug like it was no big deal, defeating a dragon. "And that was after he burned me with fire, crushed my ribs, and ate my arm."

Derision fills Yassim's eyes, and she laughs again. "I do not believe you. There is no weapon in the world that can penetrate a dragon's scales."

I shrug again and let my anger sharpen my words. "You can believe whatever you want, Yassim. It doesn't change the fact that he is dead, and my hand wielded the weapon that took his life."

Nayadi cackles. I sheathe the sword and force myself not to break eye contact with the Ilaadi princess. She is leaning forward, and a sheen of sweat glistens on the bridge of her nose. Her body language makes me think of a hunting dog being restrained when it can clearly see a rabbit.

"If you want my ship so badly, I will fight you for command of it," Yassim says.

"Me?" I ask hoarsely.

She nods once.

Golmarr steps between me and the princess, his face tight with worry. "Not worth it," he says. Lowering his voice, he adds, "Not only are Ilaadi royalty trained assassins, they are their kingdom's *best* assassins. You know that, right?"

"Of course I know," I whisper. "I studied Ilaadi history when I was eleven. I had nightmares for a year after learning about the royal family." I peer over his shoulder and meet Yassim's keen gaze. Restrained in Yerengul's arms, she looks tiny and fragile, with a delicate, fine-boned build. "I can beat her." Golmarr shakes his head and opens his mouth to say something. Before he can speak, I blurt, "I will fight you, Yassim, but only if no weapons are involved."

Yassim smiles. "No weapons?" she asks innocently. "Why ever not?"

"Because the Ilaadi poison their weapons, and I do not trust you."

Yassim shrugs. "Very well."

# Chapter 22

Yassim's eyes dance with delight, but her crew are fervently shaking their heads. She ignores them.

"Princess Yassim, the risk is too great. No one sails to the black isle and returns," the oldest man on her crew says. "I beg you to reconsider."

"You might be the captain of this ship, but I am your superior, Captain Yeb," she says. "I will be the one who decides." Yassim nods toward me and sneers. "Look at her. She might be wearing men's clothing, but she looks soft." A wide smile curls her mouth, and for a moment I am shocked by her youth and her beauty. At a glance, I would not peg her as an adult. At a glance I would not peg her as an assassin, either. But both her true age and her knowledge of killing show in the way she studies people, in the way she stands, in the sharpness of her eyes as they slice through me and find my weaknesses.

"We will fight for command of this ship," she says. "If you win, my crew will sail wherever you wish to go. If I win, I will kill you and feed your carcass to the fish before throwing your men overboard."

I push my wet hair away from my neck and smile, trying to appear harmless. "That's not exactly the deal I was looking for."

"What would you have me change? Are you *afraid* to die?"

I bite my bottom lip and shake my head. "Death holds no fear for me." I have enough memories of it to know that, despite what everyone thinks, death is a peaceful release, an end to all pain and worry.

"Then what changes do you want?"

"If you win, you feed my carcass to the fish and throw my men overboard. Fine. But if I win, you and your men forfeit every weapon you have before we set sail."

She shrugs. "Agreed. *If* you win, we will forfeit our weapons."

She already thinks she has won, which means she is overconfident. At least I have *that* in my favor. "So you accept?"

She nods, one curt bob of her head.

"Then let's get started. The sooner we set sail, the better. Yerengul, pat her down."

Still holding the knife to the princess's neck, Yerengul runs his free hand down one of her arms and then the other, patting the loose white fabric of her clothing. When he is done, she shoves him away and removes her turban, revealing deep red hair a shade lighter than her eyebrows, braided into a bun at the back of her head. Gripping the hem of her knee-length blouse, she pulls it up over her head and tosses it aside. Beneath it, she is wearing a formfitting dark blue tunic that has no sleeves, and baggy pale blue pants. A plain gold necklace circles her throat, gleaming against her deeply tanned skin. Affixed to both her wrists are very slim blades in black leather holsters. One is curved and made for slicing; the other is straight and made for stabbing or throwing. She takes them off and carefully holds them out to Yerengul. "They are poisoned," she warns.

Yerengul warily takes the knives and quickly steps away. "She's fast," he warns me, wiping the drying blood from his nose. There is respect in his voice.

"I'm sure she is." I unclasp my dripping cloak, letting it slap wetly to the deck at my feet.

Yerengul tucks Yassim's knives into his belt and motions to Jessen. "Hold her hands while I finish checking for concealed weapons." Jessen nods and clasps the princess's wrists, and Yerengul kneels at her feet. She stands still while Yerengul pats her legs through her loose pants, from her hips to her ankles, even lifting both of her bare feet to look beneath them. When he is done, he stands and shakes his head. "No weapons."

She jerks away from Jessen and studies me.

I sit down and begin working the soaked knot on my left boot, hoping the mundane task will help quiet my nerves. Both boots are soaked and too heavy to wear in a fight. My fingers are growing stiff with cold, and I realize I should be freezing, but I am not. There is too much adrenaline coursing through me for my body to be cold.

"I am pleased you picked hand-to-hand combat," she says, holding out her two small, slender hands.

I nod and tug off my boot. *Of course she is pleased,* I think. *Taking a life with bare hands is the Ilaadis' ultimate assassination feat.* I untie my other boot and yank it off, sloshing water onto the deck. Next, I roll my woolen socks down my calves and off my feet and toss them to the base of the railing. Wind plasters my wet tunic to my body, and I start shivering.

Golmarr crouches beside me, his back to Yassim. "I don't think you should do this," he whispers, his eyes blazing with anger. "I think we should try and defeat the entire crew instead."

"Why? There are eight of them and only six of us, since I highly doubt Nayadi can fight. Have you *seen* the outcome?"

He shakes his head and his brows pull tight together. "I saw Yassim blow a dart at you a split second before it happened—hence the leap into the sea—but beyond that, I have seen nothing about her or her crew, aside from the sails of their ship rippling in the wind." He puts his hand on my sleeve, and hatred sharpens his eyes. "I do not want to watch her hurt you, Sorrowlynn."

I press on the crease between his brows and give him my best smile, which is trembling and weak. "I will die by my own hand, remember? And you have seen me fight. Your brothers taught me well. I am skilled, Golmarr. I am strong." I shiver. "I'm also starting to feel the cold. A good fight will warm me up."

"But what if—"

I press my frigid fingers against his warm lips and realize my hand is shaking. He must feel it, because he closes his eyes and covers my fingers with his, stilling them. "Golmarr, my mind contains the knowledge of hundreds of warriors. You need to have faith in me." Even though the words I have spoken are strong and confident, doubt makes it hard to gain my feet. *I* am the one who needs to exercise a little faith.

With my people on my right, and the Ilaadi sailors on my left, Yassim and I face each other on the most open part of the deck. Her bare arms are thin, several shades paler than her face and hands, and lined with lean muscle. She doesn't wait for a formal beginning to our fight. Her feet barely touch the deck as she sprints forward. When she is two steps from me, she leaps, spins through the air, her foot aimed to hit my stomach.

I step to the side as her foot makes contact and grab her ankle, jerking and twisting it, and knocking her off balance. Tightening my hold, I shift my weight and slam my bare foot into the side of her head. She uses the force of my attack to her advantage and yanks her ankle from my grasp before my foot does any real damage. Her heel thumps hard against my chest, making me stumble back a step, and then she darts away.

She moves like water—swift and fluid and deceptively strong—and is faster than anyone I have ever fought or sparred with. I almost can't follow her with my eyes as she spins her body into mine again, slamming her elbow into my ribs one, two, three times in a row before I have time to react. With the wind knocked out of me, I thrust my foot into the back of her knee and slam her down onto the boat deck, landing solidly atop her. Yassim's legs wrap around my leg, and she flips me to the side and twists away before I can grab her. I climb to my feet and stand hunched over my throbbing ribs as my brain starts filtering through all offensive fighting skills I know.

"She is going to turn you into pulp if you don't get your hands up and start blocking her," Yerengul calls.

Golmarr glares. "That says a lot about the person who taught her to fight!"

Yerengul shoves Golmarr. "It was just an observation."

"I know what I'm doing," I say as I watch the desert princess. We both move at the same moment and collide in the deck's center. I swing my hand and she blocks, catching my blow with her forearm. I swing my other hand and she blocks, falling back a step. I repeat this action, and my hands blur as they fly through the air, repeatedly hitting. Yassim blocks every blow until she has been forced to the side of the ship and can either change her direction or go into the ocean. The next time I swing, she grabs my wrist and bends it backward, then rams her knee into my stomach. I stumble back, giving her enough room to spin. She lifts her leg midspin and kicks the side of my head before I have time to duck. Gasping for breath, Yassim hurries to the other side of the boat and watches me like a snake studying a mouse.

I run forward and, utilizing the length of my legs, spin and kick. Her gold necklace is my target. Before my foot hits her, Yassim ducks and grabs it. She twists my ankle and shoves me backward at the same time. I wrench my body in a half circle and fall forward, catching myself with my hands against the damp deck. Lifting my free foot, I plunge it into her stomach so hard my arms struggle to support me. Yassim flies backward, crashing into the boat's railing before landing on her bottom.

She is up and on her feet and running at me before I have a chance to stand. Her arms and legs move so fast, they become a Yassim-colored haze. I jump to my feet, ready to block an attack, but Yassim doesn't stop running when she reaches me. Her small feet sprint up the length of my body, and her elbow, as hard and swift as any weapon I've known, cracks against my cheek, snapping my head to the side.

Her small feet push off my thighs, and she flips backward through the air, landing on her feet like a cat. A satisfied smile splits her mouth. "First blood goes to me," she says, smoothing the front of her tunic. She is panting hard. The dark red hair that has come loose from the braid bun hangs in sweaty wisps around her face.

I dab at my cheek and my fingers come away crimson.

Golmarr and my father rush to my side. "She is a *good* fighter," Golmarr says, and his eyes hold more than a trace of concern.

"Here. For her cheek." My father holds a silk handkerchief out to Golmarr. The Faodarian griffin is sewn onto a corner of the white silk, right beside a letter *F*. My mother's name is Felicitia, and I wonder if this is her handkerchief.

Golmarr takes it and dabs the fabric on my cheek, using the opportunity to lean in close. "I don't know how much longer I can endure this, Sorrowlynn," he whispers. "Every hit she lands on you is more painful than if I were feeling it myself."

"I'm fine. I can barely even feel it," I say. Golmarr frowns and gently dabs my cheek again.

"You might be from Faodara, but you are built more like the Satari," my father says. "Do you know why the Ilaadi have become the best assassins in the world?"

I think about it for a moment and then shake my head. "No. Why?"

My father grins. "Because Princess Yassim's ancient neighbors, the Satari, were bigger and stronger than her ancestors. Yassim's people had to learn to fight stronger opponents, so they opted for secretly assassinating us instead of fighting face to face. That was the only way they could beat us. Use your strength, Sorrowlynn!"

Golmarr nods. "Fight like you are a man from the ancient Trevonan army. Do you know how they fought?"

I see it and feel it, the way the ancient Trevonans fought—

with no finesse, no visible skill, only brute strength. "They had competitions to see who could uproot trees," Golmarr says, "and then competitions to see who could throw the uprooted trees the farthest. They threw one another around and fought with their fists. You are bigger than her, and—no offense— slower. It doesn't mean you are weaker or less skilled. But your father is right. You are built more like a Satari woman than a Faodarian woman. Satari women are strong." He wraps his hands around my biceps and gives me a little shake. "I feel your strength, Sorrowlynn. You are powerful." A small smile graces his face. "You also know *a lot* more than she does. She has been trained to expect speed and finesse. She has been trained to fight other assassins, or kill an enemy before he knows his life is even in danger. She lurks in the shadows with a poisoned knife. She doesn't train to fight duels for ships. She doesn't train to win with strength and endurance." He cups the back of my head in his hand and leans his forehead against mine. "Please be careful."

"This *is* me being careful." I gently push Golmarr aside. The moment my eyes meet Yassim's, she starts running, fast as lightning, across the deck and brings her elbow into my ribs. As it contacts my bruised bones, I shift to the side and slip one arm beneath her armpit, reach my other arm over her shoulder and grab her tunic, and then lift her off the ground and swing her through the air, slamming her onto the deck like she's an uprooted tree—just like I am an ancient Trevonan soldier. I pounce on her, landing my weight on one of my knees, right in the middle of her stomach. The air is forced from her lungs, and her eyes bulge. Before she has time to push me off, I ball my hand into a fist, ancient Trevonan style, and slam it against her jaw with all my strength.

Yassim's head snaps to the side. When she looks at me again, eyes stunned, I ram my fist into her nose. She jerks her knee up and into my side and knocks me onto the deck. Her feet drum against my back and force me flat onto my stomach. Two small hands grab my hair and slam my face into the ship's deck, and then they are cinched around my throat.

For a split second, the deck seems to tilt and my ears start ringing, but despite my woozy brain, my body reacts with hardly any conscious effort on my part. I ram my elbow backward and feel a satisfying crunch. Yassim leaps off my back, but I dive for her, catching a handful of her tunic in my hands. With a grunt of effort, I swing her off her feet again, slamming her down onto her stomach. She yelps and tries to crawl away, but I press my knee between her shoulder blades and pin her wrists up by her head. Grinding my knee against her spine, I lean close and say, "Unless you can break my hold, your ship is mine."

She snarls and tries to force her wrists from my hands, but I am stronger than she is. "You haven't won yet," she growls, trying to buck me off. "I am not defeated!"

"Then get up and fight me." She writhes and lurches, but cannot break free. I look at Golmarr. "Does this count as winning?" I ask, and taste blood.

Golmarr nods. "If she can't get up, yes, it counts as winning . . . unless she wants you to strangle her to prove your point."

"Yield your ship to me, Princess Yassim," I say.

She pitches, testing my hold again, but doesn't break free.

"I have beaten you. I have won. Yield your ship." My voice is so quiet and commanding; my mother would be proud.

She struggles again, and my sweaty hand loses its grasp on

one of her slim wrists. Instead of ramming her elbow into my ribs, the princess wraps her fingers around the fine gold chain on her neck and snaps it. Everything seems to slow when I see the tip of a gold needle sticking out from Yassim's closed fist. Golmarr yells a warning and dives for me at the exact moment Yassim plunges the needle into my thigh. At first I feel nothing. A heartbeat later, a rush of heat expands outward from the needle.

Yassim, still pinned beneath me, lifts her foot to kick me in the back of the head, but Golmarr knocks her foot away. I take a handful of her hair, lift her head, and slam her face into the deck. Her eyelids flutter and her body softens the slightest bit beneath mine.

"Just yield your ship so I don't have to ruin your pretty face!" I growl, slamming her face into the deck again. My words are slurred, and my right thigh feels like it is on fire. "I don't want to hurt you anymore! I just need your bloody ship!"

"I do not yield," Yassim hisses. A slow smile curls her bleeding lips upward. "You will be dead before the sun sets, and the ship will still be mine. In Ilaad, that means *I* win."

The boat seems to tip beneath us, and my hold on her hair weakens as my hand begins to tremble. "Throw all her crew but the captain overboard and set sail," I say, my words slow and garbled. My tongue is too heavy and feels coated with slime. I try to swallow the slime, but it is so thick it will not go down my throat.

"What?" Yassim shrieks, fighting against my hold with renewed strength. "You have no right to throw my men into the sea!" I wobble atop her, but do not let go.

"And you had no right to poison me," I whisper, grinding

my knee harder against her back. "I won your ship fairly. I decide what to do with the crew. Based on the way you fight, I do not trust you or your men." I look at Golmarr and hope he can understand my slurred words. "Throw them over."

The Ilaadi sailors draw their weapons and eye Golmarr and his brothers warily. They will not leave the ship without a fight.

"If you lift your weapons against my men, your princess dies right now," I warn. With an unsteady hand, I slide the needle out of my thigh—it is barely as long as my pinkie finger, and hollow inside—and hold it to Yassim's neck, just below her ear. "There has to be at least a trace of poison still left in this!" Yassim goes instantly still. A single droplet of my blood falls from the needle and splatters against her skin, sliding down her neck before dripping onto the deck. "Drop your weapons *now* or she dies." Weapons clang against wood. "Jump over the side," I instruct, my voice so slurred my words are barely clear.

Six Ilaadi sailors walk to the railing, climb atop it, and jump, splashing into the icy ocean.

Taking a deep, trembling breath, I fling the gold needle into the water and fall to my side, curling my knees to my chest like a baby. Golmarr is atop the princess before she can move, pressing her face so hard against the deck she whimpers.

"What kind of poison was in your needle?" he asks.

"Blackshade," she says, the word slurring out of her smooshed mouth. Ornald crouches beside Golmarr and roughly ties the princess's wrists behind her back. Enzio kneels at my side, slipping his hands beneath my knees and shoulders, lifting me.

I swallow against the thickness of my tongue and my swelling throat. The ship's mast ripples and bends like a snake, twisting against the dull blue sky, and above it, high in the air, I see the two-headed dragon. I blink hard and look again, but find myself staring into empty white eyes.

Nayadi's hand closes tight around my jaw. "Soul to soul, I forge this bond," she whispers, "and bind my spirit to yours." Darkness gathers around her like a living, swirling cloud, until it blocks the entire sky. "Soul to soul, I forge this bond and bind my spirit to yours," she whispers again, faster this time. I open my mouth to tell her I saw the dragon, but no sound comes out. My muscles give up the ability to move, my lungs refuse to expand, and silence swells inside my ears. Beneath my ribs, my heart wrenches to a painful stop . . . and then it stays that way: silent, still. Blackness devours the ship and crawls around the edges of Nayadi's grinning face as she keeps speaking words I can no longer hear. The shadows pull at me, and my bones feel as if they are being torn from my flesh, and still my heart is not beating. I scream and clench every muscle in my body, trying to hold it together when it feels like it is being ripped apart. And then the darkness hides the world from my eyes and I simply stop existing.

# Chapter 23

I am wrapped in a cocoon of fabric, my arms and legs sweat-plastered against my body. The world is moving all around me, close and stifling, and I cannot help but wonder what I am going to be when I break free of my wrapping—a girl, or a dragon? The thought brings to mind a two-headed dragon flying high above a ship's mast. I need to warn Golmarr.

I blink at the darkness and start scratching against the cocoon, clawing it away from my face. I open my mouth to cry out, and damp hair fills it. Thrusting my arms up, they break through taut fabric, and a wave of cool, humid air breathes against my skin. I grip the sleek edges of it and pull myself to sitting, and the world swings violently from side to side.

A perfect square in the ceiling is letting in light, illuminating a small, cramped room. Beside me are three empty hammocks, and I am swinging in the fourth. The fabric is as smooth as the luxurious silk imported to Faodara from the desert. Rubbing the fabric between my thumb and finger, I realize it *is* silk.

I swing my legs carefully over the side and hop down

onto a cool floor, stumbling as my knees nearly give out. Pain shoots up my left leg and I hold the silk hammock to keep from falling. Pushing tangled hair from my face, I hobble on stiff, clumsy legs toward the square of light. Below it is a ladder, so I climb. When my head and shoulders pass from the darkness into the light, I wince and turn my face away from a blinding blue sky with the sun perched in its center.

The slap of water on wood and the snap of a sail catching the wind fill the air. A moment later, men's voices join the sounds. A pair of strong hands loop under my armpits and hoist me the rest of the way up the ladder into the bright, stifling sunlight.

"How do you feel?" a familiar voice asks. I turn toward the sound and am engulfed by a warm embrace.

"Golmarr," I breathe, without opening my eyes. I lean my head against his chest, savoring the sense of belonging I feel when I am with him. "I saw the two-headed dragon."

"It is following us, but we have managed to stay ahead of it." His arms tighten around me, and I relax against his body. "Are you feeling all right?"

For a moment, I ponder his question. "My head feels stuffed with cotton," I say, and startle at my hoarse voice. "I can't open my eyes, either. It's too bright out here. Can you help me back down the ladder?"

Golmarr laughs, the deep rumble echoing through his chest and directly into my ear. "In a minute. Let me look at your leg in the sunlight." His arms fall away, and I sway as I catch my balance. Crouching at my feet, Golmarr touches my knee, his hands warm and dry against my skin. Slowly, his hands move up my leg, fingers pressing and probing. Cracking one eye open, I peer down. I am wearing my brown Trevonan tunic and . . . nothing else. Golmarr is kneeling at my feet, focused on my thigh. My *bare* thigh.

Both my eyes pop open, and I try to step away, but he wraps his hands around my leg and anchors me in place. With one eyebrow raised, he looks up. "Why are you trying to pull away? Are you scared of the touch of a barbarian?"

All the grogginess leaves my brain. "No, I'm not afraid of your touch, but I'm not dressed!"

"Your tunic covers you well enough. This is where Princess Yassim stabbed you with a poisoned needle. I am making sure it is healing," Golmarr explains, and though he is not smiling, there is mischief radiating from his voice. "And I'm getting a close-up view of your beautiful legs," he murmurs.

"Oh," I say breathlessly, and *that* makes him smile. I swallow as he moves his hands higher, lifting the hem of my tunic. "Is that really necessary?" I whisper. Instead of answering, he frowns and leans closer, pressing against my skin with the tip of his thumb.

"Ouch!" I gasp, and force myself not to yank away as I look at his hands on my skin. On the outside of my left thigh is a perfectly round bruise with a small black scab in its center. Golmarr presses on the discolored skin, and a drip of yellow pus oozes around the scab.

"How does it look?" a deep voice asks from behind. I cringe and turn. Enzio, Ornald, and Yerengul are standing behind me, worry plain on all three faces, waiting for Golmarr's answer. Gripping the hem of my tunic, I tug it as low as I can, which is no farther than halfway down my thighs. It is absolutely unheard-of for a Faodarian princess to show her legs!

When Golmarr stands, I turn toward the ladder leading to the hammock room, but he places his hand against the small of my back, holding me at his side. "It looks a lot better. There is almost no pus coming out."

Enzio sighs and runs his hand down his weary face. "That's good news."

Yerengul laughs. "Too bad for you, brother." His gaze shifts to my legs. "I guess you won't have the excuse of a wound to put your hands on her bare skin every hour."

Golmarr shoves his brother's shoulder hard. "Be more respectful," he warns, "or I'm going to swab the deck with your face."

My father holds a bundle out to me. It is my cloak, stiff from dried salt water. I take it and wrap it around my waist, covering my legs. "Thank you. Where are my clothes?"

"Belowdecks, in the sleeping quarters with the hammocks," he says. "All of our saddlebags are in one corner, so rifle through them and see what you can find to wear."

"What about the leggings I wore onto the ship?"

Golmarr shakes his head. "They're gone. They were ruined—completely soaked with blood."

I try to remember any deep wounds I got while fighting Yassim. There were none. "One little needle puncture completely soaked them with blood?"

Golmarr's jaw stiffens. "Apparently the Ilaadi put an anticoagulant in their poisons to help them spread faster. Every nick and scratch you got bled a lot." He points at my chest. I look down and notice the bloodstains on my tunic.

I step toward the hatch, but Golmarr tugs on my tunic, bringing me back to his side. "Do you need any help getting dressed?"

I laugh. "I can get dressed on my own, thank you very much."

Golmarr smiles, but his cheeks slowly turn scarlet. His brother starts laughing, and Ornald gives him a stern look. Golmarr groans. "I didn't mean it that way. Would you like me to help you find some clean clothes?" He points to Enzio and Ornald. "Or would you like a member of your family to help you?"

I shake my head. "No. I can manage on my own."

A few minutes later, dressed in a pair of grass green leggings and a yellow tunic I found in my saddlebag, I climb the ladder back to the deck, armed with a comb and leather string. Once my eyes readjust to the bright light, I look around. Above, the sky is a clear, fathomless turquoise staring down at the dark blue sea. Golmarr, Jessen, and Yerengul are at the ship's helm talking with the Ilaadi captain. Enzio and Ornald are practicing on deck with their short swords and talking about the best Satari celebrations they've ever been to. "I miss the Glass Forest and our people," my father says.

"Why did you leave?" Enzio asks.

My father sheaths his sword and pulls a piece of white cloth from his pocket, dabbing at the sweat on his forehead.

I walk to his side and start combing my tangled hair while trying to get a closer look at the cloth. It is not simply cloth, but a finely made handkerchief. "Why *did* you leave?" I ask.

He looks at me with eyes nearly the same shade of green as mine. "Melchior the wizard gave me a bag of gold and told me if I sought my fortune with Faodarian royalty, I would find a type of love that was not waiting for me with the Black Blades." He holds the handkerchief up for me to see. It is the one embroidered with the Faodarian griffin and the letter *F* and stained with my blood.

"That is not what a soldier typically carries," I say. "Was that my mother's?"

He nods and runs a finger over the faded embroidery. "Yes, this belonged to your mother. She gave it to me the day her husband found out that we had fallen in love. That was the last time we spoke as equals." He pulls his lips tight against his teeth, whether from anger or sorrow, I cannot say.

"Was I born yet?"

"No. You were barely making the queen's belly swell."

"And was Melchior right?" Enzio asks. "Did you love the queen of Faodara?"

"I did love the queen. Very much." He laughs and looks at the ship beneath his feet. "Unfortunately Melchior didn't mention that it would only last a few months."

I put my hand on his arm. "I am sorry," I say.

My father looks at me, his eyes thoughtful, and covers my hand with his. "What I had with the queen was fleeting and wrong, and left both of us very unhappy. But you, daughter, whether you knew I was your father or not, have given me sixteen years of a truer love than I ever had with Felicitia. I believe *that* is the love Melchior was referring to—the love a father has for his daughter. You bring me joy, Sorrow, and now that you know I am your father, and Lord Damar cannot punish either one of us because of that, I am excited to discover what a life with you in it is like." He gives my hand a firm squeeze and then removes it from his arm. "I believe Golmarr is eager for a moment of your time. He has nearly worn a path in the ship's deck with his worried pacing."

I turn and find Golmarr leaning against the ship's railing,

ankles crossed, watching me. "Nice clothes," he says with a laugh. "Very . . . conspicuous. The two-headed dragon is going to see you from miles away."

I shrug and keep brushing my hair. "I believe Treyose went through his closet and found the clothes he abhors, and gladly passed them on to me. I look like an overgrown daffodil."

Grinning like a pirate, Golmarr slowly saunters to my side and lets his gaze wander over my clothing. "Aside from looking like an overgrown flower, you look all woman to me."

I feel like I went to sleep, and when I woke up the old Golmarr was back—the teasing Antharian rogue. He seems like Golmarr from before he inherited the glass dragon's hatred and tried to kill me. "Why are you acting like this?"

"Like what?"

"Like you used to act—flirting, touching me, staring at me like you're going to devour me with your eyes."

His eyebrows rise the slightest bit and the teasing leaves his eyes. "Do you want me to stop?"

"No!" I blurt, a little too enthusiastically. "It is confusing after you tried so hard not to touch me, and then tried to convince me that our love is doomed."

He reaches out and takes my hand in his. "I thought you were going to die from Yassim's poison. While you lay unconscious in the hammock, I thought about what Enzio said to me at the inn and realized how stupid I was for not taking advantage of every moment we'd spent together in Trevon. I regretted the days where I could have been close to you but let fear rule my life. I will never let fear be my ruler again." He runs his thumb across the calluses on my palm.

I do a quick visual scan of the ship's deck again. "Where *is* the Ilaadi princess?"

Hatred smolders in his eyes. "She is in the cargo hold," Golmarr says, words clipped with anger. "We gave her the chance to remain above deck, unrestrained and free to move about, but she got into a tussle with Yerengul shortly after we set sail."

"A tussle? How does Yerengul *tussle* with someone?" I ask.

"Very violently. It ended with both of them bleeding and Yerengul pinning Yassim to the deck. So, the second day, we tied her to the mast, but her incessant cursing and threats earned her a spot where we don't have to hear her."

Taken aback, I look at him. "Wait. How long have we been sailing?"

He raises his eyebrows and takes a small step closer to me. "Three days, sleepyhead, but it felt like a year's worth of worry." He touches my elbow. "Are you hungry?"

I press on my stomach. "A little."

"Well, you should be." He smiles, but it is strained. "How does pickled eel and seaweed paper sound for lunch?"

"Please say you're joking," I whisper, feeling decidedly less hungry than a moment before.

Golmarr's smile widens, moving all the way to his eyes. "Not joking. Apparently pickled eel is a delicacy in the city of Ilyaro—bones and all. Something about the pickling process turns the bones to the consistency of almonds." The smile slowly slips from Golmarr's mouth, and he cups the side of my face in his hand. "I am so glad you are awake."

I cover his hand with mine and lean into it. "Me too."

"You owe Nayadi your life."

"Nayadi?" My skin prickles as I remember the blackness devouring her . . . or me, and the terrifying sensation of my bones trying to rip free of my flesh. "Where is she?"

"Nayadi is watching Yassim. Apparently, the Ilaadi princess fears her. She fears Nayadi's magic."

Suddenly cold, I hug my chest and rub my biceps. Yassim isn't the only one who fears the crone. "What did Nayadi do to me when I was poisoned? It felt like she was trying to kill me."

"She temporarily stopped your heart to put a halt to the spreading of the poison, and then she sucked the poison out."

I hug myself tighter and try to decide which is more disturbing: Nayadi stopping my heart or sucking the poison from my thigh. "No wonder I have been asleep for three days."

"It was the only way she could save you," Golmarr says.

I nod but don't unwrap my arms from my body. "So, when the poison was sucked out, she simply *restarted* my heart?"

"She did."

When Yerengul was stitching closed the wound Golmarr gave me, Nayadi numbed it because she said she was too weak to heal even the simplest of wounds. But this time she *stopped my heart*? The thought makes me start to panic, so I change the subject. "What about the two-headed dragon?"

"When we set sail, it was circling the dock looking for us, but the moment we lifted anchor, the wind started blowing so hard we sped out of the harbor. The dragon followed, but we haven't seen it since the sun set our first day at sea."

"Golmarr," Jessen calls, his voice heavy with worry.

Instead of answering his brother, Golmarr spins in a quick circle, his eyes sweeping the sky and horizon. I know he is looking for the dragon.

"Stop searching the blasted sky and come here," Jessen growls.

The helm, the ship's wheel, is located on a raised dais at

the front of the ship. I follow Golmarr up the steps and stop beside Jessen. His arms are crossed over his broad chest, and he and the captain, Yeb, are glowering at the turquoise sails.

"What is wrong?" Golmarr asks, his gaze sweeping the horizon again, both the water and the sky this time.

"We *don't* see the dragon, so you can relax," Jessen says. "Captain Yeb, why don't you explain?"

The captain inclines his red-turbaned head and motions toward the sail. "As far as I can tell, we are moving south, as planned." His accent is thick and hard to understand, and his pale eyes are tight with worry.

"That's good," Golmarr answers, but he's frowning, waiting for the captain to say more.

"Look at the sail," Yeb says.

We all turn north, toward the sail, and study it. It is several shades lighter than the sky and swollen with wind. I lift my hand, letting the wind stream through my spread fingers. The sail is swollen the *wrong* way.

"Shouldn't the sail be bulging *southward* if the wind is blowing us south?" I ask.

Yeb nods. "Or, if the east or west wind was blowing, we would zigzag south. But if a north-blowing wind is filling the sail, like what we are seeing right now, we should be moving *north*. We are moving *south*, in direct opposition to the wind. I cannot control this ship."

# Chapter 24

"Look at the water," Yeb says.

Golmarr and I walk to the railing and peer down at the sea. It is so still, I see myself reflected in it, with Golmarr reflected at my side. The only place the water has a single ripple is in the wake created by the boat cutting through it.

"I thought the ocean was always moving," Golmarr says.

Captain Yeb groans. "In my forty-seven years at sea, the water has never been this still."

"If the wind were blowing, the water wouldn't be still," Jessen says. "So there is no wind. Yet the sail is swollen with air and we are moving." He looks at Captain Yeb. "Is this an enchanted ship?"

"No. Magic has been lost to us for sixteen years. This vessel is only eight years old." His eyes narrow. "You are the ones who brought the old woman onto my boat. Is this her doing?"

"No." Golmarr takes one more long, worried look at the smooth sea and then turns his back to it. "This is not our doing. We *should* be asking ourselves: Are we controlling the boat, or is the boat controlling us? And if the boat is controlling us, who is controlling the boat? We need to pull the sails down and drop anchor."

Captain Yeb swallows again, making his Adam's apple bob. "You should not have ordered my crew to jump overboard. We need them now more than ever."

"Put us to work. Tell us what to do. We are strong and able," Jessen says.

Yeb studies each of us individually and then nods. "Very well." He starts giving orders to Golmarr and his brothers, telling them what to do to lower the sails. When they have started working, Yeb turns to me. "Do you fear heights?"

I shake my head. I *miss* heights—miss flying like a dragon the same way I imagine I would miss air if it were ever denied me. But . . . I have never flown. That thought should not have entered my head. Yeb studies me with bloodshot eyes, and I wonder if he has slept at all since we pirated his ship. "Are you nimble enough to climb to the top of the taller mast?"

Hand blocking the sun's glare, I look at the taller mast. It has rungs sticking out on either side of it, all the way to the top. "I can climb it."

After a long moment, Yeb nods. "Climb the mast to the crow's nest and tell me if you can see Draykioch. There is a spyglass already up there. I have been warned, with a good wind, it takes only four days to reach the cursed island, and we have made very good speed."

I hurry to the mast and start climbing. The higher I climb, the swifter the air seems to be moving, whipping my hair, which I never had the chance to braid, into my face. At the top of the mast is a small, round deck with a swiveling spyglass screwed onto the railing—the crow's nest. I climb into the nest, push my hair out of my eyes, and smile. It is a little like flying, being up here with the wind pushing my clothes tight against the front of my body. The water is as flat and smooth as glass. The sea and sky seem to have no end, dissolving into each other, so it feels like we are sailing in a giant blue bubble. For a moment, I close my eyes and let the wind blow against my skin, let the sun shine golden against my eyelids, and breathe.

Looking into the spyglass, the southern horizon grows clear, the line between water and sky distinct with no land in sight. "No land yet," I call down. I swivel the spyglass north and peer through. It takes some searching, but eventually I see a dark spot against the horizon. The longer I watch it, the easier it is to recognize the uneven, flapping wings of the two-headed dragon.

Below, the heavy anchor splashes into the water. "Hold the railing, Princess Sorrowlynn," Yeb calls, and I brace myself as the ship jolts and slows down. A long, dark shadow moves out from below us, surging forward through the water before disappearing from sight. The hair on the back of my neck stands up. I stare down at the water, waiting, but the dark shape doesn't reappear.

"Did you see that?" I call down.

"See what?" my father asks.

"Something dark was swimming below the ship. When you dropped the anchor, it kept moving."

Everyone but my father and Enzio, who are still lowering the anchor, stops what they are doing and runs to the railing, peering over it. "I don't see anything," Golmarr says.

"Nor do I," Captain Yeb calls, but he does not stop searching the water.

"I have let out the anchor as far as it will go," my father says. "We are too deep for it to hit bottom, I think."

Captain Yeb stops staring at the water and starts pacing, his hands clutched behind his back. After a long moment, he looks at Ornald. "Pull the anchor back in. I cannot control this vessel. It seems we are at the mercy of the sea."

⊷⊶≍◆≍⊷⊶

I stand at the bow of the ship the rest of the afternoon, looking down into the water and waiting for the dark shape to reappear, but I see nothing aside from a few fish and my own reflection. Golmarr, Enzio, Ornald, Yerengul, and Jessen have all gone belowdecks to sleep while the captain stands tightlipped at the tiller, eyes glued to the southern horizon.

When the sun has almost reached the level of the ocean, the captain asks, "What are you looking at so intently, down in the water?"

"I am looking for the creature I saw below our ship when we dropped anchor." I stand with my back braced against the railing and study Yeb. He has the deeply tanned, wrinkled skin of a man who has seen many years at sea. His worry is evident in the taut way he is holding himself.

"How well did you see it? What did it look like?"

"It was distorted by the water, but as far as I could tell it was a long, black, snakelike creature."

Yeb's body grows even more tense. "I believe you saw the sea serpent—a water dragon with power to control the ocean."

I nod. That is the same thing I thought.

He steps to my side and braces his hands on the railing,

letting the wind whip at the faded red turban covering his hair. His eyebrows are sun-bleached to a nearly translucent white, and I wonder what color his hair is. "I am Yassim's uncle. Did you know?" He studies me with gray eyes that appear as washed out as the rest of him.

I shake my head. "I didn't. Are you an Ilaadi prince?"

Yeb smiles and shakes his head. "No. Yassim's father, King Jaquar—though he was not yet the king at the time—fell in love with my youngest sister. You see, Jaquar's first wife, an Ilaadi noblewoman by birth, died in childbirth, and my sister was the midwife's assistant. She stayed with Jaquar to help care for his newborn son, and they fell in love. Against the desires of his parents, he married her, a humble commoner, and elevated her status to royalty."

"His parents didn't try to put a stop to it?"

"Prince Jaquar had a wizard helping him. The wizard promised Jaquar's father if he allowed Jaquar to marry my sister, one of their children would help establish peace between Ilaad and Trevon."

"Did the wizard mean Yassim?" I ask, voice skeptical. I cannot imagine her promoting peace of any sort.

"We did not know to which child the wizard was referring, but as Yassim is King Jaquar's only remaining child, it can be no one else."

I think of what Yassim said the day we took her ship: the sandworm killed her brothers. For a moment, compassion for Yassim outweighs my dislike of her.

"My sister had two boys, and then bore Yassim," Yeb says as his eyes sweep the ocean. "She was killed shortly after Yassim was born. Whether by poison or illness, I do not know.

But by the time she died, the wizard had left her husband's service and never returned."

"I'm sorry," I say, "for your sister and her husband. For Yassim's brothers. But this wizard . . ." My voice trails off and I clear my throat. "Did he have a name?"

"Melchior."

Yeb's face wavers before my eyes, replaced by the face of a newborn baby, and then everything around me disappears.

⊶ ⚊✦⚊ ⊷

*The baby girl tightens her tiny fist around my finger and laughter bubbles from me. For more than a thousand years, I have walked this world, and still a newborn baby fills me with joy. The child's eyes meet mine, and a jolt of recognition sends my heart pounding. She is the one I have seen in my visions, the one who will spread her kingdom from the shores of the sea and back into the abandoned desert, making it bloom and thrive again. This is the child who will at long last sign a peace treaty with the king of Trevon and put an end to their fighting.*

*Tucking the yellow silk blanket beneath the baby's chin, I carefully lift her and whisper, "You are going to change the world." I press my lips to her tiny, warm head, right on top of a tuft of dark red hair. "What is she to be called?" I ask, turning my attention from the child to the woman sitting on the cushioned chaise beside me. I can see why Prince Jaquar fell in love with her. Though her dark red hair and olive skin are stunning, Princess Reyla's honey-brown eyes hold none of the scorn or haughtiness of a normal Ilaadi noblewoman. Her beauty radiates from within.*

*I blink and her face is replaced with the image of hands and a*

⊰ 245 ⊱

*goblet of wine. The hands hold a vial above the red drink, letting a single drop of liquid fall into it.* So that is how she will die, *I think, and look back at the baby as sorrow pricks my heart.* This child will grow up without a mother. *"Have you chosen her name?" I ask again.*

*"Yassim Reyla Jaquara," she says.*

*I nod and pronounce a birth blessing for the mother's ears alone. "Before this child, Yassim Reyla Jaquara, turns one-and-twenty, she will bring peace to Ilaad." Something shivers inside me, and I feel the wet sea air on my skin as another vision radiates before my open eyes; ocean, sunset, and my dear friend Captain Yeb staring at me with concern in his eyes.*

*"Sorrowlynn?" Yeb says.*

*"No, I'm—"*

---

"Melchior," I say, peering into Yeb's eyes.

Yeb frowns and pats his rough hand lightly against my cheek. "Are you all right? You got lost in thought."

"What was Yassim's mother's name?"

"Reyla."

"And was her hair red like Yassim's?"

Yeb nods. I force myself not to inhale a breath of surprise. As a child, I spent many hours piecing together puzzles with Melchior. He always compared the fate of the dragons, or Faodara, or Anthar to the puzzles. Every time we finished one, he would say, "It isn't until all the pieces come together that we see the whole picture, Sorrowlynn." I am beginning to see more and more of Melchior's pieces coming together.

"How old is Yassim?" I ask.

"She will be twenty at the end of spring." I feel his gaze on me, so look at him. "We have a dragon below us, and a dragon behind us. Will you please let Yassim come out of the cargo bay?"

At the thought of seeing Yassim, the bruise left by the poison starts to throb. I press on it. There is a hard, tender lump beneath my skin. "I do not trust her."

Captain Yeb takes a deep breath. "Please. If anything happens to this ship, she has no chance of surviving. She will drown, locked away down there with a *yentzee*."

I do not know that word. "What is a *yentzee*?"

Captain Yeb spits over the side of the ship. "*Dark witch. User of evil.*"

His words create a surge of anger in me. "She is a witch, yes, but the ability to use magic does not make a person evil. Think of Melchior. He was not evil." And I am not evil simply because I possess the ability to wield fire. And neither is Golmarr.

Yeb's shoulders droop, and he looks back at the horizon. "Will you climb to the crow's nest and look for land one last time before the sun sets?"

I nod, glad for the excuse to quit our conversation, and climb the mast to the crow's nest.

The sun, half-hidden below the horizon, is painting a line of shimmering gold to the side of the ship. The sky around the sun is a deep, hazy orange. The eastern horizon has faded to pale purple with a single star glowing in it.

Pressing the spyglass to my eye, I look south. A smear of gray, a scab against the blue, is visible, and I know, without a doubt, we are almost at Draykioch.

# Chapter 25

"I see it!" I blurt as I skid to a stop in front of Captain Yeb. "I see Draykioch."

All the color drains from the sea captain's face. He purses his colorless lips and his eyes scan his ship as if he is seeing it for the last time. "We will be there before the sun rises. If my ship does not stop moving forward, she will be dashed on the reef surrounding the island, and she will sink." He raises his watery gaze to mine. "Please reconsider the fate of my niece. She is the only living family I have left."

Remorse, mistrust, and compassion fire through me as I think of Melchior's memory of Yassim. I do not want Yassim anywhere close to me. Or Nayadi, for that matter. Having them both down in the cargo hold has been wonderful. I lean my elbows on the railing and look south. "I will let her up on deck before the sun rises."

Captain Yeb grabs my hand and lifts it to his forehead, pressing it on the exposed skin below his turban. "I thank you, Princess Sorrowlynn. I am in your debt and will repay you one day. This I swear." He releases my hand. "We need to prepare for the possibility of the ship sinking. Before dawn, every person needs to be on deck. The lifeboat will hold us all if the ship sinks, so I need to make sure it is stalwart."

"What should I do?"

"Nothing. There is nothing to do but wait and make peace with your life in case you die. It is all there is left."

⊷ ⚎ ⊶

Time seems to stop when one is awaiting the unknown, especially when the unknown is very likely a watery grave. Captain Yeb stands motionless at the helm as the stars slowly move across the black sky, as if he has accepted his fate and is waiting for it.

As we glide across the silent ocean, Golmarr's words from the inn begin replaying in my head: *What we have—this love—it is beautiful, and wonderful, and I cherish it above anything I have ever known, but there is so much more we have to think about.* A deep, wearying sorrow dulls my senses and makes my heart feel as if it is trying to break free from my body, so I give up waiting for fate and draw my sword. To block the things I do not want to think about, I fill my mind with the structure and discipline of sword-fighting.

I push my body through every sword-fighting routine I know. When I've run through them all, I quiet my mind and let my body move. Routines I've never done before take over my instincts, moving me in new ways and foreign patterns. My muscles conform to the routines as if they are ingrained there, and the routines mold to my body as if I am being shaped by an unseen sculptor. It is my subconscious controlling my actions, and the less I think, the more easily they come.

Midway through a routine, I hear the quiet groan of the

hatch to the sleeping quarters being raised, and then the wind carries Golmarr's scent to me. He is standing on the edge of the deck, watching, so I complete the routine. When I finish, I sheathe my sword and look at him—a dark shape against the starry horizon.

"What was that?" he asks, his voice deep with sleep.

"I don't know," I admit. "If I let my mind go blank, my body starts moving through routines I have never done before."

He steps closer and rests his fingers on the sword hilt hanging at my waist. "When I . . . when I trust myself to wield a sword again, I want you to teach me that routine."

"You still don't trust yourself with it? Even though you trust yourself to touch me?"

"One step at a time," he whispers. "I am learning to conquer this."

I close the small space left between us and place my hand on his left arm, right above his elbow. I open my mouth to speak, but no words come out. Beneath my fingers, his skin is firm and covered with bumps. Without a word, I untie the laces of his tunic and thrust my hand beneath the fabric, tracing his scales from his shoulder to his elbow.

"Twice now you've tried to tear my clothes off me. If I knew a few scales was all it would take, I would have grown them the first night we met and danced in your mother's castle," he says. "It would have spared us a lot of hardship."

I swallow against a lump in my throat and blink threatening tears back into my eyes. Not even his teasing eases my fear. "The scales have spread so much!"

"Yes. I think they like the salty ocean air." He is silent for a long moment while I study his shadowed face. And then he says, "I make a fiercely beautiful dragon, Sorrowlynn, with wings and scales as black as obsidian. When I am in the sun, the scales glow the deep blue of the evening sky right before it fades to black."

"You have seen this?" My voice breaks.

He puts one arm around me and pulls me close. "I have seen it," he whispers. He places his hand on my back, and I relax against him. The smell of him, the feel of him, and the sound of his beating heart soften a bit of the fear clawing through me. Golmarr slowly slides his hand down my spine to my lower back. His fingers probe my skin through the fabric of my tunic, and then, inch by inch, he starts lifting the fabric until his warm hand finds my bare skin. I cannot help my inhaled gasp of breath.

Golmarr freezes. "Sorrowlynn?"

"What?"

"You have scales."

His words jolt me so hard I rock backward on my heels. *"What?"*

Kneeling at my feet, he turns me so my back is to him and rolls the hem of my long yellow tunic up around my ribs. I hold the fabric beneath my elbows and stare at the outline of mast against sky while Golmarr gently runs his now-frigid fingers over my skin.

"It's only a tiny patch, smaller even than the palm of my hand. Nothing to worry about . . . too much." I don't know who he is trying to reassure—me or himself, but if it is me, it is not working. I reach back and touch my skin. In the very center of my back, right above the waistband of my leggings, the skin is hard to the touch and covered in small, rounded ovals.

My stomach twists at the feel of something so foreign growing on my body, and I have to swallow the urge to vomit. The tunic's hem falls from my elbows and settles back around my hips. "Why?" I ask. "Why am I getting scales? What is happening to us?" Fear makes my voice as tiny and scared as a child's.

Golmarr gathers me up in his arms again and presses his cheek against the top of my head. "I do not know why," he whispers, "but together we will find out and fix it."

I draw a trembling breath. "What if we don't?"

He holds me for a long time, water lapping at the ship's hull the only sound in the night. Finally, he answers, "If we don't fix it, we will become dragons." His body grows rigid against mine. "I loathe the dragons," he says between tightly clenched teeth. "I want to kill every single one!" With a burst of energy, he spins away and hammers his fist against the ship's mast. "I *hate* them!"

A polite clearing of a throat draws my attention to Captain Yeb. He is holding something in his hand, and by the dim flicker of a candle, I see it is a gold pocket watch.

"What?" Golmarr snaps.

"I beg pardon, Prince Golmarr, but it is one hour before dawn. We need to get everyone above deck in case the ocean decides to open up and devour my ship or smash it against the reef."

Golmarr nods. "I will wake my men."

"I will get the princess and Nayadi," I say.

An iron hand clamps down on my shoulder. "No," Golmarr snaps. "Nayadi can come up, but Yassim stays in the bay."

"But if the ship is dashed on the reef around Draykioch, she will drown," I say.

"A fitting fate for trying to poison you after agreeing to a fair hand-to-hand match," Golmarr growls. "In Anthar, she would have been hanged for the attempt on your life. She has no honor!"

He strides past me, but I grab the sleeve of his tunic and stop him as my own anger boils up inside me. I grip the front of his shirt and force him to turn and face me. "I will not leave her in the bay," I say, glaring. "I am the one she tried to kill, so I will decide if she is or is not allowed on deck."

Golmarr presses his lips together, as if forcing the thoughts swirling in his eyes to stay off his tongue. Finally, he grunts and pulls his tunic from my grasp. "Fine. But she's tied to the mast!" Without a backward glance, he stomps to the hatch.

<hr />

The cargo bay is dark and eerily still. The smells of pine tar, foreign spices, and eel are mixing with the aroma of a full chamber pot saturating the clammy air. My candle flickers as I wind my way among wooden crates. At the very back of the room, past all the cargo, are Nayadi and Yassim.

Nayadi is breathing so deeply the sound echoes off the walls. She is stretched out flat on her back, on the hard floor, and staring up at the ceiling with her white eyes. I gasp and jerk to such an abrupt halt, the candle splashes hot wax on my hand and almost goes out. Shoving my unease aside, I take a step closer to the old crone and peer down. Her face is slack with sleep, a trail of drool is trickling down one cheek, and her open eyes are slowly moving from side to side. Beneath her plain brown dress, her body looks as insubstantial as a pile of bones.

A few steps farther in sits Princess Yassim, back pressed against the ribs of the ship, her hands and her ankles tied together. Beside her is a chamber pot, and I wonder how she can stand the smell. She is watching me but doesn't move a muscle—only her honey-brown eyes move. I step over Nayadi and crouch in front of Yassim. "We are moving you above deck," I whisper, hoping to not wake Nayadi yet.

Yassim frowns and shakes her head. Her mouth moves, but no sound comes out of it.

"What?" I mouth.

Yassim rolls her eyes and nods toward Nayadi. She opens her mouth and speaks again, but I cannot hear a thing; not even the sound her teeth make when she snaps them back together.

"Stop playing games or I will leave you down here to die!" I whisper. I reach forward, prepared to sever the rope connecting her hands and feet, but Yassim flinches and fervently shakes her head, pressing herself flat against the ship's rib.

As my hand moves toward her, the tips of my fingers start to grow warm, and then hot. The air around Yassim ripples, and I draw my hand back. Pulling Golmarr's borrowed sword from its scabbard, I bring the tip of the blade to the spot where my fingers got burned. The air presses against it, resisting. I put more pressure on the sword, and the blue blade slices through the air, leaving bright orange cut marks that slowly fade.

"What is that?" I whisper.

"It is how I have kept her quiet," Nayadi says. I jump to my feet and almost step on her. She is sitting up, her face filled with amusement. "A simple wall of energy. I will teach you how to do it someday. There is so much you don't know."

Her eyes narrow and the hair on my arms bristles at the hungry way she is looking at me. "Such a waste of power."

I take a step away from Nayadi and put my sword back in its sheath. "We are moving Yassim up to the deck," I say. "Remove the wall."

Nayadi looks from me to Yassim and grins. "Or what? You'll kill me?"

I pull the sword from its scabbard a second time and lift it so it rests just above Nayadi's gaunt collarbone. "If I must, then I will kill you." It is a lie. I won't kill her simply because she will not do what I want. Nayadi rolls her eyes and mumbles something about me being overly grouchy from the poison, but she whips her hand through the air, and all of a sudden I can hear Yassim's breathing and smell her unwashed clothing and full chamber pot.

For a moment, guilt softens me toward her—guilt at locking her down in this tight space with Nayadi. Then I look in her eyes. They are filled with anger and loathing, and focused on me, not Nayadi, who is the one ultimately responsible for keeping her down here.

"We are moving you up onto the deck, Yassim," I say, and slide the hunting knife from my belt and sever the ropes binding her ankles. Beneath the ropes, her skin is raw. "I will have Yerengul see to your ankles."

Princess Yassim tries to stand and teeters backward, falling against the ship. I take a step away from her, wondering if she is trying to manipulate me into coming closer. "I cannot get up," she says, her voice hoarse. "I have not been able to move for days, and my body is stiff."

I glare at Nayadi. "You have not let her move?"

Nayadi shrugs. "She moved when she squatted over the pot."

"Have you fed her, at least?" I ask. When Nayadi doesn't answer, I turn to Yassim. "Have you had food and water?"

"She gave me one cup of water per day. No food." She stiffens and thrusts her chin forward. "We do not treat our prisoners as poorly as I have been treated. I consider this a declaration of war against Ilaad."

"If I knew how she was treating you, I would have put a stop to it," I say, and crouch down, helping Yassim to her knees.

"How could you *not* know? Why did you never come down and check to see how I was being treated? It is the responsibility of royalty to ensure their prisoners are treated humanely."

I laugh under my breath. "Why have I not come to check on you?" I ask. Yassim nods and glares accusations. "I have been asleep for three days. That is how long it has taken my body to heal from the poison you put into it."

Yassim blinks and lowers her blond-tipped lashes, studying the ground. "Oh." She looks back up. "How *did* you heal? My poison is almost as deadly as Strickbane. You should be dead."

I shrug. I do not have an answer. Gripping Yassim's forearms, I lift her to her feet and wrinkle my nose. "I think the smell of the chamber pot has saturated your clothes."

Yassim lifts her nose into the air and looks down on me, even though I am almost a head taller. "I do not want the Antharian prince to see me like this," she whispers.

"Which one?" I ask warily. "Not Golmarr, right?"

"I couldn't care less what that egotistical, hateful man

thinks of me. But Yerengul . . . Please let me have a moment to wash and change before I have to face him."

"As you wish. But I will inspect your clean clothing before you put it on to make sure you have no weapons, and *no jewelry.*"

Nayadi cackles and slaps her knee, and then follows us to the room with the hammocks.

⊰——⊱

When we come above deck, with Yassim smelling and looking a bit more like a princess, the eastern horizon has a thread-thin strip of red light cutting the ocean from the sky. Everyone is standing at the ship's helm, staring south. I take the length of rope that had been tying Yassim's wrists together and quickly retie them, marveling that even in the dark my nimble fingers know exactly how to make knots they have never made before, which the princess will not be able to undo.

When she is tied to the mast, I hurry to the helm and place my hand on Yerengul's shoulder to get his attention. "Can you see to Yassim's ankles and wrists? She has sores that need tending."

Even in the near-darkness, I see the sly smile that splits Yerengul's mouth. "My pleasure," he says, and opens the small medic pouch he always has tied to his belt.

I take a place between Golmarr and my father and look south. My father's arm comes around me and he squeezes my shoulders. "You are a good person," he whispers. "I am proud to call you my daughter."

"Thank you." I lean my head on his shoulder and hope

that this will not be the last time I see him. I am looking forward to spending years getting to know him better.

As the sky brightens, my heart starts hammering so hard, it feels like it is in my throat. "What is that?" I ask, craning my neck to look up. The sky seems to have a black triangular hole in it, where no stars gleam, and no light reflects off the ocean. The darkness reaches down to the water and is about to swallow the ship.

"That is Draykioch," Golmarr says, leaning forward so his elbows rest on the railing and his dark hair falls across his forehead. "If this ship does not stop moving soon, we will be dashed upon the reef surrounding the island, and if it does stop, the two-headed dragon will catch us."

"The sea serpent has been following us, too," Captain Yeb adds. "Our situation is hopeless." He touches the back of my hand with one finger. "Thank you for seeing to my niece. If the ship sinks, all I have to do is cut her from the mast instead of risk drowning in an effort to rescue her from belowdecks."

"You are welcome," I say, and the ship lurches. I am flung forward into the railing. Golmarr and Ornald hit the railing on either side of me, and then Enzio crashes into my back, nearly knocking me into the water. Only Yeb is left standing, his legs planted as firmly to the deck as the mast.

Enzio grabs my shoulders to steady me. "Are you hurt?" he asks, peering into my eyes.

"No, I am fine. What just happened? Did we hit the reef?"

"We have stopped moving," Yeb says, his voice filled with both wonder and dread. "Drop anchor!" Ornald and Enzio hurry away, and a moment later the anchor makes a deep splash as it hits the water. With every clank of the lowering chain, my heart accelerates. We have arrived.

# Chapter 26

The rising sun gleams off towering white cliffs that jut up out of the dark sea. Where the cliffs and the shore meet, the ground is black and merges with the water, making it look like ink has spilled around the island's base and is bleeding into the ocean. Smaller islands trail out from the main island, separated by thin channels of dark water. Gnarled, stunted vegetation—small blurs of dull green— shoot out of cracks in the cliff. A steep pathway switches back and forth up the stone cliff face before disappearing into a wide, jagged split in the rock. It is the only sign of civilization.

I take the telescope from my eye, and the sharp details of Draykioch shrink. The ship is a good mile from shore, anchored a mere stone's throw from a massive coral reef that surrounds the whole island as far as I can see from my perch in the crow's nest.

The water is crystal clear here, as pristine and flawless as the finest glass windows in my mother's castle, making the coral reef starkly visible. All around the reef sit the sunken remains of hundreds of ships. I am floating above a ship graveyard, and I can't help but wonder if the ship beneath my feet will be the next addition.

I climb down from the crow's nest, careful to stay wide of Princess Yassim, who is still tied to the mast, and Yerengul, who is smiling and telling her about his horses while he smooths salve on her rope burns for the second time this morning. Golmarr is at the helm, his hands resting on the ship's wheel, staring at the island, and Yeb is at his side, his attention focused on the sunken ships that have been smashed against the reef.

"Does anyone *live* on Draykioch?" I ask.

"No one knows," Golmarr says. "No one has returned from Draykioch to tell."

Yeb turns to me, his pale eyes heavy with worry. "I believe the island was once populated, but that was hundreds of years ago. No one has been on the island for as long as I have been alive, so no one knows if there is life on it aside from the gulls." He points up, and I look at the few white birds flapping through the air.

"Can we take the rowboat over the reef?" I ask.

Yeb shakes his head. "Do you see how, when the waves dip down, the reef juts out of the water in places?"

I nod.

"The boat will get stuck or shattered there, and then anyone left on ship will be as good as dead if we sink. You do know that, thanks to the sea serpent, the waters around Draykioch are known to devour ships?" He waves toward the glassy water and the underbelly of a massive ship not far below its surface.

"I have heard," I say.

"What about right there?" Golmarr asks, pointing to a

narrow gap in the reef where the waves don't splash up against it and break, but roll into the calm bay surrounding the island.

After a moment, Yeb shakes his head. "Even the best sailors would be hard-pressed to sail a *tiny* boat through something so narrow. My boat is built to hold twelve."

"I could swim it." I remember the feel of swimming in the fire dragon's lake. "It is far, but I don't think it is *too* far."

Golmarr's hand finds the small of my back, his touch both reassuring and a bitter reminder of the scales growing there. "I will swim it with you."

Enzio steps up beside me, the smell of metal residue from the anchor wafting off him. "I cannot swim, Sorrowlynn, and if I do not go with you, who is going to protect you from . . ." His eyes dart to Golmarr.

"I can swim it," Yerengul calls from the mast, where he is taking his sweet time to bandage Yassim's ankles.

Jessen leans his elbows on the railing and studies the gap in the reef. "So can I."

I look askance at my father. "Satari do not learn to swim because we are forest dwellers; otherwise I would not leave your side," he says, with a sad smile. "But we make good pirates." He pats his short sword. "I will stay aboard with Enzio and make sure the Ilaadi do not regain the ship."

"What about me?" Nayadi croaks, hobbling toward us. "Aren't you going to ask if I can swim?"

I bite my bottom lip to keep from laughing, and then with a straight face ask, "Nayadi, can you swim?"

She starts cackling and lifts her skirt, showing legs that are thinner than my wrists and bend outward at the knees. Thick blue veins bulge beneath her pale skin, and her toenails are so long they curl down and touch the deck like blunt, yellow claws. "What a senseless question to ask someone as old as me," she says, her voice bubbling with amusement. "I swam in my youth, but many have been the years since this old body has attempted such a feat. I was born more than one century ago."

A growl draws our attention to Princess Yassim, still tied to the mast. "You are going to take the fiercest fighters and leave me with the Satari forest dwellers, my ancient uncle, and an old witch? And what do we do if the ocean opens up and swallows us while you are gone?" She gives one dramatic tug to her bound hands. "We will not have enough men to man the ship!"

"I will stay behind if it puts you at ease," Jessen says.

The princess visibly relaxes. "Thank you, Prince Jessen," she says, and as far as I can tell, her voice truly holds gratitude.

"I have two cork vests in the cargo bay. They will not help much if you do not know how to swim, but if you do, they keep you above water," Yeb says.

"I know where they are. I will get them," my father says. He hurries belowdecks and returns a moment later with two tan bundles that look more like a jumble of wooden blocks sewn together than clothing. My father passes one to Golmarr and then holds the other one out for me to put my arms through. I slide the vest on and my father ties it closed. The cork blocks are awkward, making it impossible for me to put my arms down flat at my sides. Golmarr ties his closed and shrugs his shoulders a couple of times, testing the weight of the cork garment.

"I think it would be easier to swim to shore without this." I lift my hands to untie it, but a high-pitched scream fills the air, jolting my fingers to a dead stop.

Princess Yassim is motioning up at the sky with her tied hands. Yerengul follows the direction of her gaze and draws his sword. My blood runs cold as I search the dawn sky, for I already know what they have seen. A dark spot flaws the pristine blue, dipping and jerking with every flap of its wings. I don't need to see the creature up close to know the two-headed dragon has finally caught up to us.

Somehow, I am holding the reforged sword, though I do not recall drawing it. I turn to Golmarr. "You have been trained to fight them. What do we do? How can we fight something like that from the deck of a ship?"

"You cannot," Yeb says, his voice hollow with defeat as if now, finally, he has realized there is no hope his ship will ever sail away from Draykioch. "A creature that size will snap the masts like twigs and break the ship in two with one swing of its tail."

I tighten my grip on the sword. "I am not ready to give up hope. What do we do?" I ask Golmarr, but his eyes have glazed over. I grip his cork vest and give him a fierce shake. "It is going to attack us! *What do we do?*"

His attention turns to the sword in my hand, and he backs a step away as his eyes fill with panic. "I don't know what to do! I've never learned how to fight a dragon when I am confined on a *boat*!"

"But you have been trained to fight them since you were old enough to wield a weapon," I say, and hold the sword forward. He clasps his hands behind his back and fervently shakes his head. "You do not want the sword?" I ask, when really I am hoping he will take it from my hands and lift the burden of fighting the dragon. "Please fight the dragon, Golmarr."

He closes his eyes and swallows. And then he reaches for the sword. "For you, I will do it."

I take a deep breath and place the sword into his hand. "Thank you," I whisper. His fingers wrap around the hilt, and they are a perfect fit. Without a word, he crosses the ship's deck and climbs onto the railing, staring down at the still water.

"Enzio, give me your sword!" I say. Enzio slides his short sword from his belt and hands it to me. My bare feet thump on the wood as I run to catch up with Golmarr. He looks down at me, and fear darkens his eyes, but he is standing firm and sure, his head held high. I start climbing up beside him, and he asks, "What are you doing?"

"Just because *you* are wielding the reforged sword does not mean I will not fight at your side," I say. With those words, he seems to stand even taller than before, as if my presence lends him physical strength.

"Now I am the one who owes you thanks." He leans close so our shoulders are touching and points at the approaching beast. "This dragon is unbalanced because of its unsymmetrical wings and wounded tail. The left side of its body—the side with the feathers—is more powerful than the right, so we could attack the weaker right side and try to kill it ourselves, or aim for its stronger left side and weaken it. If we can weaken the left side, the right will be nearly useless, and it might drown. If it drowns, hopefully we won't inherit its treasure. What do you think?"

"Let it drown, if possible. I don't know what its treasure is, but I don't want it."

"Agreed. But we also need to stop its lightning somehow,

or dive deep below the water's surface when the lightning strikes. Have you ever seen lightning hit the ocean?"

"No."

"The energy stays on the surface. So if the ugly head draws back, it is going to shoot lightning. There is a problem, though."

I look at Golmarr like he might be crazy. "You mean a problem *besides* a two-headed dragon about to attack, with us stuck on a pile of fragile logs floating in serpent-infested waters?"

Lowering his voice, he says, "We have to lure it away from the ship so that everyone who survives the attack will have a chance of sailing home. Plus, if we fight it in the water, we have eliminated one of its strengths: its use of water as a weapon."

I peer down at the ocean, at the fleet of a thousand ships sunken beneath its surface. "You want me to jump into the *water* to fight the dragon? What about the sea serpent?" I ask, voice on the verge of hysteria.

Golmarr shrugs and glares. "You know infinitely more than me! Do you have a better idea? You're a strong swimmer. So am I. If we don't get off this ship, they all die." He nods his head backward, at Enzio and my father, his brothers, Nayadi, and the Ilaadi. "If we jump into the water to fight, *our* odds of dying don't change at this point."

The dragon is so close, I can see the sun reflecting off its scales and purple feathers, see the bones through the taut skin on its ugly wing, and see the black scab on the end of its severed tail.

"Here's the thing," Golmarr says, speaking quickly. "I have been thinking nonstop how to defeat a dragon if it tried to attack us on a ship. If the dragon is smart, the first thing it will do is destroy the ship, and chances are, everyone on it will be crushed at the same time. *You* are the one this hideous beast is coming for. If you are already in the water, it might leave the ship alone." Golmarr holds his hand out to me. "Come on, Sorrowlynn. I *know* we can do this!"

"Promise?"

He nods and flashes his beautiful, heart-stopping smile. "I promise."

My knees threaten to buckle, so I put my hand into his, and together, we leap off the side of the ship.

Water fills my ears and stings my open eyes, and something big and black and snakelike moves in the water below. Before I have time to get a good look at it, the cork vest pulls me up to the surface. I whip the hair out of my eyes. Golmarr surfaces beside me and looks up at the sky.

"Did you see that?" I splutter, treading water.

"What?" he asks, eyes begging me not to give him bad news.

"The sea serpent is in the water with us." I point in the direction of the thing I saw, and Golmarr dives. I fill my lungs and follow, struggling against the vest to stay underwater. Colorful fish dart about, weaving in and out of the ship graveyard, but nothing else moves.

Golmarr and I emerge at the same time. "I didn't see anything," he says.

"I promise it was there."

"I believe you, Sorrowlynn, but we have to put some distance between us and the Ilaadi ship." He starts paddling away from the boat and I follow.

"How do we dive below the water's surface, deep enough to avoid lightning, if we are wearing these vests?" I ask. Golmarr curses and then reaches for me, quickly untying the strings.

"Just keep one arm looped through it. If you have to dive, pull your arm out."

I am about to tell him there is no way we can possibly survive this fight when the ocean starts pulling me away from the boat. Ahead, the water is moving in a slow, lazy circle that gets tighter and faster toward its center, until it is a tight funnel sucking everything caught in the spiral under the water. I try and swim out of the whirlpool just as Golmarr yells, "Lightning! Dive!"

He grips the crown of my head and shoves me under, hard. Water fills my nose and pours into my open mouth. Before I can slip my arm from the cork vest, the ocean seems to wrap around me, dragging me downward so hard and fast my ears pop. Above, the surface flashes with blue light that illuminates the sunken ships and saturates the water's surface with an energy that vibrates against my skin. When the water has darkened to its normal color, Golmarr grabs my vest, pulling me back up.

Golmarr and I break the surface together, and I gag and cough and blow water out my nose. The ocean is still—no more whirlpool. "The ocean dragged us down," I splutter. "I didn't have to take off my vest."

"I know, but we can't worry about the ocean right now. Never take your eyes off your opponent," Golmarr orders, glaring up at the sky. "Look!" I look up and see the two-headed dragon framed by bright sky. It is hovering above us, its wings flapping.

*I told you sneaking wouldn't work,* a deep female voice whispers in my head. *We should have eaten them while the girl wasn't paying attention. Once again, you have ruined everything.* The words are accompanied by a rush of bitter hatred. The feathered dragon slams her head into the ugly dragon.

Golmarr frowns and shakes his head. "I can hear them again," he whispers.

"So can I."

*You are the one who ruins everything! It is your fault we are like this!* another voice wails, and the ugly dragon snaps a mouthful of feathers from the other's neck.

The feathered dragon hisses. *I will never be as ugly as you, no matter how you tear my feathers. Save your bouts of temper for the girl, sister. Look! She is drawing the sword that severed our tail.*

They are right that I am drawing a sword, but it is not the reforged sword. "They are focused entirely on you," Golmarr says, holding the reforged sword under the water. "Raise the sword and try to draw them down to the water, and I will attempt to wound them." Lifting Enzio's sword from the water, I wave it from side to side.

"Right before it attacks, dive under the water," Golmarr instructs. "When they hit the water's surface, go deep. I will use the reforged sword to—" His words are cut short, and we both look away from the dragon and stare at the ocean. The water is suctioning us again, pulling us in a tight circle toward a roiling center. I kick my legs and use my free arm to paddle out of the current, but the water is immeasurably stronger than I.

"Stop paddling and focus on your opponent," Golmarr calls above the sucking, hissing sound of the growing whirlpool.

With my eyes glued to the two-headed dragon, I give in to the spinning water and keep my gaze focused on the beast.

Look! Cackling laughter fills my head. Even the ocean wants her dead.

Wait until she is being sucked into the vortex before you pluck her out and eat her, then I will eat the beautiful boy at the same time.

I think we should eat them now. Or I can use my lightning again.

"They're going to use lightning again," I say, and both dragons shriek.

She has been listening, sister! the pretty dragon says. The ugly one lurches toward us, yanking them closer to the water, but the pretty one slams her head into her sister again. Wait, you fool. They are almost trapped in the center of the funnel. She will not be able to use her sword if she is being sucked underwater.

"They are waiting until we are in the vortex to attack," I say as we are rushing toward the whirlpool's center.

"I know. I can hear them, too," Golmarr says. The dragon is still hovering out of reach, waiting. When we enter the edge of the vortex—where the water grows white and foamy—I take a deep breath and tighten my hand on Enzio's sword, prepared to be sucked down into the depths of the ocean or fight the creature. The moment the water begins to drag me downward, the spinning stops and the ocean turns as smooth and silent as glass. And then the two-headed dragon dives for us.

Before I have a chance to plunge beneath the ocean, a black mass of scales, claws, and fins shoots out of the water.

# Chapter 27

Sunlight gleams off a wingless black dragon as it streaks straight up, its long, narrow body dividing the sky in two. It collides with the two-headed dragon and clamps its mouth on one of the dragon's necks—the beautiful purple-feathered one—dragging the beast down through the air. They hit the water with so much force, a wave surges up around them, washing me toward the boat.

Help me, sister! Bite him!

Gladly!

I stare in horror at the writhing, twisting mass of two bodies—one black, one purple and gray. They fight and writhe, and then plunge beneath the ocean. The force of their movement agitates the water until it looks like it is boiling.

I quickly slide my sword arm out of the vest in case I need to dive. Golmarr slowly starts paddling toward the mass, sword ready, but I stop him. "You will get killed in there."

So we wait, and the water around us slowly turns from blue to pink to red, until it is as if I am treading blood, and all the while I can hear the wailing and snarling of the two sisters in my head. Somehow, the water wraps around Golmarr and me again and starts carrying us toward the boat as the ball of dragons twists in the water, surges above its surface, and then sinks below. Feathers tinged with blood float to the surface, and the red keeps spreading until the entire ocean looks made of blood.

I need air! the ugly dragon wails. I am dying!

**We have to get away, sister! We have to work together. If we both bite his neck, we can suffocate him.** Not taking my eyes from the roiling water, I paddle backward, putting as much distance between myself and the dragons as I can. And then, as if the dragons wink out of existence, the water becomes tranquil. A few bubbles rise to the surface and pop, but nothing more.

Golmarr and I look at each other. I stop paddling and grip Enzio's sword tighter, watching the ocean, waiting. A ripple shudders across the surface. In a spray of red, the two-headed dragon shoots up out of the water and opens its ugly, unsymmetrical wings. Soggy feathers fall from its body in clumps, revealing scales that have been torn and are dangling from its flesh. The air catches in the beast's wings, and bloody water sloughs from its body and lands in giant drops in the ocean. The hideous creature pulls itself higher into the air and both of its heads whip around. Two sets of eyes focus on me.

Let us eat her now! I need the sustenance!

**Yes! I will eat her legs; you eat her head and torso!**

The dragon yanks its wings flush against its body and dives, crashing into the water right in front of me, and I am blinded by the slap of spray. I plunge into the roiling white wave and shake the vest from my arm, letting the weight of Enzio's sword carry me deeper as two sets of teeth snap the water at my feet. Golmarr dives, shooting through the water until he is below the beast. With both his hands wrapped around the reforged sword hilt, he thrusts it up against the wide, smooth belly scales of the two-headed dragon until it is buried to the cross guard. When he pulls the sword free, a fresh cloud of red follows.

The dragon spirals in the water, the force pushing me so hard I sink all the way to the ocean floor. And then I am sitting between two sunken ships, staring up through the red water as Golmarr dives and plunges his sword into the creature's shoulder.

My lungs are burning for a breath of air, so I dig my feet into the black rocks and push upward, but I can hardly swim and hold the heavy sword. I try again, kicking against the water, but sink back down. Just as I decide I have to drop the sword if I want to live, the sea serpent slithers out from between the two ships. A squeak of surprise leaves my mouth and bubbles up to the surface as the serpent coils around me, pressing my arms tight to my body. With one powerful squeeze, the serpent could crush me, and no matter how I squirm, I cannot loosen its hold. But instead of squeezing, it puts a thought in my head: **Peace, child. I am here to help you.** The creature lifts me to the water's surface and then unwinds its body from mine and slithers back under the sea. I gasp for air and Golmarr paddles to my side. He presses a cork vest into my free hand.

The two-headed dragon, far out of reach and sitting atop the sea like a bird, spreads its wings and drags its body out of the water. As it starts to fly away, the black dragon shoots straight up into the sky like an arrow springing from a bow, aimed at the two-headed monstrosity. The sea serpent opens its mouth and snaps its teeth closed on a feathered wing, but a bolt of lightning shoots from the ugly dragon's mouth.

Blue energy wraps around the sea serpent, hissing and popping against the creature's flesh. The black beast releases the feathered wing and writhes as it falls back toward the ocean, the side of its long body slapping the water. It slowly sinks below the bloody depths of the sea. The two-headed dragon is bobbing and weaving through the air, raining blood into the ocean as it flies toward Draykioch. Slowly, the water becomes as still as red glass.

Golmarr peers into my eyes, but I hardly see him. "Sorrowlynn, are you okay?" When I don't respond, he wraps his arm around my shoulders, holding the back of my body against the front of his, and starts swimming us toward the ship. After a moment, I untangle myself from his arm and swim beside him, paddling through the silent red sea.

When we reach the ship, a rope ladder is dropped over the side. As I step onto the deck, Enzio's sword falls from my fingers and thumps against the wood, followed by the cork vest. My father grabs me, pulling me so tight against him I do not have to try to stand on my weak legs.

Water is trickling in streams down my face, my sleeves, my pants. A pool of pink is growing around my feet and merging with the pool forming around Golmarr. Everyone is frozen in place, staring as we drip on the deck. After a long moment of stunned faces and uncomfortable silence, my father says, "Well? Don't you have anything to say to them? They just saved all of our lives!"

Golmarr's brothers both touch their foreheads with one finger, then fist their hands and cross their wrists in front of their chests: honored warrior. They are saluting us.

Captain Yeb presses a fist to his heart and bows. "Thank you, Prince Golmarr and Princess Sorrowlynn," he says. "For my niece's life and my ship, I thank you." Too tired to speak, I nod.

My father guides me toward the ship's helm, carrying the majority of my weight. Every step I take, Yassim's pale gaze follows. When I have walked past her, she calls out, "Wait!"

I stop and face Yassim.

"The dragons fear you and Golmarr." Her eyes move to his sword. "What is that weapon?"

Golmarr answers, "It is the reforged sword, heated by dragon fire until all the impurities were burned from the steel."

"Please come to Ilaad with me and fight the sandworm," she says, her voice trembling.

Her words stun me, and I do not know what to say. Before I fought the dragon, I was her enemy. Now she is pleading with me to come to Ilaad. Yassim falls to her knees, her hands still tied to the mast. Eyes brimming with tears, she says, "If the two of you will help me fight the sandworm, I will give you more gold than you can spend in a lifetime. Please! He is ravaging my people!"

I open my mouth to tell her I do not require gold in exchange for fighting the worm, but Golmarr shakes his head the slightest bit and touches his throat, the horse clan's hand signal for *Let me speak*. To Yassim, he says, "Sorrowlynn is a princess of Faodara, and I am an Antharian prince. We are not mercenaries. We do not fight for pay, Yassim."

Tears stream down Yassim's face. "Please! I will give you anything you ask for."

"Anything?"

Yassim nods. "Anything."

"Peace," Golmarr says.

Yassim tilts her head and frowns. "Our people are at peace with Faodara, and we have not had any disagreements with the horse lords for nearly thirty years."

"Peace with Faodara and Anthar are definitely part of the bargain I am striking, as well as peace with Satar. But I ask for peace with Trevon also." His words send a shiver of recognition through me as I see yet another piece of Melchior's puzzle fitting into place.

Anger darkens Yassim's eyes and she climbs back to her feet. She swipes the tears from her cheeks. "No."

A small smile quirks the sides of Golmarr's mouth. "Let me know when you change your mind," he says.

Captain Yeb steps up beside me, so close I smell eel on his breath and sweat on his clothes. "Are you still planning on swimming to the island?"

"Yes," I say.

"Come here." I follow him to the helm. Yeb points south. "Do you see how the water is mostly moving into the bay?"

I study the pattern of the surging waves and nod.

"I recommend you leave now. The tide is rolling in. It will pull you to the island. But if you try to swim from the land to my ship while the tide is still moving in, you will not be able to make it back. You must wait until sunset, when the tide starts moving back out, before you swim to the boat." He looks me right in the eyes. "Do you understand?"

"I understand."

Behind me, I hear the quiet slap of wet feet on wood and without looking know that it is Golmarr. He stops at my side, and he is holding a large, waterproof sack in one hand and his staff in the other. The reforged sword is sheathed at his waist.

"Your father has packed supplies for us—food, water, our boots."

A sudden image of soft sand pathways and bare feet enters my head. "I don't think we will need the boots," I say.

A hint of a smile graces Golmarr's mouth. "You just saw something, didn't you?"

I nod. "Melchior has been here before . . . only I don't remember black beaches."

"Sorrowlynn says we don't need boots," Golmarr calls to Yerengul, and the certainty in his voice, the utter and complete faith he has in me and what I just saw, makes me want to kiss him full on the mouth, right here in front of everyone.

Yerengul looks from Golmarr to me, and then back at his brother. "I'm taking mine anyway."

"Suit yourself," Golmarr says as he pulls my boots and his from the sack and tosses them onto the deck. He holds the staff out to me. "Since I am carrying the sword, I thought you would like the staff." I take it from him and cannot contain my emotions at having the burden of his sword lifted from me, and the burning love I have for him for taking it. Leaning forward, I press a quick kiss to his lips despite the fact that every person on the ship is probably watching us. When I pull away, he stumbles forward.

"Thank you," I say, taking the staff.

I walk to the starboard bow and climb up onto the railing. Golmarr climbs up beside me. We look at each other, and then Golmarr loops his fingers through mine and gives them a quick squeeze. Leaning close, he presses his lips to my cheek and whispers, "I love you." My heart starts zooming beneath my ribs, but before I can respond, he releases my hand and dives into the water.

# Chapter 28

Water splashes around me and then sucks me into its depths. I stare through the pink tinge, down to the ocean's sandy bottom and our ship's anchor settled upon it. The sand is gray here, and the sunlight shines on it in perpetually moving ribbons of light. I arch my body and pull myself to the water's surface, and emerge beside Golmarr. Yerengul, wearing a cork vest, jumps feetfirst into the water, making a massive splash and surfacing a moment later with his long hair matted to the sides of his face.

Small waves roll around us, lifting me and dropping me, pushing me gently toward the reef. I turn onto my side and use the pull of the water to propel myself toward the reef's narrow opening. With very little effort, I am sucked through the small break and spit out into the calmer water of the bay. Golmarr follows, but Yerengul bumps up against the reef, curses, and goes under.

Golmarr starts swimming toward his brother—sure, strong strokes even with our supply bags held in one hand—but the tide fights against him, holding him in place. A darkness swims toward us, and then Yerengul's head breaks the surface, his hair fanning out around his shoulders like tentacles. He coughs and wipes water from his eyes. "The water looked a lot calmer from the boat," he says, glaring accusations at the ocean.

Golmarr glowers at him. "I thought you said you could swim to the island."

Yerengul starts swimming, paddling at the water like a dog. "I can swim," he calls.

Just like Captain Yeb said, the tide is moving toward the land and pulling us in with it. Even holding the staff, it takes me only a moment to pass Yerengul and Golmarr, my body slipping and gliding through the water like a fish's. Before long, my feet touch the ocean floor, but it is not the soft, silky sand from Melchior's memories. I am standing on gravel as black as coal.

I pause and let the water surge to shore around my waist as I study Draykioch. It is exactly the same as in my dreams. The gravel shore is so black, it seems to repel the sunlight, throwing it back into the air. The beach is wide, stretching to the base of the cliff, which juts up white and pristine.

I dig my feet into the gravel and slosh out of the water, tossing my staff higher up onto the beach. My tunic and leggings suction to me, and I am grateful for the high quality of the fabric—it is not see-through. Still, as Golmarr splashes his way to me, his gaze clings to my figure just as tightly as my clothing. The intent, focused expression on his face makes my heart start to pound.

Without slowing his pace, he unties the laces at the neck of his tunic and pulls it over his head, flinging it up onto the dry black gravel. Now it is my gaze suctioned to him and the way the sunlight reflects off his dripping skin and the midnight dark scales that curl around his shoulder and dip halfway down his arm. "Yerengul is going to see your scales," I say.

"It is time he knows the truth." Golmarr strides straight to me, tossing our supplies to the ground. "I have been waiting to do this since the moment you woke up from being poisoned," he whispers, and frames my face with his hands. He tilts my chin up and our eyes meet. His eyes flutter shut as his lips find mine, and they are soft and gentle and warm despite the water dripping down our faces. I taste the salt water from our lips, and even soaking wet, his suntanned chest is warm beneath my fingers. Sliding my hand over scales, my fingertips explore them, memorizing their feel.

Golmarr's hands leave my face and find my hips, slipping under the hem of my tunic and coming to rest on the small of my back, right over my scales. He pulls me closer, eliminating every bit of space between us, and the warmth from his bare chest leaches through my soaked shirt. I wrap my arms around his neck and grab a handful of his hair.

"By the way you're kissing her, I can only assume you thought it would take me at least a few more minutes to swim to shore," Yerengul blurts.

Golmarr's lips smile against mine and he slides his hands out from under my tunic. Stepping away, he calls, "I figured I'd take advantage of your mediocre swimming skills."

Yerengul laughs and pulls off his tunic, tossing it to the black beach beside Golmarr's. "That was some kiss, brother. You had *me* blushing."

My cheeks flame, and Golmarr laughs. "Don't play innocent. You're the one who showed me the place in the barn where we could spy on Jessen and Shay when they snuck away to steal kisses."

"That was ten years ago! You still remember that?"

"Who is Shay?" I ask. I have never seen Jessen with a woman before.

The smile drops from Yerengul's face. "Shay was Jessen's wife. She died in battle four years ago."

Golmarr solemnly adds, "That was the last battle Treyose led against us. He quit fighting after he killed Shay—not because they were losing, but because he'd killed a woman. Another man's *wife*. Treyose's own wife died when he returned home."

A thorn of sorrow twists in my heart, and the scales on my back seem to dig into my skin. I wince and press on them. They are firm and hard, yet nearly as supple as my skin.

"Are you all right?" Golmarr asks, his face so worried I can't help but smile.

"I'm fine, I just—"

"What has suctioned itself to your chest, little brother?" Yerengul blurts. He steps between Golmarr and me and tries to swipe Golmarr's scales off his skin. When they don't budge, Yerengul shudders and leans in for a closer look. "Those look like—"

"I'm growing scales," Golmarr says. "I think I may be turning into a dragon."

Yerengul slowly draws his hand away from Golmarr. "What do you mean *you may be turning into a dragon?*" he asks, his eyes tight with a fear I have never seen in them before, not even when we rode out to battle mercenaries and the glass dragon.

"I'm growing scales," Golmarr snaps. "What else *could* it mean?"

Yerengul shakes his head and twists his long, drenched hair around his hand, wringing the water out. "Dragons are evil, inhuman monsters. You can't be *turning into* one. It isn't possible."

"Then you tell me what these mean," Golmarr says, pointing at the scales.

Yerengul grimaces and rubs his forehead. "Does Father know?"

Golmarr shakes his head. "They started growing after I left, after I killed the glass dragon and tried to kill Sorrowlynn." Leaning close to me, he quietly asks, "Will you show him the scar on your shoulder?"

I unlace my yellow tunic and slide the soaked garment from my left shoulder, exposing the puckered scar where Golmarr's sword stabbed me. Golmarr moves directly beside me, so we are lined up shoulder to shoulder. "This"—he points at the exact spot on his shoulder where I have a scar—"is the very first spot I got scales. They started out tiny, a patch as long and wide as my finger—the same shape and size as Sorrowlynn's scar. Now they won't stop spreading."

He turns around, showing us his back, and I cover my mouth with my hand to stifle a gasp of shock. The scales have spread from his shoulder and arm down to the hollow dip between his shoulder blades. "Try cutting them," Golmarr says. Yerengul removes a knife from his belt and scratches the tip on one of Golmarr's scales.

Yerengul's eyebrows shoot up. "Not even a mark."

Golmarr nods. "King Vaunn tried to skewer me. His blade hit me with enough force to impale me, but it slid off the scales. There was a shallow wound here . . ." He touches the top of his shoulder. "But my scales have grown over it. They deflected his sword like armor."

Yerengul grunts and nods approval. "So they're not all bad. Wait . . ." He glares. "King Vaunn tried to *kill* you?"

"He did."

"Why?"

Golmarr's eyes flash with fury. "Because I am Antharian, and he was close enough to reach me with his sword."

Yerengul laughs a cynical laugh. "That's all? You didn't provoke him? Insult his manhood or tell him that all Trevonan women look like swine? Boast about your sword-fighting skills until he wanted to kill you just to shut you up?"

Golmarr throws his hand up into the air. "My own brother, and you have so little faith in me!"

Yerengul flicks Golmarr's scales. "That's because I have known you your whole life. You have no idea how many times I have fantasized about finding a way to shut you up when you start to brag."

"I did *nothing* to provoke him—my only weapon was a staff. He tried to kill me for the simple fact that I am Antharian." Golmarr's eyes smolder with the memory. "King Vaunn's hatred for our people ran deep." He glances at me and adds, "Sorrowlynn killed him before he got a second chance at taking my life."

Yerengul's eyes slip shut for a moment as everything Golmarr told him sinks in. When he opens them, his gaze is focused on me. "Thank you," he says quietly. "If King Vaunn had killed Golmarr, it would have destroyed our father. He has lost five sons, and the grief takes more of a toll each time."

I put my hand on Golmarr's arm. "Five sons? Five of your brothers have died?"

Golmarr, his eyes heavy with sorrow, nods. "Five of my brothers have died."

"You mean, there used to be more than 'the nine sons of King Marrkul'?"

"Thirteen sons of Marrkul," Golmarr whispers. "Now eight." He looks down. His black lashes have fresh droplets of water in them.

Wrapping my arms around Golmarr, I lay my head against his chest. His hand comes up, palm over my ear, and he holds me to him, resting his cheek on the crown of my head. Yerengul clears his throat and walks away, giving us a bit of privacy.

The water dries on my skin, and still Golmarr holds me. The top of my damp head begins to warm from Golmarr's skin pressing against it, and still he holds me. Finally, his arms grow slack, and he lifts his face from my head and releases me.

"Thank you," he says, caressing my cheek with the back of his hand. He smiles despite the grief still in his eyes. Every muscle in my body starts to quiver as I am filled with an overflowing emotion I am growing more and more familiar with: *love*.

"I love you, Golmarr," I say.

He leans his forehead against mine. "I love you, too. I love you so much, it tears me up inside sometimes." He kisses me again. "It also makes me want to spend the entire day alone on this beach with you in my arms." He takes a step away. "But we have more important things to do right now. Let's go find this woman from your dreams and see what we can learn about our scales and the dragons' curses."

I turn and see Yerengul a little way down the beach, sitting with his back to us. Golmarr calls out to him, and his brother slowly gets to his feet. He has put his tunic back on, and his black leather boots are on and laced.

"Are we ready to go and see what this island is hiding?" Yerengul asks.

Golmarr gets his wet tunic from where he tossed it and pulls it on. He hands me my staff. "We are ready," he says.

# Chapter 29

The black gravel is perfect oval pebbles roughly the size of my thumbnail, just like in my visions. They look eerily similar to Golmarr's scales. As we walk up the beach, the pebbles slowly merge with silky white sand. When we pass the tide line, there is only sand. It is so fine, I hardly feel it beneath my bare feet. The sand comes to an abrupt end at the base of a gleaming white cliff, and we start making our way up a slender path that leads to a narrow fissure.

When we reach the fissure, my companions and I stop, and Yerengul and Golmarr draw their weapons. "I will go first. Wait here until I signal you to come in," Yerengul says, and steps into the narrow slot cut deep into the cliff. He is swallowed by shadows, and my heart starts hammering. "Wow. You have got to come and see this!" he calls.

I step into the shadow of the stone cleft, take five steps, and emerge into sunshine. I am standing above a valley shaped like a bowl. Nestled in the bowl is a small city made of white clay houses and buildings. None of the visible structures have doors, and those closest to us are hardly bigger than a Faodarian peasant's meager one-room dwelling. The structures are larger farther in, with those in the center of the city rising two stories into the air. The air is free of wood smoke and devoid of any human noises. Even the sandy path leading into the valley is perfectly smooth, not a single footprint marking it.

A breeze whistles through the valley and something rings out. Three strands of small blue shells have been hung from a bigger shell and nailed to the side of one of the buildings. When the wind blows, they sway into each other and make simple, rustic music. I have heard that wind chime many times before. I mean, Melchior has.

"Look at that." Golmarr points toward the very center of the city, to a building taller than any of the others, with gleaming white columns in front of it.

"What is this place?" Yerengul quietly asks, wary eyes scanning the silent, doorless building closest to us. "I do not feel good about this."

"Let's look in one of the buildings," Golmarr suggests. He ducks into the nearest structure, a small, one-story shack. Yerengul and I follow.

My eyes take a moment to adjust to the building's shadowed interior. It is cool inside, and even with no door and several small windows, darkness seems to permeate the air.

The first room has a sand-covered tile floor and nothing else. Yerengul's boots make hollow thuds as we cross the room to a hall with a door on either side. The room on the left is tiny, and holds the remains of a pallet and a rotting blanket. The room on the right makes me pause. There is a pallet on the floor, just like the other room, but there is a giant, spiraled horn nailed to the wall above the pallet.

"What is that?" I ask.

"A narwhal tusk," Golmarr says, rubbing his thumb across it. "Whoever put this here took the time to polish it."

"I wonder what happened to him."

Golmarr shudders, and I have the sinking feeling that it has nothing to do with his damp clothing. "I am worried we are going to find out."

We leave the building and continue downhill, deeper into the maze of square white structures and pristine, untouched sand trails. We pass from small structures to bigger, fancier buildings. Some of the doorways here have doors attached, and several windows have glass panes in them. The crumbling remains of knee-high stone fences separate the buildings, and more wind chimes hang here—the only sound on the island attesting to the fact that it was once inhabited.

"Let's go inside that one," Golmarr says, pointing to the biggest structure yet. It has a closed front door and glass window panes, and three shell wind chimes have been hung from the roof. Drapes hang in one of the windows, and some shattered pottery litters a tiled front porch.

The door's rusted hinges squeal in protest as Golmarr pushes it open. He and Yerengul share a look and then step through the door ahead of me. I tighten my hand on the staff, grateful for the familiar weapon as I step into the dim light.

The first room contains broken, faded chairs and the ragged remains of a rug on the sandy tile floor. Drapes framing a dingy window flutter as we walk past and cross into a kitchen. Pottery sits whole on a shelf above a small stove. A solid wood table is centered in the room, with clay plates and cups still on it, as if someone left in the middle of a meal and never came back. The food, if there ever was any, is long gone and replaced with a fine dusting of sand.

Next, we ascend a wooden staircase that moans and creaks beneath our feet. At the top of the stairs are three shut doors. Golmarr and Yerengul each take a door on the left, and I open the only door on the right.

Sunlight slants into the room through a glass window, illuminating a small bed with faded blankets on it. There are two small bulges in the bed, so I step closer for a better look. Beneath my bare foot, something crunches. I look down and my heart leaps into my throat. I am standing on a skeletal human arm connected to hand bones, stark white against the dusty wood floor. Slowly, I lift my foot and take a step away from the bones. With a trembling hand, I pull the blankets away from the bed and stumble backward. The empty eye sockets of two small human skulls are staring up at the ceiling.

"Get out! Now!" a deep voice yells.

Feet thump in the hall outside the room. Golmarr slams the door of the room I am in against the wall, shattering it into a hundred fragile pieces of wood that scatter across the floor. He runs to my side, grips my wrist with his long fingers, and pulls me out into the hall. I take one more look at the two child-sized skeletons tucked lovingly beneath the blankets, and my blood runs cold.

"Something killed them all!" Golmarr says as we sprint down the stairs and out the front door.

Yerengul is already outside, his face ashen and covered with a sheen of sweat. "We need to get back to the ship and sail away from here *now*," Yerengul says, his nostrils flaring with his accelerated breathing. "Something is horribly wrong with this place!"

Anguish battles fear in Golmarr's eyes. He looks from his

brother deeper into the maze of buildings, and then rubs the patch of scales hidden beneath his shirt. "Not quite yet, Yerengul," Golmarr says. "Give me one hour to go to the building at the center of the city to try and find some answers."

Yerengul shudders and wipes his hands down the front of his damp tunic. "Golmarr, what if the whole island is contaminated with some kind of plague? Every bed was filled with skeletons. Even the baby cradle had a tiny skeleton in it! They're all dead! Everybody is dead! That's why this place is so quiet. It's a tomb. A forgotten graveyard. We need to get away from here! Sorrowlynn?" His dark eyes are pleading, begging me to tell his brother to leave. Golmarr looks at me, his pale eyes defiant, daring me to tell him to leave, warning me that he is going to do this thing even if I do not want him to. But I *do* want him to find the answers we need. I want *us* to find the answers.

"Please, just one hour," I say to Yerengul.

Yerengul groans. Golmarr steps up to his brother and puts his hand on his shoulder. "Sometimes there are things in life more important than life itself," Golmarr quietly says. "I need to find answers. Keep a lookout from here, or go back to the beach. Make sure nothing follows us in." Golmarr glances at the sun. "Besides, we can't swim back to the ship right now, not with the tide still moving in. Yeb said we won't be able to swim out to the boat until sunset."

Yerengul shakes his head, his face grim. "Fine. One hour. But I am not going a step farther. I will keep watch." He runs his hand down his face. "What have you gotten us into, little brother?"

Golmarr grins and gives Yerengul's shoulder a shake. "Just

think of the stories we'll be able to tell at the breakfast table when we return home. We've gone where no other horse lord has gone before. Our legend will live on forever."

Yerengul's mouth softens, almost into a smile. He gently shoves his brother away. "Go. Take your hour. I will not let anything come in after you."

Golmarr inclines his head. "Thank you." Yerengul and Golmarr clasp wrists, and then Golmarr turns to me. Together, he and I start walking deeper into the silent city.

# Chapter 30

The sand seems to soak up the sun's heat and reflect it back, making me grateful for my damp clothing as we walk deeper into the maze of buildings. "It's going to be hard to go back north after basking in the sun," I say, breathing in the balmy air.

"Do you want to know what I love about you?"

I peer sideways at Golmarr. "Yes?"

He looks around. "We are out here on this godforsaken, eerie, possibly deadly island, and you manage to find the one good thing about our situation." He turns his gaze to me. In the glaring light, the flaws in his face are more pronounced—a white scar on his temple, a slightly crooked tooth, several days' growth of black beard on his face, hair stiff and disheveled from drying salt water—and I love them all. "If we get off this island alive," he says, "I will be so glad to return to Anthar, I won't care if the weather is bitter cold." A roguish gleam enters his eyes, and a sly grin lifts the corners of his lips. "Do you know what I like about the cold?"

The way he is looking at me makes my heart start beating like I am training. "What?" I ask, mesmerized.

He takes a step closer and traces my jawline with his finger. "Wrapping myself around you to keep you warm."

My mouth drops open, and I step away from him. "You are absolutely scandalous, Golmarr! Are all Antharian men so bold?"

"No. You just had the good luck to fall in love with one who is." He grabs my hand, bringing it to his lips for a quick kiss. "Let's hurry and see if we can find your dream lady. The sooner we do, the sooner we leave. I am suddenly craving cold weather."

"And if there is no one here?" I ask.

"Then we look for the answers somewhere else. We sail with Yassim to Ilaad and kill the sandworm so we can cross the desert and search the abandoned library there."

---

My feet shuffle through the hot sand and I almost wish I'd brought boots. By the time we reach the center of the city, the staff has grown damp beneath my hand, and my clothes have dried. As we approach the pillared building, the ground dips steeply downward, as if the building is so massive, the very ground beneath it has sunk. Each step we take causes a small landslide of sand as we descend.

The building is spectacular, made of pristine white stone flecked with crystals that glitter in the sun. Ten shallow stairs span the front of it, and the number makes my head spin for a moment. Pain shoots between my ears and my skull feels like it is opening up. "Ten stairs. One for Relkinn, and nine for each person who took on Relkinn's burden," I say as my bare foot comes down on the bottom step.

"What does that mean?" Golmarr asks.

I press on the skin between my eyebrows, trying to push the pain out of my head. "I don't know what that means, but I remember the names that go with each step. One for Relkinn." I step onto the next step. "Two for Saphina. Three for Naphina." A revelation is thrust upon me with so much force, it feels like a knife is being twisted in my brain. I whimper and clasp my head with my hands, and the pain immediately stops, but not the knowledge that caused it.

Hands grip my shoulders. "Sorrowlynn, what's wrong?"

I swallow and look at Golmarr. "The two-headed dragon. That was Naphina and Saphina. The two sisters whose beauty outshone all others." I see their faces—*human* faces: skin as smooth and dark as black tea, hair the color of raven feathers, eyes like gold. "The only thing that shone brighter than their beauty was their intellect."

"They were human?" he asks.

"I think so," I say, and step up onto the fourth step. "Four for Feäd. Five for Grinndoar. Six for Mordecai. Seven for Moyana." The eighth step plunges us into the shadow of a stone overhang. The stair is cool beneath my foot. "Eight is Melchior the wizard. Nine is Corritha." Again, piercing knowledge assaults my brain as the face of a woman with gleaming red hair and green eyes is thrust upon me. "Corritha was the glass dragon," I whisper. Stepping up onto the final step, I say, "Ten for King Zhun, ruler of the entire land, from Faodara to the Antharian grasslands, to Trevon, to the Ilaadi desert, and even the icy north. King Zhun was not *named* after the fire dragon. He *was* the fire dragon. They were all human once, Golmarr."

We are standing before two massive stone doors that are cool to the touch and seem to make the air temperature drop. There are no handles, so I push the door on the right. It swings open slowly, like a great yawning beast. I start to step inside, but Golmarr stops me, putting himself in front of me and creeping silently forward. I open my mouth to protest but think better of it. Speaking would alert someone to our arrival—if anyone is here.

The inside of the building is more spectacular than the outside, with a glass roof overhead, making it as bright as the outside world. We are standing in a large, hexagon-shaped room. It is at least three stories tall. At the far end of the room is a staircase that leads forward, but halfway up, splits, going to the left and the right. At the top of the stairs is a balcony with a stone railing carved to look like mermaids holding bowls of water in their hands. The bowls connect to each other, joining the top railing.

I spin in a slow circle, taking in the enormity of the room. The floor—polished stone—is completely free of sand, save where my and Golmarr's feet have trod it in from outside. The six walls forming the room's hexagon shape have each been carved with pictures, and there is a crest above each picture. I gasp and point to the wall on my left. It has a carving of the wolf cliffs of Faodara, with the Faodarian griffin crest carved above it, like a sentinel keeping watch.

"Look at that," Golmarr whispers, and points to another wall and the picture carved into it—grass that appears to be waving in the wind. Above it is the ancient Antharian seal.

On the third wall is a carving of the building that houses the Royal Library of Trevon, with the Trevonan crest above it. The fourth wall depicts the sand dunes of Ilaad, the Ilaadi serpent crest above. On the fifth wall is a mountain with a city carved in its face, and a stone knife crest above it.

"The great mountain city of Satar," I say. "And look. The

sixth wall is the lost kingdom of Belldarr." A square castle with a mountain behind it is carved into the wall. Above is the Belldarrian crest: an eagle and a sword. Belldarr used to sit northwest of Anthar, at the base of the mountains, before King Vaunn conquered it and absorbed the land into Trevon. "What is this place?"

Golmarr raises his eyebrows. "I was hoping you could tell me. You don't know it? No knowledge of it stored in your brain? No dreams about it? Surely, Melchior has been here before."

I tilt my head back, taking in the beauty of the room and trying to recall any memories of it. My mind stays infuriatingly blank, as if everything inside it has been smothered. "There are *no* memories of this place."

"But you remember the stairs leading to it, and the name of each stair. There must be *something* you remember about it."

"I don't remember anything," I snap, frustration bleeding into my words. "It's like there is a wall in my head, and nothing is getting past it!"

"Hey." Golmarr steps in front of me and rests his free hand on my biceps. "No pressure, okay? Let's take a quick look around and see what we can find. Maybe see if we discover anything about the woman from your dream."

I shove my frustration aside and nod. Golmarr's hand trails down my arm and finds mine. He lifts the sword, and we cross the glossy floor to the stairs. When the staircase divides, we turn to the right. At the top of the stairs is the balcony, with a single door on either end.

"Is any of this looking familiar yet?" Golmarr asks.

"No. My mind feels empty."

Golmarr makes a small sound of frustration and then turns

to the closer door. "Let's go in." He puts his hand on the brass door handle and whispers, "Staff ready, and just in case I never get to tell you again, I think you are the most spectacular person alive."

He doesn't wait for my answer. He twists the handle and the door swings open.

The ceiling is glass in here, just like the rest of the building, letting the light flow into it. A long, oval table is in the center of the room, with nine empty chairs around it. Nine paintings of nine different people hang on the walls: four women and five men.

I stride across the room to one of the paintings—a young, ordinary-looking man with pale brown hair and bright blue eyes. "That is Melchior the wizard. When he was young." I walk around the room, examining the other pictures, and pause in front of a woman with a white flower tucked into her long red hair. Though my mind is blank right now, I recognize her face from an earlier memory. "This woman was the glass dragon." Beside her is a middle-aged man with black hair and a crown. "And this is King Zhun."

Golmarr stands next to me, examining the painting of King Zhun. "Who are the rest of these people?"

"That girl at the farthest end, the girl who is hardly older than a child, is me," someone says.

Golmarr and I whirl around. Chills dance down my spine when my eyes meet hers, so pale a shade of blue, they look as faded as her clothes and hair. "You can't remember them because Melchior stole all Zhun's human memories from him. He passed none of the most important parts of our history on to you, Sorrowlynn."

"Why not?"

"Because Melchior didn't want the fire dragon to know what he had planned, and the moment Zhun killed Melchior, all of his knowledge was passed on to the dragon," she says. "He stored the memories in an object before he let Zhun kill him. Did he give you anything before he disappeared?"

I think only for a moment. "A knife. He said to always keep it with me." I do not tell her that Zhun ate it, along with my arm, before I killed him.

The woman nods. "Yes. The knife."

"And you are?" Golmarr asks.

The woman lifts her chin and firms her shoulders. "I am Moyana, niece of King Zhun, who was the former ruler of the six kingdoms and the captor of Relkinn. I am the daughter of Prince Mordecai, younger sister to Melchior the wizard, and wife of Grinndoar the warrior." She smiles, and even though her hair is as white and fine as clouds, there are no wrinkles on her skin. She walks forward and takes my free hand in hers, gently squeezing it, and her eyes fill with tears. "I have been waiting for you for more than seven hundred years, Sorrow-lynn of Faodara."

# Chapter 31

It is the question that has been plaguing Golmarr from the moment he learned that the glass dragon's treasure was hatred. It flies from his mouth with the sharp precision of a thrown knife: "How do I remove the dragon's treasure?"

The smile wilts from Moyana's face, but doesn't fade completely. "Are you already transforming?" she asks. Her gaze sweeps every inch of Golmarr's visible skin, searching.

"Into a dragon?" Golmarr asks, and this time the smile completely leaves Moyana's face. Lips pressed tightly together, Golmarr slips the neck of his tunic over his shoulder, revealing the dark scales.

Moyana walks across the room and stops in front of Golmarr, examining his scales, tracing them with delicate fingers. "How far have they spread?"

"They cover my shoulder and part of my back, and go down to my elbow. Do you know how to stop them from spreading?" he asks, and the thinly veiled desperation in his voice makes my heart wrench.

"You have taken all of Corritha's hatred—more than one thousand years of hatred—and that is why you are turning into a dragon." She tenderly lifts Golmarr's tunic back into place, tightens the laces, and then ties them into a perfectly symmetrical bow. Patting his chest, she says, "This building is the hall of records. It was built to house the Infinite Vessel. Every answer you are seeking has been archived in the vessel."

"The Infinite Vessel is *here*?" His hand comes to rest on the small of my back, pressing on the scales beneath my tunic. "Because Sorrowlynn is changing, too."

Now his desperation is not veiled at all. It has bled out into his words, into the iciness of his touch on my back, the stiffness of his stance. I study Golmarr's profile, realizing for the first time that his fear of *himself* turning into a dragon has never been his main motivation. He has seen visions of *me* turning into a dragon. He has known all along, and that fear is what has fueled his desperate search for answers. My heart opens with this profound realization and expands until it feels as if it is too big to be contained in my chest.

Moyana stares at Golmarr and blinks. She swallows and blinks again. Tears start streaming down her cheeks at the same moment a radiant smile illuminates her face. "You love Sorrowlynn," she says. She places her small hand over Golmarr's heart. "You already have the answer to your question within you, my son."

"What is the answer?" he asks, his voice an eager whisper.

"Love. Focus on the love, and it will overpower the hatred. If the hatred is overpowered, you will stop transforming. But you will learn more about that in a moment."

"No! I keep seeing glimpses of Sorrowlynn turning into a dragon, and the world being destroyed by darkness, and me killing her, and her killing me, and I have to know how to stop it! How to change things!"

Moyana puts her hands on Golmarr's cheeks and looks right into his eyes. "What I am about to tell you is very important. Are you listening?"

He nods.

"What you are describing to me is *not* the future. It is part of the poison you inherited from Corritha. You are seeing visions of all your worst fears, Golmarr. If you choose to focus on them, you will make them a reality. You need to choose the best possible future for yourself and Sorrowlynn, and turn all your energy into making it a reality. Believe in the good. *Be* the good." Slowly, she lowers her hands from his face. "I can see from the light that has returned to your eyes that you believe me. That is promising. At least that part of you hasn't been tainted by Corritha." She pulls a chair out and motions for me to sit. "We have a lot to discuss in a very short amount of time."

I take the seat, and Golmarr sits on my left. Moyana takes the chair on my right and squeezes my hand gently. "It is so good to finally meet you," she says, a twinkle in her eyes. "Do you know that you are the one-thousand-time great-granddaughter of Melchior?"

Memories of doing puzzles with Melchior while sipping hot chocolate fill my mind. When he looked at me, his blue eyes would twinkle and shine as if brimming with wondrous secrets. Now I know one of those secrets. "I am Melchior's granddaughter?"

Moyana nods and squeezes my hand again. "Yes, and you are my niece. I have been waiting ever so long to meet you. But we don't have time for that right now. We need to focus on the problem at hand." She drops my hands and rests her elbows on the table. "Once upon a time, there was a king named Relkinn," Moyana says. "He was a strong, fierce king, with a gift for magic stronger than any, save my brother's.

"Relkinn's greatest desire was to live forever. But he also wanted to remain in his prime for the rest of his life—eternal life with eternal youth. He was greedy. He made it his life's purpose to discover how to harness eternal life.

"One day, after a battle where he slaughtered hundreds of enemies, he realized something. When he came home from the fighting, he looked younger than his twenty-nine years. He attributed the youthful glow to the satisfaction of winning the battle. But the next battle he fought, it happened again. And then, by experimenting with killing, he discovered the more lives he took, the more life he stole. Every person he killed, the remainder of the victim's years were transferred to him. At first, my father and uncle didn't know what was happening. People were disappearing, children were found dead in the fields, bodies were simply dropped on the foggy streets at night.

"You see, he went on a killing spree, until he had killed so many people, there was no way to count the years he'd stolen. He sought out the gentlest people he could find so he didn't have to exert himself to take their lives. He would prey on the young and weak. It wasn't until I was fifteen that my father learned the source of all the murders." She sighs and stares at the carved wooden table, her eyes far away.

"What happened when you were fifteen?" I ask.

"I was walking alone through the palace gardens at sunset when Relkinn grabbed me. He didn't realize that my father had armed me with a knife and trained me to use it, should I ever encounter the murderer."

"Did you kill him?" I ask.

"I should have. My knife pierced his heart, only all the lives he had stolen healed him up quickly—but not so quickly I couldn't get away and tell my father what happened." She leans back in her chair. "Were you taught of the Great War in your history lessons, or has it dwindled down to a mere myth by now?"

"We know about the Great War," Golmarr says.

Moyana purses her lips. "That was my father's attempt to dethrone Relkinn and make him pay for his crimes. Instead, it gave Relkinn the opportunity to kill hundreds more men, making him even stronger than before. But because of the war, my father was finally able to restrain him."

"Why didn't you simply kill him?" Golmarr asks.

She opens her eyes. "We could not. Scales covered every inch of his skin, and no weapon could penetrate them. Every attempt we made on his life—poison, starvation, bodily injury—healed before it could kill him. So we locked him under a mountain. Melchior sealed him far below the Wolf Cliffs in a prison of stone, while we tried to figure out how to kill him. One year later, when they went back to try and end his life again, Relkinn was gone. In his place was a beast. *He* was the beast—the very first dragon. So now we had a dragon that would live forever, that deserved death, but was impossible to kill. At least until his lives ran out." Her eyes meet mine and hold. "His lives have nearly run out," she whispers. Her blue gaze sweeps to Golmarr. "And you hold the reforged sword. You, Golmarr, are the one who shall wield it and finally put an end to his evil."

Golmarr looks at his hands in disbelief. "Why me?"

"Because it is time, and every second of my brother's life for the last seven hundred years has been spent molding and shaping people's lives to bring the two of you here right now so I can tell you this and give you the Infinite Vessel."

Golmarr grits his teeth and looks at the sword belted to his waist.

"Also," Moyana adds, "it will break the dragon's curse. But if you transform into a dragon before you complete your quest, you will remain a dragon for the rest of your life. Do you understand?"

Golmarr looks at Moyana and slowly nods.

"If Golmarr is the one destined to kill Relkinn, why do I need to be here?" I ask.

"I am putting the Infinite Vessel into your care. Every piece of Melchior's puzzle has fit into place and brought you here. Nayadi obtaining Zhun's scale. Ornald, who is Melchior's thousand-time grandson, leaving the Black Blades and becoming your father. You choosing death by dragon over an arranged marriage and being reforged in Zhun's death fire, just like Golmarr's sword."

"What? He knew I would choose that?" I ask.

Moyana smiles. "It was his greatest hope that you would slay the beast. Melchior needed you to take Zhun's gift of absorbing knowledge for his plan to work, and the only way your body could withstand the amount of information that will be placed in your head was for you to be physically altered. After you were burned by Zhun's fire, were you changed?"

I twist a strand of my smooth hair around my finger and think of my legs. "My father whipped my legs, and when I came out of the fire, the scars had disappeared." I lift my hair, studying it. "And my hair is different."

Moyana smiles. "Yes. Those are only the visible changes. Because you are reforged, your mind has been given the means to hold vast quantities of knowledge. If it had not been altered, the strain of Zhun's treasure would have killed you."

Golmarr's hand finds my knee under the table. "If Relkinn was the only dragon, how and why did King Zhun turn into a dragon?" he asks.

"Every living person is gifted with a bit of magic. Some have more, and some have less. You, Golmarr, have the inherent talent to become a great wizard. Like you, Relkinn was gifted with strong magic. Even before he transformed into a dragon, he was wearing away the seal my brother placed on his underground prison. So the newly appointed King Zhun gathered a group of the smartest, strongest, most stalwart, brave people he knew—we were called the council of nine—and transferred Relkinn's power and stolen lives to them. All that magic was divided among nine people and a dragon, filtered to one-tenth of its normal potency."

I look at the portraits hanging around the room. "These nine people."

Moyana nods. "Yes. And of the nine, seven turned into dragons, but in the end, only six chose greed and evil as their treasures." She rolls her long sleeve up, revealing a small, shimmering patch of very pale purple scales. "I started to turn. My vice was sorrow."

Golmarr leans forward. "What does that mean?"

"First, I will give you an example of someone else's vice, a vice you know all too well, Golmarr, through no fault of your own. One of our group was a brilliant herbalist named Corritha. She could cure or heal anything with plants. When she realized some of the council of nine were turning into dragons, she tried to heal them. When she could not, she blamed

Zhun for their demise. She grew so furious with him that she started to hate him—a hate so strong and so passionate, it began to eat at her, gnawing away at her heart, at her humanity. That hatred is what made her change into a dragon. Her exterior changed until it matched her heart."

Golmarr nods. "Yes. I know her hatred intimately."

"As for me, I had taken one-tenth of Relkinn's magic and eternal life, so, like all the others in my group, I began aging very slowly. I watched my children grow old and die. Then my husband, Grinndoar, King Zhun's strongest and most loyal warrior, found something he loved more than me. His vice was physical strength, and the only way he could steal it was by killing. Every time he killed, he stole his victim's strength, until he became inhumanly strong. Eventually, he did not care whom he killed to gain his treasure, and even sought to take my life. The consequence of his choices transformed him into a hideous dragon."

"The stone dragon of Satar," I say.

Golmarr clears his throat and stares at the table. "If I do become a dragon, will I hate Sorrowlynn forever?"

"Even as a dragon, you will have the ability to choose a life of good, or a life of evil. We may not be able to change the things that happen to us, but we can choose how we respond. Grinndoar had many chances to change, but he did not. More than seven hundred years ago, I fled here with my father and we lived in peace with the natives of this island for almost a century. But when Grinndoar discovered where I was, he chose to send someone here to poison our spring. He killed every person on this island but me and my father. Because of the life we'd inherited from Relkinn, we were immune to poison. But sorrow crept into my heart. My own husband had tried to kill *me*, and he didn't care about the hundreds of others that he'd killed because he'd gained their strength."

Tears spring to my eyes, and I look at Golmarr. "That is why I am transforming," I whisper. "I have been living with so much sorrow since you tried to kill me. And then, what you told me about the world being more important than our love—the sorrow is overpowering everything else. I have never been so sad in my life."

"Yes!" Moyana says. "You are focusing on the dark part of something incredibly bright and beautiful, and it is turning you into a dragon. You must focus on the good, daughter! You have fallen in love with a man who realizes the importance of life and goodness. He is willing to put the safety and well-being of a world above his own desires. And you." She turns to Golmarr. "You already have so many things in your heart that can conquer the hatred eating you from the inside. In fact, you've already begun. Find the purpose in your life not centered on hate and make it your mission. Do not be afraid to love Sorrowlynn. It is our choices that form us into who we are. Choose darkness and you will become darkness. Choose light, and be a light for all to see. Be good. Be true. Be selfless. Let those be your focus and the darkness will not have the ability to touch you. And this"—she presses against his scales—"will stop growing."

Golmarr's chin drops to his chest and his shoulders start shaking. I do not know if he is laughing or crying until I see a tear fall from his closed eye and shimmer as it passes through the sunlight shining in from the ceiling. It splatters against the wood of the table. I wrap my arm around his shoulder and pull him close, pressing my face against his neck, feeling the warmth of his skin on mine, breathing in the familiar smell of him. My touch seems to release more tears, as this man who has been taught how to fight is learning there might be another way.

"This is good, Golmarr," Moyana says. "This is the hatred and self-loathing coming out of you."

I look at Moyana, at the depth of understanding in her wise eyes, and ask, "What did you choose to focus on to overcome the sorrow?"

"I focused my life on keeping the Infinite Vessel safe from all human eyes. Because if anyone learned the truth about the dragon's power, men—even the very best of men—would try to harness it for themselves." She smiles, but it is sad. "We have seen how that can turn out. I have kept the information for you, Sorrowlynn of Faodara—an entire library's worth of scrolls and books. You are to bring it back with you, use it to destroy Relkinn once and for all, and safeguard it until you die."

Golmarr presses the heels of his hands to his eyes and sits tall, wiping the tears from his face. "Now I know why I couldn't find the information in the Royal Library of Trevon," he says. "You had it all moved here." His eyes are bloodshot, and he looks more vulnerable than any warrior should ever look. It makes a fire simmer beneath my breast, makes me want to protect him, hold him, keep him eternally strong.

"That is why there are no early records of the dragons anywhere in the six kingdoms," Moyana concedes. "We moved all the information here and safeguarded it so it did not have the power to destroy anyone else."

I groan as realization hits. "How am I going to get it to our ship? We do not have a boat. We swam past the reef. Is there a way for our ship to dock on the island?"

Sunlight reflects off Moyana's beautiful eyes. When she blinks, a shimmering layer of tears is swept onto her cheeks. "Do not fear," she says. "I have not spent hundreds of years in solitude, planning and preparing, to fail now." She squeezes my hand in hers. Her fingers have turned as cold and hard as ice.

# Chapter 32

She pushes her chair back from the table and stands. "Come. We must get you back to your ship as quickly as possible."

"But the library? The Infinite Vessel?"

She nods. "I will give it to you."

We leave and cross the balcony to the other room. It is the exact same size as the room we just left, but a small pallet is in the center of the floor, and plants growing in clay pots cover the rest of the floor, filling the air with the smell of a lush, moist garden. "I have missed the company of people more than anything, but I have missed the forests of my homeland nearly as much as I have missed people," she says, touching the leaves of the plants by the door. "I love you, my dear friends, and I thank you for the joy you have brought to me," she whispers, speaking to the plants. Without another word, she ushers us out of the room, shutting the door behind us.

"Isn't the Infinite Vessel in there?" I ask.

She shakes her head. "It used to be, but not anymore. Come. I will show you where it is."

We leave the hall of records and walk along the hot sand path, over the footprints that we left on our way in. Moyana walks in front of Golmarr and me, silent, head held high. We pass the two-story house we entered, the one with the bones of the poisoned islanders resting silently in their beds. We pass the tiny house we first explored, and then squeeze through the narrow gap in the cliff.

The ocean shimmers and gleams and reflects the immeasurable blue of the sky. Moyana stops and stares at the horizon, the breeze whipping her loose clothing behind her like a pair of gossamer wings. "Did your ship drop anchor?" she asks.

I look at our ship, still bobbing above the edge of the reef. "Yes."

Moyana nods. "Good."

Golmarr takes my elbow in his hand and gives me a look—eyebrows furrowed, mouth a tight frown, and I know what he is intimating. *Something isn't right.* I nod my agreement. He rests his hand on his sword hilt, ready to draw it if need be.

"Golmarr!" someone calls. Yerengul ducks out of a narrow groove in the cliff face twenty paces away, and his sword is drawn. A moment later, he is running toward us. He doesn't slow when he sees Moyana, but his eyes narrow and don't leave her as he blurts, "The two-headed dragon is perched atop the cliff and watching for us. We need to prepare to fight it!"

"No," Moyana says, splaying her arms out to block us from running onto the beach. "You do not want to kill the sisters. Saphina treasured the attention and pleasures of men above everything else. It turned her into the hideous, ugly beast she is. Naphina's downfall was envy for the attention her beautiful sister got. When Naphina discovered her husband had fallen in love with her own sister, she tried to kill Saphina and use magic to steal her beauty. Naphina *did* absorb her sister's beauty—that is why she is such a gloriously beautiful dragon. But the envy and the magic also fused their bodies together." She steps out from the shadow of the cliff and calls, "Why don't you come and show yourselves, Naphina and Saphina? It has been a long time since I had the horror of looking at you in your revolting dragon body."

Above, two twin screams ring out. A small boulder tumbles down the side of the cliff and thuds onto the sand. Rubble follows, and then a shadow darkens the beach. The two-headed dragon is flying down to us. Even though my staff is useless against such a creature, I grip it in both hands.

**Be careful, sister. The man with the sword that can cut us is here,** the deep voice says, disrupting my thoughts.

I want to eat his pretty face! I hate him! cries the ugly dragon.

Golmarr clenches his teeth and presses on the bridge of his nose. "Why do I hear everything they think?"

Moyana puts a hand on his shoulder. "Dragons communicate by thought. If a dragon wants to speak to a person, it can selectively put words into his head. But if you are becoming a dragon, your mind is open to everything they say to each other. Because you are turning into one of them, your ability to hear them has been awakened."

The two-headed dragon touches down on the ground, its clawed, mismatched feet making deep depressions in the black pebbles. There are open wounds covering its body.

"If you don't want us to kill it, why did you call it down, Moyana?" Golmarr demands, his eyes fixed to the creature.

"The sea serpent is going to take care of her," Moyana

says calmly. She waves her hand toward the ocean, and I almost drop my staff. The reef is jutting up out of dry land, and beyond it, I can barely see the tops of our ship's masts poking up, for it is sitting on the ocean floor. Fish are flopping in the waterless bay, and far out to sea, a mountain of inky water is rising. Moyana, I see you gave in to your moping and never turned into a glorious beast. You chose the path of weakness. The words are not meant for me, yet they vibrate in my head.

Yes, still as plain and ordinary and mopey as ever, and to what end? You are a waste of life. That is why Grinndoar stopped loving you. The ugly head hisses and snaps its lipless mouth shut, making its yellow teeth break.

Moyana shakes her head in disgust. "You are even more hideous than I remember. How appropriate that you two have been imprisoned in the same body for all these centuries. I could never have found a more fitting punishment. How have you not driven each other mad?"

The ugly dragon shrieks, and the beast starts running toward us. I turn to face it, mentally preparing myself to fight, when Moyana thrusts her hand forward.

A loud roaring fills the air, and then all around me and my companions, sand and rock start flying outward, leaving us standing on a perfect circle of undisturbed earth. A shimmering dome encloses us, sealing us into a space where the only sounds we hear are those that we ourselves are making.

"What is this?" Yerengul asks, stepping up to the side of the dome and pressing on it. His voice echoes.

"I have made a shield of air," Moyana says, still holding her hand out.

The two-headed dragon throws itself at the shield. It

crashes into it and topples backward. The creature approaches again and slams its tail into the shield, and I can't even hear the sound it makes when it hits. One dragon shoots water at the shield, and a moment later lightning crackles from the other, spreading veins of blue light over the air dome. Beneath me, the ground rumbles, but there is still no outside sound.

"Look!" Golmarr yells, pointing out to sea. A mountain of water is rushing toward us, filling the dry ocean bed. We know the moment it reaches Yeb's ship, because the small vessel bobs high above the coral reef. And then the reef is covered, the bay is filled, and beneath my feet, the ground is trembling with the force of the approaching water.

The two-headed dragon turns its attention from us just as the giant wave reaches shore.

Fly! The word pierces my head and vibrates my brain. The dragon spreads its wings and lifts off the ground just as the top of the wave starts to curl. Caught in the midst of the wave is the sea serpent. The water tips and slams into the two-headed dragon, yanking it right out of the air. The two-headed dragon thrashes in the water, and veins of blue shoot from the ugly head's mouth. It slashes at the water with its claws, whips its tail from side to side, and rears its two heads, but it is no match for the water.

The wave surges around the air dome, completely covering it and dimming the sun's light. I love you, daughter. The thought floats into my head, warm and gentle like a summer breeze. A moment later, the mountain of water, with the sea serpent and two-headed dragon trapped in its power, bursts against the white cliff face. Both dragons are smashed against stone. The sea serpent goes instantly limp, and fire the deep indigo of twilight flares from its black body before burning out.

Slowly, the two-headed dragon's thrashing diminishes, and then the creature stills completely. A rush of bubbles erupts from the beautiful dragon's mouth. One final fork of lightning leaves the mouth of the ugly dragon. A heartbeat later, yellow fire engulfs the body and fills the ocean with light, illuminating the fish darting about and broken pieces of ships. Like a candle being extinguished, the fire flickers and fades to nothing, returning the water to murky blue. The two dragons, both perfectly still, rise and fall with the motion of the water. I step to the air dome and press my nose to it, staring up at the white cliff and the two bodies suspended beside it. "They are dead," I say.

"Yes. That was their death fire. He made the wave and killed the sisters for you," Moyana says, her voice quivering. I turn from the air dome to study her. Her cheeks are soaked with tears. "In doing so, he killed himself."

"Who killed himself?" I ask.

"Prince Mordecai. My father. When he turned into a dragon, he became the sea serpent." She dabs at her eyes with her sleeve. "He carried your ship here," she adds.

"Was his vice greed over the sea?" Golmarr asks.

Moyana shakes her head and sorrow fills her eyes. "No. His desire to protect me is what ultimately turned him into a dragon. Sometimes even seemingly good things can destroy us. He lost all trust and hope when Grinndoar tried to poison us, and started killing anyone who attempted to get onto the island."

The dome is growing brighter and brighter. Overhead,

the water parts and exposes the top of the air shield to the sun. The level of the ocean is falling as the water is draining back into the sea, until the beach is a sodden mess and we are standing on the only dry patch of land anywhere in sight.

The dome shimmers around us, and with a gust of warm wind, it disappears. Moyana turns and faces me, and there is a hardness in her eyes that was not there before.

Golmarr notices it, too. He steps to my side and lifts his sword. "Where is the Infinite Vessel?" Golmarr asks, voice rigid with mistrust. Yerengul takes his place at my other side, sword drawn.

"The vessel has all been composed into one body," Moyana says, and her shoulders firm with a strength I have never seen in another living being. Her gaze grips mine. "I am sorry," she whispers. Something glints in the sunlight, and I tear my gaze from hers in time to see the knife in her hand. With a simple flick of her wrist, air slams into Golmarr and Yerengul, knocking them backward. Moyana steps forward and lifts her blade so the sharp tip is pricking the skin above my heart.

I scream and wrap my hands around hers, and everything happens so fast that I am nothing more than a pawn being moved by another's will, by a plan that was put into place centuries before my mother conceived me. Moyana turns the knife in our joined hands so it is pointing at her own chest, and thrusts with a thousand years of preparation, of sorrow, of solitude, of purpose.

The knife pierces skin, grinds against bone, and finds the living, beating heart that has been waiting centuries for release. And it is *my* hands holding the blade to Moyana's chest, embedded into a heart anticipating this moment for an eternity.

"Thank you," Moyana whispers. She falls to her knees and the knife slips from my frozen fingers, still firmly implanted in her chest. "Now you can take the Infinite Vessel with you. Thank you, Sorrowlynn," she whispers again, blood soaking through her white clothing and splattering the sand in big, thick drops. Moyana totters and falls to the side. Golmarr lunges and throws his arms around her before her head hits the ground. Gently, he eases her onto her back so she is in the exact center of the dry circle of sand, surrounded by a beach soaked with salt water and littered with debris.

With her last bit of strength, Moyana turns her head. Out in the water-filled bay floats the corpse of the two-headed dragon. Already, gulls are dipping down from the air and pulling chunks of flesh from the body. At the place where the water meets the black beach lies the sea serpent. The scales are raining from his body, revealing pale, human-looking flesh underneath. Moyana turns her head back up to face the sky, and the air filling her lungs seems to leak out.

Golmarr kneels at Moyana's side and takes her beautiful, thin hands in his. He crosses them above her heart, beside the time-worn leather hilt of the knife—the final burial pose of a dead warrior. Together, Golmarr and Yerengul each touch a finger to their foreheads and cross their wrists—*honored warrior.*

And then I feel it. My head, my brain, my very soul opening and expanding as everything Moyana was enters me. It is not like the slime and vileness forced upon me when I killed King Vaunn, and it is not the mental agony that nearly burst my skull when I killed Zhun, the fire dragon. Moyana's knowledge is filling me in the same way that my love for Golmarr fills me. I am a vessel being filled to the brim with light and truth, and any darkness hiding in my depths is forced out. I am like a flower opening to a sun I did not know existed and drinking in its energy for the first time. And now I know what her treasure was. Love.

When the transfer is complete, the tears come, because I know the depths of sorrow Moyana endured and the pain she experienced. The struggle she underwent to defeat her trials is staggering. And then the liberation she was given when she dedicated her life to the storing of knowledge, to becoming the Infinite Vessel and devoting her life to the hope of making the world a better place, steals my breath. I know the intense goodness of her heart and the sincere gratitude she had for her life, despite every earth-shaking, heart-wrenching trial she fought through. I am touching her very soul, and it is brighter and more glorious than the sun beating down on me.

Beneath the layers of Moyana's long life, I feel the hall of records embedded within my mind, a knowledge so vast I cannot sense its beginning or ending. It is eternal, and it is infinite. I am within the hall of records, and the hall of records is within me. *I* am the Infinite Vessel.

"She was the Infinite Vessel, Golmarr. I inherited her knowledge."

He cups the side of my cheek. "You are the Infinite Vessel now?"

I nod, and a sob shudders through my body.

Golmarr wraps his arms around me, and I cry against his chest. His hand slowly moves over my hair as he holds me close. When my tears have stopped, he tilts my face up and kisses my left eyelid, then my right. "Sorrowlynn." His voice stirs my heart, and I open my eyes. He slides his sword from his belt and thrusts it into the ground between my feet. Kneeling, he looks up at me and says, "Sorrowlynn of Faodara, I vow to protect you all my life, to love you with all my soul, and to follow you to the ends of the world and back. I am yours until I die."

I place my hand on top of his head and close my eyes as the pieces of Melchior's puzzle slip perfectly into place.

# Epilogue

We hoist the sails and catch the wind moments after the sun has hidden itself behind the western horizon. As the ship starts slowly pulling north, I lean my hands on the railing and stare at the sea. It no longer looks like a layer of glass placed above a ship graveyard. The water is moving, small white-capped waves rising and swelling and slapping against the ship's hull, hiding the sunken vessels beneath its uneasy surface.

Hands come down on the railing on either side of mine, and the warmth of a body presses against my back. "Have you decided where we are going?" Golmarr asks, and nuzzles my hair. I turn, still encircled by his arms, and face him.

"First, we need to stop the sandworm from destroying Yassim's city. Then we are going to Satar—to the abandoned stone city built in the mountain."

His eyebrows rise. "We are?" he asks, surprised. "What is in the ancient kingdom of Satar?"

I put my arms around his neck, not caring who sees how forward I am, and run my fingers through his damp hair.

"There is a dragon in Satar who treasures strength above everything else."

Golmarr nods. "Grinndoar, Moyana's husband."

"Yes." I stand on my toes and kiss Golmarr's right cheek. "You need to slay him and gain his strength."

Golmarr's mouth falls open for a moment before he asks, "I do?"

I nod and kiss his left cheek.

He removes his hands from the railing and places them on my waist, taking a tiny step closer. "Why do I need to slay Grinndoar?"

I brush my lips against his. He tightens his hands on my waist and tries to deepen the kiss, but I pull away and press my fingers to his mouth. "If you slay Grinndoar, you will inherit his strength. You will be the strongest man in the world. And when you are the strongest man in the world, you will be ready to face Relkinn."

Golmarr glowers and clasps my hand, removing it from his lips. "That sounds incredibly *impossible*, Sorrowlynn."

"But . . . the pieces of the puzzle," I stammer, shocked at his reluctance. "If you inherit Grinndoar's strength, you will be unstoppable."

He stares into my eyes, and his glare falters as one corner of his mouth turns up. "I might need some convincing. Or you could completely addle my thoughts by kissing me, and then ask me again. But . . ." His eyes grow thoughtful. "Yes. I know how to solve this. The only way you're going to get what you want is by kissing me," he whispers.

I shove his chest, but he tightens his hold on my waist and grins. "You are a rogue, Golmarr of Anthar!"

"You're right. I *am* a rogue. You'd better hurry up and addle my thoughts, or I might have to addle yours, and if you can't think straight, there's no hope for us."

I laugh and place my hands on his cheeks, and then gently pull his face to mine and proceed to thoroughly addle both of our thoughts.

# Locations

**Kingdom of Faodara:** proper northern kingdom from whence our fair heroine hails; though governed by a queen, women follow very strict rules of etiquette

**Kingdom of Anthar:** grassland kingdom south of Gol Mountain, where men and women train as warriors and fight side by side in battle

**Kingdom of Trevon:** greedy, war-hungry kingdom due west of Anthar; ruled by an evil king and a prince who conquered the kingdom of Belldarr at the tender age of fifteen

**Kingdom of Ilaad:** desert kingdom and home to the best assassins in the world; terrorized by the sandworm

**Kingdom of Satar:** abandoned kingdom located inside the Satar Mountains; former home of the Satari migrants known as the Black Blades; home of the stone dragon

**Kingdom of Belldarr:** small kingdom conquered by Treyose of Trevon

**The Glass Forest:** densely wooded home to mercenaries, cutthroats, and a group of Satari migrants who call themselves the Black Blades; former home of the glass dragon

**Draykioch (aka Serpent's Island):** desert island feared by all sailors, for a serpent sinks any ship that approaches its shores

**Gol Mountain:** lofty mountain between Faodara and Anthar; the fire dragon's former prison

# Characters

## Kingdom of Faodara

**Sorrowlynn (aka Suicide Sorrow):** destined to die by her own hand; slayer of the fire dragon and inheritor of his treasured knowledge

**Queen Felicitia:** Sorrowlynn's indifferent (except when loose corsets are concerned) mother

**Lord Damar:** queen's husband; *not* Sorrowlynn's father

**Diamanta:** sister destined to outlive three husbands

**Harmony:** sister destined to make peace wherever she goes

**Gloriana:** sister destined to bring joy to all

**Ornald:** former captain of the guard; Sorrowlynn's father

**Melchior the wizard:** giver of fate blessings; the fire dragon's last human meal

**Nona:** Sorrowlynn's loving nursemaid

## Kingdom of Anthar

**Golmarr:** wielder of the reforged sword; inheritor of the glass dragon's hatred; searching for the Infinite Vessel

**Yerengul:** brother trained as a medic; Sorrowlynn's arms teacher

**Jessen:** somber brother whose wife was killed in battle

**King Marrkul:** ruler of Anthar

**Ingvar:** oldest prince of Anthar, heir to the throne

**Olenn:** brother stationed at the western stronghold

**Arendinn:** brother stationed at the eastern stronghold

**Nayadi:** witch who sees visions and gives counsel to King
   Marrkul . . . when she feels so inclined

**Leogard:** oldest living swordsman

**Evay:** Golmarr's former love interest

## KINGDOM OF TREVON

**King Vaunn:** greedy old man determined to rule all the
   kingdoms

**Treyose:** King Vaunn's grandson, pawn, and only living heir;
   conqueror of Belldarr

**Reyler:** Treyose's most trusted man

## KINGDOM OF ILAAD

**Yassim Reyla Jaquara:** princess and trained assassin

**King Jaquar:** Yassim's father; ruler of Ilaad

**Yeb:** captain of the ship Jassar; Yassim's uncle

## THE GLASS FOREST

**Edemond:** patriarch of the Black Blades; Ornald's brother

**Enzio:** Edemond's son; Sorrowlynn's cousin and sworn
   protector

**Melisande:** Enzio's mother, saved from a mercenary's blade
   by Sorrowlynn

## ISLAND OF DRAYKIOCH

**Moyana:** keeper of secrets

## DRAGONS

**Zhun the Fire Dragon:** treasurer of knowledge; killed by Sorrowlynn

**Corritha the Glass Dragon:** treasurer of hatred; killed by Golmarr

**Naphina and Saphina, the Two-Headed Dragon:** sisters; wielders of water and lightning; corrupted by envy

**Mordecai the Sea Serpent:** Moyana's father; treasures her safety above all else

**Grinndoar the Stone Dragon:** Moyana's husband and King Zhun's strongest, most loyal warrior; manipulator of rock and treasurer of physical strength

**Sandworm:** terrorizer of Ilaad; lives beneath the sand and devours any living creature that sets foot in the desert

# Glossary

**Antharian hand signals:** sign language used by Antharians, especially in battle

**Black Blades:** former inhabitants of Satar

**black stone blades of Satar:** two ancient stone blades passed to Enzio by his father; one of them was given to Sorrowlynn, to be returned only after Enzio fulfills his promise to save her life

**citadel:** Antharian fortress built into the side of a mountain, where children are sent to be trained as warriors

**council of nine:** ancient alliance of nine of the wisest and strongest people

**death fire:** fire that burns a dragon's remaining life and magic upon its death

**dragon tears:** black pebbles that glow as if lit from within, found on the shores of Draykioch

**Great War:** (possibly mythical) war that nearly destroyed the six kingdoms more than a thousand years ago

**hall of records:** building that houses the Infinite Vessel

**Infinite Vessel:** fabled vessel in which all of dragon history is stored

**Mountain Binding:** spell bought by two kings to lock the fire dragon beneath Gol Mountain

**pell:** wooden post used for building strength and precision in sword-fighting

**proxy wedding:** wedding in which one or both of the individuals are not physically present

**reforged sword:** sword burned and purified by death fire; the only weapon that can penetrate dragon scales

**King Relkinn:** man who started the Great War

**six kingdoms:** ancient name of the unified kingdoms before they were divided by the Great War

**Strickbane:** dragon poison, lethal to humans

**transference:** transfer of a dragon's treasure to its slayer

**Vinti:** ancient language of the six kingdoms

**waster sword:** cheap, sturdy, dull sword made specifically for practicing

**weighted waster sword:** heavy, unbalanced practice sword used to build strength

**Prince Zhun:** defeater of Relkinn, creator of the council of nine

# About the Author

BETHANY WIGGINS is the author of the Transference trilogy, as well as the novels *Stung, Cured,* and *Shifting.* Bethany lives in the desert with her husband, five quirky kids, and three black cats. You can follow her on Instagram and on Twitter at @wiggb, and visit her at bethanywiggins.com.